# Praise for the works of Janet Lynnford

### *Bride of Hearts*

"Rich with historical detail and insightful characterizations, this intricately plotted story skillfully entangles its characters in a deadly web of murder and political intrigue as it credibly—and occasionally chillingly—depicts the political undercurrents, jockeying for influence, and royal meddling and manipulation so typical of the Elizabethan court." —*Library Journal*

### *Firebrand Bride*

"Lush and sexy . . . a compelling read that brings the romance of the Scottish countryside to life."
—Tess Gerritsen

"Lively action [and] vividly rendered scenes . . . recommend this fast-paced, intricately plotted tale."
—*Library Journal*

"Rich in historical detail and personages. . . . A strong heroine and equally powerful hero, an exciting backdrop, colorful details, and fascinating characters make this a not-to-be-missed read." —*Romantic Times*

### *Lady Shadowhawk*

"A provocative tale with intense characters and some heart-pounding twists." —*Rendezvous*

*continued . . .*

Historical Romance by Janet Lynnford

*Bride of Hearts*
*Firebrand Bride*
*Lady Shadowhawk*
*Lord of Lightning*
*Pirate's Rose*

# SHETLAND SUMMER

## Janet Lynnford

AN ONYX BOOK

ONYX
Published by New American Library, a division of
Penguin Putnam Inc., 375 Hudson Street,
New York, New York 10014, U.S.A.
Penguin Books Ltd, 80 Strand,
London WC2R 0RL, England
Penguin Books Australia Ltd, Ringwood,
Victoria, Australia
Penguin Books Canada Ltd, 10 Alcorn Avenue,
Toronto, Ontario, Canada M4V 3B2
Penguin Books (N.Z.) Ltd, 182–190 Wairau Road,
Auckland 10, New Zealand

Penguin Books Ltd, Registered Offices:
Harmondsworth, Middlesex, England

First published by Onyx, an imprint of New American Library,
a division of Penguin Putnam Inc.

First Printing, May 2002
10  9  8  7  6  5  4  3  2  1

*This book is dedicated to:*

*My family, whom I cherish—*
*husband, son, mother, in-laws, cousins,*
*my departed father, and his mother,*
*Lynnferd, from whom I took my pen name.*

*My writer friends of Central Ohio Fiction Writers,*
*my supportive friends of my "e-mail authors loop,"*
*and my special author/mentor friend, Connie Rinehold,*
*who also writes as Eve Byron.*

*My editor, Cecilia Malkum Oh,*
*who is, in my eyes, a rising star in her profession.*

*And my colleagues, who support my writing at*
*The Ohio State University.*

*My love and thanks to each one of you.*

# Chapter 1

*The Shetland Islands Main Isle, 1599*

Sun at midnight. He'd never seen anything like it. Drummond Graham trudged along the wind-swept coastline, watching his younger brother enjoy the silver rays of the sun that never set, and envied his innocent awe. Iain Lang alternated between staring at the luscious green meadow rising to his left, then whipping his head right to admire the brilliant blue waves that crashed over the rocky seabed. The midnight light lent a magical air to the land, but Drummond couldn't appreciate it. He had too many worries on his mind.

" 'Tis so bonnie here," Iain breathed. "I'm glad we're travelin' by night.'Twould have been a pity to miss such sights."

"Aye." Drummond grunted, shifting the heavy pack on his back.

Iain glanced at him, clearly anxious about his mood, but he couldn't help it. During their twelve days on the island, the farther they'd traveled up the coast, the angrier Drummond had become. Few things infuriated him, but now he was taut with rage. Last night, Iain had likened him to a catapult, loaded with deadly ammunition and primed for attack.

If only he were, Drummond thought ruefully. He would enjoy unleashing such a dangerous weapon on the injustice he saw here, correcting it with brute force. But he was in an impossible position, a guest on the island due to the generosity of the very man whose actions incited his wrath. That man held the illustrious titles of Earl of Orkney and Laird of the Shetland Isles. As such, he should have been a beneficent ruler of his people.

Nothing was further from the truth, which left Drummond hot with rage.

He couldn't live with such anger indefinitely. It was what had set them on their journey at eleven that night. Earlier, he'd dropped into bed, exhausted from pushing himself. He had fallen into instant, blessed sleep, but it had been short-lived.

Long before midnight, he'd jolted awake, hounded by an old, recurring nightmare. Seven years since he'd had it. With his father's death, he'd thought it gone forever.

Instead, it returned with a vengeance. Anger, in its ugly way, assumed different forms, rearing up when you were unequipped to hold it at bay. Drummond had known he wouldn't sleep again that night.

Iain had been delighted to continue their journey. He'd not closed his eyes at all, being too enthralled with the midnight sun. So they'd said farewell to their crofter hosts, hoisted their packs of Shetland wool, and set out.

"Mayhap we could go for a swim," Iain ventured, a hopeful expression on his sensitive face. "I see a sandy stretch ahead." He pointed out a distant break in the rocky shoreline. " 'Twould cool ye down."

"Nothing can cool me down." Drummond tried to control his black mood. "Not since I talked to the mother of that lad who was hanged at Sandwick. Someone said he'd stolen a sheep, and a carcass was found, yet the earl had no evidence the lad did it. It could have been someone else." It could have been the earl, he added to himself.

Iain shivered at his words. "I agree 'tis terrible, but

what can we do? He's laird of the isles. Have ye changed yer mind about acceptin' his invitation to the castle?"

Drummond shook his head, noting Iain's nervous swallow.

"Mayhap a swim would be best," the lad tried again.

"You go. I need to think." Drummond let go of his dirk, realizing he'd been clenching its hilt until his fist ached.

Iain shifted the pack on his back with an uneasy movement. "Ye're not forgettin' yer purpose here, are ye?" he began. "That ye've come to—"

"Dinna say it," Drummond snapped, startling Iain. What was wrong with him, snapping at his brother? "I asked you to keep my true purpose secret." He steadied his voice. "We've come to buy Shetland wool. Nay more."

"If ye say so, Brother," Iain said meekly, clearly wanting to keep the peace.

*To buy Shetland wool and no more.* He might say he would stop there, but he'd come for more than that in the first place. Now, his anger would take him farther. Even Iain could see that something drove him tonight. And it wasn't just the local earl. Thanks to the nightmare, the old burden wore on him, heavier than in the past.

Drummond passed a hand before his eyes. "I'm sorry, Iain. I dinna mean to be unkind, but I need to keep moving. Have your swim, but dinna linger. It's going to storm." He nodded toward the black thunderheads building to the north, concerned for the lad.

"If the weather's bad, I willna get another chance to swim for days," Iain insisted with his usual stubbornness. "If ye stay on the track, I can catch up with ye." He indicated the path ahead that curved left, no doubt crossing the island and running straight to the earl's castle at Scalloway.

"Very well." Drummond halted. "But dinna be caught without shelter. I promised your mother and father no harm would come to you on this journey. I promised myself as well." He regarded Iain with affection. "You're important to me, lad."

Iain flushed scarlet with pleasure, an answering grin spreading across his face.

He reminded Drummond of a young colt trying to rise on awkward legs for the first time. But then Iain was only seventeen. Drummond grinned back at him, glad for the companionship of a kinsman on his quest. He was a loyal lad, well worth the time and effort Drummond had spent seeing him educated. Entirely worthy of the place Drummond had requested for him in their father's clan of the Grahams. Although he was young and still made errors, Drummond felt certain the lad wouldn't repeat his most recent ones. "Get on with you." He clapped Iain on the shoulder a last time. "Enjoy the water, and dinna be too long."

Iain Lang waved to his brother and headed down the track toward the shore, delighted by the chance to escape duty. Halfway there, he turned and looked back. Drummond stood exactly where he'd left him, chin raised, staring into the wind of the approaching storm as if it blew a bad omen his way. Maybe it did.

Iain idolized his older brother, and not just because of the many things he'd done for him in recent years. It seemed Drummond had endured nothing but hardship most of his life. Iain had been fortunate in comparison. Though he was illegitimate, his mother had wed a good man who'd given Iain his name. He'd known little of his real father, Will Mosley.

In contrast, as Mosley's eldest illegitimate son, Drummond had had many doings with their father until his death when Drummond was eighteen. All Iain knew was that Drummond had been forced to assist with Mosley's illegal schemes so that he and his mother might eat from day to day. Though dead, Will Mosley had clearly laid a heavy burden of sorrow on his eldest son, which he carried yet today.

It probably explained Drummond's strong reaction to the local earl's injustices. Which made Iain decide he *would* linger at his swim.

He resumed his trek toward the water. If the carl proved the ogre that rumor painted him, Iain expected an explosion once Drummond met him at Scalloway, a meeting he intended to miss. Getting caught in a storm would be a treat in comparison.

"Ting, where are ye, love?" Gemma Sinclair approached the wild ponies grazing on the moor, calling softly. The coal-black stallion that was lord of the herd raised his head and stared at her with suspicious eyes. Other than that, there was no reply.

"Ting? 'Tis Gemma, come to see ye."

Nothing.

Loneliness sliced through Gemma. Her life was about to take a downturn, and if something had happened to her pony, the only remaining friend she was able to protect, she didn't see how she could bear it.

"Ting!" She called louder this time, panic rising. Still no reply. Perhaps Ting couldn't hear her, as Gemma was upwind of the herd. Her voice might be lost on the wind. Yet she dared not shout or whistle. No one from Scalloway Castle must know where Ting was hidden. Even far away, on the moor where the wild ponies roamed, her caution ruled with the memory of the recent horror, so fresh in her mind.

Tears stung Gemma's eyes as she remembered the bloated human body that had once been a kindly tinker. With no mark on him, he'd been pronounced an accidental drowning. Yet Gemma had thought it suspicious. She'd sought his help, and this was how her supposed savior ended. Drowned in a tide pool south of Scalloway. Everyone had thought him in Edinburgh this month past, but in truth, he had never left the Shetland Isles.

The rise in the earl's temper had come the same day the body was found. Patrick Stewart, Earl of Orkney and Laird of the Shetland Isles, had been in a fury since his chief magistrate brought the body to the castle yesterday morning. The earl had been punishing people for the smallest offense. After three years in his household, Gemma had learned that whenever he wished to punish her, he struck out at Ting.

So she had hidden Ting and waited for the earl to act, but he had not. If he'd discovered the letter she'd written, why didn't he confront her? Or had he harmed Ting and now awaited her reaction? The thought was horrifying.

"Sweetheart, where are ye?" Frantic, she called louder. Still no reply. Changing direction, she approached the stallion, knowing his approval would let her move among the herd to look for Ting. He stood on a small hillock, neck arched and head upflung, his thick mane and tail frothing in the wind.

He was beautiful, proud, and free, unlike most of the males on the islands. Even her dead husband, who had been an important district official, had not been so free. At any other time, Gemma would have enjoyed the sight of the stallion, poised against the darkening sapphire sky. She would have basked in the scents of heather and upland grass whipped by the powerful winds of an oncoming storm. Yet despite her love for the midnight sun of summer, the magic she usually felt on the wild moor was absent tonight.

Not only was there the tinker, but her uncle's plight hung heavily on her mind. As the chief stone mason in charge of the men building the earl's new castle, Andrew Crawford was frequently deprived of his evening rations and locked in a storage chamber for contradicting his lordship's chief magistrate, Lawrence

Bruce. Tonight had been such a night, as had been the prior night, and the one before that.

Of course Gemma had smuggled food to him. Her uncle and aunt had raised her from an infant, loving her as tenderly as if she were one of their own eight. She would repay them with her life. But tonight, she'd managed only bread and cheese for her uncle, and a big man who hauled stone all day couldn't maintain muscle on that. Not for days on end.

Resentment against Bruce roiled through Gemma as she approached the stallion, turning her body sideways and lowering her gaze. The herd leader offered no welcome, though he knew her well. But he was being protective, and she must forgive him, not transfer her anger to him. All the past carrots and care she had lavished on them meant nothing if she threatened his herd. It was a miracle she could approach them at all, or that they accepted Ting.

But then Ting had come *from* them, a runt whose mother had died. She would never have survived but for Gemma, who had nursed the foal like a babe. They understood what she did for them, caring for their health, Gemma thought, for the stallion always tolerated her. No other human could get as close.

Gemma drew nearer, then stilled, waiting for the stallion to make the first move. As expected, he stepped forward after a moment of scrutiny, lowered his neck with an imperious motion, and sniffed her. Gemma waited for his sign of approval.

With a regal arch of his neck, the stallion flicked his tail and moved away to nudge a straying youngster back to its dam. She was accepted once more.

"Thank ye kindly, yer worship," Gemma said softly. At least one dominating male in her life responded as desired. "Ting?" she repeated as she moved toward the mares.

An answering squeal rose from the middle of the

tightly packed ponies. Her heart contracted with relief as the press of horseflesh parted. Pushing her way among the mares, Gemma met the tiny animal halfway. Ting nearly bowled her over with her enthusiastic greeting. The creature's withers barely came to her thighs; her ears were level with Gemma's waist. A runt for sure, and therefore all the more dear.

Gemma chuckled as she knelt to embrace her friend. "Praise the saints that you're well."

Ting poked her soft muzzle into Gemma's hand, soft whickers announcing her joy. *I'm so happy to see you.*

"I'm happy to see you, too." Gemma read the action as clearly as if Ting had used words. "I brought you a carrot. Guess where 'tis." Standing straight among the ponies, Gemma held up both hands, the signal for Ting to search. The pony stretched out her neck to sniff. "No' tucked in my bodice." Gemma smiled as Ting tickled her hip. "Nor in my waistband."

Ting moved to the leather pouch strapped at Gemma's waist. Pulling back her lips, she grasped the closing thong in her teeth and pulled it free of its loop. Thrusting her nose under the pouch flap, she flipped it up and rooted, then pulled free a stumpy carrot with a victorious snort.

"Excellent!" Gemma praised as Ting crunched the carrot with relish. "You're no' the least out of practice, though I guess 'tis been only a day. But it seems like a year, I've missed you so." Gemma scratched Ting's poll as the pony finished crunching the carrot, then butted her pouch for more.

Gemma smiled. "I only brought the one carrot, Ting, but I did bring your brush." She pulled it from her pouch and began on Ting's withers. The pony stood stock-still, eyes closed, an expression of ecstasy on her face.

"I see you've enjoyed yourself. You've been rolling in the mud." Gemma lovingly whisked away a patch of the dried substance. "Well, 'tis good you're frisking with friends, because you canna come back to the castle yet. At any moment, the earl is going to be furious with me, and I dinna want you there. I canna let you suffer for my sins, though they're sins in no one's eyes but his."

The idea of the earl's anger brought her back to the tinker, and suddenly a new fear sprang into Gemma's mind. Bruce had found the body. Had he guessed what the tinker carried when he left Scalloway Castle? Was he the reason there was a body in the first place?

The thought froze her in place, and Ting, sensing something was wrong, rubbed against her, whiffling concern through velvety nostrils.

Saints above, Bruce might be a murderer, and she had complained about him in her letter to the king. Now that he had seen what she wrote, he might seek revenge.

She thought of applying to the earl for relief, but it seemed of little use. Though the earl was no fool, he seemed unaware of how Bruce dominated the people, taking what he wanted of them. He was aware of how she clashed with Bruce regularly though. She had argued with him often enough on behalf of the islanders. How Bruce must have enjoyed finding her letter, knowing she believed it on its way to Edinburgh.

What to do now? Thinking furiously, Gemma attacked the burrs stuck in Ting's tail as the pony stood, a model of patience. She'd meant to appeal to the flame-haired stranger who would arrive at Scalloway any day. Drummond Graham, a Lowland Scot come to buy Shetland wool, was reportedly the delight of women. She'd heard it from Marjorie Tillman, the Scalloway cobbler's wife, who'd heard it of Helga Carnegy of Cunningsburgh, who'd heard it of Lizzie Kennedy of Sandwick, and on down the coast.

Those who'd met him said he was kind and sympathetic. He'd helped Margaret Jones of Lochend cut her summer hay, refusing any payment because she was newly widowed. He'd tended Elsa Strang's new bairn for a full day so she could finish a weaving to pay her rent. He'd listened patiently as she talked of her troubles. Elsa had sworn she'd felt as if a burden had lifted from her shoulders, just being able to speak of her hopes and fears.

The news of his rare understanding spread quickly, as did all information among her network of friends. 'Twas said that Drummond Graham was a brawley man with piercing green eyes that saw into a woman's soul. On Shetland, women knew each other, confided in each other. They had to. There were few other ways to protect themselves. And all the reports from her trusted cronies were the same. He inspired confidence in a woman and kept his mouth shut about what she said. He had seemed the perfect one to ask for assistance, but in light of yesterday's events, she must not.

The task resettled on her shoulders. She must find a way to deal with the earl. Everyone had weak spots. The trick was to learn what they were.

As for the Lowlander, she must stay as far away from him as possible. Another innocent man must not die. She swore it by the miracle of the midnight sun.

Drummond stood for some minutes after Iain left him, assessing the change in the wind. Moisture hung on the air, portent of a storm. A rumble of thunder confirmed his belief. Although the dark clouds had not yet blotted out the midnight sun, a storm boded ill in ways he couldn't completely fathom. He would move along, and Iain had best be quick about his swim.

Hefting his pack, Drummond turned his face toward the hill. He wasn't sure what lay ahead, but from what he'd seen and heard on the island thus far, it wouldn't be good.

Two hectares later, Drummond crested the last rise in the center of the island and spied a herd of horses spread out on the moor below him. What he'd expected, he wasn't sure, but this sight delighted him.

They weren't full-sized English horses. Nor were they the short Scots garrons to which he was accustomed. They were the sturdy draft ponies that originated on these isles, and Drummond had never seen so many in one place. Their muscular bodies could be a miracle of power when required, and he admired the spirited creatures with their lush manes and tails blowing in the wind.

Alert to his presence, even at this distance, the matriarch on the perimeter of the herd raised her head to assess him with intelligent, limpid eyes. Their patriarch, a fine black stallion, whipped his head in Drummond's direction, but he did not move the herd. Not yet.

Drummond sank to a crouch and went very still, hoping they would ignore him and stay. Their untamed beauty awoke an awe in him that he wanted to savor. How many were there? He counted in silence. Perhaps four dozen, and each as wild as the wind.

They were beautiful in their natural setting, against a backdrop of roughening sea. The blue waves were tipped with white caps, another portent of the coming storm.

Far off, a speck that must be a ship tossed on the waves. Tiny islets dotted the water, so small that no one lived on them. Instead, they were covered with sheep, rowed there by their owners to graze on the lush sea grass, puffs of white against green.

A bonnie land, to be sure, full of people who were used too hard by both weather and laird. The nobleman who ruled the Shetland Isles was slowly extracting from them everything they held dear.

As he gazed at the sea, he mourned for them. Would that he could change their lives of poverty. But he had seen worse as he traveled the length of Scotland, always seeking. And when he found what he sought, he *did* change the worse to better, if he could.

That must remain his purpose here—righting the wrongs that were his legacy. Yet along the way, he might relish such innocent joys as gazing upon wild ponies. They were everything he yearned to be, replete in their freedom as he drank in the sight of them, vowing to carry their strength and beauty in his heart.

How ironic that the hated nightmare had led to this pleasure. In the years it had plagued him, that had never happened before.

But then he wasn't the same person he'd been before his father died. His appreciation of the ponies proved that. Once, he would have planned to sell one so he could buy food for himself and his mother. Now, as a flicker of lightning frosted the ponies in silver, he thought instead of ancient verses about elven lords and ladies who rode on silver steeds. Although he didn't believe in fairies, he saw how this sort of scene must have inspired the ancient harpers to sing of the power of enchantment. It certainly entranced him.

A movement captured his attention, and he turned to look. Odd. The hair color he glimpsed seemed inconsistent with the rest of the herd. Instead of being dun or gray or black, it was silver.

Drummond narrowed his gaze, then gripped the hilt of his sword, unwilling to believe his eyes as a human female rose from the midst of the herd.

# Chapter 2

Drummond blinked and looked again. He didn't believe in shape-changing magic. But if a pony hadn't changed into a human female before his eyes, where had she come from?

He must have seen wrong. Illusion caused by the midnight sun and the coming storm. That was it. The twilit moor was changing before his eyes into a darkling, windswept land. Confusing shadows crept across the earth.

He looked away, rubbed his eyes, then looked again, expecting to see ponies and no more. Blast it, she was still there, as tall and willowy as the ponies were short and muscular. She stood in profile among them, her face turned to the sea. Her loose hair formed a fair stream of silver, fluttering behind her slender form. Her cloak and gown were the palest blue-gray, the color of a summer dawn.

Very well, he wasn't seeing things. She must have been crouching among the ponies, he decided, yet would he not have seen her? He had not, for all his keen sight. She had appeared magically among them, as fair as Venus who had risen from a seashell in the sea.

The sight of her was as stimulating as the potent aroma that foretold the storm. She moved among the animals with astonishing grace, and they accepted her as if she were one of their kind.

Unheard of. Yet she was living proof of such power, a queen of enduring majesty, moving as if created by the magic of the storm.

Drummond shook his head, wanting to deny it. Perhaps she fed the ponies so they would accept her. Yet wild ponies didn't let humans come among them, not even for carrots. Besides, he didn't see her feeding them anything.

*The eerie magic of the storm is making me see things. Thunder magic of this enchanted isle.*

As if in answer to his thoughts, thunder clapped. Lightning shot across the sky, a jagged bolt gilding her in silver as she reached the far edge of the herd. She stepped forth like a fairy queen leaving her spellbound throng. One tiny pony broke from the others and trotted after her. Sensing the creature's presence, the woman turned and dropped to her knees, embracing the charming creature, who returned the endearment, rubbing against her affectionately.

*A fey female, beloved of untamed beasts.*

A painful feeling stirred in the region of his heart as he witnessed the amazing bond. Woman and pony, each seemed so wild and free, yet bound to each other by choice. If only he could live that way. But he was chained to a destiny that had dawned in the past and refused to set him free.

A droplet of rain spattered his face, then another. As if she too felt the rain, the woman rose and turned toward the sea. Suddenly, she hugged the pony a last time, guided it back into the herd, and raced off toward the shore as if the devil were at her heels.

Drummond looked to the bay and saw why. The speck had grown large enough to see that it was a ship, listing to one side, its sails flapping uselessly in the wind. It was sinking. The crew, like ants at this distance, plopped from the sides to cling to the jagged rocks littering the sea.

He clutched his pack and raced after her, his interest in the woman overshadowed by tragedy. In the face of death, magic meant nothing. It was powerless to hold evil at bay.

She was already in trouble, Gemma reasoned as she raced for the shore. What matter if she disobeyed the earl on this score? He forbade the islanders to aid damaged ships so he could claim the rich cargos after the crews drowned. But she would defy him, in this and more.

There was no time to lose. The currents offshore flowed strong and deadly. Even if the crew and owners managed to cling to the rocks, they could still be overcome by fright, cold, or the growing waves. She refused to ignore people whose lives were threatened, no matter who ordered it.

Anger burned in her at the earl's injustices, but at least her mood aided her purpose, she thought grimly, as she slipped and slid among the rocks and heather. The shore lay some distance away, despite the excellent view from the moor. Her wrath fueled her feet, so that she ran at record speed.

By the time she pelted onto the shingle, she labored for breath. The wind snatched at her wet cloak and tugged at her hair. No matter. She must rally the men she'd spied huddled together, sharing a dram of ill-gotten liquor. She would never report them. She was too glad to find them when and where she needed them.

"Come," she panted, racing up to where they sat and gesturing furiously at the sinking ship, then at two nearby sixerns pulled up on the shore. "We canna let those people drown." She had to shout to be heard over the rising wind.

The three men, whom she recognized as a fisherman, a laborer, and a cook, stirred, their expressions guilty, though they did not rise. Damn the earl, she thought, frightening them so that they failed to respond to others in need. "Walter, ye almost drowned last Easter." She appealed to the fisherman, whom she knew to be a leader among the townspeople. "Ye will help, will ye no'?"

Walter Douglas grimaced with embarrassment. "The earl says foreigners wish to take advantage o' us."

"Damn what the earl says." Gemma stamped her foot on the hard, wet sand, too enraged to care what they thought of her unladylike outburst and treasonous words. "What does your heart say? Would you turn your back on your fellows? Could you sleep with such a thing on your conscience?"

The three men heaved slowly to their feet, as if torn between her appeal and their fear.

"We'll be punished," Simon Brandie said. As the castle cook and a friend, he had already taken too many risks helping her feed her uncle.

"I'll take the responsibility," she insisted. "I'll tell his lordship I threatened to deny you your daily rations. I won't, of course, but pray help me. We must not stand by and let people drown."

Instead of moving toward the sixerns, the three looked from one to the other, brows furrowed. They glanced at the sinking ship, then back at their feet, refusing to meet her gaze.

"Must I go alone?" she demanded, feverish with fear for the ship's people. "Will no' even one of ye help me?"

"I will, though I hate to take the risk." Simon raised his gaze bravely to meet hers. "The earl lets Lawrence Bruce decide punishments, and I dinna relish another fortnight in the castle dungeon," he added heavily. " 'Tis dank down there, and the swill they give us isna fit for swine."

"At least ye were fed in the dungeon," Manss Olla-son said to Walter. " 'Tis better than layin' stone all day under Bruce's watch without a noon ration. I've had all I can stand."

Gemma wanted to scream with frustration. "Come then, Simon. We'll manage somehow." She moved toward the sixerns, her heart sinking. How would two row the boat meant for six?

"Hold!" a man's voice cracked out behind them.

Her companions gaped at someone behind her, and Gemma whirled in horror, sure it was Lawrence Bruce.

A thunder god from the old Norse tales confronted them, wielding bare steel in a powerful hand. A black cloak whipped around his muscular body, his magnifi-cent mass of flaming red hair flying in the wind. He brandished the sword, and it glittered with savage strength as a bolt of lightning flashed across the sky. His brilliant green eyes leaped with the fires of deadly determination. "You will all help in the rescue," he commanded, shouting into the teeth of the wind. Training the point of his sword on Walter's throat, he gestured toward the boats, his features a grim mask. "Move. Now."

The men scuttled toward the boats as if they'd merely awaited a good excuse to do what they knew was right.

Gemma stood rooted to the spot, too astonished to move as rain trickled from her soaked hair down her face and neck. The tempest whistled in her ears, and still she stared in idiotic awe at the powerful god who had appeared before her, the answer to her prayers.

"We have people to save. Come." He motioned toward the boats. When she failed to obey, he sheathed the sword and stepped forward, the frighten-ing stance of the thunder god receding. " 'Twas your idea to effect a rescue, was it no'?" He offered her a winning, conspirator's smile.

Gemma felt her knees weaken like softened sea sand. With his vivid red hair and piercing green eyes, this had to be Drummond Graham, the man she'd sworn to avoid. An insane feeling of relief washed through her. " 'Twas," she said.

"Then come." His voice gentled as he took her arm to lead her toward the boats.

His touch flashed like lightning through her veins. Her blood laughed in jubilation.

Appalled by her response to him, she pulled away and ran to join the others.

"We won't even ask who ye are," Simon said over his shoulder as Drummond Graham arrived behind her. "We'll tell the earl we were forced to the rescue at sword point by a stranger."

The man nodded, tacitly agreeing to take the blame on his own shoulders.

But as they all heaved to guide the first sixern into the water, Gemma realized she was glad to know who he was, even though the knowledge was a double-edged sword.

As the storm buffeted them, Gemma chafed with impatience. They must hurry, especially since she'd wasted valuable minutes staring at the stranger. Manss and Simon waded into the water and climbed into the lead sixern, as she, Walter, and Graham launched the second boat. Then Walter roped it to the first. As they piled into the lead boat, scrambling for places, a shout hailed them.

"Ho, wait for me. I'll help." Another stranger, younger than Graham but with similar hair of flame, raced after them, his powerful legs churning the water.

Without a word of introduction or explanation, Graham clasped the younger man's hand and hauled him into the sixern.

Another miracle, Gemma thought, shaking her head in bewilderment. Not only did the thunder god appear at the right moment, but he brought an assistant. They had lacked a sixth person to row the boat properly, and at the last moment, one appeared like a gift from above.

She couldn't think how she had merited such good fortune, but she accepted it.

The rowers rearranged themselves, and Gemma found herself sharing a thaft with Drummond Graham. As she fit the peg of her oar into its rooth, guilt swiftly hooked her with its barbs.

Graham should not be involved in this venture. It would further enflame the earl and trigger more of Bruce's punishments. She had vowed to keep him as far removed as possible from the island's affairs. Instead, she involved him and his friend.

Too late to change it. Lives were at stake.

Later, she must find a way to oust him and his friend from their difficulties, but for now . . . Determined to concentrate on the good she could do, she dipped her oar and bent to the task.

The storm lashed the water into choppy waves as they left the shore and moved into the colder, deeper waters of the bay. Gemma struggled to keep rhythm with Walter, who set their pace. Their journey to the rocks was hard-won, and as they neared them, she spied men clinging for their lives, their faces terrified.

*Soon you will be on dry land,* she promised them silently, *safe from the rage of the sea.*

The ship, what was left of it, looked German. Probably full of timber and salt for curing fish. A valuable shipment of items scarce in the isles. The earl would be disappointed if the merchants survived.

But he hadn't reckoned on her, Gemma thought. Tonight, despite his wishes, she would hold death at bay.

Walter, with his skill on the water, brought them alongside the rocks in a thrice, but it was Drummond who lifted the ship's boy to the empty sixern. "There now. In you go." He helped the lad to safety, then the ship's cook, who clutched a beloved iron kettle. A seaman with a gash on his brow joined them. Under Drummond's command, they loaded the extra boat with nine people. The remaining two stared at them with wild-eyed fear as Walter prepared to return the boats to shore.

As Gemma lifted her oar, her gaze locked with that of a man cowering on the rock. Terror radiated from him, wrenching her heart. "Wait!" She half rose to signal Walter. "I'll stay on the rock until you return for me. You, sir. Get in." She reached out to the seaman, who did not wait for another invitation. He gripped the side of the boat and slung one leg over the side.

"*You* shall not. *I* shall." Drummond Graham jerked her back onto the thaft.

But he couldn't enforce his order. As the panicked seaman plunged headlong into Drummond's lap, arms and legs flailing, the boat rocked like a thing gone mad. Drummond released her to grapple with the seaman.

Rising, Gemma yanked up her skirts and straddled the side of the boat. Not content to save only the one man, she gestured to the other. "Get in," she shouted, meaning the two to sit with Drummond on the thaft. It was wide enough, she thought, shifting her weight onto the rock and following with her other foot. She had more strength than these exhausted men. She could easily wait on the rock for the sixern's return.

But as the second man clambered after the first, she slipped. Her movement thrust the boat away, and she plunged into the sea. The shock of icy cold froze the gasp in her throat.

*I can't swim in skirts. I'll drown.*

Gemma lost all track of coherent time as she kicked at the wet fabric wrapped around her legs, waist deep in the water, clawing at the slippery rock for a solid handhold. Images from her childhood on Fair Isle flashed through her mind, an incoherent blur. The family pony nuzzling her with love in its bright eyes. Her aunt's kisses, warmer than her cozy trundle bed. Her uncle's booming laugh tickling her heart as she sat on his knee, secure in the circle of his arms.

*The warmth of his arms.* She felt them now, dragging her from the cold. She grasped instinctively for the hands that lifted her, desperate for safety. Miraculously, she found it. As she found firm footing, she collapsed in a heap on the rock. Wind compounded the cold, and she shuddered violently, appalled by how close her rash decision had brought her to death.

Strong hands drew her against a massive chest, enveloping them both in a warm wool cloak.

Startled, Gemma looked up, irrationally wondering if a crewman on the rock had grown overly familiar.

For the second time that night, she went mute with astonishment.

She was stranded on a rock in the midst of a raging storm, held fast in the sheltering arms of Drummond Graham. It was the most dangerous place she'd ever been.

# Chapter 3

Gemma ducked her head, shivering with cold, feeling thoroughly embarrassed as Drummond drew her onto his lap. She had vowed not to involve him in island affairs, yet here she was, with both arms locked around his middle, clinging to him fiercely.

Nor was staying behind on the rock at all what she had imagined. She had thought to sit in safe tranquility until the sixern returned. Instead, waves alternately buffeted, then tugged at them, seeming intent upon dragging them into the sea. Wind and rain lashed them from all sides.

But her greatest danger was this unexpected intimacy with the captivating Lowland stranger.

"Thank you for staying with me." She winced as her voice cracked. "I had not realized 'twas you who pulled me from the water."

"Impetuous female." He spoke against her hair, tantalizingly close. "You shouldna have left the boat, but I understand why you did it."

He understood her? The idea made her nervous. Her female friends had said he seemed in perfect sympathy with them, but she hadn't expected him to understand her. No man besides her uncle ever had.

They had also said he was bold and bonnie to look upon, though she wondered if any had seen him from this vantage point. She stole a glance at him through her lashes, mortified by the shivers of excitement coursing down her spine. Or was she simply freezing?

Saints above, she sat directly on his lap, feeling the masculine strength of his thighs against her bottom. Their contact sent tides of weakness sweeping through her. Or was it the waves sweeping over her legs, making her dizzy with fear?

Either way, Drummond Graham's well-defined mouth hovered mere inches from hers, infinitely appealing. She realized she was growing hysterical, thinking wild thoughts about sampling them when propriety made it impossible, if not absurd, given their circumstances. Yet she felt entirely alone in a raging world, with no safety but in his arms. She had no intention of letting go for any reason. Not until they were on solid land. Mayhap not even then.

"I had to save the men." She wanted to explain but had to raise her voice to be heard over the storm. "They looked exhausted. I'm sorry to endanger you as well."

"You acted on the impulse of a loving heart."

He did understand her—a shocking experience. In her world, men were either too care worn or work worn to take the time, or they weren't to be trusted.

An icy wave crashed against her back, and Gemma clung to him with all her strength, glad to have saved the men. She disliked her response to the thunder god, especially at this vulnerable moment, yet what choice did she have but to cling to him? She had never before been at the mercy of the raging sea. If they lived despite her mad decision that put them here, she would owe him a great debt.

How would she repay the debt if the best thing for him was to leave the islands? Dismayed by the dilemma, she whimpered as another wave battered them.

Drummond shifted her on his lap and tugged at her knees, pulling them up to her chin. He tightened his cloak around her, binding her more securely against his chest.

*Heavenly warmth.*

Gemma felt a moan build within her, not of suffering but of perverse pleasure. She hadn't been held in so secure and comforting an embrace since she was a child, sitting on her uncle's knee to have a hurt soothed. How ridiculous to feel bliss in the midst of the worst danger of her life.

"Are you cold?" He bent his face near to ask the question.

"No' t-too cold," Gemma stuttered between chattering teeth. Embarrassed, she leaned her head against his shoulder and closed her eyes, devastated by the tender concern in his gaze, by the feel of his one strong arm wrapped around her shoulders, the other around her waist. She couldn't really compare him to her uncle. Not when she was acutely aware of his muscled torso beneath her hands, of how he held her firmly, insisting on their intimate contact to keep her safe. His touch seemed to cherish her, kindling such a fierce glow of excitement within her, she dared not look him in the eye.

As she struggled to maintain control of her emotions, a hard object struck Drummond from behind with sudden force. Gemma felt the shock reverberate through him, heard him suck in a breath. "Are you hurt?" she cried, struggling upright to see.

"Dinna look," he ordered, blocking her view with the cloak.

"Are you injured?" she repeated, running both hands over his back, anxious for him.

"Nay." He captured her arms to stop her urgent inspection. " 'Twas the body of a man from the ship."

Gemma cringed against him, horror prickling through her. Her second brush with death in two days, but this time, someone wished to shield her from its bleakness. The generosity of his effort unnerved her. "Were you ever this near death?" she gasped.

"Aye."

His calm assertion appalled her. "When?"

"I was caught once in a battle. A long story. I was unarmed and on foot among mounted men with axes and swords."

She couldn't believe such a thing had happened. "But that's terrible. Did you come through unscathed?"

He nodded and patted her shoulder, the strength of his broad hand reassuring. Surely he led a charmed life, to have faced death and lived. "Pray tell me more," she said.

"No' now. One day, if you like."

Would they ever have a day together for her to hear his story? Gemma doubted it, but he seemed sure they would. Shivers racked her body, and she realized she was chilled to the bone yet suffused with a tingling excitement from their intimacy. Confused, she bent her head and closed her eyes against the beauty of his strong features. "How did you know we needed help?" she asked, trying to deny she enjoyed his touch so much.

"I was watching you from above the moor. I saw you run for the ship."

Disturbed, Gemma raised her head and met his gaze. "You saw me with the ponies?"

"Is something wrong with that?"

Everything was wrong with it. If he mentioned to anyone that she'd been with the herd, the earl would learn of it and know where to find Ting. "Dinna breathe a word," she begged. "I have no right to ask anything of you, not after what you've risked. But I'll do anything you wish if you'll no' mention you saw me with the ponies, or that the ponies were on the moor."

He looked puzzled by her plea yet convinced of her

urgency. He nodded slowly, gazing deeply into her eyes. For the first time, Gemma felt exposed. Bare to the soul. Her wet clothing seemed a scant barrier between her yearning flesh and his warmth.

Drummond Graham really could see into a woman's thoughts and spirit. And surely he saw within her the animal urge to lie with him, to change them from remote strangers to intimates bound by a shared risk. Though she had not meant it to happen, they were intimates already, locked in each other's arms. It was a disaster.

He must have sensed her concern, for he pulled her head against his chest and cradled her, arranging her arms to hold him as well. "Hush. Don't think about it now," he murmured into her ear. "Everything will come right in the morning. Just hold on to me."

She caught her breath as he pressed his cheek against her hair. His grip on her tightened, as if he never meant to let her go.

*Don't think about it.* As if he knew that her mind wasn't on the rescue. If he understood that, she was doomed. Before this moment, no man had inspired passion in her, but now it blazed to life in her heart and mind. She could think of one thing only. And that was of lying with Drummond Graham, naked, in a place of great serenity. Of holding him, and of his holding her, until the moon had set, and the stars had long ago gone to their heavenly beds.

Sitting on a rock in a raging storm was no banquet, but as Drummond spied the returning sixern, battling its way through the waves, he felt a stab of regret. From the moment he'd seen this woman rise like Venus from among the ponies, she had touched something deep within him that he usually denied in his workaday world devoted to his quest. The wish to fulfill his own needs, not just the needs of others, had attacked him with savage intensity, taking him by surprise.

Desire as powerful as the storm enveloped him. He wanted to throw discretion to the winds, to touch her, kiss her, make love to her right there on the rock, with the scent of the sea and the wild waves surrounding them. Nor would the urge respond to reason and depart.

The fact that they were stranded in the middle of the bay, savaged by wind and weather, intensified the desire, and he was at a loss to explain why.

The sixern maneuvered next to the rock, and his brother, ever reliable when he needed him, reached out to help the woman on board. Iain sent him a questioning glance as Drummond followed into the safety of the boat. "We're all right," he reassured Iain, settling the queen of the ponies on the bench beside him.

She slid as far away from him as possible, as if mortified that anyone should know of their recent intimacy. His body stirred in response to the sight of her lips, flushed rosy from the chill, the firmness of her breasts and thighs evident through her wet clothes.

His body's timing was terrible. They had people to care for who were in shock from being cast into freezing water, perhaps from losing comrades. The ship had surely carried more than the eleven they had rescued. Lives had been lost. Mastering his errant emotions, he plied his oar.

As they climbed out of the sixern and dragged it to shore, Drummond saw the rescued men moving up the shingle toward the castle. Under the woman's direction, the few who couldn't manage on their own were helped by the other rescuers.

Who was she, to direct them?

Rather than entering the imposing, unfriendly castle, she sent them to the byre. The warmth of the oxen and cattle assailed him as they entered the clean, cozy stone building with a thatched roof. Those who had the strength climbed the ladder to the loft and collapsed in the hay.

"Pray help them out of their wet clothes," she directed Drummond without preliminaries. "The others will fetch dry clothing. I'll bring hot soup and drinks."

She whisked off, all remote efficiency despite her obvious exhaustion. She returned in dry clothing, followed by a lad wheeling a barrow. On it sat a steaming kettle and stacks of wooden bowls. Some of the sailors, now in clean though ragged garments brought by her three associates, gathered at the front of the loft, eager for the soup she ladled out and passed up the ladder.

Once she'd fed those on their feet, she climbed the ladder and moved among them, checking those who'd fallen asleep from exhaustion, assisting those too weak to eat on their own. Drummond worked at her side, propping up a sailor with a gash on his brow so she could apply healing ointment. When they were done, she pointed to the barrow below.

"I brought blankets," she said crisply. "I pray you fetch them, for this man is still cold."

As Drummond climbed down the ladder, he saw her slip a slender arm around the shoulders of the ship's boy and help him sit for his soup. The young fellow slurped the hot broth, clinging to her as if she were a guardian angel come to save his soul.

Not until they were all asleep did she descend the ladder and speak to Drummond in hushed tones. "Are you well?" she asked, as disappointingly distant as if she had not molded her body to his a short time ago.

"No harm done."

Drummond said the words with cool composure, but they weren't true. Infinite harm had been done to his peace of mind as he'd leaped from the boat to haul her from the threatening water and into his arms. He studied the tired line of her shoulders, the heaviness of her eyelids, and felt the reckless wish to return to the rock if it earned him the privilege of holding and protecting her. An absurd notion.

"I only held to you so tightly on the rock because I feared being swept away. I do apologize." She sent him a cautious glance, as if reading his thoughts and afraid of them. "It felt so safe, like when I was a child and my uncle would hold me after I'd had a nightmare."

Drummond understood nightmares all too well. "I'm glad you think of me as kindly as of your uncle. I take it he is no longer living. You speak of him as if he were not."

Her expression turned tragic, and he regretted touching a sore point for her. "He is living, but . . . that is, he . . ." She paused, then seemed to collect herself with self-conscious effort. "Excuse me. 'Tis naught to involve you. Pray forget I mentioned it."

"I am glad to be of service." He felt immediate concern for her uncle, who clearly worried her. "And will continue to be, if possible. Is your uncle ill?"

"Yes. I mean no, but he will be. That is . . ." She paused again, looking stricken. "Pray dinna ask. You have already put yourself in danger by helping us. You should leave here at dawn."

Drummond shook his head, unable to believe that *she* expected to protect *him*. Clearly he was the one who should do the protecting. "I *chose* to help."

"You have my gratitude for saving these poor people," she said. "You must tell me what I can do to serve you before you depart." She touched his arm in a pleading gesture.

He felt a poignant response, sure that she didn't ask many things of others, that when she did, her requests came in this form—asking others to say what she could do for them. "Very well," he conceded. "You can tell me why the ponies on the moor love you so. What is your secret, pray?"

She sucked in a breath and glanced around, obviously alarmed by his question. "You promised not to mention them."

"There's no one to hear." He looked around too but saw no one. What did she fear? Even Iain had bedded down in the hayloft earlier, saying he was too tired to move.

"You must tell no one I was there." Her pale brow creased in a frown, and her eyes, the same clear blue as the Shetland sea, burned with fear. "Why were *you* there at such a time?"

He couldn't think why it mattered, but as she'd gone to the moor at midnight, she must have her reason. "I couldna sleep, so my brother and I decided to walk on to Scalloway. I happened on you by chance. I'll no' mention it to anyone if 'tis so important to you."

Despite his promise, she seemed to lose confidence in him. She stepped back, stiffening her spine with a dignity meant to keep him at arm's length. "Thank you. I'll leave you now so you can sleep. As I said, you should depart at dawn."

He couldn't think why she kept insisting he leave. "I have business with the earl."

She blanched. "Can you not go your way?" she urged.

"Why?"

She hesitated. "Because . . . the earl will be displeased that we rescued the crew. He wants whatever cargo is salvaged for himself," she blurted, then winced. "I shouldna have said that."

Drummond was glad she had. So the risk he'd taken was braving the earl's wrath. No wonder she wanted to protect him. "I'm staying," he said with force, furious at this new evidence of the earl's tyranny.

She took his anger wrong, drawing back with an air of haughty disdain. "If you insist, but I hope you can improve on your ability to keep out of our affairs. For your own sake."

The withdrawal of her trust hurt more than he liked

to admit. "I intend to tell the earl that the rescue was my idea. I'll tell him that I forced you and the others to aid me."

A degree of stiffness deserted her spine. "That is good of you, but he willna believe you. He knows me too well."

He wondered who she was to the earl, that the man knew her so well. "I'm still staying. The earl corresponded with me some months ago and invited me to the castle. I expect he has enough breeding to know how to treat a guest."

"He'll find a way to punish you, guest or no."

The idea of anyone being so vindictive made him even more determined to stay. Her brave resignation in the face of the man's ruthlessness touched him, even as his blood boiled with rage. "Then 'twill be my duty to deny him the pleasure."

Her face tightened, and worry brooded deep in the twin lakes of her eyes. The battle lines were drawn between him and the earl, and she appeared terrified of what that meant.

The desire to protect her overwhelmed him as he guided her to the shadows of the stable entry. "Let it go for tonight. All I want is an answer to my question about the ponies. Then you must go to your bed." He wasn't afraid of the earl, and he thought he might finally be able to sleep. But first, he wanted to understand the magical attraction she held for the animals, as well as for him.

Her expressive eyes changed yet again, this time becoming enigmatic. " 'Tis no secret." She shrugged evasively. "I simply lack any interest in exploiting them."

A dart of irritation stabbed Drummond. She thought to push him away by suggesting he would ill-use the ponies. "You know I have no wish to exploit them, yet I doubt they'd trust me to walk among them," he pressed.

"No? Well, since they're mostly female, perhaps they dinna want to be like the many women you've met since you landed on Shetland."

"What do you know of the women I've met?" he demanded, disliking the veiled criticism in her tone.

She lifted her chin, her eyes snapping with sudden reproach. "I've heard about ye, Drummond Graham. They say ye've broken hearts all the way up the coast."

Her announcement brought Drummond up short. Him? Breaking hearts? "How did ye hear that?"

"We women talk to each other, that's how."

"They *said* I broke their hearts?"

She met his gaze, a challenge in her eyes. "You cast a spell that makes them trust you. They say you're the perfect man."

He smiled wryly at that. The perfect man. If only she knew. "What does a perfect man do with such trust?"

"He makes a woman want to pour out her heart."

She made it sound so easy. An interesting way of looking at the painstaking technique he'd developed to question women. It usually began with backbreaking or tedious labor on the women's behalf to win their trust, followed by patient hours of listening to their thoughts, the majority of them irrelevant to his quest. Despite this, he had come to enjoy the confidences shared, to appreciate the depth of their dreams, their desires. The companionship, however fleeting, relieved the tedium of his life. "I dinna hear *you* pouring out your heart," he said.

A wistfulness flitted across her face, as if she were sorely tempted to do what she decried. "The fault lies in the women, I suppose," she said pensively. "They find you so sympathetic, they imagine they're in love. You break their hearts without even knowing it."

"Mayhap you're afraid I'll break yours?" He didn't

know what possessed him to tease her, but she didn't seem to mind.

Irony tinged her low laugh. "Of all the things in the world I fear, that is the last. I have more pressing issues at stake."

"I've a mind to hear them."

"Nay!" Her manner changed again to apologetic. " 'Tis too dangerous. You'll miss nothing, I assure you," she added hastily. "In fact, you're better off not knowing. Buy our wool, profit from it, and go your way. The sooner the better. I wish you nothing but well, Drummond Graham."

After the depth of their involvement, he didn't appreciate her continual insistence that he leave, especially after he'd made his intentions clear. "You have the advantage of me, I fear, mistress, as I dinna ken your name."

"That's a rarity. A woman seldom has the advantage over a man." Her mouth quirked sweetly at the corners. "I'll keep it for a while, if you dinna mind."

He did mind. He didn't like anyone, male or female, having an advantage over him. But if she had to live under the earl's rule, perhaps it was the only advantage she was likely to have. "Very well. If you will explain about the ponies," he coaxed.

Anxiety dominated her features once more, and he remembered the beauty of the bond he'd witnessed between her and the tiny white pony. Clearly she wanted to protect the creature.

"One of them is very precious to you. Is that it?" he asked.

"Precious. Aye." Her admission was reluctant yet tender, coming on a soft exhalation. Her eyes misted, and he knew she was far away, on the moor with her pony. Her face glowed with radiant beauty as love illuminated her from within. "Have you ever had someone give you their complete trust? Someone whose devotion is selfless?" she whispered, touching his arm. "You know you'll always be loved, no matter what you say or do. Always forgiven your errors."

He ached within as she spoke, remembering the pangs of hunger he'd endured so his mother could eat. The ragged skirts she'd worn so she could buy books and teach him to read. He had loved her utterly, and she had loved him, forgiving him the things he'd done.

"I can see that you have," she observed, catching him in his moment of weakness. "But you don't like remembering it. Something about it is disturbing. What?"

Her perception hurt almost as much as the old pain knifing through him. "Many things in life are difficult," he said stiffly. "We get along in spite of it."

"Some don't." She gazed at him with a keenness that made him squirm. "Some of us never can," she said pointedly, "unless we believe in magic."

She looked as regal as the storm that ruled the wind, daring him to accept her answer. Yet he couldn't believe in magic. He had come to the Shetland Islands on a deeply personal quest, given him by his dead father who had loved wreaking havoc with personal vendettas and illegal ventures, leaving others to repair the damage.

With a history like that, Drummond had no time for magic. His life was devoid of it. So was hers, it seemed to him.

But as she turned and hurried toward the castle, leaving him alone, he closed his eyes . . . and suddenly he stood above the moor once again. The billowing green land spread out below him, and the wind sang in his ears. The fairy queen, with her hair a fair stream of silver, stepped forth in his mind's eye, leaving her enchanted throng to embrace the white pony. The richness of their love sang between them like the wind, high and sweet, and as the storm swept the sky, he was rocked by the thunder magic of the isle.

It made him see the hole in his life, and it yawned before him, as black and empty as the void.

# Chapter 4

"You have dark circles under your eyes, Gemma."
Gemma froze in place as the earl entered the cavernous great hall from his private entrance behind the dais. His choice of words seemed innocuous, as always, but his tone blistered with disapproval. All sound died from the fifty-some men, women, and children breaking their fast at the long trestle tables before her.

Realizing their moment of confrontation had arrived, Gemma gathered her courage and rose from her place at the high table. The earl towered over her, obsidian eyes boring into her.

So he wanted witnesses to their quarrel. Very well, she must fight on his terms, but she had her weapons ready. "Aye, I could scarce sleep last night, my lord, after—"

"You were *out* most o' the night, Gemma," he interrupted in harsh tones. "I have it on good authority that your bed was not slept in." He paused and narrowed his eyes to disapproving slits. "Members of my household must be above reproach in behavior. If you expect to remain here, reputation intact, this must no' happen again."

Gemma straightened her back in outrage. She had expected a battle over what she'd done, not this roundabout attack. "You make it sound as if I were having a illicit liaison.'Twas nothing of the kind. You know what I was doing."

"I do," the earl said grimly. "And I dinna approve." He nodded at something over her shoulder, and from the corner of her eye, Gemma saw Drummond Graham and his companion from last night enter the hall.

Guilt hit her like an unexpected blow to the gut. *Stay away,* she wanted to cry, her agitation compounding. She had never meant to bring them into the island's troubles. How could she protect them, as she must, when she was under attack?

Yet for an instant, the comfort she'd felt in Drummond's arms last night returned to haunt her. Oh, to be back on the rock, held against his warmth, the safety she felt in his arms stronger than wind and waves.

But she could not expect him to offer her refuge. It must be the other way around. Shifting her attention back to the earl, she found him studying her. He glanced in Drummond's direction, raised his eyebrows, and sent her a subtle, knowing glance.

Heat flooded Gemma's neck and face as she took his meaning. He knew all about the improper, illogical longing she felt for Drummond Graham. The arousal she'd felt as he'd held her. The satisfying intimacy of their exchange by the stable door. He'd always had the uncanny ability to read her thoughts. Now he ripped away her privacy, leaving her vulnerable and exposed.

At that moment, Lawrence Bruce swaggered into her line of vision. As the earl's uncle, Bruce had served the Stewarts since long before Gemma was born. Tall of stature, with massive arms, legs the size of small trees, and dark, glittering eyes, he offered Gemma a satisfied sneer. Clearly he knew the subject of their dispute. Bruce might even be the one who had reported her unslept-in bed, as he often told the earl about household misconduct. He seemed to relish meting out the punishments, a task the earl left to him.

Had Bruce or one of his lackeys watched her with Drummond in the stable last night and reported to his lordship? That, coupled with the softening of her expression just now, would have been enough for the earl to guess her feelings.

Gemma schooled her expression, determined to reveal nothing, to feel nothing, either about the earl's discovery, about Bruce's cruel smirk, or about Graham.

Despite her resolve, sweat bathed her body, followed by cold.

*Be calm,* she cautioned. She must make the earl believe her interest in Drummond was easily forgotten. And she must defend what she had done to help the crew of the wrecked ship. "Your lordship, I did what I did because I was concerned about—"

"I know what concerns you, and it does not please me," he rapped out with unnerving force. "There are other matters requiring your attention. Where is that pony of yours?"

Fear surged through her. He *would* use Ting to hurt her. She must attack first. "Your lordship, I believe that Master Bruce had a hand in that tinker's drowning," she blurted, ignoring Bruce's furious frown. "I saw that his clothing was wet after he'd been out the night before."

"Wet clothing proves nothing." The earl trivialized her accusation. "What you *should* have seen is that your undisciplined pet soiled my favorite carpet two mornings past. You should have spent last night cleaning it, as you promised when I let that creature into the castle. Instead, you traipsed about the island for most o' the night. The animal will be punished. A dozen lashes. See to it, Bruce." He snapped his fingers, and the magistrate bowed, indicating his willingness to do his duty.

Before quitting the hall, he paused to capture Gemma's gaze. His dark eyes glittered with fury at her accusation about the tinker. He would be avenged.

Dismayed, Gemma watched a slow smile slither across his swarthy features as he saw his threat register. Then he was gone in search of Ting.

The earl nodded curtly, satisfied that his orders would be obeyed. He turned to leave the hall.

Gemma gasped, startled by the swiftness of events. She'd not even had a chance to argue the rightness of what she'd done. Knowing Ting was safe, at least for the moment, she squared her shoulders and raced after the earl. She would not to let the matter drop.

"Whip *me* if you wish, for rescuing the men last night," she cried, catching his sleeve, speaking so that the entire hall could hear, "but do not bring Ting into *our* disagreement."

He swiveled and met her gaze with surprise. "Whip ye, Gemma? I've never done such a thing. Why do ye imagine I would?"

She lifted her chin to confront him. "For rescuing the men from the ship last night."

"They are not the subject of our dispute."

"They are. You are displeased with me for assisting them, so punish me, no' my pony." There. She had accused him in public, come what may.

He smiled gently, as if she were a wayward child. "People in need of food and shelter are welcome at Scalloway. 'Tis Scots hospitality, Gemma. Ye ken that."

Gemma seethed as he said one thing but meant another. "What of their cargo?" she challenged, waiting to see if he would claim the timber, tools, and other goods for himself.

He regarded her with a contemptuous expression. "I have studied the position o' the wreck and 'tis too dangerous to retrieve the cargo. We canna risk more lives."

Gemma's anger rose. His decision meant one thing. The owner of the ship was among the survivors. If the earl couldn't have the cargo, he would ensure that no one else did, not even the one entitled to it.

As he turned to go, she clasped his arm once more, fury overcoming fear. "If King James knew what happened to foreign ships that—"

"Gemma, we have guests. Where are yer manners?" he barked, his counterattack swift and brutal. "Perform the introductions at once."

Gemma whirled in confusion to find Drummond Graham and his companion standing a mere pace behind her. Drummond's concerned gaze sent a dart of hope through her, yet what could he do to change the earl's ways? "They have not told me their names," she said, averting her face as she told the partial lie.

"Then go to yer chamber and stay there," the earl snapped. "I shall speak to ye anon."

Gemma glared at him. Once more he rendered her powerless, unable to defend herself or others in critical matters, and she resented it. "I'll be in the byre, seeing to our other guests, the crew from the ship who, as ye say, are entitled to our care." Lifting her head with defiance, she swept from the dais, aware that every eye followed her retreat.

Including Drummond Graham's.

The hole in his life grew deeper and blacker as Drummond watched the woman called Gemma leave the hall. He had learned from a stable lad that she was companion to the earl's wife, though the countess often had her supervise her children. Despite her servant status, Gemma clearly did not accept the earl's tyranny. The mixture of rage and desolation in her expression cut him to the core.

Patrick Stewart, the Earl of Orkney and Laird of the Shetland Islands, stood a length away, clad in trunk hose and doublet like a Lowland Scot. Here was the source of the island's misery, girded with dirk and sword. Although the earl was in his fifties, though his hairline receded, he looked every bit the vigorous warrior. His high forehead sloped down to a regal Roman nose and a fierce expression that spoke of power. His eyes gleamed with a ruthless light, suggesting he was hot for battle and would relish the excuse to crush anyone in his path.

Drummond had once lived in the shadow of such a man. He knew the mental terrain, had walked it, waking and sleeping, for many a year.

Unable to abandon the coming conflict, he steeled himself for the first skirmish and saluted with a slight inclination of his head. "Drummond Graham, at your service, my lord. My brother, Iain Lang."

"Brother?" the earl rasped. "You mentioned nay brother in your letter." Even as he accepted Iain's presence, his tone accused Drummond for failing to ask permission to bring an extra guest. He meant to put Drummond in the wrong and keep him there.

Drummond ignored the power play. "We have business to discuss, I believe."

The earl grunted and nodded toward the table. "Have you broken your fast?"

"I have, though my brother has not."

"Lang may dine, then. You shall follow me."

Iain approached the table, clearly eager to escape the coming confrontation.

The earl led the way through his private door and down the passage. As they entered his withdrawing chamber, Drummond felt his blood boil with resentment. The luxury of the wood-paneled, tapestry-hung room as compared to the impoverished stone cots of the islanders was inexcusable. As the earl motioned him to a chair and ordered spiced wine, he had to restrain his desire to launch an all-out attack.

"Terrible weather last night," the earl began congenially. "Ye arrived before the storm?"

"I was caught in it. It made the work harder, but we managed."

"The . . . work?" The earl set the words like a trap.

Drummond refused to play games. "The work of rescuing the poor souls from that damaged ship. German, I believe. I saw it sinking and commandeered the first people I found to assist. I suppose I frightened them, but they were able enough once I put my sword to their throats. Until then, they were uninclined to do my bidding. Why is that?"

The earl frowned. "I canna say. What are their names? I'll strive to learn."

Drummond frowned back, sure the earl meant to use the men's reluctance as another excuse for punishment. He wasn't falling into that trap either. "I have no idea of their names. I dinna think I would even recognize them again. But I'm guessing they hesitated because you've forbidden such rescues."

The earl shook his dark head, his expression perplexed. "Gemma told ye that. I canna think why she tells tales. I've issued nay such order."

"You dinna have to." Drummond was in no mood to mince words. "Those who go against your wishes know soon enough that they've trespassed. Your punishments speak for you."

For the first time, the earl reddened. He leaned forward in his high-backed chair. "If someone accuses me o'—"

"They would never dare accuse you," Drummond interrupted, venting his anger in rudeness. "They're too afraid."

The earl sank back in his chair, his eyes radiating cold fury. "I am laird here. I could discipline ye for such audacity."

"But you won't. I have too many friends in high places. They know I'm here. Specifically, they know I'm visiting you and staying at your castle." He stared back at the earl, challenging.

Momentary fear flickered in the older man's eyes. Before it could harden into rage, Drummond leaped to the offensive. "I heard you order that pony whipped. You did it to punish Mistress Gemma for her part in the rescue. Let's just say I'll do nothing for now about how you treat foreign traders if you spare the beast. I'll even pay for your soiled carpet, so you lose nothing."

"Disciplining a dumb beast is entirely appropriate."

"But sabotaging international shipping is not. King James would be displeased to know that you purposely let drown merchants who come to trade on Scots soil."

The earl narrowed his gaze, but Drummond thought he detected a glimmer of discomfort. "So then," he pressed, "what is the price to replace your carpet? I'll pay in gold."

"Ye like ponies so well?"

His tone suggested Drummond had a perverted interest in the creatures. The man was a champion at twisting a person's meaning, using it to attack. "What is its value?" he repeated.

"I canna understand yer interest in an animal ye've never seen."

So the earl hoped he would admit to seeing the pony and thus locate it. Drummond remained stubbornly silent.

The earl grunted, as if admitting defeat. "Six pounds will cover the carpet's value. And *I* will tell Mistress Sinclair of my decision to spare her pet. Ye'll say nothing to her."

Drummond nodded, but as he counted out gold coins and the earl urged him to discuss his plans to buy Shetland wool, he knew the friendly overture was a farce. They were now open enemies, and the earl was a dangerous man. Today, he chose to play the magnanimous lord, accepting the gold. But Drummond knew he would bide his time, waiting for the right moment to strike back. This extraction of gold was only the beginning of what Drummond would pay for his foolish audacity of challenging the man in power.

Yet he had learned audacity all too well from his reckless father. He couldn't suppress it now.

As he approached the door to leave, a small girl trotted into the chamber, holding one hand aloft. "Papa, Papa. I hurt my finger," she sobbed, wiping away fat tears with her other hand.

The earl leaped to his feet, radiating concern. The child of perhaps four or five ran into his arms, and he swept her into a bear hug. "Show me where." He settled her on his knee and made a great show of examining the thumb, which clearly was not severely injured. "How did it happen, Elizabeth?" he asked gravely.

"Gordie bit it." She favored him with an ingenuous smile.

The earl threw back his head and emitted a vibrant laugh. "Gordie is but a wee babe, my bonnie Elizabeth. He has only a few teeth."

"I ken that, Papa. But he bit me just the same."

They shared a laugh over the jest, and the earl pressed the child's thumb to his lips. "There. I kissed it better." Then he tickled her, making her giggle.

Drummond watched in silence, suppressing the futile hope that a man who so loved a child might be convinced to have more compassion for his people. He could not put much value on the earl's easy way with his own offspring. Some men saw love and hate as two sides of the same coin. They were capable of both passions in equal measure, especially the second if someone threatened what they considered theirs.

Drummond returned to the great hall and stood in the private entry, brooding. What idiocy had driven him to interfere in island politics? In doing so, he compounded the difficulty of his task.

The earl had given him permission to continue buying wool in the Scalloway area, but clearly did not believe it his only interest. What could he believe after Drummond had had the audacity to interfere in his affairs? The man was suspicious. Drummond sensed it lurking beneath his smooth exterior. He sensed a good many other things about the earl and his plans, none of them good.

Drummond drew the imaginary cloak of his disguise closer around him. No one must learn his purpose here, especially not the Laird of the Shetland Isles. He should buy wool, conduct his business, and cause as little stir as possible.

Unfortunately, his anger didn't permit it. He couldn't bear to see a tyrant abuse people. Though he couldn't expect to accomplish much in defending the islanders, he had at least bought Gemma's pony a release from punishment. A small victory, yet a victory, nonetheless.

The earl had apparently finished his tête-à-tête with his daughter, for she skipped up behind him as he gazed at the company in the hall. She flicked him a pert, fearless smile as she brushed by and went to sit at table. As the child slid onto a bench, the bright gleam of a silver head caught Drummond's eye. He fastened on it, and his chest tightened.

Gemma must have checked on the men at the byre, then returned, because she now sat at the high table between a young man in his teens and a lovely girl of similar age with hair of flame. A babe, undoubtedly the few-toothed Gordie named by Elizabeth, squirmed on Gemma's lap, and she dropped a kiss on his head as he chuckled and drooled.

These must be the earl's children, and between them sat Gemma Sinclair, as shining as her name. Beautiful jewel, like the island where she lived. Her fair hair shone, incandescent with morning light. Her sky blue kirtle skirt and bodice molded to her curves, reminding him of how she had felt in his arms last night.

He would dearly like to hold her again. To peel away the blue fabric and explore those graceful curves in detail. He imagined the full swell of her breasts without their covering. The images his mind conjured were maddeningly erotic. It fired his lust.

Curse the illogical drive of male appetite, he didn't want to be aroused. Not now. Not when her eyes were full of sadness and longing. A woman so bright and tragically beautiful should be treated with respect.

He forced his gaze away and searched the hall for Iain. His brother was seated on the other side of the flame-haired lass. The girl parted rosy lips and spoke. Iain answered eagerly, his mouth stretched into a smile so broad, so ingratiating, it reached from ear to ear.

Drummond knew that smile and groaned inwardly. It couldn't be. Iain had promised.

But as he watched, Iain captured the girl's hand and carried it to his lips in a gallant gesture. His expression of adoration spoke volumes.

Just what Drummond needed to complicate his problem with the earl.

Iain was in love. Again.

# Chapter 5

"Did it go badly, Drummond? What did the earl say?"

Drummond snapped his attention from Iain to find Gemma gazing up at him, the chuckling babe in her arms. Her blue eyes were wide with concern.

Always thinking of others before herself. Her pony was to be whipped, or so she believed. She had slept poorly last night, if at all. Yet her first care was for him and his confrontation with the earl. Her gentle consideration touched him more than he liked to admit.

*I paid him not to whip your pony,* he wanted to say, but stopped. He'd promised to let the earl tell her. Although Drummond didn't trust the man, he must wait a reasonable interval before breaking his word. "Who is the young lady next to my brother?" he asked gruffly.

"Lady Rowena, the earl's eldest daughter." She studied him with an air of tender anxiety that broke him into a thousand pieces. He'd met many women on his travels. Many were attractive, yet Gemma Sinclair touched him as none had before, with her innocent courage in the face of oppression.

"What did he say?" she quizzed him again. "I can see you're distressed."

He grimaced at her ability to read him. "I am distressed. My brother has just fallen in love."

Gemma's gaze flicked to Rowena and Iain, her face revealing surprise. "Impossible. They've only just met." She looked so earnest, so sure of her statement as she tipped up her face to contradict him.

The position put her soft lips at just the right angle for kissing. Interest shot through his loins, and a fit of devilment overtook him as he studied the dewy texture of her mouth. "What's impossible about it? Short acquaintance has nothing to do with male-female attraction." He loaded his tone with sexual innuendo, raking the curves of her breasts and waist with his gaze.

Ruby-rich color flamed her cheeks as she stared at him, appalled.

He lifted his eyebrows, enjoying her response. "You should save your judgment for things you understand."

Her embarrassment shifted to indignation. "I do understand such things, sir. Better than you think." She tossed her head.

Intrigued by this suggestion, he couldn't resist letting his gaze fall once more to the blue fabric pulled taut over her breasts.

She blushed brighter, if that were possible, and stepped back.

Drummond didn't consider this the response of an experienced woman. "You understand in theory, but not in practice," he said dryly, stabbing in the dark. "Am I right?"

She bowed her head, seeming suddenly humbled, and he realized he'd hit another sore point for her. At once, he was sorry. She didn't need more pain. He'd let lust guide his words and hurt her in the process, which was unforgivable.

"We're not talking about attraction," she countered

unexpectedly, her head jerking up in defiance. "We're speaking of love. There's a difference, which *you* obviously dinna understand."

Now she'd hit *his* sore point. "I understand it perfectly," he snapped, angry that she'd caught him off guard. Immediately regretting his harshness, he tempered his tone. "Whatever our opinions about love, Iain believes in his own. He's been in love more times than I can count and he's only seventeen. It turns him into an adulating puppy, unable to see anything but the object of his obsession. He makes disastrous decisions. Not that the earl's daughter isn't charming and all that is proper," he amended. "But he is far below her in social status. His lordship willna approve."

"He willna, indeed," she confirmed. "She's promised to the son of a Highland chieftain."

Drummond nodded. "I dinna approve either. Iain goes to such extremes when he's in love, he becomes impossible to manage and good for nothing. He forgets his duty, his friends, his kin. He even forgets to eat, sleep, or drink."

"What will you do?"

He noticed she did not suggest he depart. Good. She'd given up that tack. "I must convince him he's not in love."

"If he really believes he is, it won't matter if you think he is not."

Drummond winced inwardly. Mayhap she knew more about the subject than he'd thought. "I can limit his time with her, and you can keep her out of his sight."

"You sound as if you intend to be here a while. What are your plans?"

"I intend to purchase wool in the Scalloway area. The earl welcomed me to the island and gave me free rein." He felt guilty lying to her. They both knew there was nothing welcoming about the earl. She was so perceptive, she might even suspect he concealed other reasons for coming to the isles.

"You have good reason to leave if you're right about your brother. I warned you last night that you should not remain. I suggest you depart," she said.

There it was again, her insistence that he leave, which infuriated him. "I suggest you keep your suggestions to yourself."

She frowned, seeming annoyed with him but in full possession of her temper.

He couldn't think how she maintained her peace of mind after last night, or after her public quarrel with the earl. Unless she were used to living with tyranny. Accepted it as an unpleasant but ever-present aspect of life. And she believed her pony was safe for now, hidden away with the wild herd. In truth, Ting was safer than she knew. The idea gave him satisfaction.

But Iain's dumb expression of worship as he gazed at the beautiful Rowena did not satisfy him. He must separate the pair at once. Without another word, he moved toward the table.

Gemma followed and quickly performed the introductions. Rowena was fourteen. The lad next to her was Robert, the earl's heir, sixteen and sullen. He left the hall as soon as he'd been introduced, exiting through the earl's private door. Elizabeth was five, and Gordie, only a year old. Though the infant was a bundle of wiggling warmth in Gemma's arms, Drummond saw at once he was a terror to anything at his level. Within minutes of being set on the floor to amuse himself, the child yanked the cat's tail. It screeched and leaped onto the table, upsetting a pitcher of milk.

"Oh, dear." Gemma soaked up the spill with linen toweling.

As Drummond grabbed a napkin to help, Elizabeth jumped up and captured Iain, as energetic as a spinning top. "Play quoits with me," she demanded.

Iain agreed, though he never took his gaze from Rowena.

As Gemma finished mopping, a page entered and bowed before her. "His lordship wishes to see ye in his withdrawing chamber, Mistress Sinclair."

There. The earl would tell her about her pony. She would be relieved when she returned.

Drummond let out his breath and sank into a chair. He hadn't realized how tense he'd been. "I do believe I'll accept the earl's earlier invitation to break my fast." He reached for a loaf of bread.

Gemma produced a little pearl-handled eating knife from a sheath on her belt and cut him a slice. As she placed the brown barley bread on a trencher and handed him the crock of butter, she regarded him, her head cocked to one side, seeming puzzled by his decision to stay.

Drummond drew out his own eating knife and concentrated on buttering the bread.

Gemma shrugged, as if to say she would never understand him, and padded away. Her soft slippers made little sound as she disappeared down the passage to see the earl.

Drummond eyed Iain, who had coaxed Rowena to join him and Elizabeth in the game. Much as he would like to whisk away his moonstruck brother, his desire to remain was greater.

He *must* see Gemma Sinclair after she knew her pony had been spared. If he had guessed aright, and he thought he had, judging from her response to his jibe about love, she had little experience with such happiness.

But at least one wrong in her life would now be put right.

"Come in, Gemma. Aye, I want a word wi' ye."

Gemma entered the earl's withdrawing chamber, stiff with anxiety, expecting the worst. Was he going to issue a worse punishment in private than he had before everyone in the great hall?

He pointed his long, bony finger at the chair across from him, and she sat. He rarely asked her to sit in his presence, especially not if he intended to reprimand her. The unexpected courtesy worried her, and she waited as he lounged in his black velvet chair, fingering the gold tassels ornamenting the arms.

"I'll come to the point, Gemma." He sat forward. "Drummond Graham has been sent by King Jamie to murder my sons. Ye ken my father was the son o' James the Fifth? Wrong side o' the blanket, but in some people's eyes, it puts me and my children in line for the throne. James wants to be sure my branch of the family never inherits. When I die, he'll give the earldom as a reward to some other man."

Gemma stared at him, unable to believe this news. "Graham told you this just now?"

"O' course he didna tell me," the earl snapped. "But I ken why he's come, and so do ye.'Tis yer fault he's here." He paused and squinted at her, as if waiting for her confession.

Gemma squirmed, her mind in a whirl. She wanted to deny his accusation, except for one fact. She had written to King James. Not just once, but twice. She knew he'd found her letter in the drowned tinker's pouch, and that letter hadn't reached the king. Did that mean the earl knew about the one she'd written six months earlier? Or was he merely guessing?

Even if her first letter had reached James, the king wouldn't send a man to murder the children. James had two perfectly healthy sons to inherit after him. Nor could she believe such a thing of Drummond Graham.

With his uncanny ability to read her, the earl seemed to know exactly what she was thinking. "Ye're a rauckle fool, Gemma. Graham is here to destroy our way o' life. If my line fails, how do ye expect to live?

As the mistress of a murderer? Or mayhap ye thought to be the wife of a murderer?"

She flinched. "He is no murderer," she denied with heartfelt vehemence.

"Nay? Ye think no' because he lusts for ye? He's a hardened warrior. Look at his weapons. Ye'll find them scarred by use."

His point spurred her memory even as she blushed at his words. Drummond had said he'd faced death before, which meant the earl was correct. Drummond had the look of a hardened warrior. Yet what man didn't have to fight for his land and rights these days, especially if he lived on the Border? "How can you be sure he intends to harm the children?" she argued, refusing to accept this.

"I *believe* that is his purpose. Can we afford to take the chance that I am wrong?"

"I suppose not." Though she disagreed with his conclusion, she would never do anything to endanger the children. Better needless caution than a risk to the children's lives, no matter how small. "What do you intend to do?" she asked warily.

"We mun treat him with courtesy, lest he complain to the king, but I can thwart his purpose." The crafty expression that Gemma knew so well stole over his features. "Robert and Gordie will be guarded at all times."

His orders to her followed, as she'd known they would. She was to attach herself to Drummond Graham as often as possible, the earl said. Watch him. Become intimate with his thoughts under pretext of a romantic interest.

"Ye disapprove of my interest in him," she protested, uncomfortable with this charge.

"So ye *are* interested. Ye admit it."

He'd caught her, and it didn't matter that he was inconsistent in his directives. "I'm interested enough to have learned a few things about him, and I'm sure he's no' capable of murdering a child," she said.

He brushed aside her opinion. "It doesna matter what ye believe. We canna take the chance. Since Graham lusts for ye, ye'll have no trouble sticking close to him. But do not involve youself too intimately. I meant what I said about your behavior."

She flushed. "How can I win his trust if I'm to remain above reproach in my behavior?"

The earl snorted with disdain at her naïveté. "Tease him. Lead him on wi' a few kisses. Women are good at that. Encourage him to reveal his innermost thoughts. But do not lie wi' him, or I'll make ye sorry. Do I make myself plain?"

He did. He meant she would be torn in her loyalties if she became with child by Drummond. A woman must be loyal to her child's father, whether she approved of him or no. It was a universal law of survival. Yet she felt insulted that he believed she would engage in relations with a man outside of wedlock. Didn't he know her better than that after her six years on the main island?

"If I do this, will you no' whip Ting?"

"I will reduce her sentence to five lashes. The animal deserves punishment. She purposely defecated on my carpet."

"Only because you kick her and hit her all the time," Gemma accused, not at all satisfied by the reduction. "Animals are like people. They respond to love and affection. You've hated her from the moment I first brought her to the castle."

"Wi' good reason," he snarled back. "Ye had to bring her to the great hall so she could nose around, making a nuisance of herself, stealing food from people's trenchers, including mine."

"Ye could have asked me to remove her from the hall," Gemma protested in an argument they had repeated many times. "Ye didna have to hit her with the trencher and chase her away, shouting at the top of your lungs."

"I didna, eh?" he grunted. "Ye ken she hasna done it since."

No, Ting hadn't, Gemma thought with resentment, because she kept them separated. He'd kicked and cuffed her often enough for minor offenses that Ting had learned to hate him. A year ago, he'd tied her up and beaten her with a horsewhip for delivering what Gemma considered a well-deserved bite to Lawrence Bruce. She had been distraught by the severity of her pet's wounds.

Now, whenever Ting saw the earl, she laid back her ears and bared her teeth. Gemma had had to ensure they did not meet. It made life difficult, but the castle had many chambers and she managed most of the time. But now he was going to beat Ting again, and she must find a way to prevent it.

As if dismissing her, the earl rose and poured himself more mulled wine.

"Is there anything more, my lord?" she asked, rising also, desperately trying to think of a way to save her pony. Unable to formulate a plan, knowing she needed more time, she edged toward the door.

"Offer to escort Graham on his wool-buying jaunts." The earl swung around to block her retreat. "Take Rowena wi' ye."

"You just said he wished to kill the children," she protested, baffled.

"Idiot. He's doesna want the lasses," he snapped at her. "Do as I say. Why do ye argue all the time? Ye're as bad as Rowena. Worse."

Gemma knew why he wanted Rowena to come. So he could question her later about her own behavior with Drummond. Clearly he hadn't noticed yet that his daughter was attracted to Iain.

"Well, what are ye waitin' for? Get on wi' ye," he

roared, growing impatient with her angry silence. Waving his arms, he shooed her from the room.

Disheartened, Gemma fled. She would do as he commanded. She had no choice. But she did not believe Drummond Graham meant to harm the children, and she intended to find out the real reason he had come to the Shetland Isles.

*What a stroke of genius,* the earl congratulated himself as Gemma left the chamber. She was upset by the story about the children. Well she should be. Graham's coming was her fault. She must take the consequences of what she'd done.

Since she loved the children, he'd deliberately used that against her. If she felt terrible, believing she'd put them in danger, she'd earned the agony. Now she would do anything to protect them.

He personally didn't believe Graham would murder the children, but he might well take them away as a caution against their father's behavior. Or he might do something worse. He might encourage King Jamie to summon him to Edinburgh.

The earl was taking no chances. Gemma had an admirer in the form of the king's man, Drummond Graham. She admired him in return. He would use those facts to his advantage.

# Chapter 6

Gemma didn't look relieved when she returned. Drummond rose as she stepped through the private entry into the hall. He was disgusted with the earl. Whatever he'd said, he hadn't told her that her pony was spared. The tension in her face should have dissipated. Instead, she appeared as tightly wound as a clock spring. Now *he* would have to tell her.

The more he learned about her, the more she intrigued him. The countess considered her special. So much so, she entrusted her children to Gemma while she rested because she was expecting yet another child. He'd gleaned this information from Elizabeth as he sat at table, awaiting Gemma's return. Gemma had unusual spirit and courage. Clearly, she resisted the power of the islands' sole ruler when few others dared.

He itched to get her alone, to ask many questions as well as to tell her the news about her pony. Yet he suspected the earl had inflicted some substitute punishment. Surely that was the source of her tension. Though their acquaintance was brief, Drummond knew the difference between Gemma filled with joy, like last night when she was embracing her pony, and today's tight, nervous posture. It meant trouble.

He didn't relish his two tasks. He must extract Iain from Rowena's company, difficult enough. He must find a way to see Gemma in private, which had its problems. Though he would relish a moment with her, after the earl's insinuations about her interest in him, her reputation was in jeopardy. He must protect her at all costs.

Deciding to think about it later, he strode to his brother. "Come, Iain, we must be about our business. The earl has approved our buying in this area. Let us set out." He paused behind his brother, clapping his shoulder with a firm hand.

Iain's gaze never wavered from Rowena. " 'Tis raining. We canna buy wool today."

Drummond tightened his fingers on Iain's shoulder. "We can," he warned.

"If you will permit . . ." Gemma's voice trailed off as Drummond looked up. She appeared confused and embarrassed for a moment, but then straightened. "I will serve as your guide around the island," she said. "I know all the women who raise sheep and sell their wool."

Her offer struck him as odd. Would her reputation not be compromised if she were alone with him and Iain? Though he accepted, he puzzled over it.

"Might the Lady Rowena join us?" Iain had fastened his gaze on the girl, as if he were a button finally matched to the right sized buttonhole.

Annoying lad. Drummond sent him a baleful stare, but Iain had eyes for no one except Rowena.

" 'Tis perfectly proper wi' Mistress Gemma along," Iain nagged, ignoring Drummond's subtle signals of protest.

"I'm sure Rowena has more important affairs to occupy her." It might be proper, Drummond conceded, but he must do all he could to thwart Iain's wish to be alone with the girl.

"All the children can join us. We can walk out after noon dinner," Iain pleaded. "The rain will surely stop by then. Are the children in yer charge, Mistress Sinclair?"

"Elizabeth and Robert must work with their tu-
tors," she said a bit slowly, "and Gordie will be nap-
ping, but aye, Rowena can join us." She hesitated, as
if awaiting Drummond's refusal. When he said nothing, she cleared her throat. "Shall we depart at two
of the clock?"

Drummond nodded his ascent. He couldn't think
why the women were being so easily offered to them.
He disliked the idea of Iain being alone with Rowena,
but he didn't see how to prevent it. Not if he was to
be alone with Gemma, as he intended. And he did
intend it.

Though his purpose was practical, he couldn't deny
the stab of desire that shot through him at the memory
of her earnest face and soft, kissable lips tilted upward
toward his.

As the two Lowlanders strode from the great hall,
Gemma's mind swirled in confusion. If the king had
received her letter, perhaps he *had* sent Drummond,
but not, as the earl thought, to murder the boys. No,
he would be here to check her accusations of injustice.

Feeling hopeful, she sat at the table, took Gordie
from Rowena, and began on her porridge. The king
would gain nothing by murdering the boys. It seemed
so unlikely, she doubted the earl believed it. Surely
he had invented the idea to force her to help him.

Sickened by his machinations, Gemma put down her
spoon. How she hated intrigue.

"Gemma, please come quickly," Marione called
suddenly from the musician's gallery, waving to catch
Gemma's attention. "Her ladyship needs ye."

At mention of her mistress, Gemma passed Gordie
back to Rowena and raced up the narrow staircase
leading to the gallery over the hall. She beheld the
Countess of Orkney and Lady of the Shetland Islands,
great with child, collapsed on a low stool in a swoon.

"Oh, dear." Kneeling, Gemma loosened her lady-ship's collar and felt her pulse. To her relief, the pulse was quick but firm, allaying her fears. Margaret Livingston was forty-eight years of age and should never have become with child so soon after Gordie. Yet she was almost due to bring forth another infant. In her last weeks, the midwife had confined her to bed to ensure a healthy delivery, yet her ladyship often defied her orders and got up. "Do you know what happened?" she asked Marione.

"I dinna ken." The serving maid was shaking like a leaf. "She craved a wee walk, so we came here, as we oft do, to see ye and the children breaking yer fast. We'd nay mare than entered when she dropped into a swoon." Marione gestured helplessly. "She spoke o' the devil wi' red hair, but it makes nay sense as she has red hair o' her own. She grows more and more fanciful as she nears her time."

Gemma felt the countess's forehead, noting that, though pale, it was cool and without fever. "I canna understand it either, Marione, but she needs her bed. Will ye fetch two of the footmen to assist us?"

As Marione departed, the countess drew a deep, shuddering breath and gripped Gemma's hand. "Och, stay wi' me, Gemma," she whispered.

"Of course I'll stay with ye," Gemma soothed, glad to be present when needed by the woman who was both mistress and friend. In the last three years, the countess had been a pleasure to serve. She was ever concerned for Gemma's welfare, her happiness, her needs.

Gemma guessed that she was fortunate indeed, as such caring for a companion was rare. "What is wrong, my lady?" She smoothed back stray wisps of her friend's red hair that had escaped from their braids. The wisps were touched with first gray. "Have the labor pains begun?" she asked with concern.

" 'Tis no' that." Margaret covered her huge belly in a protective gesture and continued to grip Gemma with her other hand. "Bide a wee, will ye?"

"Of course. As long as ye wish." Baffled as to what had caused the swoon, Gemma put an arm around her friend and urged her to lean against her rather than the hard wall.

The countess rested her head against Gemma's shoulder and closed her eyes, breathing deeply. " 'Twas the shock, is all," she murmured. "Two men wi' red hair. Red as the devil's own."

The comment made no sense. Gemma could only conclude, as Marione had said, that the countess was becoming fanciful as her labor grew near.

"I'm sure we have no devils here," she said in comforting tones, wondering if the countess referred to their two Lowland visitors. "But even if we did, I would not let them harm you," she added, in case the countess persisted in her fear. "I would send them packing in a thrice."

The countess seemed reassured by this vow, for she relaxed and a little color returned to her pale cheeks. "Thank ye, Gemma, for being so good to me," she said softly. "Even if the devil himsel' came, ye wouldna let him harm me. Ye're no' just a companion to me; ye're a loyal friend."

"I hope so. You offer me far more than a mistress is obliged to do."

The countess straightened on the stool and smiled at Gemma. "I dinna want to be a mistress to ye. I consider ye like my own child. Ye're a good, hardworking lass, and I would see ye happy in life."

"I am happy," Gemma said, eager to show gratitude for the countess's care.

But Margaret saw through the pretense. "Ye're nay such thing," she scoffed. "Dinna pretend that life isna hard under his lordship. He's in a temper all the time, he is."

Gemma fell silent. It was no use belaboring difficulties that could not be changed.

"I intend to make it up to ye," the countess continued. "I have an idea o' how."

"There's nothing to make up. Ye've seen that I have Ting and time to care for the wild ponies. I ask nothing more," Gemma vowed.

"Ye would like more time outside o' this heap o' stone."

Gemma nodded, recognizing that the countess understood her well. " 'Tis a very nice dwelling, but yes, I prefer the outdoors," she agreed.

The countess patted her hand, then struggled to her feet as the voices of Marione and the footmen were heard in the passage. "Ye're a good child, Gemma. Good as the day is long."

Gemma smiled her appreciation. The countess did her best to compensate for the earl's injustices, never failing to show her love. Just now she had offered Gemma the supreme compliment, for at this time of year in the Shetland Isles, the days were so long that no night darkened the land for weeks on end.

For the countess's sake, she put a good face on her difficulties, but it wasn't easy. And trying to get information from Drummond Graham, whom she believed innocent, then deciding what to tell the earl, would be one of the hardest things she had ever done.

# Chapter 7

Gemma sat on the stoop of Katrine Taylor's cottage later that afternoon, playing cat's cradle with Katrine's youngest daughter, four-year-old Brenna. Behind her, Drummond talked sheep and wool with Katrine.

Just listening to the way he guided the conversation, first winning Katrine's trust, then urging her to tell her history, made it impossible to believe he'd come to kill the children. He was the perfect man, honest and caring, just as her friends up and down the coast had said.

"Yer turn, Gemma." Blond-haired, barefooted Brenna waved her hands, strung with her cat's cradle string.

Gemma obligingly performed the correct motions. The string twined on her own fingers, its complexity like the intrigue swirling around her. How she hated it. If only life were simple and people could be honest with one another.

Instead, she was supposed to ferret out Drummond's purpose in the islands. But while she industriously obeyed her orders, she had realized what the earl would do.

He cared not at all why Drummond had come. Her efforts to find out were unimportant, because before she could discover it, the earl would arrange an

innocent-looking accident. Perhaps it would happen
out on the moor, or perhaps somewhere else, with no
one as witness. 'Twould be the end of Drummond
Graham.

Rigid with concern, she passed the cat's cradle to
Brenna. How foolish of her not to have realized it
immediately. The earl was vicious with adversaries.
Since he held the power in her life, she could not stop
him. Her only choice was to warn Drummond, and
she had tried. Thus far, Drummond had refused to
heed her and depart.

"Ye're no' attending, Gemma. 'Tis your turn."
Brenna interrupted Gemma's thoughts, eager for the
all-too-rare attention of a castle dweller.

"I'm sorry, dear." Gemma took the cradle onto her
fingers, but after another turn each, they gave up. She
was too distracted, listening to Drummond and worrying. Brenna hopped up and went to beg Iain to play.

*Good choice,* thought Gemma, knowing Brenna was
entranced by their male visitors. She wanted Iain to
herself as much as Rowena, though for different reasons. The earl's daughter was pouting by the well at
losing her new sweetheart's full attention.

Rowena had never had a real sweetheart before.
Neither had Gemma, unless you could call her sixty-
year-old late husband a sweetheart. Memory returned
of her disappointed desire for someone as young and
full of life as she'd been at eighteen.

*Knit,* she told herself. *Don't dredge up the past.* She
pulled her knitting from the pouch at her waist and
sorted out the needles. She couldn't help but sympa-
thize with Rowena. Many of the local lads idolized
her, but none were of a class to woo her.

Neither was Iain Lang, except that as a guest at the
castle, he was thrown into her company. But that
didn't make him a proper match. The earl would be
furious when he learned of the pair's attraction to
each other, especially since he had promised his eldest

daughter to the son of the Earl of Caithness on the mainland.

Drummond's voice lilted behind her as he questioned Katrine, then deepened, husky and masculine, as he chuckled at her reply. The sound vibrated through Gemma, rocking her body with shivers.

How could a man stir her so with a mere laugh?

*Don't let him,* her mind warned. *Danger lies in becoming too involved with a man who must soon depart.* She bent over her knitting, wanting to resist. Yet she couldn't help but listen.

"How do you make the fleece such a beautiful pale brown color?" Drummond asked Katrine.

"Och, 'tis natural. My sheep are that color."

Happy pride tinged Katrine's words, and Gemma imagined her pleasure at Drummond's attention. A spurt of jealousy surprised her.

*Stop it. Katrine is your friend.*

Yet desire hummed through Gemma, and she admitted she longed to have Drummond's pulse-quickening gaze fastened on her and her alone.

"You must spend long hours carding and spinning," Drummond continued. "What do you think about as you work?"

"My children. My husband." Katrine giggled, as if thrilled to be asked. "My man is a fisher and away to sea just now, but you'll meet him if you bide a wee. He provides for us fine."

"I'm guessing 'twas love at first sight for the two o' ye," Drummond observed.

Gemma imagined Katrine's blush. "Aye. From the time we were bairns, our mithers said. We grew up in neighboring cots, as close as two peas in a pod. I loved him as a lass, and I love him still."

"Ye never looked at another man, I'll wager."

"No' I." Katrine's stout denial rang with pride. "I were a true goodwife, wi' two bonnie lads and a lassie to show for it."

"How old are the lads?"

"Grown, wi' wives o' their own. They're fishin' wi' my man. We had one other bairn eight years ago, but she's alying in the kirkyard." Her voice clouded with sorrow.

"I understand." Drummond's quiet sympathy wrung Gemma's heart. "Iain's mother was heartbroken when she lost a bairn some years back. He and I are half brothers, and our families are close, so I understood her pain. Some mothers try not to become attached to a new babe, in case they lose it. But my guess is 'twas no' your way."

"Indeed!" Katrine was adamant. "I loved my wee anes from the moment they squalled their way into the world. It hurt so to lose our one. Is it wrong of me to pine?"

"A person becomes better for the love she gives away, not for what's held back," Drummond said.

Gemma's heart contracted. He was as sensitive as he was cordial, drawing Katrine out. She knew Katrine's history, but had never known her to wear her heart on her sleeve. Yet here she was, proclaiming her love to Drummond Graham without reservation.

*Devious.* Gemma remembered the earl's warning. He had said Graham was devious and warned her not to trust him. No matter how much Gemma disliked her master's ways, his words held a grain of truth. She wanted to learn Drummond's true purpose on the island, for it seemed evident that he had not come to buy wool. He seemed far more interested in the women than the goods they offered. His many questions probed for something, she guessed.

None of her friends had mentioned this in their tales about him. They had been lulled by his enchanting voice, which was as pleasant as drinking the sweet, intoxicating bramble berry wine her husband used to love. Little wonder they had failed to notice.

She might not have noticed either, save the earl's

task made her question everything. How she would prefer to forget it, to close out everything else in the world except those beguiling masculine tones.

The dilemma drove Gemma to her feet. She must move to where she couldn't hear or see the man. Finding a sunny spot at the far side of the well, she spread her skirts on a sun-warmed rock. This was better. She could watch Rowena and still be within hailing distance of the cot.

As her fingers clicked the ivory knitting needles, the beauty of the day soothed her. The rays of the sun, so missed during the dark months of winter, caressed her cheeks and the wind teased loose tendrils of her bound hair.

At length, Drummond concluded the purchase and emerged from the cot with Katrine, who was all smiles. Still taken with Iain's attention, Brenna begged to accompany them to the next cot, and Katrine gave her permission. The child could help by bringing back a bag of meal from the neighbor when she returned.

As the party of five continued across the hills, Gemma pretended calm indifference to Drummond, who walked at her side. Yet she couldn't help but admire him. Clad in a simple brown leather jerkin, white shirt open at the throat to reveal sun-browned flesh, he looked carefree and in command of his life. How she longed for such freedom as he seemed to enjoy.

Ahead, Brenna pushed between Iain and Rowena, separating the two whose hands had all but touched. Gemma was relieved to have the child along. But as they continued along the route, Drummond's pace lagged, and Gemma was forced to slow her step. The three young people moved farther ahead.

As they came to a deserted, partially tumbled-down cot, Drummond stepped off the path. "I have something in my boot." Without ceremony, he sat on a heap of stone, hauled off the boot, and turned it upside down. A pebble tumbled out.

Gemma felt a sudden certainty that he'd put it there before they set out. How else would such a large object enter a sound boot? It was an excuse to speak to her alone. The thought both pleased and annoyed her.

It pleased her because of the thrill she felt as he looked up, appreciation in his piercing green eyes. She wanted him to keep looking at her, to appreciate her some more, which was embarrassing. The thought of what he would do if he acted on his appreciation turned her knees wobbly, and this reaction annoyed her most of all. "Why in heaven were you talking to Mistress Taylor of such odd things?" she bit out with a resentment that surprised her.

His green eyes questioned. "What odd things?"

"Love. Her husband and children."

"You and I spoke of love earlier."

"We were discussing someone else, not ourselves." His assessing gaze filled her with secret longings. She stared back, spellbound by the sensation.

"Do you wish to tell me of your love?" he asked softly.

She caught her breath, taken aback. She seldom thought of love in relation to herself. Love was for people like her aunt and uncle, before her aunt's death, or Katrine Taylor and her husband. Not for her. "I have no love of that sort, sir. I am a widow."

He started, as if surprised by this news. Sympathy radiated from him. "I am sorry to hear of your loss. I did not know."

"People don't, because I don't wear black. The earl bid me put it off." The explanation he hadn't requested spilled from her as sorrow welled up. "But I cared for my husband. He was the head man of our district. The foud, such officers are called, though I believe you call them bailies on the mainland. I was brought from Fair Isle to wed him, and he was very good to me. Everyone respected him, especially me."

"I'm sure ye did."

She blushed hotly, knowing *respect* wasn't the word Katrine Taylor had used to describe her relationship with her husband. Drummond was comparing her to the cottar woman and the difference gaped. To her as well as to him. "Did you learn what you wished to know of Mistress Taylor?" she asked, to hide her embarrassment.

"What do I wish to know?" he asked, all easy affability.

"You tell me, Drummond Graham," she countered, realizing her attempt to surprise him into a confession had failed. She would try the direct approach. "Ye arena here to buy wool. I can see that as easily as I can behold the sea."

He grinned at that, for on the sea-surrounded island, few places existed from which the water was invisible. "You seem to know a good deal about me, Mistress Sinclair, but what of your own affairs? What of your pony, for instance? Did the earl speak to you of her?"

If he meant to distract her from her questioning, he couldn't have chosen a better subject. "He reduced her sentence, but he will have difficulty carrying it out, as you know." She struggled to subdue the painful tightening in her throat as she answered. "If Bruce guesses to look among the herd, he will not easily spot her. Once he does, 'twill take time for him to catch her. Before then, I must work out something so she is spared." Overcome by anxiety for her pony, she turned away. Ting might still be beaten, despite her best efforts to prevent it.

Drummond's hand on her shoulder from behind startled her. "Then he didn't tell you?"

"Tell me what?" Her voice sank to almost a whisper

as terror gripped her. What was the earl plotting behind her back?

"He isn't going to whip her."

She blinked, unable to believe she had heard correctly. "He isn't?"

"He promised me he wouldn't whip her. You may bring her back to the castle whenever you wish."

She stood transfixed as comprehension seeped into her mind. "You asked him not to punish Ting?"

"Aye."

At the single word, the floodgates burst within her. She spun around, wanting to fling her arms around him.

She hugged herself instead, nearly dancing. "You're so kind, so generous to intervene for her." She beamed, turning on him the full intensity of her joy and relief. "How did you convince him?"

"I was persuasive." He seemed uncomfortable with her praise.

"The earl doesn't change his mind once it's made up," she insisted. "You've worked magic with him. Tell me how you did it. Please."

A grimace darted across his expressive face, and he spoke with seeming reluctance. "My gold was persuasive."

But she knew the earl liked power better than coins. He had to have another reason. A new, unpleasant thought surfaced in her mind. "He exacted payment from both of us, intending that we should never know," she pointed out.

Drummond snorted in disgust. "I canna say I'm surprised. What did he demand from you?"

She didn't want to admit she was supposed to extract information from him. She need not admit it. She wished to know Drummond's purpose on the island, but she wouldn't necessarily tell the earl what she learned. "Nothing important," she said. "I'm just grateful that Ting is spared." At the thought of her pony, a rush of thanksgiving overwhelmed her. She'd been right; the earl, wrong. Murderers didn't precede their dire acts by rescuing pet ponies from beatings. "You gave up your gold for Ting," she marveled, wanting to know exactly what had moved him to do it. "Why?"

Her question had an odd effect on him. He shifted his gaze to the hills, suddenly remote. "I canna abide people who abuse helpless creatures," he muttered darkly.

She wondered what past experience spurred this reaction. Despite her concern, happiness overcame her, and she reached out, grazing his shoulder with her fingertips.

At her touch, his attention snapped back to her. She could have sworn that a feral pleasure burned in his eyes. Not for the first time, she realized that something troubled her about those eyes. He was bold and bonnie to look upon, as the island women said. She had recognized his strength and caring since his arrival, even felt they shared a closeness after he'd rescued her on the rock.

Yet his eyes were always guarded, even now, despite the sensual interest she felt leaping between them like potent sparks. Though he coaxed others to open themselves to him, he opened nothing in return.

But just now, she didn't care. She had missed Ting so. The tap of her hooves as they went about the castle together, the warmth of her soft muzzle as she begged to be petted. And now her pony could come home. "Thank ye," she whispered, knowing she was mad.

Except that she wanted to keep being mad. As mad as the summer storm of last night.

# Chapter 8

As Drummond gazed into the twin lochs of Gemma Sinclair's blue eyes, he felt rocked by the thunder magic of last night. By St. Andrew, he hadn't anticipated her response to the news about her pony. Or his to her joy.

As relief and happiness illuminated her face like candle glow, heat raced through his veins. A delirium took hold, demanding he pull her into the shelter of the tumbled-down cot and explore her bewitching, smiling mouth with his own. The mere thought of her expressive hands on his body stirred his masculine interest.

He was becoming as bad as Iain.

"Did you save Ting so I would stop telling you to leave the island?" she asked, all innocent sincerity.

Her question jerked him back to reality. In a sense he had, though now he had even more reason to avoid her. She had just openly questioned his purpose on the island. "You're no' going to suggest it again, are you?" He sat to adjust his boot, avoiding her gaze.

"You've been so generous, I dinna know what to say. I still dinna understand why you did it."

He looked up, concerned that her enthusiasm would go too far. "Perhaps I did it for selfish reasons."

Wariness flitted in her eyes, then disappeared. "I don't believe it. I think you really do hate to see the

helpless abused." The sweetness of her voice deepened. "I think someone you loved was once made to
suffer while you were forced to look on."

Her words stung his memory alive, conjuring up
painful scenes he didn't want to remember. "We stray
from the topic," he stated with harsh finality. He
wasn't accustomed to women who noticed such things,
or who dared to mention them if they did.

"Don't say I'm wrong," she insisted. "I can tell from
the look in your eyes. Just now, you seemed to be
remembering someone dear and how she or he had
once hurt."

She stepped closer, skimming his arm with her fingertips. "Come, tell me how old you were when it
happened."

He adjusted his boot, avoiding an answer.

" 'Tis no use being stubborn," she persisted. "I willna
be put off."

He straightened, annoyed that she expected to cut
through his barriers. "Why do you ask?"

"Why?" She seemed surprised by his question.
Gliding closer, she sank to her knees and rested one
hand on each of his shoulders. "Because confiding in
a friend can be comforting."

The idea that talking about the past could provide
relief struck him as impossible, yet she offered friend-
ship, and he had no wish to refuse. He closed his eyes
and sat stock-still as the warmth of her palms and
fingers spoke to his flesh.

"You couldna save your loved one back then," she
whispered, as tender as the new leaves in spring. "You
were too young, and it wasna your fault. But now
you're strong, and you've saved Ting for me. Let me
thank you the way I wished to earlier."

She leaned forward to brush his cheek with her lips,
and the scent of the windswept moor enveloped him,
reminding him of last night's lightning gilding her in
silver. The new, coveted sensation chased away the

reminders of past pain that she had unleashed with her words. Instead, he thought of her sweet body pressed to his as they had clung together upon the sea-lashed rock. How he wanted to immerse himself in her, drugging himself into forgetting his unpleasant past and committed future. It took his full power of concentration to resist.

"You must not blame yourself for what happened," she said in that earnest, consoling tone he was coming to crave.

"You blame yourself for yours," he challenged, recognizing a point with which to trip her.

A shiver ran through her, but she held her ground. Gripping his shoulders, she shook him slightly, making him open his eyes. She captured his gaze. "Not for the ones I couldna help." A beseeching smile tugged at her lips. "You've helped me. You must let me help you in return."

He looked away, disgusted with himself. He had beguiled her into caring, and despite her fragile position, she still found the strength to offer *him* aid. Yet she was the one needing protection. Though the earl had promised not to beat her pony, Drummond believed he would find another way to punish her. She'd hinted it was the earl's way the night they'd met.

Nor was Drummond safe. The earl had probably prompted Gemma's questions about his purpose on the island. If he suspected Drummond of some illicit mission, what wouldn't he do?

"Gemma? Where are you, Gemma?" Brenna's voice intruded.

Gemma jerked to her feet, clasping her hands before her. A shadow crossed her face. As if she were transparent, he saw what she was thinking. She felt guilty of illicit passion, despite the fact that she'd done no more than touch his cheek in an innocent gesture of thanks.

He, on the other hand, had imagined her naked.

Had thought how it would feel to drive his hardened length into her breathtakingly sweet flesh. His response to her made him so furious, he forced himself to sit on his stone and pretend to adjust his boot. By St. Andrew, half a second alone with her and he lost his self-control.

He was even more annoyed with the way she patted her hair and straightened her bodice, feverish with guilt. He had to tell her she was guilty of nothing. "Gemma," he called softly.

She turned, and the reassurance froze on his lips as her gaze met his. Her blue eyes spoke of a longing so ardent it was almost palpable.

In a flash, it came to him that she felt guilty neither because she had embraced him in an unseemly manner, nor because they had been talking in private for longer than was proper. She felt guilty because she wanted him.

He was amazed.

He was also more aroused than he'd been in years, his body crassly demanding he act on his interest. And hers.

"There ye are, Gemma." Brenna popped around the corner of the cot, followed by Rowena and Iain. "What are ye doin'?"

"Master Graham had a stone in his boot. I was waiting for him," Gemma explained.

As Drummond subdued his unruly body, he had to admire Gemma's calm confidence. As she hid her emotions, she revealed a new side of her nature. She was a woman of many qualities. A woman who controlled her thoughts and feelings in the face of a tyranny she could not fully acknowledge. Even more daunting, she wielded a power to soothe and comfort others. The wild ponies on the moor recognized it, letting her walk among them. Their behavior confirmed what he had sensed in her that first night, then experienced himself just now. His heart felt unexpectedly lighter that it had in days, though their situation had not changed.

"Let us walk on." Gemma took the child's hand and set off down the path. "Come, Rowena." Rowena dragged her feet as she followed, glancing over her shoulder at Iain.

Iain waited until Drummond rose. "It doesna take all this time to get a stone from a boot," he remarked once the others had moved out of earshot. Curiosity was written all over his face. "What else were ye doing?"

"We were talking."

"I imagine ye were. I've never seen ye so taken by a female," Iain observed with cheerful aplomb, as if Drummond's weakness mitigated his own.

"I am not *taken* by her, as ye so rudely put it. I admire her courage, that's all. Few women have such backbone."

"A very pretty backbone it is, too," Iain teased. "She's courageous *and* she's comely, a rare combination. I can see why ye want to bed her."

"I dinna intend to bed her," Drummond flared. "As if I would with the Earl of Orkney looking over my shoulder. I want to stop him from ruining his people's lives."

"I see." Iain pondered this. "She's the first one who's really needed ye. She'd use ye to fight her battles for her. Beware."

"She's no' like that."

"You seem to know her well on such short acquaintance. Very interesting," Iain observed. "I predict she will ask."

"She hasn't and won't," Drummond snapped, irked by Iain's implications. "She keeps telling me to leave."

Iain whistled in surprise. "That so? Then I have it backward. Ye're the one who will ask something o' her."

"What makes you so damned perceptive all of a

sudden. Just because you're in love with the earl's daughter."

"Who says I'm in love?"

Drummond scowled at his brother. "I know the signs. You promised it wouldna happen again."

"I canna help it if Cupid fires his love darts where he will." Iain grinned, annoyingly self-confident and brash when he was in love. So different from the appreciative younger brother he usually was, deferring to Drummond in everything. "This is such a beautiful island," Iain said, bending over to pluck a sea island pink and inhaling deeply of its scent. "I wouldna mind weddin' and living here."

Drummond wanted to shake some sense into his brother. "The only way the earl would let either one of us stay here, Brother, is as hides nailed to a byre."

# Chapter 9

She had failed to warn Drummond of the danger of remaining on the island. Knowing the earl as she did, she should have insisted he leave. Instead she'd let him distract her that afternoon with his kindness in saving Ting. Foolish in her weakness, she had succumbed to the desire to kiss him, not even pressing him about why he'd come to the islands.

Gemma rebuked herself that evening as she collected Gordie from his nursemaid and took him, nestled in her arms, to see his mama. The questions wouldn't stop tormenting her. Why did Drummond Graham wish to talk to Shetland women?

He said he'd come to buy wool and knitted goods, and buy them he did, seeming very knowledgeable about quality and prices. He spoke of the market in Edinburgh, where he expected to make a tidy profit.

Yet he also spent long hours questioning the women he bought from, asking about their lives. It seemed unnecessary. He could make his profit without the trouble.

Few men cared so for women's thoughts. It ingratiated him with her cronies, as well as with her, she admitted. He was generous in lending assistance. Despite the brevity of their acquaintance, he had done much for her. He was a man beloved by women for good reason.

Yet she'd thought she'd felt more than impersonal courtesy from him on the moor. He'd rescued Ting, then told her of it while gazing upon her with bold, unsettling eyes.

The intensity of those eyes lingered in her mind. She'd thought them shuttered, but she realized she'd read something in them today on the moor. What?

It came to her suddenly.

Need.

His eyes were full of a craving that reached inside and touched her own desire. He longed for her tenderness. She'd known as she kissed his cheek. Dare she think that meant he needed her?

Unfortunately, she wanted him. In his presence, she'd felt the heady ecstasy that came from being admired by a lover. This was why she hadn't insisted he leave the island. She wanted him to stay.

But that was selfish. His peril was growing. Her life was not threatened, despite the tyrant who ruled her. Yet Drummond Graham would never be safe until he left the earl's holdings of Orkney and the Shetland Isles.

That led to the immediate problem facing her. What would she tell the earl when he questioned her? She cuddled Gordie as she descended the stairs, thinking of how she'd caught Drummond in the upper castle passage that afternoon, talking to the maid who cared for the bairn, along with the wet nurse. She could tell the earl about the incident, which would frighten him.

Though Gemma knew Drummond wasn't interested in the boys, the fact that he'd talked to the girls who cared for Gordie piqued her curiosity. The girls had blushed and giggled under his attention, all too obvious in their delight. When they saw Gemma, they had fallen back guiltily.

It seemed Drummond had been asking them questions, just as he did the women from whom he bought knit goods. Why?

Did the man enjoy making every woman alive fall in love with him?

Even if that wasn't his purpose, they fell in love with him anyway. Or at least they liked him far too well. As did she.

She must insist he depart at once, she decided as she stepped into the countess's chamber and curtsied to her ladyship. "Here's Gordon, my lady," she announced, glad to brighten her friend's evening. As Margaret had said, they were friends. She had never felt the countess looked down on her. Rather, she trusted her implicitly.

"Och, my wee one. Ye're good to bring him, Gemma." The countess held out her arms from where she sat in the huge canopied bed, propped against heaps of cushions.

Gemma settled on the edge of the bed, Gordie on her lap. Margaret's delight in seeing her child, her loving coos as she stroked his head and rubbed his back, soothed Gemma as well. She was sorry her mistress could not hold Gordie, but the midwife had forbade such a big bairn's pressing on her abdomen where the new child grew.

"I hope you're feeling better, my lady," Gemma said, as Gordie, remembering a previous romp on the bed, crawled off Gemma's lap and headed for the pillows heaped on the featherbed.

As he giggled and rolled among them, the countess gazed at him fondly. "I'm recovered," she said. "How did my other children fare today?"

Gemma obliged with a recitation of the day's activities. "Quite well, my lady. Rowena and Elizabeth worked with their needles this morn. Then after noon dinner, Elizabeth studied her French and singing, and Rowena accompanied me on a walk. Robert completed his Latin and history lessons in the morning and, during the afternoon, was tutored in riding and use of the sword."

The countess beamed at the reports. "Robert is becoming such a brawley lad. Big and strong, as his father was at his age." Melancholy shadowed her green eyes. "If only he were like his father in his youth, instead o' as he is now. My Patrick has changed so."

"Was he different when he was younger, my lady?" Gemma asked, startled by this unusual reference to the past.

"Oh, aye, he was so gallant, I loved him on sight. He was so taken wi' me, he proposed."

This was news to Gemma. "I thought your marriage was arranged."

" 'Twas arranged by our fathers," the countess agreed, examining one of her red braids as if she wished away the gray strands. "Patrick didna have to love me, but he did. Och, he were a bold, bonny one, riding into our baily on his chestnut stallion, his dark hair shinin' in the sun." She sighed deeply. "If only he had stayed the way he was, lovin' and honest, but he's moved away from me. And taken my Robert wi' him. My firstborn is becoming just like his father. Intent on ruling everything in sight. I wish I could change him back."

Gemma discretely said nothing to this wistful confidence. She could hardly imagine the power-obsessed earl as a kindly, love-struck youth, though she supposed people did change over the years.

Yet if he had once been the way the countess described him, the earl had changed more than a little. He had become an entirely different man. He'd also influenced his eldest son to follow in his footsteps. Robert regularly used his status to take advantage of others and gain things for himself. As the countess sighed, looking sorrowful, Gemma's heart went out to her friend.

" 'Tis naught I can do save bear it, I suppose." The countess reached out to tickle Gordie. "And take

comfort from my children and from ye, my friend."
As her child rolled on his back, giggling, she caught
Gemma's hand and pressed it, sending her a loving
look. "And speaking o' those we love, where is Ting,
Gemma?" She smiled fondly as Gordie kicked his feet
and waved his arms at her. "I havna seen her for two
days. You always keep her near."

"She is . . . outside just now, my lady." Gemma
evaded the question, knowing it unsafe to involve others in her quarrel with the earl.

The countess searched her face with concern. "I
heard his lordship was angry with her but reduced the
severity of her whipping. I wish he'd spared her entirely. He didna used to be that way."

Gemma couldn't imagine the earl as anything but
liberal with punishments.

"I hear we have a Lowland visitor," the countess
continued, but Gemma sensed a new tension in her
as she raised the subject. "I've seen him. Nay, chide
me no'." She raised a hand to block Gemma's protest.
" 'Tis why I was in the gallery this morn. I wanted to
see this god among men."

"There are two Lowlanders visiting," she answered,
taking care not to single out one over the other. "I
find them to be courteous guests."

"But the elder is handsome, is he no'? All the
women like him. They say he's the perfect man." The
countess tickled Gordie's tummy with her loose braid.
Gordie crowed and grabbed it.

"They do." Gemma wondered what the countess
would make of this fact.

"Och, Gordie, do not pull so." The countess gently
disengaged her braid from the child's fist. "Well then,
so many canna be wrong. He mun be a good man."

Gemma knew she must proceed with caution. If she
betrayed special interest in Drummond, the countess
could accidentally convey this to the earl. "We know

very little of him." She kept her tone neutral. "All we
know is that he buys knitted goods and women enjoy
his company."

The countess sniffed, dismissing the theory. "We
ken a good deal more than that. I hear he's done
many a kind deed for our women. He rescued that
ship's crew, and he saved ye from drowning. Nay man
wi' an evil nature does such things. Still, ye mun learn
more o' him and tell me, aye? I'm thinking ye should
wed again, and mayhap he'll suit. Master Thomasson
was a good man, but old, and ye've been widowed
three full years."

"Not so old," Gemma protested, amazed at the tack
of this discussion. She had not been so attached to
Alexander's memory that she would never consider
remarriage, but what had prompted the countess to
choose Drummond? The idea, dropping out of nowhere, amazed her.

The countess smiled at her shocked expression. "We
all admired yer husband, o' course. But ye would like
a young man this time, I trow, and I would see ye
happy. This Drummond Graham could take ye away."

Gemma knew the earl never let his people leave
the isles if he could stop them. Why would the countess even suggest it? "Do ye wish to see me wed
again?" she asked.

"Only if ye wish it, but his lordship plans to give
ye to William Fermour," the countess admitted with
a rueful shrug.

A toady to Lawrence Bruce, Gemma thought, horrified by the idea of wedding the foud of Dunrossness
at the southern end of the isle. "I will not wed him,"
she declared with vehemence, realizing her friend was
warning her. If she didn't want Fermour for a husband, she must marry someone else. Quickly. Before
the earl forced him on her.

Putting this unsettling news aside, Gemma strove to

entertain her friend with talk of the children. But as she described Elizabeth's latest words and deeds and Rowena's favorite accomplishment of learning to read Greek, she couldn't help but wonder. Why would the countess suggest she marry Drummond Graham?

She left the chamber an hour later, no closer to the answer. But she understood now why the earl had ordered her to leave off her mourning. William Fermour had asked for her, and it seemed the earl intended to grant his wish. Knowing this, the countess must have fixed on the first eligible man who could remove Gemma from the earl's power.

Though such an escape seemed unlikely, the countess's kind wish for her happiness filled Gemma with appreciation. Could anyone have a better friend?

After putting Gordie in his cradle under a nursemaid's watchful eye, Gemma made her way to the earl's withdrawing chamber. The countess was kind, but she would fight her own battles. She didn't like his lordship's plans to marry her off, nor did she like the way he'd failed to tell her about Ting. And she intended to say so.

"Enter," the earl called in response to Gemma's knock at his withdrawing chamber.

Gemma pushed open the door and stepped inside. "Your lordship." She dropped the customary curtsy. "Why didn't you tell me you werena going to whip Ting?"

The earl smiled and beckoned her to come closer, as if he weren't at all surprised by her question. "Why do ye think I am not?"

Gemma cringed inwardly as she realized her outspokenness had landed her in a trap. If she said Graham told her, the earl would know she trusted the word of a stranger. Yet in truth, she did.

"I overheard Bruce say she would be spared," she

said, the uncustomary lie clumsy on her lips. She forced herself to meet his gaze. "Why did you no' tell me?"

"I wasn't ready for ye to ken."

She scowled. He had his own reasons for everything and didn't care if he hurt her. Nor did he care if she knew he'd lied to her, exacting payment from her in return for nothing.

"What have you learned of Graham?" he demanded, turning the tables unexpectedly.

Here was the question she'd dreaded. "Very little. He seems to be buying wool. And talking to Gordon's nursemaids." She spoke calmly, but she felt the telltale color burn her cheeks. Was she giving away her wish to mislead him?

The earl interpreted her agitation as interest in Drummond. "There. We have proof. He intends Gordie harm. Aye, and ye've learned he beguiles the lasses, using them to gain his ends. I tell you he is a seducer. Lead him on if 'twill trap him in a confession, but remember what I say."

"You say he's an assassin. Yet you trusted him to walk out with one of your children today," she countered, hoping to trip him into explaining.

"I told ye afore. He's no' interested in the lasses," he growled. "He wants the lads, who can inherit the earldom. Dinna be fooled by his pleasing countenance. I know King Jamie and the sort o' man he chooses to do his work. Ask Graham about his background. Ye can be sure he didna grow up in honest toil, tilling fields or raising sheep or learning a trade. Take a good look at his sword and dirk. What sort o' man carries weapons scarred by use? Nay fisher or crofter, that's sure."

Though Gemma did not find this argument convincing, she put it aside to ponder later. "I canna wed William Fermour of Dunrossness," she said, moving without hesitation to her next subject. "Her ladyship needs me to help with Gordie and Elizabeth. I canna leave her."

He betrayed no surprise at her new choice of subject or her unsubtle rejection of a rich and favored bridegroom. "Why do ye think Fermour's interested?"

Gemma shuddered, realizing that if she told the truth, she would implicate the countess, who must have betrayed her husband's confidence. "Lawrence Bruce talks too much when he thinks no one is listening," she said, which was true enough.

The earl shrugged. "The children like ye, but ye will wed where I decree. You owe it to me."

Anger erupted in Gemma. His demands never ended. Yet from experience, she knew that protest would only make matters worse. "Bruce has disagreed with my uncle again over the laying of the castle stone," she bit out, leaping to the next issue at hand.

"I dinna interfere with Bruce's direction o' the work," he replied, unruffled.

"My uncle directs the work. *He* is the stone mason." She knit her brow in her fiercest frown, but he seemed too busy sipping mulled wine to notice. "He is being confined during the hours when he is no' at work," she argued. "There is nay reason for it. You could order him freed."

The earl sighed and stroked his short, trimmed beard. "*Yer* uncle may direct the laying o' the stone, but *my* uncle directs the stone mason. However, as it seems important to you, Gemma, I will look into it. But I wish ye would attend to yer woman's duties and leave the building to the men."

Gemma seethed as she left the chamber. Such a small request and he acted as if he had granted her the world. His comment about her woman's duties also left her raw with rage. Why was her uncle's well-being not her duty? Why could he not see that people disliked Lawrence Bruce? Even King James didn't like the sound of him, if he'd sent Drummond Graham in

response to her complaints. And how dare the earl
suggest that he had done so much for her, that gratitude should compel her to forsake all happiness by
wedding Bruce's oily associate, William Fermour?

"So ye're thinkin' to take a secret bridegroom
when I'm no' lookin', eh."

Rowena spun in her chair as her father's accusation
startled her. He stood at the door to her chamber,
radiating anger and suspicion. "I didna hear ye enter,
Father," she gasped, trying to cover her fear. The earl
had a way of slipping up when she least expected it.
She never knew when he was watching her. "Why
would ye say such a thing?"

He sauntered into her bedchamber and pinned her
with his dark-eyed gaze. "Ye were flirting with that Lowland Scot this morning. *And* this afternoon, I hear tell."

Trembling inside, knowing he had heard correctly,
Rowena fastened her gaze on the book before her and
turned a page with a show of serenity. "He's ages
older than me. I'm no' interested in him, Father."

He jerked the book from her hands. "I'm no' talking about the elder, and well ye ken it," he shouted,
making her jump and face him. "Ye're flirtin' with
Iain Lang, so dinna deny it. Is he what ye fancy? A
baseborn bastard with no power or land?"

"A low birth canna hide his noble spirit," Rowena
shouted back, enraged by the accusation. She did like
Iain Lang. More than she'd ever liked a man. "He is
far worthier of my attention than some I know, who
are noble of birth but crass in their hearts." She
gripped her rosewood writing table, afraid of how he
would respond.

Before she could draw breath, her father's palm
connected with her cheek.

Rowena clutched her face. Unable to hold back the
tears of outrage and hurt, she sobbed aloud.

"I would take my belt to ye, but ye're too old," he

muttered, holding up the book to see the title. "Tristen and Isolde," he read aloud, "in Greek, no less." He flung the book aside. "I give ye a fine education and ye use it to fill ye head with romantic trash. It does ye nay good. Did that pair nay good either. Tristen died. My belt used to bring ye to yer senses."

She wept harder, remembering the blisters he'd raised on her backside in her childhood. She'd had a pert tongue, but he'd been unreasonable. Hard with her. Unforgiving. And worst of all, unloving. "I don't know why ye're so angry with me all the time," she sobbed. "Ye're no' with Elizabeth."

"Elizabeth is a sweet lass. No' like ye."

"I've always obeyed ye."

"No' without a rude word first. But ye'll obey me now. Tell me about Gemma. Was she alone with Drummond Graham this afternoon?"

Rowena sealed her lips into a tight line, sure her father's question meant trouble for her friend.

"Answer me," he snarled, raising his hand.

Rowena flinched but remained silent. She must not betray Gemma. Rowena knew what it was to be watched by her father's spies and to be betrayed. Someone had watched her with Iain Lang and reported her to her father. She did not wish to do the same to Gemma.

The earl's arm swung up in a long arc, then descended toward her. Instinctively, Rowena ducked, and his hand connected with nothing. Enraged by her evasion, he grabbed her by the shoulder. Rowena felt herself dragged to her feet. As she struggled uselessly in his iron grip, the slaps began. Left cheek, right cheek, left, right. She closed her eyes and tried to clutch at his arm to stop him.

The earl paused, his chest heaving with exertion. "Well?" he demanded.

"I-I dinna ken what ye mean," she stammered, struggling to hold back tears. "Gemma walked with us, 'tis all." She knew he would slap her for as long as she refused him, humiliating and paining her without ever leaving a bruise.

At her refusal, he began again. She steeled herself against the assault. Perhaps she could bear it longer than he would continue. "What did ye see?" he demanded. "They were alone, together, aye?"

"I . . . saw . . . nothing," she sobbed as the battering continued.

With a roar of rage, he delivered a last, vicious blow. Blood spurted from her nose, a bright stream of crimson soaking her gown as he released her. Rowena dropped, sobbing, into the chair.

"I'm writing to John McCree to fetch ye at once," he growled, looming over her.

Rowena shivered at the repulsive image of the black-haired barbarian that formed in her mind's eye. John McCree, son of the Earl of Caithness, had sued for her hand last year, but only because he wanted her father's gold and her body. In that order. "Nay," she cried, despairing. "He's a butcher, murdering his neighbors, feuding and reiving. I hate him."

Bracing herself for another battering, she waited as her father considered her statement.

He merely smiled, frightening her even more. "Then tell me what ye saw today. Did Gemma and Drummond contrive to be alone together? If ye say, I'll no' write to McCree at once."

Desperately mopping the blood streaming from her nose with a handkerchief, Rowena struggled to compose an answer. Before she could speak, he grabbed her chin and forced it upward until she met his gaze.

"Were they alone together? Ah, I can see they were from the look in yer eyes. Excellent." Releasing her abruptly, he strode for the door, wiping her blood on his trunk hose.

"Dinna write to McCree," she begged.

"I'll no' write to him yet, but ye'll wed him before

the autumn's done. Ye'll wed him or I'll see ye dead,"
he said before slamming the door.

Rowena found her handkerchief and, pressing it to
her face, groped her way to the washbasin. Once the
bleeding had stopped, she quietly turned the key in
the lock of the door. Then she threw herself on her
bed and sobbed.

He didn't care if she lived or died. He only saw his
own desires and his plots, and his latest plot didn't
bode well for Gemma. He had forced her to give away
her friend. To what purpose, she didn't know, but she
didn't expect it to be good.

Hopeless. Her life was hopeless.

# *Chapter 10*

*I must be on guard every waking moment. The earl means to have his revenge.*

Drummond sat in the huge stone kitchens of Scalloway Castle that evening, pretending to be relaxed and calm as he chatted with the cook. Yet even as he challenged the earl, his mission must remain his primary purpose. So he had questioned the three kitchen women as they scrubbed the worktables, swept the floors, and tidied the chamber for the night. Not one of them was the person he sought.

Disappointed but determined to continue his search on the morrow, he pondered the earl's latest action. He must have ordered Gemma Sinclair to question him. Why else would she have asked if he'd learned what he wanted of Katrine Taylor?

People rarely cared if he listened to the gossip of crofter women. Or even that of more highly placed women. Women in Scotland were not always prized by their men, an error in his estimation. But because he had helped save the ship's crew and Gemma's pony, his motives were questioned.

By St. Andrew, he would not be put off his search, though today had been both unproductive and unsatisfying. Katrine Taylor was not the person he sought. He'd also ruled out the next four women he'd interviewed.

All the other times, he'd had more details to find

the person he was looking for. A name. A description. This time he had nothing except the location and a few unhelpful details.

"More ale, Graham?" the cook said, interrupting his thoughts. "Drink up, and I'll tell ye a tale that'll give ye the belly cramp from laughin'."

Drummond pulled his attention back to the cook and nodded in appreciation. "I've enjoyed your tales, the ale, and your excellent stew, Brandie. My thanks, but I believe I should retire and let you find your bed as well. You've been most kind, but 'tis late."

The three kitchen women gazed at him as he gained his feet, clearly wishing he would stay. He thanked them all again and climbed the stairs to an upper floor of the castle.

The earl had directed that he and Iain have the rare luxury of private chambers. A cheery fire blazed on the hearth of his room as he entered. The coverlet on the canopied bed had been turned down, as if tempting him to take his ease. *Lie down and sleep,* it coaxed.

He knew he couldn't sleep yet. He had too much on his mind. Having lived under his father's tyranny, he had learned much about obsession with power. As he'd traveled up the coast, he had heard and seen much evidence of the earl's abuse. Two men had disputed over land. The foud had ruled that since they could not agree, the land became the earl's. They might use it only at his pleasure and for a fee.

A boy had been hung for stealing and killing a sheep. The sole evidence had been blood on his hands. Yet why would a young person kill an animal but not take it for eating? Why leave it in a pasture to be found?

Unless someone else had killed the sheep and blamed him. Drummond had asked the women he met and learned the lad was sole heir to his ill mother's property. With the boy gone and the mother soon to follow, the earl would gain more land.

Where doubt existed, decision always favored the Earl of Orkney and Laird of the Shetland Isles. But such details were hidden from Gemma and the earl's family. It was a conspiracy to keep them ignorant of his oppression. Even Gemma's friends seemed privy to the plot, hiding the truth from her so she could bear her fate of living under the earl's thumb.

As Drummond leaned against the window ledge, gazing into the twilight of the northern night, he felt no inclination to sleep. The chamber was pleasant, its window looking inland toward the castle outbuildings. The view was beautiful, the lush green hills embellished by flocks of sheep. Despite it, he felt the tight rein of authority checking the land. No peace existed here.

Above him on the castle wall, he knew a guard walked, securing his wing. Drummond watched the man's shadow, cast by the midnight sun, counting how long it took him to pace his segment. Out of habit, he searched for a route by which to leave the castle without being noticed. Not too difficult. As the guard reached the far corner and turned it, one could slip from the kitchen door and make for the stables. He had noted this from outside during the day.

He counted the moments the guard was gone. By the time his shadow reappeared at the corner, a good minute had passed. The outbuildings had been unobserved during that time. Too short for a major invasion, but long enough for a man to slip in or out if he chose.

Useful information if he needed it later.

At that moment, a skirted figure slipped from the castle and bolted for the stables. He waited, knowing the guard would return like clockwork.

He counted, aware that he was cheering for her. Ten seconds. Twenty seconds. As he reached four-and-forty, she disappeared into the stable. He breathed with relief as the guard's shadow reappeared.

She was safe, whoever she was. Probably a serving maid trysting with a stableman.

But seconds later, he saw two cows move with far more purpose than expected toward the stone dyke that bordered the farthest outbuilding. One of them stopped to graze, but the other continued doggedly on until it reached the dyke.

A figure, indistinct at this distance, slipped over the stile built in the stone wall. As he watched the shadow climb the hill, pausing to hide behind flocks of sheep in case the guard looked, a new idea came to him. Could this be Gemma Sinclair, going to fetch her pony while the castle slept? Did she go by stealth to conceal where she'd hidden her pet?

She had offered her aid, and he began to admit he might need it. He didn't want to reveal his purpose, but he was beginning to recognize that he needed assistance. Without it, he might never achieve his purpose in the islands.

He checked the passage outside his chamber and found it empty, but caution sent him back into the room. Wanting no one to realize he was out meeting Gemma, if indeed he was so fortunate, he arranged bolsters in his bed to resemble a sleeping body under the coverlet. He added a nightcap to complete the appearance.

The fire had died down. He stepped back to observe the effect. Anyone looking in would think he slept soundly in the bed assigned by the earl. With the deception complete, he used the same stealthy techniques as Gemma to leave castle and its outbuildings.

Halfway to the moor, he came to the deserted cot where he and Gemma had paused earlier in the day. He settled to wait among the riot of sleeping sea pinks. If by chance the figure he had seen was not Gemma, he would hide behind the wall as she passed and no one would be the wiser.

But it was Gemma Sinclair. She came toward the cot, the tiny pony frisking at her heels. The midnight sun shone behind her, its muted light encircling her bright hair like a halo. It illuminated her beauty, transforming her into a gilded fairy queen of the windswept isle.

He stepped into her path, filled with an overwhelming urge to taste her sweetness.

Startled, she leaped back, almost stepping on Ting. The pony skittered out of the way but regarded him calmly, as if she'd smelled him all along and considered him no threat.

Gemma appeared shaken. "You frightened me," she said. "I didna expect you here. You were said to be abed."

So she'd deliberately asked his whereabouts. Interesting. "I saw you slip out and realized you were fetching Ting," he said.

She looked about her, seeming to check for spies, though the moor was as empty of hiding places as the earl's soul was devoid of feeling. "You will not mention where I keep her?" she said, stepping near and speaking low.

"O' course not," he assured her, "if you'll do me a courtesy in return." The sort having to do with the glorious feel of her lips against his cheek, he hoped. He couldn't stop coveting the feminine warmth radiating from her, waiting to be enjoyed.

She seemed filled with nervous energy. Was it anticipation? If so, it wasn't of anything pleasant. She was not a maid hoping for kisses. She was a frightened woman who most likely realized her situation on the island could only become worse.

Yet why be anxious with him? She hadn't been this afternoon, and he offered no more threat now. Or did he?

He supposed she sensed his lust. Expectation had heated him like a fever the entire time he'd waited for her. Now, with her only an arm's length away, his body burned with awareness. More than that, he sensed she was equally aware of him. The air between them sizzled, as if waves of energy connected them.

"I'll do you a courtesy you may not like," she said with low urgency, "but you must believe 'tis for the best. You must heed my warning. Leave the Shetland Isles at once and never return."

Drummond wanted to shake her. Why must she insist on his departure? He didn't want to argue with her, but he was not leaving.

Something warm and damp thrust into his palm, and he looked down to find Ting sniffing his bulging pouch. Welcoming the distraction, he pulled out the carrot he'd lifted from the kitchens and offered it to her.

Ting closed her teeth over the end and snapped it off with obvious relish. "Rascal, you knew I'd brought you a treat." He scratched her poll, marveling at her diminutive size, as Gemma stared at him, her eyes filled with anxiety.

"Does this mean you refuse to go?" she asked.

Drummond grunted. Things were bad, but not so bad that he must leave. "Why did you name her Ting?" he asked, deliberately avoiding the subject.

"I named her after the town of Tingwall. And after the Lawting that is supposed to rule the island. Her mother died and I raised her from a foal.'Twas three years ago, just after I lost my husband. We had no children, and I suppose I wanted a substitute. Everyone said I did."

She seemed inspired to tell him a good deal, despite her anxiety. Mayhap if he persisted, she would tell him other things. He offered the pony the last of the carrot on the flat of his palm. She swept it into her mouth with velvety lips and crunched it happily, then nuzzled him in thanks.

Sweet creature, so affectionate and trusting. Now he understood why Gemma loved her, why she protected her from the earl's wrath. The animal had a special sensitivity to human moods and intentions. She had liked Drummond at once, and he, her.

He rumpled her ears, scratched her poll some more, and, kneeling, ran his hand down her left foreleg and lifted it. "No shoes on you, eh? I suppose there's no need." He checked the hoof. "But you are caked with mud." He produced his dirk and flicked away dried mud and stones with the tip.

He noted how Gemma watched his movements, gaze locked first on his weapon, then on his hands. He moved around and cleaned Ting's other front hoof.

"You're stubborn, Drummond Graham. You won't listen to me," she said.

"And you're worried because the earl has been talking about me," he stated, no question in his mind.

"Aye," she admitted, the mixture of concern and worry in her blue eyes deepening.

So much for his hope that she might return his lust. "And what does he say, besides being angry that I rescued the ship's crew and interfered with your pony?" he asked, pressing to the heart of the matter.

"He would never admit anger, but he does want to know why you're here." Her grip on Ting's mane tightened, the slender knuckles whitening.

Drummond considered the question. The earl was a wily opponent, so it was better to keep him guessing. This meant he must not tell her. Anything Gemma knew, the earl would find ways of extracting. She might know her master well, but the skill required to outfox a fox was foreign to her trusting nature. "I prefer to approach the question from the other direction," he countered. "Why does he think I'm here?"

She inhaled deeply before speaking, as if seeking courage to answer his question. "He suspects you of having no interest in buying wool."

No surprise there. "What does he think interests me?" After his encounter yesterday with his lordship, he wanted to know exactly what was in the man's mind.

He studied her as she hesitated, letting his gaze wander over her body, willing her to remember their intimacy on the rocks, when she had trusted him completely. *Tell me, sweetheart,* he urged with his eyes. *Bare your soul to me.*

She shivered violently in response, and the delicate pulse in her throat quickened, betraying his effect on her. "He believes you are here," she began slowly, "to assassinate his two sons for the king. Not that I believe him," she finished in a rush.

"Assassinate his . . ." Drummond clutched the hilt of his sword as he took in this monstrous revelation. "How did he come to that conclusion?"

She fidgeted uneasily with Ting's mane for a long moment before looking up. Her gaze, as it locked with his, was earnest yet defiant. "I wrote a letter to King James complaining about his lordship, Lawrence Bruce, and conditions on the islands, but it never reached him. The poor tinker carrying it drowned, and when his body was found, I believe the earl and Bruce saw my letter." Her voice dropped to a tortured whisper. "Once the earl knew I'd appealed to the king, I'm sure he suspected I'd done it before. And I had. I'd written an earlier letter and sent it by way of a Dutch trader. I received no response, but when the earl told me about the children, I realized my first letter must have reached the king. He sent you in reply."

Drummond was incredulous. Of all the things he had expected, it wasn't this. Tension radiated from every bone and sinew of her body, and he recognized what the confidence had cost her. Instinctively, he knew she had never told anyone what she had done. Little wonder. Her audacity went beyond anything he could have imagined. By confiding her secret, she showed tremendous trust.

His mind reeled as he took in the other implications of her words. Little wonder the earl feared him, if he thought he'd been sent by the king. He had the potential to destroy the man.

As for Gemma, he was the answer to her prayers, but what an answer. Not that he would murder the children. With her accuracy of judgment, she said she didn't believe him capable of such evil. Nor did he think the earl believed it. No, he was using the idea to try to control Gemma. But the earl might believe he was the king's spy, sent to assess the truth of her letter.

"You quite astound me. I dinna ken how to respond," he said honestly, struggling with the morass of information. He was used to having women confide in him, but never news this explosive.

"I know you wouldna murder children, no matter who asked it of you," she stated with passionate conviction.

"Ye trust me." This simple fact touched him beyond words.

"A man canna behave as you do, offering many kindnesses to others, sacrificing your own time and comfort, and do such a thing. I know I'm right."

He nodded, unable to deny it in the face of her logic. "I would never agree to kill children, no matter the circumstance," he said carefully, wanting to dispel any doubts she had on that score.

But he was willing to let her and the earl believe he was the king's man. The threat could prevent the earl from killing him outright. What an excellent way to keep his lordship off balance.

At his confirmation, a smile lit up her face, more radiant than the midnight sun. "I am so glad to know it. So . . . very . . . glad." She turned away, her shoulders shaking, and he realized she wept with relief.

Glad to have eased her mind, yet concerned for her, he touched her arm. When she didn't pull away, he slid one arm around her shoulder and drew her into his embrace.

With both hands before her streaming eyes, she leaned against his chest and cried. She fit against him with perfection, and desire reared its demanding head, eager to crowd out his more benevolent instincts.

What an incredible coincidence it was that had brought her into his arms. She thought him her savior, come from the king. Though he did spend his days rescuing women and their children from lives of poverty and hardship, though he was on a mission to the islands, it wasn't the mission Gemma thought.

"I couldna believe, as the earl does, that the king would kill children," she said through her tears. "If he were angry with the earl, he would kill *him*. Nor could I believe you capable of murdering children, but I wanted to hear it from your own lips. The children are dear to me."

With effort, he controlled his lust, confining his caresses to soothing murmurs and pats on the back. What a burden it was for her to fight the earl alone. Look at what the man had done. He had coerced her into questioning Drummond.

"That brings us back to where we started," she said, as if her moment of crisis were over. Finding a handkerchief, she moved from his embrace, wiping away her tears. "I dinna ken exactly why you're here and I willna ask." She put away the square of linen and became all business. "Yet for your safety and mine, I propose to tell the earl you are from the king but that I learned no further details. He can draw his own conclusions."

Her quick grasp of his thinking relieved Drummond. The less said about his purpose, even in denial, the better. Despite her innocence, despite her obvious wish to think him from the king, Gemma understood that. "My thanks," he agreed, wishing she had not moved away. "I appreciate your support."

In truth, he felt more than appreciation. When he could see past his lust, he realized he was deeply honored that she trusted him so completely. "I will assist you in any way I can, but more than that, I canna say. I feel I should be as honest with you as you've been with me, yet I'm here on behalf of another. I canna betray the confidence." He nodded solemnly, hoping she would think he meant the king's confidence.

"I understand." She regarded him shrewdly. "There's more to it than meets the eye."

"Precisely." He cleared his throat as she waited for him to continue. Now was the moment to enlist her aid. He felt awkward, admitting his need, but admit it he must if he expected to achieve his goal. "There is just one difficulty. While I am here, I am conducting a bit of personal business as well, and find I require assistance."

"Ye seem so self-sufficient. How could that be?"

He grimaced at her gentle needling, recognizing it for what it was. She encouraged him to be honest with himself and with her. "None of us likes to admit to weakness. But in this case, I could use some help."

She seemed to recognize the effort it took to admit failure and had pity on him. "Just as I needed help the night of the shipwreck. Perhaps I can assist without knowing the details. Tell me what I can do."

"I am searching for someone," he said simply.

"So that's why you talk to the women." Understanding dawned on her face, along with more relief.

"I ask that you say nothing of this," he added, concerned that she might openly speak of it.

Gemma cocked her head and regarded him in puzzlement. "Of course not, if you wish to keep it quiet. But is it a secret I must keep from the earl?"

Drummond considered. If the earl believed he was from the king, nothing else would matter to him. "The earl wouldn't care. I am merely delivering a message to the woman from her family, who is looking for her. But she may not wish others to know."

Gemma nodded. "I confess I am curious, but say

no more. I can keep a personal secret. As long as the person you seek is guilty of no crime."

"I assure you, she is not."

"What is her name?"

His hope of help dissolved into anxiety. He wasn't prepared to answer this question. "We can speak of her later. I shall preserve her secret a while." He wished he could tell her all of the truth, but he hadn't lied. He did wish to preserve the woman's secret. Forever, if he could.

She seemed to consider his wish, moving to the heap of stones where he'd adjusted his boot earlier in the day. Spreading her skirts, she sat among the sea pinks. "I will help you find this woman, but do you mean to wed her once she is found?" She folded her hands precisely in her lap and regarded them, as if not the least interested in the answer to her question.

She was more beautiful than the flowers among which she sat, and he itched to pluck her like the blossom that she was. "Would you be disturbed if I did?" he asked, sitting beside her.

She looked up, unexpectedly grinning. "Would you change your plans if I were?"

He raised his eyebrows, realizing she gave as good as she got. He must have a care how he teased her in the future. "She would have no interest in wedding me," he confessed. "I will simply deliver the message. She will decide what she wishes to do about it."

"Heavens, how mysterious." Gemma shivered. "I love pleasant mysteries."

"I canna say there's anything pleasant about it." Silently he cursed his father, who had saddled him with this legacy.

She relaxed, more sure of herself despite his denial. "I willna tell a soul. I promise. There. We've exchanged secrets."

"Mine is rather small compared to yours," he said morosely, sorry for that fact.

"Then tell me a larger one. A personal one. Something sweet or touching from your youth."

He could think of nothing. His youth had been devoid of things either sweet or touching. Guilt and fear had been his daily fare.

"Start with something simple," she urged. "Where did you grow up?"

"I lived with my mother in Lockerbie," he obliged, knowing this line of questioning was harmless but would lead nowhere. He could not fulfill her wish for a pleasant memory. " 'Tis a small town, inland from Solway Firth on the southwestern coast of Scotland."

"Did you learn a trade from your father?"

He refused to answer that question. He'd learned what his father had demanded, but "trade" was too nice a term.

"Tell me of your mother, then," she said, recognizing his reluctance and choosing another path. "What was she like?"

Her interest was endless, though he recognized it as kindly and not the least prurient. "I'm pleased to say that she's living in comfort at Castle Graham where my cousin is clan chieftain. I could not see her cared for without his help, but once I thought it a possibility, I willingly went through hell to ensure she had it. My reward is seeing her take her rightful place. She was and is loyal, levelheaded, and hardworking. In my youth, she had nothing but undeserved hardship."

Gemma rewarded his confidence with a smile. "I'm happy to hear she is well settled. It is hard to see those who raised us suffer, especially if 'tis for our sake."

He flinched as she once more used her uncanny skill to touch his deepest value. But then she lived under a tyrant, just as he once had. It made her more perceptive than others to the source of his pain.

"I quite understand how ye feel." She touched his arm with tentative fingers.

He pulled away, sure that she didn't, at least not

about how he burned to possess her. One look at her gleaming hair, her creamy skin, the hint of soft breasts beneath her stiff bodice, and he had to fight the desire to take her in his arms.

"I see you dislike speaking of yourself," she continued, oblivious to his arousal. She was as brisk as a goodwife setting her cot to rights. "But I felt certain a parent taught you to be trustworthy, and I was correct. Your mother trusted you, and though you dinna mention your father, I'm sure he trusted you as well."

"You have an unusual view of things." He grimaced, realizing his father *had* trusted him, though it was to do the unsavory deeds he demanded. Under threat of harm to his mother, Drummond had faithfully carried out his father's commands from the time he was five. Not until he was eighteen had his chieftain given him a way out.

Pain of the past roused within him, clashing with desire for Gemma, one emotion tearing him apart, the other beckoning, offering a moment of comfort.

Gemma studied him, her blue eyes darkened to sapphire in the twilight. For the first time, he wondered if perhaps she did sense his inner turmoil, if not his desire. "I'm glad you shared with me," she said. "Airing details from our pasts can be good for the spirit."

"Ye make the spirit sound like damp bedding. Air it properly and all will be well."

She turned pensive as Ting approached and nuzzled her, asking for attention. She ran her hands over the sleek white back in a rhythmic motion. The pony lowered her head, eyes closed, enjoying her mistress's touch.

Desire shot like a current through Drummond as he watched. Her hands were strong and expressive, containing her essence of caring and integrity. How he envied the pony, able to seek her attention at will, knowing she would receive it.

"I know it sounds odd," she mused, "but I like your

comparison. When our spirits are dampened, if you hide what troubles you inside, it grows into something unpleasant, like mildew on damp bedding. Our hearts need fresh air and sun."

"Does *your* heart get such things?"

"When I am with my uncle, my cousins, the children, and the countess, aye. And with Ting and the wild ponies." An engaging smile played at the corners of her mouth, and once more, her bonds with loved ones brought a light to her face, more heartwarming than candle glow. "And when I exchange confidences with a friend like you."

That pushed him over the edge. He reached for her.

# *Chapter 11*

Drummond felt Gemma move eagerly into his embrace, and he realized she *had* sensed his arousal. Perhaps she even returned it in kind.

Ah, yes, she did, for she wrapped both arms around his neck and turned her face to his, inviting his kiss. She hadn't been oblivious after all.

Clasping her waist, he reveled in her warmth. It burned through his veins, driving him to want more of her. She was achingly exquisite, in spirit as well as in body. She was a woman of formidable mettle, daring all to call the king's wrath down on the earl.

In return, he had offered her his aid, and at least a small piece of himself. A bold step for him. He wasn't used to it. But it helped to share his burden, satisfying him to know he would have her help in his mission. Now his body lustily demanded satisfaction of another kind.

She smiled faintly, and he claimed her lips. Sexual desire crackled between them. He hadn't been mistaken about her interest in him. She responded to his kiss like a deprived flower, eager for sun and rain, as if both flowed from his touch.

Delighted to have awakened her ardor, he buried one hand in her amazing silver hair. Cupping her head in one hand, he tasted her lips hungrily. With the other hand, he explored the sumptuous line of her throat and neck, then shifted to trace the path with his lips. At the end of the path, he found the treasure—her breasts, heaving in response to him.

Nearly stupefied by desire, he returned to her lips. Lord save him. If he loosened the laces that confined her beauty, he might be lost.

*Beauteous curves and hollows.*

*Feminine flesh speaking to male.*

Ting crunched grass nearby, as if in tacit approval, and the soothing spell of the windswept island rocked him. Gemma seemed to embody the island with her own personal magic, which fascinated him further. He tasted her deeply, offering himself in return.

With a sigh, she pressed her body to his. It drove him wild, and he felt suddenly reckless, as he hadn't in years. She wanted him. And his need for her was a driving force, refusing to be stilled.

Unable to think of anything but satisfying both their wishes, he pulled the laces at the front of her gown. Her bodice gaped. She shuddered as he pulled away the stiff fabric and found her linen smock beneath, then drew it down to expose her flesh.

Her firm breasts begged for his touch. He bent to lave one budding tip with his tongue, feeling himself lengthen and harden as she gasped with pleasure. A new ripple of shudders swayed her body as she twined one hand in his hair, the other gripping his waist.

"We shouldna do this," she whispered. "*I* should not. The earl said if I lay with you, he would see me punished. He doesna make idle threats."

She was right to fear the earl's wrath. And lying with him had more difficulties than the earl's anger. Though Drummond wanted to make love to her, longed to take her from the island and make her his, he had nothing to offer her. Not a home nor the opportunity to have a family. Thanks to his father, he had no future. At least not one worthy of a woman of dignity like Gemma. One must earn the privilege of making love to a woman, and he had not done so.

With a curse, he dragged his hands away, pulled up her smock, and sat back.

He knew how to cultivate women, how to win their trust, but he'd never reached out to one in personal need. Nor had he permitted a woman to sense the need in him. He raged at his loss of self-control. The moment she had appeared, he had let it slip, with this disastrous result.

"I apologize," she said, retying her laces. "That was my fault. I wanted you to kiss me. I wanted more than for you to kiss me. It was wrong."

In the luminous twilight, she looked for all the world like the delectable fairy queen of the summer night, fresh from her bower, lips swollen from kisses. "Your fault? That would be true only if I had been unwilling. I was not."

She smiled at the vehemence of his admission. "Never mind. I will help you find this woman you seek and all will be well."

He nodded his thanks. "And once I complete my task here, I will take you back to the mainland where you can find a new life."

Her smile of appreciation nearly knocked him backward with its intensity, but it faded quickly. "The earl would no' permit it. No one born here can leave the island without his license. And I couldna leave the countess or my uncle.'Twould be heartless."

"You havena told me about your uncle." He seized the subject to subdue his still rampant need. "You're worried about him."

"My uncle is the chief stone mason responsible for building Scalloway Castle," she answered, straightening her hair where he had tangled it. "The earl's magistrate seems to look for reasons to punish him. Just now, he is depriving him of food. A man who works hard all day cannot afford to go without, but my uncle's rations have been cut and he is locked away each night in a storeroom to ensure he receives no supplements. I suppose I should be grateful he isna put in the dungeon, but that's mere selfishness on the magistrate's part. He knows my uncle would fall ill at once from the damp. He wants him on his feet, though subdued by hunger, so he can still work."

Outrage filled Drummond. "He torments someone you love while forcing you to stand by and watch." He leaped to his feet, wishing he could challenge both the magistrate and the earl to duels. He much preferred the direct method rather than secret machinations. "I will bribe someone to feed your uncle better," he swore.

She rose to her feet also, an expression of sorrow rippling across her delicate features. "You've already spent your gold for me, rescuing Ting. I will manage to feed my uncle." She produced a key from the pouch at her waist and held it up so that it caught the sun's rays, glinting faintly.

He realized it must be the key to her uncle's prison.

"But you understand very well what the earl does to us," she said, returning the key to her pouch. "The tyrant isolates his subjects. We begin by avoiding confidences in our loved ones because we know they will suffer if they're detected. Eventually, we get out of the habit of trusting others. I see it in the countess. She must not confide in anyone. And she still wants to believe in her husband, though she knows better."

Drummond thought of the ugly stories he'd heard as he traveled up the coast and knew this was true. "You have my support now. We'll find a way to help your uncle."

"You are kind to offer." Her faint smile suggested she didn't think him capable of providing relief in their situation, despite his ties to the king.

Mayhap he wasn't. Only drastic measures would improve conditions on the islands. The pain of her situation pierced him. Despite her trust in him, despite his support, the web of treachery thickened around her, making it impossible to put complete faith in anyone or anything. The opponent was too strong and held all the advantages.

"When you live under the rule of a man like the earl, you learn that no one dares tell the complete truth about themselves," she said, her anguish increasing. Ting pressed against her in a tender, protective gesture. "To protect our loved ones, we tell them lies, but the worst of it is, we tell them to ourselves. We can't live with ourselves if we don't." A sob caught in her throat. "I hate it," she choked out. "I hate everything about my life, but I can't do anything about it. Many people think me virtuous because I try to help them, but I'm not. In many ways, I'm as bad as the earl. I suspect the evil he's done, but I canna speak of it." With a sob, she gained her feet and rushed past him, and the ever-faithful Ting followed.

As she broke into a run, moving away from him down the track, Drummond wanted to rage against the earl. The man put Gemma in an impossible position, ensuring her enslavement. She was cared for kindly by the devil himself. She could try to run away, but she must know that if she tried, his kindness would vanish. She would be hunted down like a dog, for as she said, no one could leave the island without a license from the earl.

She was no fool, blindly obeying the one in power.

She was fighting for the survival of those she loved, willing to sacrifice her own happiness, her life itself. And her adversary had all the strength of a dragon, waiting in the safety of his lair until he wished to attack. Which would be soon. Too soon.

Gemma knew that Drummond followed her back to the castle, but he kept his distance, respecting her wish to be alone. She had wanted his lovemaking up on the moor, had unkindly encouraged him, yet her situation was too dangerous for such indulgence. He had offered to help her leave the islands, but her obligations would not permit it. Despite their attraction, nothing was possible between them. Life was full of unpleasant ironies.

As she entered the rear door of the stables, Gemma looked back. Drummond stood high on the windswept hill, watching her, as if standing guard over her. Grateful to know he was near if needed, she entered the stable and took Ting to a straight stall.

"I'm sorry, love, but you must stay here tonight." She pulled hay from between the slats of the hayrack and encouraged Ting to munch. " 'Tis too soon to risk an encounter between you and the earl."

After exchanging last caresses with her pony, she went to the tack room to set a pot of herbs simmering on a brazier. By the time she emerged, carrying her chest of ointments and remedies by its strap, the odor of pungent herbs filled the stable. She nodded to the stable lad on duty, a particular friend of hers, indicating that she needed nothing.

Knowing she had two more tasks to complete before she slept, Gemma stood on a mounting block facing the earl's huge black stallion over the wood partition of his stall. The sorry truths of her life throbbed within her like new wounds. Healing a wounded animal often helped soothe her own pain.

"Hello, Jupiter. How's your leg tonight?" she asked quietly.

Known for his savage disposition, not to mention his tendency to kick and bite stable workers, Black Jupiter, the earl's prize English stallion, tossed his head and rolled his eyes in a show of temper.

Gemma cast him a wry look. "No' ready to admit it hurts, are ye? At least eat the carrot I brought." She held out the treat and waggled it to tempt him.

Black Jupiter sidled over to the partition and snatched the entire carrot from her. As he crunched it greedily, Gemma saw Drummond from the corner of her eye, slipping into the stable. He found an observation point some distance away but did not intrude on her solitude.

Glad to know he was nearby, she hung over the partition and placed both hands on the horse's finely chiseled head. "There now, 'tis your old friend Gemma." She lowered her voice to a mesmerizing chant. "You remember me. I'm the one who takes away the pain."

At her touch, the horse quieted. With the carrot devoured, his breathing calmed and he stared straight ahead, as if in a trance.

Rising on tiptoe, Gemma placed her cheek against the great stallion's, bathing him with her breath, the surest way to communicate her benevolent intent. "You need not be wary of me, as with some of the others," she whispered. "Amos beat you yesterday, didn't he, and you have no way to tell the earl. But you bit Amos first. Why, Jupiter? Did he cinch your saddle too tightly?"

The stallion's ears swiveled to take in her pacifying litany, but other than an occasional flick of his tail, he moved not a muscle.

Having woven her spell, Gemma moved from the mounting block with smooth, deliberate motions. Picking up her chest of remedies, she slipped into the stall.

Once at the stallion's side, she ran a hand down his broad chest and left leg until she came to the bandage swathing the fetlock. "Easy there, laddie," she reassured as he flinched. "I know it hurts. Let me see what I can do."

The stallion shifted uneasily as she touched the leg, but steadied under her comforting intonations. After unwinding the bandage, she tested the swollen flesh for heat.

"It has improved," she assured him. "One more poultice should have you free of pain. I'll just fetch the hot herbs. You'll be right as rain in a few days."

With a sense of achievement that compensated for her upset over the encounter with Drummond, Gemma took fresh bandages from her remedy chest and headed for the tack room. She must not think of how badly she'd wanted Drummond's lovemaking. She could accept neither it nor the freedom he offered. Not now. Not ever.

Drummond watched as Gemma completed her ministrations to the earl's stallion. No wonder the wild ponies on the moor let her walk among them with easy acceptance. If the black hellion of a stallion craved her healing, the ponies undoubtedly welcomed it as well.

Her skill with the beasts also explained the power behind her touch. She had an uncanny ability to heal, to comfort. He'd responded to it just as the animals did.

As he watched, she patted Ting a last time, then left the stable. Through the open double doors facing the castle, he watched her time her dash to the kitchen just as the guard disappeared around the corner. Apparently she didn't mind if the stable lad knew she'd been in the stable, but she didn't want the guard knowing as well.

The dragon's great lair of stone swallowed her up.

Drummond shifted on his feet, knowing the dragon slept within. He didn't want to encounter the fiend tonight, nor even one of his minions. Now that he knew what the earl believed, he wanted to rage rather than sleep.

He moved down the aisle of stalls to Ting. She would be lonely, robbed of both her mistress and her fellow ponies' company. Poor creature. He believed he knew just how she felt. He would keep company with her and the soothing aroma of horses and hay.

As predicted, Ting stood tethered in a straight stall, looking dejected. She whickered and pulled at the rope as he slid in beside her. "You were hoping for something else of Mistress Sinclair tonight, weren't you?" he said softly, running a hand along her sleek back. "Looks as if we're both to be disappointed. Except that your desire is admirable. Mine is not."

He untied the rope and removed it from her halter. She rubbed against him in thanks, showing how much she trusted him, just as her mistress had done.

He was grateful for both, and he had no intention of letting either of them down.

He would like to find a way for them to leave the island. Unfortunately, with the many people depending on Gemma, it seemed an impossible task.

# Chapter 12

Gemma slipped into the kitchens, trying not to think about Drummond. Yet how could she not think about him?

Twining her hands in his thick hair had been divine. She had longed for that from the instant they'd met. The masculine tickle of his emerging beard as he'd kissed her had been a titillating pleasure. Her body craved more of Drummond Graham, threatening a riot if she refused to meet its demands.

Most disquieting.

Just as disquieting had been their discussion. He'd offered her a glimpse of freedom, a chance to leave the island. Out of love and loyalty, she had shut the door on that idea with depressing finality, but oh, how she longed to accept.

For six years, she had lived on the main island under the tyrant earl's rule. Any sane person in her place would flee. Yet she could not walk away, leaving her friends and kin at his mercy.

But Drummond wasn't ready to leave, and much could happen in the coming days. She would think about it later. Drummond must first find the woman he sought, as well as complete his mysterious mission.

The idea of his mission intrigued her. Though she had sworn not to pry, to be satisfied with the idea that he came from the king but would never harm innocent children, she couldn't help but wonder. He hadn't said for certain. Was he or was he not from the king?

The earl believed he was. He expected an attempt on his boys' lives, and she and Drummond meant to let him believe it. The ugliness of this tactic struck her squarely between the eyes. The only way to control the tyrant was with tyranny. Evil bred evil. And pain.

Saddened by these thoughts, Gemma set them aside. She had promised her uncle a meal before she slept tonight, and after the recent chaos, she longed for his comforting care.

After lighting a lantern, she found the fish stew left from supper. She ladled out a bowl, tore off a hunk of barley bread, then made her way to the small storage chamber where Lawrence Bruce had ordered her uncle locked when he wasn't at work.

Bruce had given the order, but to goad Gemma, he'd given her the key. She must be the one to lock her uncle away after work, must suffer the torments of being his jailor. Each night, she was to return the key to Bruce, but tonight, she hadn't. He must have forgotten to ask for it, and she had purposely failed to seek him out.

"Uncle, I brought ye something to eat," she whispered as she opened the door.

"Och, Gemma." He roused from his pallet in the tiny room full of grain bags. "Ye're a good lass."

"Now Uncle, ye ken that Mary is the good lass o' the family. You never could keep us straight. From Ellen on down, 'tis all mischief, as you oft said." She relaxed into the old family jest, born of the occasional lapse when he'd called one of his nine children by the wrong name.

He chuckled, then drank eagerly from the bowl. "So I have," he quipped, pausing to wipe his mouth. "But ye ken I meant naught by it. I've always loved ye, Gemma, as if ye were my own bairn."

"I love you, too, Uncle." She watched him wolf

down the bread and knew that his hard day of labor, followed by the light evening meal, had left him ravenous. Why hadn't she pulled off a larger piece of bread? Andrew Crawford was a big man, and as the chief stone mason, he worked as hard as any of the workers, hauling and mortaring stone all day.

Not only did Bruce force him to endure hunger, but humiliation as well, knowing the men he directed ate their fill in the great hall. But Bruce said that her uncle unsettled the workers, made them uncooperative. And now she knew the earl wholly approved of the punishment ordered by his magistrate.

With the perception born of long familiarity, her uncle seemed to know something troubled her. Once he had eaten, he leaned against a sack of meal and opened his arm, urging her to nestle against his side as if she were once more a bairn.

"Bide o' wee, my Gemma." He patted her shoulder drowsily. "How did ye come by the key, eh? I thought Bruce collected it from ye each night."

Replete in the warmth of his love, tired from her long day, Gemma snuggled against him. "He forgot tonight, so I kept it," she murmured. "Being your jailor has its advantages." She forced her voice to lightness, though inside she raged at both magistrate and earl. "I wish I were a wee lassie again and ye could make everything right with a kiss and a hug."

He must have heard the despair in her tone, despite her effort to conceal it. "Tell yer ald uncle what's wrong."

So many things were wrong, but she had no wish to upset him. He had protected her for many a year from the fate of being an orphan. Now it was her duty to protect him. "Your being here. That's wrong." She gestured to his cell.

"The earl wants his castle. I'm willing to build it for him."

"But Lawrence Bruce should not be permitted to abuse you," she protested. " 'Tis no' right. I spoke to the earl about it."

"He willna listen to aught against his man. He has greater matters on his mind."

Unhappily, she knew too much about those greater matters. "The earl wishes me to wed again," she blurted out.

"Does he, now?" Her uncle sat up straighter, as if sensing her unspoken fears.

She hadn't meant to tell him, yet she could not hold back the words. She confessed everything. Well, not quite everything. But she told him about the countess's astounding idea that she marry Drummond Graham, then Drummond's offer to take her to the mainland. "But I canna accept his offer. I wouldna leave you or the countess."

"Ye're a good child to stay because o' me, but I wish ye to be happy," her uncle admonished. "Go wi' him. Start life anew, as he says."

She shook her head vehemently. "I must see you safely back to Fair Isle."

He seemed to think on this for a moment. "Verra well. Once I'm back, ye mun go." He patted her arm, as if the plan were settled.

Gemma despaired at what she must tell him next. "His lordship has demanded that I wed William Fermour."

Her uncle flinched at the name. "Ye canna wed him. He cheats people at his district market by adding to the weights and measures. People pay taxes to him on goods they never get. Go wi' Drummond, Gemma. He saved ye from the sea. He's a good man. All the women say so." He nodded, as if sensing her wonder at the news he'd managed to glean. "Aye, I heard o' him, even here. The earl rules our acts, but no' our minds. Nor some women's tongues." He chuckled at his jest but then turned thoughtful. "But if Drummond takes ye from the isle, 'twould be better if he weds ye, as the countess says."

"Why do you both think of marriage?" she asked, blushing in the dark, glad he had no way of knowing about her two trysts with Drummond on the moor. "We've just met. Besides, the earl says he has a disreputable background, and I'm wondering what he knows. He said Drummond's weapons would be scarred from use, and they are."

"What does he carry?" her uncle asked with his usual practicality.

"A razor-sharp dirk," she admitted. "He used it to clean Ting's hooves, and he's very skilled with it. I could tell from the way he handled it. His hands are as nimble as eels."

"Is it new?"

"The leather on the hilt is worn, and 'tis nicked and ground thin in places from sharpening. I'm guessing 'tis years old."

"That doesna make him disreputable. Most men carry a dirk or two all their lives," her uncle scoffed. "What of his sword?"

Gemma tried to remember. "I havena see it out of its scabbard." At least not by daylight, she thought, recalling how skillfully Drummond had wielded it the night of the sinking ship. "But the scabbard looks far from new. I'm guessing they were both given him by his father. Since he refuses to speak of him, mayhap he's the one who's disreputable. Drummond speaks freely of his mother, though. He said he willingly went through hell to ensure her security."

"There." Her uncle pounced on this detail. "The father might be a villain, but the earl misses a piece of the puzzle. He doesna see a mother as able to give nobility o' character to her son, as Drummond's obviously did."

Gemma raised her eyebrows. "Ye think Drummond Graham noble of character?"

"Every woman on the island thinks it, and well they should." He laughed. "Any man who labors for women in exchange for nothing save their thanks has a valiant heart. 'Tis proof enow for me."

If he gave to others but received little in return, Gemma thought, his purpose in life might also be as difficult as hers. She certainly could not live as she wished. Nor could Drummond, it seemed. "It matters naught if I wish to wed him or leave the island with him," she argued. "Either way, the earl would stop me. 'Twould ruin his plans."

"Ye canna blame him for making his plans. We all do."

"I blame him for the nature of those plans, though."

"It does nay good. Hate the sin but never the sinner."

Her uncle's fatalistic acceptance was typical of the islanders. Though a strong man with many skills, he could not hope to escape the tyrant who ruled the land of his birth. But she would not accept it. Not now that she saw a possible path of escape. "I do not wish to leave the islands, but the earl is so miserly. I would like him to be more generous. More just."

"Just and generous are no' his way. Those o' us who mun live under him take him as he is and bear our lot. Good will come o' it in the end. When yer auntie's sister died after givin' ye life, 'twas our lot to take ye in, yer auntie and me, and we did. We've been rewarded many times o'er for it."

Gemma sighed, missing her aunt, who had died of a fever two years past. "My mother would not say who my father was?" she asked for the thousandth time.

"Nay. She went to the main isle to ply her knitting skill. A six month later, I took yer auntie to visit her and learned that ye were growing in her belly, an' her unwed."

"How did she live, if she had no husband and was clearly with child?" Gemma had never asked about this aspect of her mother's life.

" 'Twould seem her fine lace knitting was greatly coveted, despite her shame. She had plenty o' coin."

The sorrowful story of her parentage, of a man who had deserted her mother, reawakened Gemma's rage with her predicament. "Uncle, I will see you out of here," she swore, slipping from his embrace and rising. "I'll ask Drummond Graham to help convey you back to Fair Isle."

"Ye'll no' succeed 'til my labors are done. Bruce has given me a special task."

Gemma tilted her head, wondering what he meant.

"Ye ken I'm workin' in the south corner o' the new wing. No one is permitted to come near." He touched her skirt, pulling her down again, and she knelt before him. "I'm buildin' a secret chamber. A hiding place for the earl, his children, anyone he wishes to protect. It opens from what will be the countess's new bed-chamber. By the hearth is a secret panel. I'm finishin' the stonework inside."

She knew he shouldn't be telling her this, but the secret clearly ate at him. He needed to confide in a loved one, just as she had. She grasped his leathery, calloused hand and carried it to her cheek. "I hear you, Uncle. You need say no more."

"There is more." He pulled her closer. "I mun tell ye how the secret panel opens, before 'tis too late. On the panel to the left o' the mantel, ye press the middle ornament and the one at the top left, both at the same time. They release a spring—"

A scrape sounded at the door, and they both started. Filled with cold dread, Gemma gained her feet and opened the door a crack.

Embers glowed on the distant hearth, the only light in the depths of the darkened kitchen. Nothing moved. Bruce knew she had the key tonight. She didn't doubt he had set someone to watch for her. Perhaps he listened himself. If he'd heard them, she was in deep trouble. The earl's secret was exactly that—a secret. No one was supposed to know.

The idea took Gemma's thoughts in a new direction. The earl would have hired a master carpenter to craft the secret panel. Scalloway had such a man by the name of Magnus Jamison. Except that he had died last week from eating bad fish.

The earl and Bruce had accorded him all honor at his funeral. Gemma had comforted the widow and children and brought them food and gifts of coin in the name of the countess.

Gemma had thought it an odd way for him to die. The man knew fish as well as his own name. Everyone in the islands knew when one went bad or was still good.

Now, with a sinking feeling in the pit of her stomach, she wondered. What if Jamison had not died from eating bad fish? What if he had died from poison put in his food because he knew too much about a certain task he had just completed?

Sickened by the possibility that her uncle, and now she, knew too much as well, she kissed him and took the empty bowl as he settled on his pallet. "This willna last forever," she promised. "Soon, the castle will be done and ye can return to Fair Isle and Cousin Ester." She referred to her eldest cousin, now a widow, who kept her uncle's home.

"Soon," he grunted in agreement, pulling up his blanket, seeming unwilling to admit his danger. "Aye, soon."

As she closed the door of her uncle's prison and relocked it, she hated her life for all the reasons she'd told Drummond. Because they lied to each other. And they lied to themselves.

# Chapter 13

Unwilling to light a taper and announce her late-night roaming, Gemma felt her way along the corridor toward her chamber, eager for bed. Best get some sleep, for she needed her strength. On the morrow, she must rise and fight her battles anew.

She sensed rather than saw a movement ahead. In the next instant, two great fists grasped her around her neck and tightened, threatening to cut off her air.

"What do ye here?" rasped a voice.

Gemma gasped for breath and clawed at the man she recognized as Lawrence Bruce.

He released her neck but transferred his grip to her left arm. "Haimsone, bring light," he shouted down the corridor.

A guard descended the stair that led from the castle wall, a smoking torch in hand.

"Release me, sir," Gemma hissed with indignation. "I am for my bed. 'Tis all."

"I dinna believe ye." He twisted her arm behind her and pushed her down the corridor toward an open door.

"Master Bruce, you are hurting my arm. What has gotten into you tonight?" She struggled against his brute strength, but his grip tightened.

"Ye'll be hurtin' a deal more afore the night is out. Look here."

Bruce shoved her over the chamber lintel. Haimsone followed, holding aloft his torch.

Gemma started, unable to make sense of what she saw. Chaos reigned in the room. Feathers swirled in the air and settled on an overturned chair and writing table. Broken pottery from the washstand littered the floor. The bed had suffered thc worst damage. One of the deep blue bed curtains had been torn from its rod and lay tangled on the floor. The thick quilt, mounded into a big hump on the bed, had been slashed many times, releasing its feathers. Snowbanks of them lay around the chamber, rising in swirls at the least draft from the window, hearth, or open door.

"What has happened?" She tensed, knowing this was one of two chambers assigned to their Lowland guests. As Drummond had still been in the stable when she left, it must be his. But why would someone destroy his chamber? Were they looking for something?

"What's the stir, Bruce?" The earl stalked around the corner, coming from his bedchamber in the next wing. His attendants followed, carrying lamps and candles. More guards joined them from the castle garrison, their lanterns lighting up the corridor.

The countess peeked from her bedchamber three doors away, her face anxious.

"Go back to bed, my dear," the earl ordered his wife. "Ye shouldna be on yer feet. All is well," he assured her more gently when she didn't move. "Call for one o' yer ladies. They should be attending ye."

"Yes, madam. We will take care of everything," Gemma added her reassurance, concerned that her mistress not be upset.

The door closed on a muffled sob. Was the countess crying? Gemma wondered. She must be upset already, and Gemma longed to go to her, but first she must help solve this mystery of the destroyed chamber.

"Speak, Bruce," the earl ordered.

" 'Tis my night for the watch up on the wall." Bruce prided himself on taking his monthly turn at guard, as if he were part of the garrison. "I heard a scuffle below and came at once to see what was wrong. I found this chamber as ye see it, my lord. I found Mistress Sinclair skulking nearby. Is it not the chamber given to one o' the Lowlanders?"

Gemma braced herself. Was he going to accuse her of improper behavior?

The earl gave him no chance to do so. "These two chambers were indeed assigned to our Lowland guests." He indicated the next chamber farther down the corridor. "Quickly, knock on the other door. Rouse the occupant."

A guard banged on the door. Iain opened it after several minutes, his eyes heavy with sleep, his nightcap askew.

"I knew it," Bruce shouted. "This chamber was given to Graham, and this woman"—he jerked a thumb at Gemma—"has just tried to murder him, for I found her knife on the floor." He held up a small, pearl-handled knife such as ladies use to cut their bread or fish.

Aghast at this unexpected accusation, Gemma started to protest. Iain yelped in surprise and demanded to know Drummond's whereabouts. Bruce ignored them both. He strode into the ruined chamber. "Let us see what mayhem she has wreaked on our innocent visitor as he lay in his bed." He tore back the shredded quilt.

Everyone gasped, expecting the hump in the bed to be a dead body, its blood soaking the sheets.

Bolsters lay beneath the quilt, slit from end to end, feathers spilling from them like milkweed from ravaged pods. Bruce's motion stirred the feathers into a furious dance.

"Ye see," she cried. "He's no' here. Of all the ridiculous nonsense, that I should kill him or anyone else."

"No, ye didna succeed, murderess," Bruce snarled. "He wasna in his bed. But ye shall be punished for the attempt."

"No' in his bed?" The earl appeared overcome by this announcement. "Where would he be but in his bed at this time o' night? Find him at once! He is our guest and his safety is vital. Check the entire castle."

Members of the garrison raced off to obey. The others stood, awestruck witnesses to Bruce's accusation.

The earl took the small pearl-handled eating knife from Bruce and inspected it. "This is indeed yer knife." He rounded on Gemma. "The verra one the countess gave ye as a New Year's gift two years ago." He waved it in her face. "Is it no'?"

Gemma stared at the knife in the earl's hand, then at the small sheath at her belt. To her surprise, the sheath was empty, nor did she remember when she had last seen her knife. "It may be, but—"

"How could ye try to murder our guest?" the earl sputtered in outrage.

"I did not!"

"Don't attempt to play the innocent," Bruce ground out. He stepped forward and gripped Gemma tightly by the shoulders. "Ye are guilty. Admit it."

Gemma recognized the glint of triumph in his eyes. This was his revenge for her accusation that he had killed the tinker. And for learning about the secret chamber. She glanced at the earl and realized he wished to be rid of her. She had become a greater liability than asset. Well, let them try. She would not succumb meekly to this trumped-up charge. "I didna do it," she said stoutly. "When Drummond Graham is found, he will bear me out."

"If ye did not attempt to murder him, what were ye doing in the corridor?" the earl demanded, towering over her, filling her with dread.

"I was late to my bed after caring for Ting."

"Liar," Bruce growled. "Ye were talking to yer uncle in the kitchens, sneaking him extra food."

"A liar as well as a murderess." The earl picked up the new accusation. "I see exactly how it is. Ye're in love with the Scot. You admitted it to me the other day. I warned you to keep yer behavior above reproach, but ye didn't listen. My own innocent Rowena, whom I entrusted to yer care, swears ye contrived to be alone with Graham on the moor this afternoon. Ye lured him to couple with ye. But when he wouldna offer marriage, ye tried to murder him. As luck would have it, he was no' in his bed. You cut his bolsters instead."

The earl's attendants and the remaining garrison eyed each other, clearly scandalized by this testimony.

"I couldna have slashed those heavy bolsters with such a small knife," Gemma protested, knowing it was no use denying her interest in the Scot. "Only a strong man could manage that."

"I can only assume yer rage gave ye the strength. Gemma, I am ashamed and saddened by yer actions. Ye will have to stand before the Scalloway foud to be judged," the earl said.

"But I've done nothing," she cried. "Let me loose." She tore away from Bruce's grasp. "Where is Graham? What have you done with him?" Had the earl managed to murder him, despite the fact that he was not in the bed?

"Go join the garrison, Bruce," the earl ordered. "Find him. We will await ye in the great hall. Guards, bring her." With an imperious wave, he moved down the passage, his ermine-trimmed robe billowing about him.

A single feather from the ruined bed drifted through the air and settled on Gemma's nose. She felt a shriek building in her throat as two guards closed in on her. Grasping her arms, they forced her to follow the earl.

Gemma shook them off. "I will follow him of my own accord," she said, delivering each a scathing stare.

They fell back, and Gemma turned. With all the dignity she could muster, she walked toward the great hall, wanting only one thing in the world—for Drummond Graham to appear unscathed. She had seen him whole and well only an hour earlier. Surely no one could have killed him and disposed of the body in so short a time. Nor was Drummond a man to be caught by surprise and easily murdered without raising a hue and cry.

Drummond must be alive. And once she was assured of his safety, she knew he would testify that she had not done this terrible thing.

Tension mounted in the great hall as a growing number of people gathered, waiting for Drummond Graham to be found. The scullery maids, the cook, the stewart and his assistants, the earl's household treasurer, the countess's maids, even one of the two nursemaids who tended to young Elizabeth, arrived. And of course all fifty men from the garrison assembled.

Whispers and gossip filled the hall. The earl kept no secrets. Gemma saw within minutes that everyone knew his version of the story. According to him, Drummond Graham had scorned her, and in a fit of murderous rage, she had tried to kill him.

Iain Lang entered at a trot, his jerkin buttoned wrong, his face drawn and anxious.

Gemma pressed his hand. "I'm sure your brother will be found."

Iain pressed hers in return and leaned close to whisper in her ear so the guards would not hear. "Ye've been accused of murder and ye worry first for him?"

"Of course I'm worried about him. The earl could have murdered him."

"No' Drummond. He wouldna be so careless as to

let that happen." With a confident smile, perhaps to keep up her spirits, Iain retreated from the guards' intimidating glares.

Lawrence Bruce entered the hall and went to whisper to the earl on the dais.

The earl whirled to confront Gemma, where she stood between the guards. "Graham canna be found in the castle. Ye have killed him and disposed o' the body. Bruce, lock her in the storage chamber next to her uncle."

Gemma gasped as the guards pulled her toward the kitchens, but at that moment, a stir rose at the hall entry. Everyone turned as Drummond Graham appeared. Though his red hair was tousled and his eyes heavy with sleep, he was very much whole and alive.

Shouts of welcome flooded the air.

Gemma wanted to weep with relief.

"Come forward, Drummond Graham," the earl thundered, his voice rising above the others.

Drummond moved to the dais, his gaze falling on Gemma, questioning. "What's the stir, my lord?"

"Master Graham, ye are unharmed. Praise the Lord." The earl gestured to the heavens, palpable relief lighting up his features.

Drummond frowned at him. "Of course I am unharmed, sir. Why would you think otherwise?"

"Because this woman tried to kill ye." The earl brandished Gemma's knife. "We must thank God she succeeded only in cutting up yer quilt and bolsters, but she meant to carve ye into small pieces. I apologize for her madness. She will be punished, I promise."

Blood suffused Drummond's face, but he uttered not a word. Instead, he stepped deliberately onto the dais and stood toe-to-toe with the earl.

Despite the nobleman's size, the younger Scot loomed over him, his height and breadth powerful and intimidating. The earl seemed to shrink to insignificance in comparison.

"What makes ye think she did this?" Drummond

demanded, his low voice tinged with a dangerous edge.

Gemma had never seen the earl retreat, but as Drummond confronted him, he inched back. "The ruined bed and bolsters make me think it. Her knife was on the floor. We found her skulking in the passage nearby. She has also engaged in questionable conduct of late." The earl waxed eloquent, and the entire hall hung on his words. He had the upper hand with his subjects and knew it. They would see things his way, for they depended on him for shelter and bread.

"The night ye arrived, she stayed out all night," the earl continued. "One o' my men attested to seeing her in intimate discussion with ye at the stable door early that morn. She even admitted to me that she is in love with ye. My innocent daughter Rowena told me that ye and Gemma were alone on the moor today. I conclude that Gemma has ignored my advice and behaved immodestly with ye. When ye refused her wanton demands, as well ye should, she tried to murder ye as ye slept."

Gemma shuddered. It sounded so convincing. Everyone would believe him. They always did. For six years, she had blinded herself to the truth as well.

But Drummond Graham merely shrugged. "I'm sure ye mean well, my lord, but yer conclusions are incorrect. Gemma could not possibly have tried to murder me, for she has been with me in the stable until a short time ago. I sent her to her chamber for the night while I finished removing the mud from her pony's coat."

He turned to the crowd with a nod, winning them with his sincerity, destroying the earl's story with astonishing ease. "She has never behaved with anything but the utmost modesty and propriety toward me, and my admiration is such, I have asked her to be my bride. She has agreed, so she has no reason to slash my bolsters, let alone wish me dead."

He stepped to Gemma's side, and the guards fell back, Lawrence Bruce with them, his mouth hanging open in shock. Drummond looped his right arm around her waist and squeezed, as if warning her to follow his lead. With a winning smile, he turned to the earl. "I pray ye bless our union, yer lordship. We wish to be wed as soon as the banns can be cried."

A vast hole of silence opened in the hall. Gemma stared at Drummond as he captured her right hand and raised it to his lips. His bride? Her?

"Tell him 'tis true," Drummond hissed between clenched teeth without moving his lips.

Gemma's gaze darted in terror to the guards. They were far enough away not to have heard, yet she could not speak. Her tongue sat in her mouth like a dead fish, useless. He squeezed her waist again, and she started, then rallied. "Indeed," she croaked feebly, hoping it would do.

The earl looked disinclined to accept the story. "If this is so, how did Gemma's knife come to be on the floor of yer chamber?" he ground out.

"I borrowed it of her earlier to cut the pages of a book," Drummond said. "It must have fallen to the floor when the table was overturned. Your lordship, I'm sure you can see that someone else has done this wicked thing. I pray you put all energy into discovering him at once. In the meantime, I'm sure you will understand if I feel unsafe in the castle. With your permission, Gemma and I will remove to another abode at once. As it isn't entirely proper for us to live together before the marriage ceremony, I will handfast with her now."

He released Gemma's waist but caught both her hands in his. He spoke in ringing tones that reached the farthest corner of the hall, vowing to be her mate for a year and a day.

"Your turn," he prodded Gemma in low tones.

Could this possibly be real?

Drummond squeezed one of her hands sharply. "I do," she babbled, unable to repeat the words he'd just said. "I vow to do exactly what he vowed. With him."

She sounded like the village idiot, but Drummond smiled as if well pleased with her. He turned congenially to the earl. "Thank you, your lordship, for witnessing our union. God'den to you all." He executed a bow that encompassed the awestruck populace and drew Gemma from the hall.

Such a liar. So smooth. Gemma marveled at his skill.

Yet even as Drummond lied to save her, she realized the earl's purpose. Her master had meant to do away with Drummond, and she had been his weapon of choice.

# Chapter 14

"He meant for you to die and to blame me for it." Drummond nodded agreement with Gemma's choked whisper as he hustled her into the stable. Stablemen and lads scattered, deserting their posts in the confusion that followed in the wake of his announcement in the hall. Everyone knew he had defied the earl's attempts to accuse Gemma of murder. They were now both outcasts from the noble household. Word spread quickly in the islands, and now Drummond knew how. His lordship's loyal minions were everywhere.

Nevertheless, elation bore him on triumphant wings. He'd outwitted the earl. Stymied the old bastard in his tracks as he'd sought to destroy both him and Gemma.

Satisfied by the memory of the earl's dumbfounded fury as he snatched Gemma from the death trap, Drummond cursed him with a string of choice expletives.

"You canna undo what he's done with curses," Gemma said, resisting him for the first time. She stopped in the middle of the aisle and stared at him with confused, haunted eyes, as if beseeching him to explain what he'd just done.

Drummond wished he could, but they had no time. "If I could challenge his lordship to a duel and cut him to pieces, I would. As I canna, I choose to curse, and you, who have just sworn to be my wife, will humor me." He moved into Ting's straight stall, took the pony's halter, and urged her backward.

"Yes, sir, lord husband." Despite her sarcasm, she looked confused by what he was doing.

He halted Ting beside Gemma. "We're going to stay at the deserted cot near the moor," he explained, hoping to erase the dazed look from her eyes. "The pony, too."

His explanation failed to produce the hoped-for reaction. Gemma's blue eyes widened. "The cot has no roof. One of the walls has a gaping hole."

"I'll build up the wall and we'll thatch the roof on the morrow. If it doesna rain tonight, we'll be all right."

"I dinna think anything will ever be all right again."

Her voice had a hollow quality, and Drummond considered the best way to reassure her. "It will. Trust me and you'll see. We're going to live on the moor until I finish my mission here. A few weeks should do it. Then I'm going to remove you from this hellhole."

Of course it wasn't as simple as he made it sound. Open war had been declared between them and the earl. His lordship would see him dead before he permitted him to leave the island.

Drummond's ruse of being from the king offered some protection, but not much. Tonight's drama proved how easily a king's spy could be dispatched without a hint of blame sticking to the earl or his man, Bruce. Little wonder Gemma still looked bleak.

Iain entered the stable, and Drummond waved him over. "We're going up to the abandoned cot on the moor. Join us, but pray fetch food from the castle kitchens first. Whatever you can take quickly. Dinna let anyone delay you." He gathered several wool blankets from a stall partition. "We'll sleep with these. Anyone mind the scent of horse?"

"Not I, sir. I'm off for food." Completely serious for once, Iain scuttled back to the castle.

Drummond took Gemma's hand and Ting's halter. Buoyed by his success, he led the way out the back door of the stable. Both woman and pony obeyed him without protest.

He set a fast pace for the stone dyke that surrounded the castle. Once Ting was through the gate, he did not slacken their speed as they mounted the hill toward the moor. The earl infuriated him with his tyranny and greed. Although Drummond had won the first battle, it would not be their last. He must rally his resources.

But as he strode into the deepening twilight, he felt a profound desire to enjoy one of his resources. He glanced back at Gemma, pleased to see her following him.

He hoped she would remain quiet. In his present state of mind, it would take little encouragement for him to do what he'd wanted from the start—to take her in his arms, to taste her warmth, and make her truly his.

He must not, his sense of honor argued. He was not free to live as he chose. Not until he fulfilled the legacy left him by his father, and that would take years.

Yet fate had made her his when he least expected it. He'd wanted Gemma from the moment he'd seen her, rising among the ponies. Since that night, he'd come to appreciate more than her beauty. He could not regret his actions in the hall, despite all the reasons he should not wed.

There had been no choice. She had been without defense, and he had done the only thing possible to protect her.

Tomorrow would be soon enough to right the terrible wrong he had done her.

Tonight, it would be all he could manage to keep from claiming her as his own.

Gemma stood in the cot, watching Drummond, unable to think straight. As Ting fell to cropping grass, she stared at their new home in a daze. It looked even less habitable than she remembered it, but Drummond didn't seem to care.

Still numb with disbelief, she found an old stool with one short leg and sat on it. With the blankets piled on her lap, she watched him restack stones on the wall. He worked with a feverish energy, a grim smile that puzzled her haunting his lips.

Having placed the stones as high as possible without mortar, he found a broken broom and began to clear debris from the single-roomed dwelling. The midnight sun illuminated the unyielding line of his jaw, still set as it had been when he faced down the earl and won. From time to time, he glanced at her, a possessive, smoldering light in his green eyes that set her shivering with anticipation.

But then his expression would harden as he returned to his task, looking angry. Was it with her, or perhaps himself?

They were handfasted. Gone were all the reasons for them to keep their distance. No longer was she bound to spy on him by the earl's command. Her relief was so great, she wanted to kiss him.

"Thank you for saying you would take me away from this hellhole," she blurted, overwhelmed by the sensations storming her from every direction. Fear of the earl. Relief at being rescued. Doubt that it was real.

"I didna just say it. I'm going to do it." He swept harder, faster, his movements stiff, unyielding. The air between them seemed to crackle, as if a storm approached.

"*After* I care for my friends and kin."

"We'll talk about them later. You're my wife now and must obey my every command."

He wasn't being logical or reasonable, but this didn't seem like the moment to argue with him. "I'm sorry I took so long to thank you properly," she managed. "I *am* grateful. But I want you to know we can separate later. I dinna expect you to go through with a real ceremony, given the circumstances."

He looked infuriated. "As you said so succinctly in the stable, that bastard tried to use you to kill me. It's become a personal matter between him and me. I'll no' let him succeed."

"You'd marry me to stop him?"

"I'd go through hell to stop him."

She wasn't sure how to take this statement. "I dinna hold you to any obligation. I'm sure you dinna want to wed," she tried again.

He tossed the broom aside and approached her, as if he'd just made a decision. As he towered over her, his potent masculinity leaped from him like sparks from a fire. "Dinna tell me what I want."

Suddenly, her confusion fell away, and she knew exactly what to do. Rising, she faced him. "I dinna need to tell you," she said softly, reaching out a hand. "We both know what you want. I want it as well. Now."

She trailed off as he grasped her hand, but he didn't stop there. In response to her bold invitation, he tumbled her off balance and into his arms, molding his body to hers. She had enough experience to recognize his arousal, flagrant against her thighs, and her mind whirled.

Excitement deluged her at his obvious passion, a flood of such force that it weakened her knees. They wobbled precariously, threatening to desert her when she most needed their support, and she gripped his shoulders to keep from falling.

He crushed her lips beneath his own. His demands stunned her, so unlike his courteous restraint earlier in the evening. His body, hard against hers, was intoxicating, and after her shock and fear, she welcomed the comfort of his arms. Yielding, she parted her lips beneath his sensual onslaught.

He emitted a rough groan of appreciation, and the horror of the night's events retreated to a distant place. Gemma answered his invasion, inviting him to taste her, tasting him in return.

She didn't know much about men aroused by danger, but she'd heard it had that effect. If this was what rescuing her did to him, she meant to enjoy it. As a widow educated in the ways of Eros, she had craved Drummond's kisses, his touch, from the first.

As his lips slid to her ear and he tugged at the lobe, shivers rushed through her body. Anticipation of further intimacies hummed through her until she felt as taut as a finely tuned harp. "This canna be real," she murmured, dazed.

"No? Is this not real?"

His hands unlacing her bodice felt very real indeed, as did the cool air on her shoulders as he stripped away the garment and tossed it aside. Her breasts ached for his touch.

He pulled down her smock. The flat of his palm brushed, then circled and cupped her sensitive flesh. Then came his mouth.

"Good heavens! *Drummond.*"

"At last you call me by my given name. Is this what it takes?" His tongue danced over her flesh.

Time stood still for Gemma, and when she closed her eyes, she saw Drummond as he had appeared the first night, a Norse god charged with potent power, the answer to her prayers.

"Mmm." The purr of appreciation rumbled from her throat unbidden. "Thunder god," she whispered as a fierce need rushed through her lower body. "Kiss me again."

His mouth caressed hers. "What did you call me?" he murmured against her cheek.

"The night I first saw you, I thought you a thunder god arrived from across the sea."

"I'm no god."

"But you can give us both thunder. Aye?" She grasped a handful of her skirt and pulled it up. Catching his hand, she placed it on her bare thigh above her stocking.

His body quivered with ill-contained excitement. "Do you know what you're doing?" he growled.

His touch on her thigh set the earth beneath her in motion, as if shaken by thunder. She clutched his shoulders desperately as she felt desire radiate from him. "I told you I'm a widow. I know exactly what I'm doing."

"Then God help me, I cannot refuse."

She felt him easing his hand toward her most private place, and a sudden thought panicked her. "Do thunder gods do it, er, like this?"

He paused, his hands tightening on her flesh. "Does standing up offend you?"

"My husband always said a respectable couple must be in a proper bed. With the man on top."

"I disagree. A man and a woman can be face-to-face, equals in pleasure."

He touched her gently, then more firmly, sending bolts of lightning through her. She threw back her head, drinking in air, feeling more alive than she had in years.

"Have I found the right spot?" he asked, his breath harsh and ragged.

"Oh, yes." Since he'd found it, she couldn't think why he would leave it, but instead of continuing, he raised her right leg and draped it around his waist. Then he gently eased two fingers into her feminine corridor. She started to protest, but stopped as unexpected thrills of pleasure dazzled her. "Gracious, Drummond, are you *entirely* certain this is what proper couples do?"

"Your first husband never did this either?"

She shuddered with enjoyment as his fingers moved within her. "No, never. He would not have considered it fitting."

"I think it fits very well. He never did anything remotely resembling it?"

"For certes, he did not." Drummond's touch awakened her senses in a manner most unlike her first husband's uninspiring fumblings. His further motion drove her to distraction so that she couldn't concentrate on his questions.

"Do you dislike my touch?" His fingers continued their exotic motion, fascinating her senses.

"Nay." Gemma could scarcely answer, she was nearly delirious with delight.

"Sure? What if I do this?" He tugged gently at the spot he'd found earlier.

Closing her eyes, she saw flashes of lightning, lighting up her life, and wanted more of him. "I am . . . quite . . . certain I don't dislike it." She sucked in her breath as he stopped the friction. "Drummond, do you wish me to beg?"

"Pray do." He was watching her, his green eyes searching for her response, lingering on her bare breasts, as if wishing to devour her.

She drew a deep breath. "More, please."

He grinned, a tantalizing, sardonic look. "Too lady-like." He teased her again. "Can ye no' muster a bit more enthusiasm?"

"More!"

"Better." He resumed the friction, the pleasure awing her before he ceased.

"Stop teasing." Closing her eyes, Gemma stood on tiptoe and pushed against his hand. "Why don't we just—" She reached for him and found his arousal, fully defined within his trunk hose.

He growled and dragged her hand away. At the same time, he captured her mouth in a devouring kiss.

"Not too fast, sweetling. One thing at a time." Short and labored, his breath warmed her cheek as he continued to stroke her.

"There! Oh dear, yes!" She moaned in ecstasy as he brought her to the edge. Unable to contain herself, she moved against his hand, and the pleasure compounded. Her world shook with nerve-tingling euphoria as he pressed and rubbed, again and again.

An unexpected storm tore through her, drawing her upward to a moment of exquisite culmination. She convulsed against him, her fingers tightening on his shoulders as the rays of a midnight sun pulsed behind her closed lids.

As she drifted back to earth from her completion, she reached for the ties holding his trunk hose. With a groan, he bore her to the floor, onto the blankets where she had dropped them earlier. She helped loosen his clothing, then parted her legs, eager to guide him in. Let her please him as much as he had pleased her.

Merciful heavens, but he was larger than she had imagined possible. Far more formidable than her first husband, but excitingly so. The exhilaration she had thought finished reawakened as he pushed his way in, then waited, braced on his arms above her.

"So beautiful," he whispered, his breathing ragged, betraying his urgency. "I want to taste all of you. Everywhere at the same time."

She smiled and slid her hands under his shirt to explore his sculpted chest. His body trembled in response, and desire flashed like fire in his eyes. He bent to catch her breast in his mouth, growling his hunger.

Her entire body hummed with appreciation. In answer to his need, she arched against him, drawing him deeper.

"More thunder?" he asked, moving within her for the first time.

A flash of urgency gripped her. A gasp of surprise escaped her throat.

"Nay?" he asked, meeting her gaze.

"Aye! As thunder gods do." She grasped his shoulders, suddenly aware that a repeat of her recent fulfillment lay within her reach. "Again," she cried, pulling his head down, meeting his mouth in a voracious kiss.

"So eager?" His whisper was rough as he obliged with a degree of enthusiasm she would once have considered unseemly. Compared to her staid, elderly husband, he ran rampant in his need for her, thrusting over and over.

"More than eager," she declared boldly, meeting him stroke for stroke. As she clasped his hips, she was shaken by the storm of sensation pounding through her. She wanted to go on forever, reveling in his strength.

Just when she thought she couldn't bear any more ecstasy, Drummond seemed to swell within her. As he groaned to fulfillment, she rose to completion with him, her cries of pleasure mingling with his.

Was this true passion? If so, surely its power would unite them and give them strength to overcome the danger ahead.

But if they couldn't overcome it, she was willing to die trying, for now she had Drummond Graham.

No words of love had passed between them, but none were required. They needed each other.

It would suffice for now. In the volatile existence she must lead as the earl's enemy, now was all she could be sure she had.

# Chapter 15

Good lies and bad. As Gemma had said, they lied to others, they lied to themselves, and now the lies had tied them together in a knot of deception.

Drummond awoke slowly the next morning, haunted by this knowledge. Then he opened his eyes to behold a magnificent blue sky overhead.

How could life juxtapose two such disparate things against one another? The azure field, on the one hand, dazzled him. The ugly snarl of their troubles lay on the other. They existed side by side, the perfect and the perfidious. Amazing.

Even more amazing, in the midst of impossible difficulties, he lay flesh to flesh with a beautiful half-naked woman who was now his wife.

She stirred against him, sparking his senses to life, a warm seraphim wrapped in purity.

Drummond knew he took advantage of her need for him. Given the choice, she would never wed a man who could offer her no future.

Yet the earl had said she loved him.

Could it possibly be true? If so, he would have liked nothing better than to settle down with her at Castle Graham. To start a family, to raise sheep and sell their wool. But such stability might never be his lot. He was doomed to wander, perhaps forever. Nor had his past taught him to give his heart freely, and she deserved that from a man.

No, although he recognized the hole in his existence for what it was, he must not use this tender, sensitive woman as if she were a plug to stop the leak of vital substance from his life. Only time and completion of his quest could make him whole.

Yet the warmth of her flesh tempted him. Last night, all unpleasant thoughts of his past, all nightmares had retreated. Gemma's generous invitation seemed to have held bad dreams at bay. He wanted to repeat last night's experience, but he'd just vowed he would not.

"Good morrow, Gemma," he said softly, aching to stroke her inviting flesh. Memories of her moans as he had pleasured her last night returned, immensely tempting. Initially, he hadn't meant to have her, but at her invitation, he'd lost control.

He should not have done it. He'd taken advantage of her vulnerability.

With her back to him and eyes still closed, she burrowed deeper beneath the blankets, brushing against him as she did so.

The male part of him responded, rising and swelling. "Sleep well?" he asked, forcing his mind elsewhere.

"Better than I've slept in years." She smiled languidly, eyes still closed.

"I owe you an apology."

"How so?" She sounded drowsy.

He smiled grimly, surprised that she had to ask. Clearly she had not only slept well but was still wrapped in glorious dreams. Unfortunately, he must interrupt them. "I regret reminding you of unpleasant facts, but it *is* morning." He sat up and pulled on his shirt.

"I would rather it were not." She pulled the blanket over her head.

"Sorry. I canna work miracles."

A slight giggle emanated from beneath the blanket. "I disagree."

Refusing to reply to this bit of provocation, he rose, finished dressing, then built up the fire. When it smoldered, beginning to burn off the morning chill, he sorted through the bundle Iain had brought last night and found a small kettle. "I apologize for springing that handfast strategy on you last night, but I had nothing better at hand."

She peered over the edge of the blanket, her eyes wary, as if to assess his meaning.

"I know you were surprised," he continued. "You have my profound apologies."

"Drummond Graham, you saved my life." She sat up, pushed aside the blanket with deliberate hands, and stretched bare, elegant limbs, driving him mad with her beauty. "I wouldn't think of complaining about the manner in which you did it. Your decision is quite acceptable."

He raised his eyebrows and studied her gravely. "The handfast is but a temporary solution to protect your reputation. As soon as I take you from the islands, you will be free."

She reached for her netherstocks and smiled at him as she pulled one on. "It was an excellent way to deal with the problem. I'm glad you thought of it."

The soft pink areolas of her breasts teased him through her thin linen smock. Unbearable. He tightened his control on his insistent arousal as he thought through the situation. If she agreed they were handfasted merely for convenience, he couldn't believe she accepted his lovemaking out of anything but gratitude. Equally unbearable. So he would not question her motives. He dare not. "I also apologize for my unseemly behavior last night. I should never have touched you."

Seeming undaunted, she pulled on the other netherstock before regarding him pensively. "We both wanted it. Besides, I wouldna call your behavior last night unseemly. I would call it"—she paused, as if searching for the right word—"extraordinary. I had no idea I could feel that way until you showed me."

Extraordinary? Drummond stared at her. After last night, he'd expected either a demanding or tearful reception, but she seemed to accept both the handfast and his lovemaking with equal appreciation. The thought unnerved him. "Nevertheless, I promise you it won't happen again."

Yet even as he spoke, he wanted to feel her hands on him, grasping and guiding. He'd thought of nothing else last night as she'd slumbered, dreamed of having her again and again once he finally slept. He wanted to remove her smock, baring her breasts, her waist, her thighs. He wanted to please her as he had last night, then bury himself in her magic to seek his own release.

She seemed to sense his dilemma, for she regarded him in surprise as she finger combed her hair to remove the tangles. "You dinna wish it to happen again? Why ever not? I realize I refused you on this very spot mere hours ago, but things have changed. Given our new situation, intimacy seems quite reasonable. We are two consenting adults."

He clenched his fists as anger rose at her blithe offer. She had no conception of the complexity of sexual relations. "I canna use your person simply because we both enjoy it."

"But you wouldna be using me," she pointed out, ever rational. "You've made me your handfast wife. A respectable position that can be respectably dissolved upon mutual agreement."

She spoke with a calm he could scarcely fathom. He was becoming so hot and aroused, he could find no sensible reply as he watched her draw on an article of clothing, then pause to make a point about how he should bed her. She filled him with the insatiable urge to tear away each garment and explore her marvelous flesh. "We can only dissolve the arrangement if we are no' intimate," he insisted.

"Ah, but you forget," she said, as if unaware of his rising lust. "That rule would apply if I were a virgin. Since I'm a widow, the only way of verifying that we were intimate is if there's a child."

"*We* would know if we were intimate," he insisted. "I would consider it wrong to leave you after regular intimacy."

"*We* would learn from it if we wanted to stay together. If we did not, we could part as we chose."

Her logic confused him. Or perhaps it was the nether region of his body confusing him, urging him to accept her reasoning. "Regular intimacy breeds children," was all he could think to say.

"You may put your mind at ease on that score, for 'tis not likely. I never conceived during the three years I was wed. As neither frequency of effort nor timing resulted in conception, I must conclude that I cannot bear children. So you have no reason to hesitate. Intimacy seems a reasonable benefit of our temporary union."

Drummond was dumbfounded. How, in one breath, could she speak so objectively of her possible barrenness, then of his lovemaking as a reasonable benefit of their relationship in the next? He never knew what to expect from this woman. "Let me understand this. You enjoyed last night and would like to repeat the experience?"

"Indeed, yes." She shrugged, her expression apologetic. "Pray excuse my bluntness, but I'm tired of pretending. My first husband was not . . ." She paused, then continued with determination. "He was much older than I, and age takes its toll. 'Tis unfair to judge him on that basis, for he was a good man, but I wearied of pretending to be pleased. You, on the other hand, go about things much differently, so I can honestly say I enjoyed bedding with you. I did let you know, did I not?" She smiled faintly, surveying his body with innocent appreciation.

Drummond groaned inwardly as a lick of flame shot up his groin. Did she not understand how she fired his lust? Clearly, she had less experience than she said if she was unaware of how her new invitation affected him. "The reason for barrenness is not always easy to pinpoint in partners," he managed to point out. "You might be surprised to find you are not."

Hope flickered in her gaze for an instant, then died. "My husband had three children by his first wife. And his former mistress bore his child shortly after our marriage. He kindly gave up the mistress when we wed, but I think that serves as adequate proof of who was to blame for our lack of children. I regret it, of course, but one must look for the benefits in life and relish what is offered. Since I canna bear a child, we could dissolve our union later with no loss of honor to either party, as you will surely want children when you wed. I have Ting, which must suffice."

Her loving gaze strayed to the pony just outside the doorless cot, and he marveled at how she accepted what seemed to be her fate with such serenity. Her argument tempted him unbearably, yet he still must not touch her.

He had vowed that last night would be their first and last time together. Yet now that he had crossed the threshold of desire . . . "Madam, passion can be so powerful that, once indulged, some people cannot resist."

She regarded him with wide eyes. "Before last night, I would not have understood your meaning. Now, I believe I do."

He nodded as the fire in his groin urged him to reach for her. If she felt one fraction of what he did, she would be as tempted as he. Yet it would be unfair to indulge if they were to part, and she seemed to agree that they would. "Trust me, passion can be irresistible. I have seen people who care nothing for each other, indeed who hate one another, unable to avoid exercising their base instincts together."

Her smooth brow puckered. "But we dinna hate each other. I was led to believe, last night, that perhaps you found me comely. I'm no' completely inexperienced, either, though I fear I acted it. I would strive to please you better next time."

She was driving him mad with this conversation. She was more than comely, and she had pleased him without striving, more than she could ever know. "Gemma, it would be wrong of me to accept a commitment at this time. In truth, I consider the great sacrifice you've just made, along with your willingness to help me find this woman I seek, more than enough." Firmly he led them away from the treacherous subject.

"What sacrifice is that?"

"You've given up your place in the castle. You can never return as one of the household."

"I did not give it up," she said with indignation, her mood shifting. "The earl took it from me. You see how desperate he is, willing to sacrifice me to get at you."

"I still dinna understand why he did it. I thought you were important to his household, or at least to the countess, who influences him."

"Now I know why her ladyship was crying last night," she said half to herself. "She knew or suspected what he was up to." She returned to meet his gaze. "I wore out my usefulness by writing to the king. Or I was more useful to him as a lure to catch you. Either way, I'm glad I've been cast out of the castle, because I hated being one of his creatures. Now I have no choice but to be free of him. Except I fear more than ever for my uncle." She pressed a hand to her forehead, as if in sudden pain.

"What is it? Is he ill?"

"He . . ." She hesitated. "He is in greater peril than I thought, but 'tis dangerous for you to know the details."

"What could be more dangerous than one of the earl's men trying to murder me in my sleep?" He was unable to resist a bit of sarcasm.

She grimaced. "I forgot. 'Tis deceptively peaceful here. I didn't want to think about why we'd come."

"You had best tell me," he urged. "I hate ugly surprises from unexpected sources."

She swallowed hard, as if summoning the courage to tell him, and he had an unpleasant premonition. Something even worse than he'd imagined was about to be revealed.

"My uncle told me he is building a secret chamber for the earl," she blurted. "My guess is that when 'tis finished, he will be killed to protect the secret. I think someone eavesdropped on us as we spoke in his prison last night. Now that I know about the chamber, my fate is sealed as well."

A red haze formed before Drummond's eyes as anger besieged him. "How dare he rob people of their lives for his convenience. He willna kill your uncle. I shallna let him."

"You canna marry my uncle, too, to save him." Her expression turned bitter as she moved toward the single window, tying the laces of her bodice. "You of all people should realize how ruthless the earl is."

"You think I do not? I suspected his plotting the day I met him," Drummond snarled. "I shall find a way to help your uncle leave the island."

"And I shall continue to feed him. You need not trouble about that."

He surveyed the defiant tilt of her chin, finding it and her doubt annoying. "And how will you continue to render that service from this location?" he asked with mock politeness.

She seemed to have forgotten that detail once more.

Her defiance retreated. She bowed her head. "If you can arrange it, then I thank you. If only you could tell the king what the earl is doing, perhaps he would listen to you."

He knew at once that she still wondered if he came from the king. Yet he dared not satisfy her wish for knowledge. As long as the earl had possible access to her, it wasn't safe for her to know the truth. "We shall see," he said in a noncommittal tone. "In the meantime, we must be on our guard. Ting is a great help. She doesna allow anyone near the cot without giving a warning."

Gemma's eyes glowed with pride as she reached for her petticoat and, nodding earnestly, stepped into it. "She's as good as a dog for standing watch, but then you sleep lightly. Like a cat, alert and prowling at the first scent of danger on the wind. I heard you get up last night when she came to the door and snorted. What was it?"

"Probably some animal hunting for its dinner. She quieted after I took a look around."

Her eyes fluttered half closed again in a dreamy, drowsy look. "I drifted off before you came back. I knew you would see to whatever it was."

He liked the idea that she felt so secure in his care, she could sleep undisturbed. She trusted him implicitly, which he found heartening. "As you say, 'twas nothing, but 'twill not remain that way if the earl is desperate. Did you have a chance to speak to him last night?"

She lifted the bundle Iain had brought and rummaged through it. "Nay, I did not. He had his surprises waiting for me," she said sadly.

Surprises, indeed. Good lies and bad lies swirled around them. They troubled Drummond, reminding him of how he hated anything less than honesty. But clearly, the earl believed him to be from the king.

He would not have taken such decisive action against him otherwise.

Gemma found a loaf of bread and a knife in the bundle and, placing them on the stool, proceeded to cut them each a slice. As she took a bite of hers, she scowled. "No one born here can leave the islands without the earl's license. How will we depart with my uncle?"

"I dinna ken. I'll manage something."

Her smile of appreciation so aroused him, he wanted to drown in her beauty. His fury was not all she thought it—for the earl alone. He was furious with how much he wanted her this morning. He had hoped a vain hope that his lust would vanish by light of day. Instead, it returned, stronger than ever.

She didn't seem to notice his stare. Finishing the remains of her bread, she rose gracefully, stepped into her kirtle skirt and tied it. "Well," she said briskly, "what would you like to do first?"

What he wanted to do was kiss her. He wanted her to be his sweet sin, for he understood such things well. His father had rewarded him with sin when he performed his tasks well, putting him to bed with a young, comely strumpet at only fourteen. He'd partaken for years, knowing it was wrong. Unable to resist the passion.

Yet he must not accept Gemma's offer.

The life she lived was not wild and free, as he'd thought when he first saw her. Yet she loved with a heart that refused to be chained, despite the fetters of her life. She deserved for her emotion to be returned in equal measure.

*Someone whose devotion is selfless.*

She'd said it of her pony, but *her* devotion was selfless. He wanted the thunder magic within her, waiting to explode to life.

Drawn irresistibly, he gathered a handful of her silver hair in one hand. When she did not move away, her gaze remaining riveted on the fire, he bent to kiss her neck. The creamy quality of her flesh urged him to commit greater folly. He slipped one hand down her bodice, closing on the enticing softness of her breast.

She tilted back her head against his shoulder and uttered a sob.

He released her abruptly. "You're crying."

"Nay." Her eyes remained closed as she laughed through the tears. "I'm being ridiculous. The earl tried to kill me. I'm living like a heathen on the moor, and I'm happy. I am as wanton as he said." She opened her eyes and stared fully into his face. "I wanted to lie with you from the moment I first saw you," she whispered fiercely.

Her passionate declaration nearly unleashed his control again. "Wanting isna what's wanton. It's acting on it regardless of circumstances. You didna do that, nor will I let you. Not that I don't welcome your offer," he added with an insinuating grin.

To his surprise, after her calm discussion of sex, she blushed furiously, and desire roared through him. Every nuance of her response filled him with unaccustomed exhilaration, knowing she wanted him.

He desperately wanted her, and she sensed it, wanting him in return.

He longed to accept her offer, to join his flesh with hers. Yet he must remain strong to stave off disaster. For danger stalked them on the moor, and they must prevail over the earl. Somehow.

# Chapter 16

*He is a man beloved by women, but he refuses to love one of them in return.*

As Gemma folded their blankets a short time later, she thought about the puzzle that was Drummond Graham. Women fell in love with him, but he clearly had never allowed himself to respond to one of them.

Judging from his behavior, he liked women, wanted to protect them, but refused to take gratification from anything but giving them aid. Although he had married her, although they felt a mutual attraction, he said he expected to behave the same way with her.

Very well, she respected his wishes. She understood that he must pursue his mission unfettered. They each had their separate commitments. She would leave him alone.

She had liked him better last night, though. Without his iron self-control, the perfect man came alive. Flawed but more human, lusting for her. Far better, indeed.

Annoyed with the direction of her thinking, she chased the ideas away. Their situation didn't allow for indulgence in personal relationships. Danger stalked them on the vast moor. Though she loved the island, loved living outside the oppressive walls of the castle, she had never wished to live here under the threat of death.

Nervous about their vulnerable position, Gemma watched Iain disappear down the track toward the castle. "Do you think 'tis safe to send him there?" she asked Drummond. Though he barely glanced after his brother, she sensed his tension even before he spoke.

"Since we need food for three, which is a good quantity, 'tis best he go. We could ask food of the cottars we'll visit today, but I would rather not. Their fare is too meager. He and I would hunt, but we need the time for other matters."

"Iain could hunt while we search," she ventured, troubled by his reluctance to describe these other matters. He could mean business for the king, or simply his search for the woman. Perversely, she felt irritated that he did not confide in her now that her allegiance belonged solely to him. "He wouldna have to go to the castle for food," she said, biting back the questions she wanted so badly to ask.

"He could, but we have more pressing requirements. For one thing, we need a roof."

He gestured upward, reminding her that their shelter was still less than adequate. Their entire existence was precarious, and although she didn't wish Iain to take a risk, they were all at risk now. The earl had made it clear that he would stop at nothing to see them dead. Yet the means must be subtle. Open murder would not do.

Determined to keep busy, she tidied the cot, trying not to be annoyed by Drummond's reticence. The longer he remained silent about his true purpose, the more she believed he was, indeed, here on the king's business. But he would tell her only if he wished her to know. Asking would be a waste of breath.

Drummond drew water from the well and filled the stone trough by the door for Ting to drink, then brought Gemma a bucket in which to wash. As she doused her face in the cold water, she hoped Iain would return soon. The lad had slept outside all night, politely leaving them in privacy, such as it was without a roof or a door. He was a likeable lad, with hair and eyes the same color as Drummond's, but he was different from his elder brother in every other way. Iain wasn't nearly so handsome, but he was much easier to know.

She had prepared their morning meal using what Iain had brought from the kitchens last night. While they had eaten cold bannocks and cold, cooked white fish, the lad had chattered like a magpie, telling her all manner of things about himself and his family. He had learned a carpenter's trade from his adopted father, but at thirteen Drummond had introduced him to the chieftain at Castle Graham. There, he'd begun his education in the many skills needed by a clansman. Once mature, he would join the chieftain's men. Gemma found him a delightful companion.

"You and Iain have the same father?" she asked as she washed.

"Had. He's dead," Drummond said.

His curt answer showed he had no wish to pursue the subject. Gemma concluded that Iain had been born on the wrong side of the sheets, sired by Drummond's father, who was of the Graham clan. Unfortunately, she understood being baseborn all too well.

"Iain will probably try to see Rowena while he's at the castle. I thought you didn't approve of his interest in her," she said.

"That was before," Drummond replied tersely. "This is now."

His abbreviated response maddened her. "But they might be caught by the earl," she pressed as she finished putting away their few cooking utensils.

"He had already arranged a tryst for today. I told him to keep it. Rowena is an intelligent lass. She'll know to bring him food."

"The earl might punish her if he catches them together," she said. "He can be harsh with Rowena."

"I asked yesterday. Everyone at the castle said that the earl doesna beat his children."

"Aye," Gemma agreed, "but he slaps them, especially Rowena, as they disagree often. He never actually injures her, but 'tis humiliating to be struck."

"I'm sorry to hear it," Drummond said without a shred of compassion, "but as long as he does no physical harm, she might have to endure a slap or two. Iain will do everything he can to ensure they're not caught."

This attitude seemed so unlike Drummond that Gemma stared in surprise. "Are we so desperate that we must sacrifice Rowena's physical well-being?"

Drummond rounded on her, tense with irritation. "You just said her father doesna beat her, and since we have a threefold purpose in sending Iain to the castle, aye, we must take the risk, though I believe it slight. We will gain food, information, and if the earl learns that we come and go at will, 'twill unsettle him, which is to our advantage. He needs to be reminded he's no' the only power on the island."

Gemma grimaced, realizing that he employed battle tactics. In times of war, the path to victory might be unpleasant, yet it must be endured. Even Rowena would be asked to take her share of risks if she truly cared for Iain and wished to help them. "The earl might capture Iain and hold him hostage," she said.

"He wouldna risk anything so obvious that could be reported to the king," Drummond contradicted. "You are worrying overmuch. Iain will return soon, and all the earl will hear is that he came for food and departed. If he and Rowena manage properly, Rowena's name will no' be mentioned. Come now. We have work to do if you're to help me find the woman I seek."

She let him seat her on a rock in the sunshine, but felt much was amiss this morning. She'd enjoyed their mutual confidences on the moor last night, then been thunderstruck when he'd snatched her from death by

announcing their mutual wish to wed. She'd been ex-
hilarated by his lovemaking that followed. Her joy had
known no bounds when he'd stated his wish to take
her and her uncle from the island, no matter how
impossible that seemed. He was a vital, living force
who had swept into her life and brought stunning
change.

Yet today he was remote as he stood opposite her.
His austere expression reminded her of the uninhab-
ited, windswept stone stacks of the outer isles. At the
very least, she had thought they were friends, but it
was difficult to maintain a relationship with a stone
stack.

"Tell me what you know of this woman," she began,
taking refuge in the task at hand.

"A member of her family visited her here in 1584.
She conceived a child at that time."

"What is her name?"

He hesitated. "I . . . dinna know."

She frowned in surprise. "You dinna know? But
didn't the family tell you?"

"Nay."

Gemma squinted at him, his terse answer failing to
register. "But when I asked you before, you said you
would tell me later. You must know it. Think and
'twill come back to you."

His body went rigid with tension. "I told you I
dinna know it and her family didna tell me," he exploded. "You must accept what I say." He glared at
her, then looked away abruptly, seeming to regret his
harsh words but unwilling to apologize for them.

A wave of disappointment engulfed Gemma as the
last shred of their intimacy from the night disinte-
grated. How she had cherished their joining, believing
he would now open himself to her. But their handfast-
ing had apparently earned her no lasting right to his
trust.

Saddened but determined not to show it, she

squared her shoulders and continued. "I'm sorry, but I simply cannot understand this family. Why would they ask you to find her without giving her name?"

"*That* is the difficulty." He glanced up at her, irony twisting his face. "I told you I had made no progress. Now you know why."

Gemma could not give up so easily. "Are you sure this person exists?" she pressed.

"She could be dead by now, but I think not. She exists. I must find her. I dinna have a name.'Tis all I will say, Gemma," he warned. "Dinna needle me."

The finality of his response discouraged her. He might be telling the truth about the lack of name, but she sensed he was holding something back. Something important. The omission concerned her, as did the growing challenge of the task before them. "What time of year was it when the family member visited the island?" she asked.

"June."

"And you say she had just conceived the child?"

"Aye, at that time."

Relieved that these questions had not provoked another flare of anger, Gemma calculated aloud. "So if she delivered nine months later, that would be March or April. The child would be fourteen years of age now. That helps. We can search for a woman with a child that age, born in one of those months. Pray continue."

He stared off into the distance, as removed from her as the Americas. "That's all I know." He left her abruptly and went to stand by the well, as if to escape her inevitable reaction.

"That's all?" she repeated in disbelief, following him. He moved to the other side of the well as she approached, keeping the stone barrier between them. "Who is this person who expects you to find his relative without any details?" she demanded. "He must be insane."

"He's no' important."

His answer came far too quickly, and Gemma sensed the crux of the problem. "On the contrary, he is very important," she said, watching him carefully. "He gave you an impossible task, and because of some past obligation to him, you accepted, despite the likelihood that you would not succeed. That makes him very important, I would say."

A ripple of distaste crossed his face, as if he were remembering the person and disliked the memory intensely. Would he now divulge the person's identity? Gemma leaned forward, holding her breath.

Drummond ran one hand through his hair and looked at her with exasperation. "Gemma, are you going to help me or no?"

It was her turn to feel exasperated. "I need to know *something* if I'm to help you," she cried. "I am your ally, not your enemy. Who is this person and why is he withholding important details?"

"I have no more to say on that score."

His eyes became remote again, and she realized how deeply the habit of privacy ran in him. Ingrained for years. Impossible to shake. Gemma sighed. His private nature might be an asset as the king's spy, but it proved a definite detriment in this situation. Nor did it recommend him much as a mate. "Very well," she said with resignation. "I'll do what I can. I will identify all the women who have fourteen-year-old children. It will narrow the number somewhat, but you'll still have dozens upon dozens to interview, unless luck allows you to happen on her soon." She drew the bucket from the well and drank from a cupped hand, more concerned by the enormity of the task than she liked to admit.

" 'Tis no' that I dinna trust you," he said.

Gemma jerked up her head. She hadn't expected him to justify his refusal to share details. "Nay?" she encouraged. "Is it a secret, then?"

"To the family, it is. And people so enjoy gossip, I'm no' in the habit of telling anyone, even those who might help." He paused. "I've never had to ask for help before."

A trickle of hope assuaged her disappointment. Although he wouldn't tell her, he had told no one else, either. "I am honored you have chosen me to assist," she said. "Does Iain know?"

"Everyone in my family knows. But outside the family, no."

"Then it's *your* family who seeks this woman." She pounced on the detail in triumph, but it was short-lived. He clammed up like the mussels they gathered from the sea, easy to obtain but the very devil to crack in order to reach the delicacy inside.

"I am sorry I pried," she apologized, recognizing the need to respect his desire for distance. "I guess I just wish you were more like Iain."

"We're much alike," he grumbled, clearly discomfited by his slip. "Red hair. Green eyes. Same height."

"Iain has red hair and green eyes, just as you do, but the two of you are nothing alike."

Drummond cast her a disbelieving glance. "We share many of the same features. Our mouths, for example, are both like our father's."

Gemma shook her head, unable to agree. "I see the resemblance, but it stops there. His mouth turns up in mirth most of the time, whilst yours does not. Your smile is more noble, however, on the rare occasion that you show it." She wanted to move to his side, to touch his arm and encourage his confidence, but she knew he would reject such a gesture.

He stared off into the distance, confirming her belief.

"Try to think of some little detail that will speed our task," she coaxed, unable to give up. "Anything."

"There is nothing."

"Surely you can remember some small particular,"

she wheedled in her most convincing manner. "Eye color. Hair color. Close your eyes and try to think. I won't press you, but do try. It might help to sit here." She rounded the well and patted the stone seat built into its low wall. "The sun is so pleasant. Enjoy its warmth."

He frowned, clearly not wishing to obey. Nonetheless, under her guiding hand, he sat.

She felt certain that he could share some small detail. It wasn't that he didn't remember. He was unaccustomed to trusting anyone with even the tiniest detail. She must win his confidence before she could coax anything from him. "Can you feel the light on your eyelids?" she soothed, seeking the healing croon she used with injured animals. "Think of nothing save its pleasing warmth. We Northerners value the sunlight. It brings comfort and confidence. We *will* find this woman you seek. I swear, we will."

She paused, waiting for the lines of tension to leave his face. Gradually, he relaxed beneath the sun's calming rays. His forehead, formerly molded into ridges, smoothed. His expression eased. "Much better," she praised. "Now then, imagine you are speaking to the man who visited this woman. Can you see him? It is a 'him,' is it not?"

"Aye," he admitted grudgingly.

Good. Her tactic was working. "Dinna open your eyes. He is speaking of his journey. What did he say about the woman?"

"He said he had been to the Shetland Isles and met a beauteous female."

"Did he describe her further?" She paused, noting that the man must have had a romantic interest in the woman, given his description. "Did he say why he came to the isles? That might help us know where to begin."

His scowl returned and he shifted on the stone seat, a clear sign that her probing unsettled him. "I was a child when he told me. How the devil should I know why he decided to visit the islands? You ask too many questions."

Despite her care, Gemma knew she had pushed too hard in her questioning. But she still suspected he kept something from her. His deliberate refusal to discuss the man was a sign of distrust, which saddened her. Only through trust did two people build a true relationship. "Suppose I tell you something about my past instead," she proposed, knowing that if she did so, he might feel encouraged to share in return. "I will tell you about my home on Fair Isle if you agree to stay where you are," she bargained, "with your eyes closed."

Though his scowl remained, he complied.

"That's right. Enjoy the sun." She reached deep for the tones that lulled ill or frightened ponies. "Our northern sun is most pleasing. Not too bright, not too hot. What shall I tell you? Fair Isle is a beautiful place. I grew up there with my aunt and uncle and my eight cousins. All eleven of us lived in a stone cot much like this one, though bigger. Three chambers for humans. One for animals. And, of course, a kiln for drying corn."

"Of course." He seemed to relax now that he was no longer the subject of their discussion.

"Auntie and Uncle had the first bed in the sleeping chamber, though it was not the largest," she continued, hoping to lull him into complacency, then coax some information from him. "My three boy cousins slept in the box bed. We girls slept in the third and largest bed. It was built into a nook, so we had to squeeze in, all six of us, but it was most cozy in winter. Ingrid kicked in her sleep, so we put her by the wall and she kicked it. Anna had bad dreams, so we put her in the middle where one of us could comfort her in the night."

"You love your cousins."

She nodded, suddenly missing them dreadfully. "I think of them daily, though it's been so long since I've seen them."

"You dinna visit them regularly?" His eyes flew open to regard her in disbelief. " 'Tis not that far to Fair Isle. I passed it on the way."

"Keep your eyes closed." She brushed his eyelids with her palm, and obediently, he lowered them. "I have not seen them of late," she said. "In six years, the earl only permitted me to see my family twice. Once when they came for my wedding, and three years later when my husband died." She closed her eyes for a moment, the ache for her family like an unhealed wound. "He said the countess needed me, and 'tis true her health has been poor since Gordie's birth," she said, forcing herself to continue. "But before that, he could have spared me. He wouldna even let me visit when my aunt was dying. I've been fortunate to see my uncle, but he has been here less than a year and is kept busy with his labors each day."

"That's grossly unfair." Drummond's tone was outraged.

He was right. Ships and small boats traveled too and fro continually. It would have cost the earl nothing to let her visit her family. The countess had many times said she would gladly spare her for a few days. "The earl is too selfish to think of others," she said. "I asked many times, but nothing would happen. When I reminded him, he would say he'd see to it. But he never did."

"What of your husband before he died? Did he not insist to the earl that you go?"

"He agreed with the earl, saying it was best that I forget my roots. My place was with him. He did not like me to knit either, as I had on Fair Isle. He said it was a lowly occupation, for peasant women. He taught me to write and do sums and manage his household instead. Once I entered the earl's household, he also forbade my knitting. I knit only when I'm away from the castle, as I did yesterday." Sadness coursed through her. She missed her cousins so, all of them living on Fair Isle.

"I shall buy you needles and wool at once. You may knit all you like here," he said. "You say your aunt and uncle raised you?"

His sympathy and kindness brought a lump to her throat. "Aye. My mother and aunt were sisters. When my mother died, my Aunt Maude and Uncle Andrew took me in, though they could barely manage another mouth to feed. They loved me well," she added, struggling to swallow past the lump, "despite that."

"Was your father a fisherman, unable to care for you?"

Gemma felt tears trickle down her cheeks. Why must he ask now? She was crying because she missed her family, not because of her past. But she'd meant to tell him eventually, so she ought to do it, tears or no. "I never knew my father," she said, her throat tight. "He refused to wed my mother, or mayhap he couldna because he was already wed. Either way, she bore me out of wedlock, then died from milk fever when I was a few weeks old. I never learned who he was."

His eyes flew open. He stared at her, seeming appalled.

She wiped away the tears, determined to continue since he'd introduced the subject. "I dinna mind, for I've been fortunate. I was never degraded for my birth. My family loved me. The others on Fair Isle appreciated my skill with ponies and knitting. My first husband gladly asked me to wed, though I suppose my youth was the reason for that." She took a deep breath, determined to finish the task without being maudlin. "I felt honor bound to explain, in case my birth troubles you."

# Chapter 17

Drummond felt as if the world had turned upside down, dropping him in the last place he expected to land.

Mistress Sinclair was baseborn?

She was the bastion of goodness and caring in the earl's household.

She was obeyed by the servants, beloved by the countess and her children, respected by all on the island.

How could she be baseborn? His mind revolted at the idea. It simply wasn't fair to her.

"Trouble me?" he growled, rising and moving to the other side of the well, needing a moment to adjust to the idea. "Why the devil should your birth trouble me?"

"It would trouble some people." She watched him as she dabbed her eyes with her handkerchief. "I felt you had the right to know, so you could decide if you find it undesirable."

"If you're undesirable, I'm the King of Spain." He was beset by the maddening wish to pull her into his arms and murmur words of comfort. "By St. Andrew, I didn't mean to make you cry."

"You didn't make me, and I'm not crying about my birth or my barrenness," she insisted flashing him an indignant glance. "You asked at a bad moment, 'tis all."

She wasn't devastated by her birth? He turned back to study her, noticing how the sun turned her hair to silver. Silver had great value, as did she, and he recognized another facet of that value: She didn't care about her birth. She cared how he felt about it. "My father refused to wed my mother as well," he offered, then leaned on the stone well to observe the effect of his words.

Gemma's eyes widened, becoming as large as half-pennies. "No. You're just saying that to make me feel better."

Annoyance flickered through him. The idea of comforting her with his own secret had come to him in a flash of inspiration. He had never felt the need or desire to share it with anyone. Now that he had, he wanted a different response. "I tell you the deepest secret of my soul and you think I made it up?"

"Deepest secret?" She regarded him with wary distrust.

Despite their physical attraction, despite her trust in his ability to protect her, he realized they were realms apart in personal trust. And likely to remain so if he couldn't manage to bare his soul in a convincing manner. "My father must have promised my mother marriage. She would never have surrendered her virtue otherwise, but he refused to wed her after I was conceived," he explained, hiding his impatience. "The only reason I'm legitimate is because our clan chief, my father's cousin, arranged my mother's marriage on paper when I was eighteen. When my father found out I had encouraged my mother to agree, he beat me bloody."

Her disbelief vanished. "I *am* sorry," she cried, compassion glinting in her eyes.

Triumph mingled with relief as he felt the comfort of her caring response. But he wanted her to feel comforted as well. "There's naught to be sorry for. Not anymore.'Tis over, for you as well as for me. We're free of them and can be who we are, not someone's idea of what a baseborn person should be."

She smiled faintly. "How kind of you to reveal your own pain so I would not feel badly about my past."

His frustration returned. This was still not the effect he sought. "I didna tell you merely to make you feel better, though I did want that, too. I told you because it seems we understand one another. We endured the same thing."

"The same thing." She tried on the words, as if measuring their fit. "Perhaps in part, but no one ever said a hard word to me because of my birth. I suspect you cannot say the same."

Once more, her perception about him was deadly accurate. "I was taunted, true, but I grew up quickly and was soon able to beat the boys who called me a bastard and make them take it back. What I resented were the women who refused to buy my mother's weaving because they said she was a harlot. That damage I couldna undo."

She shifted her gaze from him to the azure waters of the sea. "People can be cruel. I told you of my birth for that very reason, so no one could spring it on you as an ugly surprise. But I learned to live with it long ago. I accept who and what I am."

He wanted to round the well, to touch her and feel her tantalizing response, but he would not. He could share only this small piece of himself. No more. He didn't have what she really required. "I accept it as well. Though you may wish to start life without me after we reach Scotland, you will always have my regard."

Her expression softened. "My uncle said you had a noble spirit. I was convinced of it from the moment we met. Your mission here is one of noble truth, is it not?"

He winced inwardly at this. In his rush to convince her that birth didn't matter, he had reinforced the idea that he was some sort of hero. Unfortunately, there was nothing heroic about his daily life. He spent most nights in shelters little better than their roofless cot.

She wasn't yet horrified by living on the moor, but she would be, given time, especially after the comforts of a castle. And when she learned he was always traveling, even in inclement weather, most of the time on foot, she would not be so enthusiastic about what she called his mission of noble truth. For that reason, he had no intention of making their union permanent, though he had to fight to keep his hands off her.

"Well, we must return to our task." Gemma straightened briskly, seeming to interpret his silence as an end to the discussion. "If you must interview every woman with a fourteen-year-old child, we had best start." She found a stone and crouched to draw with it in the soil. "We'll begin in Scalloway with the Williamsons, the Smiths, and the Fetters. They each have a child who is fourteen." She drew a W, an S, and an F in the loose soil. "But John Smith was born in the winter. December, I believe, so he is unlikely to be the one." She rubbed out the S. "There are two other children who are fourteen years of age living in Scalloway, but I do not know their birth months." She added a G and a T to her list. "Let me see." She tapped her chin, thinking through the families she knew.

He let her work, free of interference. The moment of confidences had passed. He had broken a principal rule of his life because someone else's need was greater than his. But it hadn't set him free. Far from it.

"I have an idea," she said, unaware of his turmoil. "I'll ask Jean, the shoemaker's wife, to discover their birth months. She loves to gossip, though she never injures anyone with her chatter. She will ask in such a roundabout way, no one will realize what she's after.

Or if they realize she's interested in their birth month, they won't know why."

He moved closer, drawn to her as she laid out the plan.

"Since you've already covered the southern part of the main island," she said with her forthright efficiency, "if we find no one in Scalloway, we can move north."

"Aye, to Lerwick," he agreed.

"Indeed. I have a friend there who will help me identify likely candidates. But once we find them, 'tis your turn," she warned. "You must question the women, although that should be no difficulty for you."

He couldn't resist the opening. "Are you still jealous of how the women confide in me?"

She shook her head, as if embarrassed. "What I really wish is to do what you do. To draw people out. To win their trust."

Her revelation intrigued him. "Your friends trust you. You have only to reach out and draw them closer. I'll show you how 'tis done, if you like."

" 'Tis not important." She brushed it aside. "We should begin before the day slips away from us," she said. "What do you wish to do first?"

He didn't answer, and she glanced up. He saw her swallow hard at the interest in his eyes. She had unwittingly reissued her earlier invitation, and he longed to accept. To do the things they had done last night. Again.

Beneath his stare, she hugged herself with both arms, lowered her gaze, and shivered. The simple response jolted his senses alive. He'd been impersonal this morning, emphasizing the importance of restraint. She had disagreed but bowed to his logic. Now he did not wish to obey his own decree. Nor did she. She had told him so openly.

It shook his resolve to honor their agreement.

But for the moment, circumstances forced them to honor it, for they had no time to lose.

They must find this woman so they could leave the Shetland Isles. As long as they remained, one wrong move and they would be gallows ornaments for the earl.

Drummond felt discouraged as he, Gemma, and Ting returned to the cot that evening. After Iain had returned from the castle, they had taken food and set out. In his first foray with Gemma's help, he'd hoped to find the woman and her child straightaway.

Instead, his efforts had been doomed to failure. He'd interviewed six women, each discussion more demanding than the last, despite Gemma's help. Since she knew the women, he'd asked her to sit with them, to join in the conversation as she saw fit. She had put the women at ease because they trusted her, which made the questioning go faster. Still, he'd had no luck.

Though he enjoyed talking to the women, he would have enjoyed it more if he hadn't felt driven by circumstances. The concentration needed to guide the discourse exhausted him, leaving him drained.

Now they were both tired, hungry, and, since the clear weather had deserted them, wet. Rain beat a tattoo on their heads as they plodded up the hill. Gemma appeared to have caught his gloomy mood, which worried him. She walked with her wet head bowed, her feet dragging. Ting seemed equally dejected, trudging dismally, head lowered against the rain.

So much for what Gemma had called his life of noble truth.

"I'm sorry it's been a terrible day. I'll prepare food so you can rest," he apologized.

She looked up to meet his gaze. "I am tired, but it was one of the most amazing days I've ever spent."

"How's that?" He couldn't think what she meant.

She stopped in the muddy track, seeming surprised. "You dinna ken?"

He shook his head, stopping also. Ting halted, then wandered off the track to crop a tasty growth of clover. " 'Twas a long day, probably boring for you, and unfortunately, unproductive," he said. "We can hope for better luck on the morrow, but chances are, we won't have it. It takes time to find a needle in a haystack. Perhaps I can purchase that wool and knitting needles for you on the morrow. 'Twill help you pass the time."

She stared at him for a long moment, then suddenly tilted back her head and laughed. Raindrops had gathered on her eyelashes, making her eyes sparkle. As he stared in even greater surprise, she wrinkled her nose at him and laughed again. "My day was amazing because you're amazing, Drummond Graham. You work like a slave for hours, then think only of my comfort and whether I was bored. But I wasna bored. I had never listened to you conduct an entire interview before, and I was fascinated. You had me mesmerized through all six visits, from start to finish. You did far more for each of those women than listen to their stories. You gave their lives dignity by acknowledging how they have endured cares and hardships for their loved ones. You celebrated their joys and grieved with them for their trials. For those with lives of suffering, such recognition is a blessing seldom received. You have an uncanny ability to touch the human heart."

Drummond could think of no response. He'd learned to put women at their ease, to probe gently for the information he needed, to care genuinely for what they shared with him. But he'd never considered what he did amazing. "I canna think I'm a blessing. 'Tis not a term applied to a man."

"Priests give blessings," she said. "They're men."

He narrowed his gaze and grasped her arm, suddenly aware of how her wet garments clung to her shapely figure. Pulling her closer, he felt the burn of awareness rake through him. "I'm nay priest," he said. "I'm an ordinary man." His mouth hovered mere inches from hers, and having experienced her softness, he longed to claim her again.

"A man, aye, but not the least ordinary." She smiled up at him.

He thought of that morning when he had revealed his past to her. Now she called the long, dull day with him amazing. Most women wanted gifts, flowers, or compliments from a man, but Gemma was delighted by glimpses of who he was.

Touched by her generous nature, he sought her mouth with his. She tasted of the cool rain, her lips moist with it. He delved inside to taste her warmth, dazzled by the contrast. His hands stole around her waist.

"Mmm." She leaned against him, wrapping both arms around his neck and kissing him back with abandon.

His blood roared in his ears as he hungrily melded his mouth to hers. This jewel of the island tasted better than—

"Have ye gone completely mad?" Iain's rude shout intruded. "Kissin' in the cold rain? Get in the cot before ye catch yer deaths."

Drummond looked up to find his younger brother glaring at him.

"And ye accuse me o' behavin' like a fool over a woman." Iain folded his arms across his chest and looked aggrieved. "Ye're soaked to the skin."

"So are you, Iain," Gemma said in her sweetest tones. "Your hair is matted to your head."

"Bosh!" Iain exploded. "I have an excuse. I've been making a roof all day." He grabbed Gemma's hand, jerking her away from Drummond. "And ye're to get under it at once." He hustled her up the track toward the cot.

Gemma glanced apologetically over her shoulder at Drummond as she followed Iain.

Drummond followed, mocking himself. On the most difficult search he had ever encountered, unruly desire distracted him. What was he to do? He suppressed his lust, denied it, but it refused to go away.

As he mounted the crest of the hill, he saw the new roof of simmons and straw covering the cot. Iain guided Gemma inside, then reemerged, muttering to himself in irritation.

"There's a clean, dry shirt in my saddlebags, Gemma," Drummond called as Ting disappeared inside after her mistress. "You're welcome to it, if you like." He halted before the cot and Iain. "Well done, Brother. I knew I could count on ye to manage." He nodded toward the tightly packed straw roof. " 'Twill keep the rain out well."

"I had help, but I'm bound to secrecy else my thatch suppliers be punished," Iain muttered, apparently appreciating the praise but still resenting the kiss.

"We must find a way to repay them. And you . . . Come, you must be thirsty from your work." Drummond drew him toward the stone-ringed well and pulled up a bucket of clear water. "What said Rowena this morning?" he asked, once they were beyond Gemma's earshot. "I wanted to speak to you about it before we left for Scalloway but didna wish Gemma to hear. She carries too much of a burden as it is."

Iain smirked cockily at him over the rim of a new pottery dipper, clearly a gift from Rowena. "She says she loves me."

Drummond wanted to smack him. "No' about that. About her father," he growled.

Iain shrugged, seeming pleased to have annoyed his brother. "He's in a lather, swearing vengeance on the person who slashed yer bed. The countess weeps at his anger. The entire household is paralyzed, afraid to move for fear of being the brunt of his lordship's wrath."

"Good. He hasna decided what to do yet. Does work on the castle continue?"

"Aye. I saw the men at their labors in the unfinished wing. Why?"

"Gemma's uncle is the chief stone mason. I must make some arrangements for him. What else?"

"Rowena says her mother intends to arrange yer wedding to Gemma."

Drummond hadn't expected the countess to take such a decisive action. "Does the earl know?"

Iain shrugged. "I doubt it. At least no' yet, though he will. Rowena says his spies are everywhere, and as I had some difficulty meeting wi' her, I ken 'tis true. But I'm willing to run the risk on the morrow to see her again. Shall I?"

"No' so soon," Drummond said. "We dinna want to set a regular pattern of visits the earl can anticipate. I hope you didna tell Rowena to expect you."

"Nay, though I wanted to. I had to convince her my regard was steadfast, though I canna see her every day."

Drummond raised his eyebrows. "I can imagine how you induced her to believe you."

Iain preened, clearly pleased with himself. "I let her know how I feel. And she vowed to see we have a basket of food on the morrow as well as today. She'll leave it hidden behind the dyke near the dairy."

"Excellent. Did you give her my message for Brandie, the cook? And the money?"

"I did."

Drummond nodded. "I trust Brandie will relieve Rowena of the risk she takes. Ye did well, Iain. My thanks." The arrangements were excellent, but he didn't feel as contented with them as he'd implied to Gemma. He intended today's tryst between Iain and Rowena to be their last. Seeing the girl was dangerous to Iain's already inflated opinion of himself, and Drummond didn't like the sound of the earl's brutality toward her. He had permitted the meeting only because Rowena had been their most readily available source of accurate news from the castle. Now he would work through the cook if the man agreed.

Oblivious to the danger, Iain nodded his appreciation to Drummond and started toward the cot.

Drummond cleared his throat loudly.

Iain halted. "Something more, Brother?"

"Iain, you didna tell Rowena you love her in return, did you?"

"O' course I did. I proposed marriage and she accepted."

Drummond wanted to explode with frustration. This is what he hated about Iain in love. Iain out of love was reasonably cautious and displayed decent judgment. In love, he turned impulsive and blind to all danger. "You do her a discourtesy," he barked. "If you have to let her down, she will be hurt."

Iain tossed his head, all devil-may-care. "I willna let her down. She requires my aid, for last night her father slapped her until her nose bled."

Drummond didn't like the sound of this. "I will not have her injured because of us. We will avoid her from now on."

"I dinna mean to avoid her," Iain snarled with indignation. "I mean to rescue her. The earl forced her to admit you and Gemma had been alone together, then wouldn't let her explain that 'twas only for a moment." Iain looked disgusted. "She says he's promised her to the eldest son of the Earl of Caithness. She canna wed him. He's a madman."

Drummond shook his head. It was one thing to remove Gemma and her uncle from the island. Both were of age and not legally obliged to the earl, but the earl was Rowena's father. "Dinna be hasty, Iain. I understand how you feel, but—"

"Dinna tell me what to do," Iain shouted, putting down the dipper. "I'll do as I see fit to ensure her happiness. Besides, I dinna notice *ye* remaining celibate. I never thought ye capable of hot-blooded, reckless abandon, but ye are." He frowned with a knowing air.

Drummond had to delve deep for the strength to remain calm. He would be every bit as celibate as Iain from now on, but his brother wouldn't believe him. " 'Tis no' the same thing."

Iain glared at him. "Nay, I suppose it isna. Ye're no' in love with Gemma, as I am with Rowena, though I have ears and you made a good pretense o' it last night." He nodded as Drummond scowled at him. "So the way I see it, Brother, if you can wed for lust, why should I no' wed for love?"

Drummond continued to scowl as Iain went inside the cot to seek shelter from the rain. Lust or love was not the point at this juncture. He wasn't sure they could all escape with their lives.

# Chapter 18

Gemma woke with a start in the middle of the night. She lay beneath her blanket, warm and cozy after the chill of the day's rain, but cursing her laxness.

She hadn't meant to fall asleep. She had meant to go feed her uncle after Drummond and Iain slept.

Drummond had promised to see to it, but after their long day with the women, he had forgotten. She felt quite certain, because he hadn't asked her for the key to her uncle's cell. Lawrence Bruce had another, but it would do Drummond no good. He had no access to it.

She must do the task, she supposed, though it annoyed her. Men insisted on being all powerful, taking charge of everything. Half the time they didn't keep their promises.

Gemma sat up cautiously, not wanting to wake Drummond. Then she realized the space beside her was vacant. Earlier, he had wrapped himself in a separate blanket and insisted she do the same, putting a barrier between them. Now he was gone.

All the better. He wouldn't know what she was about to do. Neither would Iain, who lay rolled in his blanket against the far wall, breathing lightly but evenly, indicating sleep.

Ting dozed on her feet just inside the door. As

Gemma stepped past her, the pony awakened and followed. No harm in that, she thought. The dogs at the castle knew Ting. They wouldn't bark.

At the stone dyke beyond the farthest outbuilding of the castle, Gemma let Ting through the gate, then crouched behind her to make the journey to the dairy. She hoped the castle guard wouldn't notice an extra pony among the other animals in the yard.

From the deserted dairy, she and Ting slipped to the byre. The men from the German ship were gone, having joined a ship from their country for the return home. Alone in the byre, she studied the castle, not wanting to enter the stable. Her friend, the stable lad, must not know she was here. "Wait for me, love," she whispered to Ting.

Accustomed to remaining outside when Gemma wanted her to avoid Bruce or the earl, Ting ambled calmly through the door and lowered her head to crop grass. Gemma patted her a last time and skirted the stable as the castle guard disappeared around the corner.

The kitchen door stood ajar, as always, to allow the stableman or lad access during his night duty. She let herself in. After lifting a wheel of bread from the pantry, Gemma unlocked the storeroom door.

"Uncle," she whispered, squinting to make out his form in the dark. " 'Tis Gemma."

"My child, I thought ye gone from Scalloway." The scrap and rustle of movement sounded in the pitch-dark storage chamber as he sat up.

She locked the door behind her this time. "Nay, we're living on the moor. I'm an outlaw, I suppose." She sank to her knees, feeling for his hand in the dark.

He pulled her into a bear hug, his fatherly concern warming her. Peace seeped into her, along with nostalgic memories of her youth.

"Ye're nay outlaw in my eyes, Gemma, lass. You've

handfasted with a fine man. Leave with him, child. Ye deserve a better life than ye'll find here."

The peace fled. "I wouldna leave ye, Uncle. You deserve better as well."

"Ever faithful." He stroked her hair, his work-roughened fingers catching in the strands. Strong hands. Caring hands. She had loved watching them build a life for his wife and eight children, plus her. When his hands were at work, all was right with the world.

"Oh, I near forgot. I brought you bread."

Her uncle took the loaf but did not tear into it, as he had the previous night. "The cook smuggled me extra food afore I was locked away tonight. I dinna ken why or how, but he did. I ate my fill."

Gemma pondered this news. "Drummond said he would see that someone fed you." Guilt crept through her for doubting his word.

" 'Twould seem ye can rely on him. Do ye love him, child?" he asked, surprising her.

"I scarce know him," Gemma protested. "He rescued me from the earl. In return, I am assisting him in finding a lost family member here on the islands. 'Tis a convenient bond for us both. No more."

Her uncle tsked. " 'Tis more than convenient. A handfast was unnecessary if he didna wish it."

"Oh, that." Gemma tried to make light of what Drummond had done. "He did it to protect my reputation."

"Why trouble?" her uncle persisted, ever practical. "If he took ye from the island, no one would ken whether ye were wed or no. Ye could say whatever ye wished." He paused, as if to let this sink in. "Surely he appreciates yer beauty," he went on. "He's no' blind."

She wished he would leave the subject. "He is a gentleman, despite being a Lowlander," she stated firmly.

"In truth? He hasna touched ye?" He chuckled as if feeling her answering blush in the dark. "Dinna be 'shamed. He handfasted wi' ye for a reason and will do what men do wi' women. He'll learn to love ye, as ye will, him."

Steamy memories beset Gemma, of Drummond's tempestuous lovemaking and her joyful response. She shrugged them off. "Why do ye think so? Ye ken little more of him than I."

"I know what he did for ye. Twice."

Twice was too often. Drummond went to extremes, then offered more. "He said he wishes to help me free you, as well," she confessed. "He will, too," she hurried on, unwilling to let him deny the possibility. "After we find the family member he's seeking, we can all depart."

The deep silence that followed worried her. Surely he wouldn't refuse to go.

"If he means to remove me from the earl's clutches, child, he mun be quick about it," he said at last. "Two days o' work remain on the chamber. I'm no daft, either. When I'm done, I dinna expect he'll let me return to Fair Isle, to tell everyone his secret."

So he realized his days were numbered, and now they were reduced to two. Gemma wanted to scream in panic. "Why did you not say so at once? 'Tis too little time. We have dozens of women to interview. Mayhap more. I would depart with you now, but I need help to do so." Her mind darted in one direction, then another, seeking a solution. "Can you draw out the work, Uncle? Require a special material? Something the earl does not have and must order from the mainland?"

She felt his tension in the silence that followed. "I think I have it," he said at last. "I'll ask the earl for cork to line the chamber. 'Twill seal in sound. Otherwise, anyone hiding there will be detected if they make the least noise."

Gemma's hopes rose. "Excellent idea. 'Twill take him some time to find sufficient cork. We can locate this woman by then." She held his hand to her cheek, willing her words to be true. "I'll return on the morrow, to learn if the earl has agreed."

He patted her shoulder with his free hand, ever the giver of comfort. "Ye mun get yer rest now, lass. Go, and think on this." He paused, as if gathering his words. "Yer auntie and me, we were together a year or two afore she died." Gemma knew he understated. They had been wed for more than thirty years. "Look for what's to admire in yer Drummond Graham, and 'twill grow to affection. Look to affection, and 'twill grow to love."

"There is much in him to admire," she admitted.

"Nay more than admire?"

"He has many good traits."

"Then why the long face?" he queried. "All the women envy ye, being handfasted wi' him."

Gemma sighed. He seemed to hear everything, despite his confinement. "They envy living in a one-room cot on the moor, with no sure source of food? I tell ye, there is no future for us. He seems the perfect mate, but he's unyielding in his ideas and he is secretive, which is not the least pleasant to live with." She broke off as she put into words the idea that so troubled her.

"Are ye yielding and open wi' him?" her uncle asked.

"I have tried, but he refuses to respond." Gemma shook her head in despair.

"He wants ye. How could he no'?"

"I wish that were so, but I think not. Many women love him, but he has no feelings to give in return."

Her uncle tsked, shaking his head. "Nay, Gemma. Dinna be so sure o' that. He has feelings, but he's walled them in, as sure as I'm walling in the earl's secret chamber. Ye can count on that."

*   *   *

Gemma wondered about her uncle's words as she relocked his storeroom door. She'd felt certain Drummond had rescued her solely out of habitual heroism. Could he possibly have feelings for her besides lust?

If so, what were they? He'd spoken of a passion so strong, it took hold of people and refused to let go. He said he understood such things.

She'd felt certain that lust was part of why he'd rescued her. But why had he refused her offer that morning? The idea of his hands on her body, his lips seeking hers, made her blood sing with pleasure. She had told him honestly that she would enjoy it with him, and the chance that she would conceive was slim to none.

The answer lay in his rigid nature. Only an intensely private man responded as Drummond did. The ability to keep secrets served well at times, but in personal relations, Gemma knew it could wreak havoc. Take her uncle, for instance. Drummond hadn't told her he'd made arrangements for his care. He had let her worry instead.

Irate with his purposeful omission, Gemma stood at a window, watching the shadow of the guard on the wall, backlit by the midnight sun. As he disappeared around the corner, she slipped out the kitchen door and quietly closed it.

Rough hands seized her from behind.

Fear jolted through Gemma and she bent double, wrestling against the confining grip. Wrong choice. Her attacker bore down on her, his weight giving him the advantage. She struggled futilely against his strength.

A hand jammed a huge wad of coarse cloth to her mouth, muffling her screams.

"Stop yer strugglin', mistress," her assailant ordered. "His lordship wants to see ye."

His lordship wanted worse than to see her. Desperate to escape, she kicked, aiming for his shin. As her foot connected and her assailant grunted, she glimpsed a white form shooting forward. Ting sank her teeth into the man's arm.

He shouted in rage and pain, released Gemma, and wrestled with the pony, who hung on to his arm with a savage intensity Gemma would not have believed possible.

"Go. I'll handle this."

Startled, Gemma jerked around to behold Drummond. Her wide-shouldered thunder god had materialized out of nowhere. "He'll hurt Ting," she protested, moving away to show she meant to obey.

Drummond stepped forward and plucked the man from the ground as easily as if he separated a flower from its stalk. Ting let go and backed away, her ears still plastered to her head, her eyes flashing with rage.

"Ting, come," Gemma ordered softly, knowing the guard on the wall had probably seen them. He would give the alarm. They must run.

The last she saw of her assailant, he was wrapped in Drummond's grip. The man flailed with both fists, but to no avail. Drummond cuffed him once, not hard enough to kill him, it seemed to Gemma, and flung him aside. He collapsed to the ground, and Drummond pounded after her.

They let Ting through the gate in the stone dyke. As they sprinted up the hill, Gemma heard the kitchen door bang open against the castle wall. Pausing, she glanced back, her heart pounding in her chest. A figure emerged, holding a lantern aloft. The guard had given the alarm, but no men poured from the castle to give chase.

The figure stood immobile in the stable yard, staring after them, and suddenly she knew it was the earl. He would not give chase, for he meant to catch them another way. A more silent, secretive way, so that he could not be blamed.

Horror licked at her heels as she whirled and fled,

knowing the Earl of Orkney and Laird of the Shetland Islands would never willingly release her. She would never be free of him.

Ting nudged against her side as they ran, and she grasped a comforting handful of mane. "Thank you, friend," she panted. "You're always there when I need you."

Someone else had been there when she needed him. For a third time, Drummond had saved her.

She thought of how he had stormed into her life, emerging from the rain, brandishing a glittering sword. He'd saved the seamen, then pulled her to safety on the rock, cradling her as dangerous elements raged. He had snatched her from the hangman's noose, guarding both her reputation and her life as he made her his handfast wife before the entire hall. Last night, he had given her a gift she'd never imagined existed as she shuddered to fulfillment in his arms.

Now, he rescued her once more. Yet it would have been unnecessary if he hadn't been secretive. She felt as if she were being dominated by another sort of tyranny, despite its benevolent nature. She was expected to leave everything to him, including all thought.

"You should have told me," she raged, whirling to confront Drummond as he caught up with her. "I said I would feed my uncle. Why did you go behind my back?"

"I didn't go behind your back. *I* said I would see to him and you agreed. Why should I have to tell you again, once 'twas done?" He cursed as he labored for breath. "Dinna call me to account when you're the one who ran off in the night like a madwoman. I never dreamed you would go to the castle alone. If Ting hadn't fetched me, I wouldn't have known where to find you."

This news momentarily distracted Gemma. "Ting fetched you? You're sure?"

"I should think I would know if I'm fetched or not. When I discovered you missing, I headed toward the sea, hoping you had been unable to sleep and had gone for a walk. She met me and insisted I follow her to the castle, where I found you being attacked."

"Good heavens, Ting must have seen the brute skulking outside the kitchen door and known he was waiting for me." Gemma stooped to caress the pony, who rubbed her muzzle against Gemma's cheek. "You knew just what to do, didn't you, love?" Thrilled by her friend's keen instincts, she turned back to Drummond. "Never say that ponies are not intelligent."

"I never did."

He was just cross because she embraced Ting instead of him, Gemma thought, assessing his frown. Her uncle had said Drummond, being a man, would want her, and men understood men. "Dinna put yourself in a temper. I appreciate what you've done, for both me and my uncle." Her rage diminished. She stepped forward and caressed his cheek.

His stare remained as cold as the North Sea. "I'll be in more than a temper if you continue this rash behavior. Why didn't you tell me your concern? Ting trusts me. Why you do not, I canna comprehend."

Her hand dropped. "There's more you don't comprehend," she snapped. "I need direct news of the people I love, updated often. You've been alone so long, you keep everything to yourself. If this happens once more, I think I shall scream." With a huff, she continued up the track, in despair of reaching him.

He sprinted after her, grasped her arm, and jerked her to a halt. "You didn't tell me what you wanted. You just took matters into your own hands and charged off."

The distance between them widened, making her even more angry. She hated being nothing to him but the needy recipient of his care. "No, I didn't tell you what I wanted, because when I do, it makes no difference. You understand the women you talk to so well. I thought you understood me as well, but I see you do not.'' She tugged, trying to break his hold.

His fingers tightened on her arm, refusing to yield. ''Will it satisfy you if I report to you daily about your uncle?''

She glowered, hating the need to concede. But she must, for her uncle's sake. ''You have word of him daily?''

''I expect to now that I have a paid spy in the earl's household.''

Another secret he had not shared with her. One that would have put her mind at ease. She wanted to turn her back and stalk away in outrage, yet she must not. ''I must have news of him on the morrow. He may be in grave danger unless the earl agrees to line the secret chamber with cork.''

''Cork?'' The word seemed to mystify him.

''Yes, cork.'' She stamped her foot, made impatient by her fear. ''The chamber is almost done. Unless my uncle can convince the earl to let him line it with cork, drawing out the work longer, he'll be dead within days.''

Understanding dawned in his eyes. ''I'll check first thing on the morrow, to see if cork is being ordered. Does that satisfy you?''

''It helps,'' she agreed grudgingly.

''Then 'tis settled. No more midnight trips to the castle. No more reckless acts.'' He released her and walked on, leaving her to stand in the track, annoyed once more by his heroic generosity.

She hurried after him. '' 'Tis *not* settled. You've spent too much of your gold for me already. Now you're paying a spy to watch over and feed my uncle.''

He shifted a seemingly impersonal gaze to her. '' 'Tis a small price if 'twill prevent you from doing something so rash. 'Tis a great deal of trouble, rescuing you from scrapes.''

"I dinna do rash things, as you term it, simply to give you trouble."

"No, but you might have told me earlier in the evening of your concern. It would have saved me a fit of apoplexy when I found you gone."

"Did you have apoplexy?" she asked, curious but doubting.

"Would you care if I had? You didn't appear to consider the possibility before you left."

His sarcasm destroyed any hint of possible caring. "Well, of course I would. I wouldn't wish apoplexy on anyone," she said indignantly. "But if I'd told you where I wanted to go, you would have stopped me."

"I would, indeed. With good reason, too. I had already taken care of the problem."

Infuriating man, she wanted to kick him. "You fail to see the point. You should have told me first. I love my uncle, but you don't understand love. Feelings mean nothing to you."

"You canna do something just because your feelings tell you to. You must only do things that make sense."

His unending logic, so devoid of emotion, sent her over the edge. "You're so stubborn, Drummond Graham, acting only on logic. I cannot bear being near you."

Gathering up her skirts, she sped up the steep track, her anger giving her strength. He was impossible, and she could scarce wait until they found a way off the island. She never wanted to endure the torment of living near him again.

# Chapter 19

If he was stubborn, she was worse, Drummond thought as Gemma sprinted up the track, followed by Ting. He had just rescued her from capture by the earl. For a fraction of a second, he relived the relief he'd felt as he had flung her attacker to the ground. But relief swung back to annoyance. Why did she say she couldn't bear being near him?

Last night she hadn't behaved as if she disliked him. Far from it. This morning she had invited him to repeat their sensual experience.

She was right. He didn't understand her.

Infuriated by her willfulness, he followed at a distance. As they approached the cot, she passed it, laboring on up the track. Wasn't she going to bed, where she belonged? He picked up his pace. What in hell did she mean to do?

By the time they crested the hill, he realized she was going to the pony herd. By St. Andrew, she preferred horses to him. It vexed him even more.

He wanted to return to the cot, to ignore her as if she were an irrational, ill-behaved child having a tantrum. Yet she did not have a child's effect on him. She drew him inexplicably.

The places she'd touched him last night still burned as if seared by fire. He wanted more of her lips on his body and her capable hands on his flesh. They were hands of infinite tenderness, used to comforting ponies and babies and, as she had said, to satisfying the man who was her husband.

Disgusted with himself, he admitted that as the man presently playing that role, for whatever space of time, he wanted to feel her competent hands on him, caressing his naked flesh.

Yet he wanted more than that of her. Something he couldn't name.

At a distance, her pale hair glowed like molten silver by the light of the midnight sun. Yet the source of that light did not seem external.

It was her spirit that burned. *She* was light.

He wanted to taste her life-giving energy until he, too, glowed from within.

He followed the pair, the pony like a small beam radiating from a greater sister moon. The herd leader saw Gemma coming. Ensconced on an outcropping of rock, he stood as still as a stone, watching her approach. The stallion moved not a muscle, indicating his acceptance.

Drummond ran faster. It was wrong, but he couldn't let Gemma go. Not tonight.

The midnight sun glowed low on the horizon, a ball of molten copper streaking the sapphire sky with bronze ribbons. She fled before him, a wild swan stretching her wings, as untamed as the wind.

He strained every muscle in his body, pounding the ground, willing himself to arrest her in her flight. Just before she reached the mares, he caught her. He clasped her around the waist and spun her into his arms.

As she crashed against him, he saw a thousand biting insults form on her lips. She would fight him, but he wouldn't give her a chance. He crushed his mouth to hers.

She wrenched away, breaking the kiss but not his grasp. "Leave me be," she cried, her blue eyes flashing fire as she strained against his hold. "I tell you I hate you."

"Then you tell me lies." Her soft body against his urged him to commit folly.

"Why should I not?" she demanded. "Should I repeat what I said this morning? Degrade myself by admitting I want you? You refused to let me make love to you, as you did to me last night."

"Is that what you think I did? I simply refused?" The raging need in him escalated.

"Yes," she hurled at him. "You're so perfect, all you want is for me to tell you how grateful I am."

He didn't want her grateful. He wanted her hot with yearning for him. Begging for his touch, as she'd been last night. "I give in," he panted, feeling the guttural growl in his throat, seething with primitive passion. "You have bested me."

"I don't want to best you."

Her words made no sense to him. At this moment, all he understood was the urgency of the sexes, pushing him to join with her in feral heat. But if she didn't want it, he wouldn't force her. He let her go, throwing up both hands.

To compound his confusion, she flung both arms around his neck, crushing her body against his. "You're impossible, Drummond Graham. I don't mean I don't want you."

He couldn't decipher her meaning. Not now. His blood sang in his ears, goading him to join with her in reckless abandon among the heather. "Let us be very clear about this. Tell me what you want of me," he urged, not sure he could give it to her, knowing he must try. "I will do everything within my power to obey."

"I don't believe you can obey anyone, but I don't care anymore," she cried in a new contradiction, her lips against his hair. "I've turned into an animal. I want what you want."

He couldn't follow her reasoning, but her last words resonated clearly in his mind. "You want me to have you? Here? Now?"

"I want you to make love to me. Here. Now."

He didn't care what she called it. He awaited no second invitation. With a groan, he bore her to the soft grass, pulling up her skirts as they went. Her nimble fingers helped free him of his clothing. He met her eagerly rising hips with his own.

Heat shot through him as he thrust within her. So tight. So eager for him. She clutched his back, writhing beneath him, pulling him deeper. Unable to contain the torrent of passion dammed within him, he burst into marvelous release as she bucked against him, building toward her own fulfillment. As he spent the last of his seed, she cried his name, the note of triumph and satisfaction unmistakable in her voice. Her body convulsed as he held her to his heart.

"Extraordinary," she breathed with satisfaction, relaxing beneath him, eyes closed, a smile curving her lips. "You are extraordinary, Drummond Graham."

He felt himself rising and hardening again in response to her praise. "Not I. You, Mistress Selkie." He brushed himself against her.

She opened her eyes. "What, again?"

"Only if you wish."

"Oh, God, how I wish."

She didn't specify the exact nature of her wish, but he knew it went further than the moment. As did his. Yet he intended to capture the fullness of the here and now, memorizing her every nuance, every sensation she imparted to him.

She kicked off her slippers as he untied her bodice. He helped her out of it and flung it aside. Her blue skirts sailed away like a ship to become lost in the sea of waving grass. Her petticoats and smock joined them, floating like white birds through the air, then sinking out of sight. As he pulled off her netherstocks, he felt ravenous for her bare flesh against his, like smooth cream.

Her deft fingers worked on him next, stripping away his leather jerkin, neatly nipping his shirt buttons through their openings. He knelt in the grass, free of all clothing at last.

" 'Tis my turn," she whispered. "I want to make love to you."

Her offer transfixed him as her fingers explored, caressing the nape of his neck, arousing him unbearably. "I love the way your hair falls here," she said on a sigh.

He closed his eyes as her lips touched the back of his neck. Here, a man was most vulnerable, most exposed. The back of the neck was open to the assassin's surprise attack or the lover's touch, both equally devastating in their own ways. He struggled to hold back his rising arousal.

"And here, where your beard changes from rough to smooth." She kissed the place where his day-old beard began, her lips satin smooth and slipping lower. "And here. I've wanted to kiss you here."

Her mouth anointed his shoulder, sending paroxysms of pleasure shuddering through him. Whether or not she knew it, she had graduated from grateful to gloriously sensual. She acted out her desire, which was far more provocative than words.

"And here, you are even more extraordinary. I've yearned to kiss you here." She pressed her moist mouth to his chest, sinking lower by the moment.

"Aye," he whispered as she cupped and stroked his hardened length, gazing at him in wonder.

"Perfectly extraordinary," she murmured, testing him with her tongue.

With sensitive fingers, she went to work on him, arousing him to fever pitch. So small and fragile, those hands seemed, yet they were fraught with a perilous power. She held him tightly, driving him to distraction, using both her strength and her softness. The enchanting blend made him want her. Now.

"Come. Quickly." He rolled to his back, bringing her with him, urging her on top.

An alabaster goddess, she mounted him with hesitation. "How is this done?" Her lips pursed in puzzled concentration.

"I think you can guess. You learn quickly, my queen of the midnight sun." He showed her what he meant.

With a grin, she moved forward and descended on him.

He moaned as she took his full length into her womanly depths.

She answered with a wordless chuckle, moving experimentally.

He grasped her waist and pulled her down hard.

She moaned with pleasure and threw back her head, her long hair tickling his thighs.

"Ride me, sweetest," he urged.

"I've never had a steed such as you. We'll frighten the ponies."

"They're no' frightened. They ken what we're doing, for they do it as well." He gestured toward the calmly dozing mares.

She rode him hard, then harder. This type of abandon he welcomed. Let her expend all the reckless impulses she wished with him.

Just when he thought he could bear no more, they crested the pinnacle. As he convulsed within her, he pulled her down into a kiss. Her moist lips parted at his demand, and he tasted her with a hunger that had not been satisifed for years. Forever, it seemed. The thunder of her magic shook him.

They lay in each other's arms for a long time afterward. The wind touched his heated flesh, a welcome cooling. Catching her hand, he kissed her palm, was rewarded by her contented sigh.

How he had wanted her here, on the open moor

where he had first seen her. Here was where she belonged. Not in the oppressive earl's castle, but dwelling among the steeds of Apollo, creatures of the
midnight sun. Here, she walked the world of wild sea
grasses blowing in the wind, her celestial blue garments billowing about her. Here, she was one with the
herd, so wild and free, she made his heart ache.

The vast circle of sapphire sky stretched above
them, and he realized she was irrevocably linked to
this enchanted isle, as elemental as its earth, air, water,
and fire. When he joined his flesh with hers, he
touched this wild island, adrift in the tempestuous seas
of the north. For a short space of time, he was one
with the wild swan spreading her wings, taking him
with her as she soared to the skies.

In return, she called his lovemaking extraordinary.

What she didn't realize was that she had made it so.

# Chapter 20

Drummond didn't want to think as he lay down back at the cot. After the release he'd found with Gemma on the moor, he wanted to sink like a stone into the still waters of sleep.

No luck. He tossed and turned, unable to quiet his mind.

Gemma had not rolled herself in a separate blanket this time. She had spread one blanket on the floor, then curled up at his side, the other blanket over them both. Her soft breathing, the knowledge that she lay within easy access, clad in only her chemise, drove him nearly insane. He had had her twice on the moor, yet lust stampeded through his body like a herd of wild horses, out of control.

*A passion that refuses to be denied.*

He had told her he understood such things. But his passion for Gemma exceeded anything he had experienced with the females supplied by his father. She touched him in places that went beyond flesh, arousing a need in him that only she could fulfill.

It didn't make things better. It made them worse. Their uncertain future hovered over them like a threatening cloud. How the devil was he to complete his mission, then get four people and a pony safely off the island?

He stared at the roof of the cot, sorting through

options and discarding one after another. The hard-packed clay floor seemed to grow harder beneath his back. Restlessness plagued him for hours before he finally drifted into a fitful sleep.

The bloodred sun of morning cast its rays across his face, waking him after too little rest. Heaving to his feet, he went outside to assess the weather, only to find that the earl's man had appeared, as he'd feared. In truth, he'd expected one sooner. The guard stood some distance down the track, watching their cot.

Drummond knew he would exchange places with a new man that evening. A steady stream of them would come, relieving each other. Watching. Stalking. Biding their time.

"I suppose there's no chance of raiding the castle larder this morning." Gemma peered over his shoulder at the man. "He'll run and announce us the instant we take a step in that direction."

"Aye," he agreed, surprised as always by her calm analysis of an unwelcome development. She might be as wild as the island ponies, but she managed adversity, which explained how she had survived under the tyrant's rule. "I could snare some rabbits, but that and cooking them would limit our time for my search. I would rather buy food in the village if we can," he said.

Iain sauntered up and eyed the guard. "I'm ravenous. Is he guarding the castle larder?"

"Aye, and dinna make any plans to sneak past him," Drummond said firmly. " 'Tis one thing to slip into the castle unexpected. Quite another for the earl to know you're on your way. We're for Scalloway village, to find food there." He donned his leather jerkin and led the way, sorry to see that the red sky of morning heralded more rain. Patches of mist dotted the hillside. Not for the first time, he wished away the need to live on the moor.

Despite two nights in a makeshift cot, despite their

precarious existence, Gemma looked fresh and alert this morning. As they walked toward the town, he recalled the prior evening's events, reliving the powerful satisfaction he'd felt at smashing her attacker's jaw.

A torrent of sexual energy raced through him as he remembered what had come after. But he must not dwell on it now, or his energy for his work would be diverted. He must find the woman he sought. Quickly.

Despite his resolution to remain aloof, he allowed himself the pleasure of watching Gemma as she walked at his side, head held high, swinging her arms to match her strides. Her blue garments, though wrinkled and beginning to soil, still accentuated her graceful form. She had said she was happier than she'd been in years.

The slight smile curving her lips proved she had spoken the truth. Perhaps she was relieved to fight the earl openly after so many years of suspicion and doubt. If so, he was glad to have contributed to the first stage of her liberation.

"Do ye think anyone will dare to sell us food?" she asked.

"Someone will," Drummond said. But as he glanced over his shoulder at the earl's man following them, he realized that most would be too frightened. They dared not risk the earl's wrath if his guard reported them.

A short time later, they returned up the hill, having garnered a few eggs and some knobby turnips. Barely enough to feed three, and both required cooking to be palatable. People had disappeared into their stone cots as their small party had advanced down the main path through the village. Gemma's friends had begged her not to ask anything of them, for fear of reprisal. Those who knew her less well had simply refused to open their doors.

Drummond was sorry to see that Gemma displayed less vigor as they returned up the hill. She might not

yet be downcast, but she was daunted by the villagers'
rejection. Anyone would be.

"Gemma, wait." They all turned at the sound of a
female voice. A girl ran after them, bearing a big basket
that bumped against her knees as she ran. Drummond
recognized her as one of the countess's handmaidens.

"Her ladyship sends ye this cuddie," the girl panted,
offering the basket to Gemma. As Gemma took it,
the girl cast a baleful glance at the earl's man, who
returned the favor with a castigating frown.

"How kind of her ladyship to think of us. Thank
ye, Marione." Gemma lifted the linen cover. Within
lay a tall stack of oatcakes and a pot of jam, a crock
of pickled herring, and a bowl of fresh bramble berries
clotted with cream.

"Such a feast. Where did she get the berries? All
the bushes I saw were picked clean," Iain breathed,
looking ready to pounce on the food.

"From her kitchen garden. She honors ye by sharing
her private store." Marione pressed a small note into
Iain's hand, then pulled a pair of knitting needles from
a pouch at her waist and began to knit.

Iain's face brightened. "Thank her ladyship for us,"
he said with fervor. "We're grateful."

But he was clearly more grateful for the note, which
must be from Rowena, Drummond concluded. Despite the ravenous appetite he'd professed, he retreated to read the note in private.

"We are indeed grateful to her ladyship, but Marione, how is she?" Gemma asked as Drummond relieved her of the basket.

The dark-haired girl appeared anxious. "Her ladyship is most unsettled, Gemma. She says she mun have
ye at her side or the babe will come too soon. She
and the earl quarreled terrible about it last night."

"Were you able to calm her? Did you give her the
herbal brew, as I instructed, when she is distraught?"

"Aye, but she wants ye. Says only ye can soothe

her. The pony, too." She paused in her knitting to pat Ting, who bobbed her head in a friendly manner, showing long acquaintance.

Gemma's expression pinched with concern. "Oh dear. I *am* worried about her. Tell her I would come to her, but I dare not. Thank her for the food. Tell her to have a care the earl doesna learn she sent it. He would be displeased."

"She says she doesna care about his temper. She swore she's going to send food regularlike.'Tis another reason why they quarreled. An' he dares no' cross her because o' the babe. She told him she will arrange yer weddin' as well."

Gemma appeared discomfited by this announcement. "Tell her no' to let it concern her just now," she said evasively.

Marione shook her head until her dark curls bounced. "Och, her ladyship has set the date. The twenty-fifth of June, says she, an' will let none gainsay her, even his lordship. She says she wants ye wed to a brawley gentleman, as is yer due." The girl delivered this speech with passionate emphasis on the word "brawley," accompanied by a shy glance at Drummond.

"Tell her ladyship she is most kind," he said as Gemma's anxious gaze darted to him. "But she must not do more to anger the earl."

Instead of accepting this message, Marione shook her head again. "I've never seen her ladyship defy the earl, but she said that baskets mun be sent twice a day. Said she'd fill 'em and walk 'em up here hersel' if he wouldna see it done. His lordship roared like a lion at her. Everyone heard 'im, but she wouldna be swayed. An' she says to tell you that his lordship has ordered cork, whatever that means. But she told me to tell you special-like."

Drummond noted that Marione's dark eyes glowed with respect for her mistress's daring in defying the tyrant. At the mention of cork, Gemma appeared re-

lieved, though she pressed Marione's hand and murmured words of concern for the countess.

Yet nothing could be done for her ladyship just
now. He concluded that they should eat and gather
their strength. Perhaps he could think more clearly
then.

He thanked the girl again, and as she returned to
the castle, he guided Gemma and Iain back toward
the cot. Iain had finished reading his note. His lovesick
expression told Drummond he would be good for little
today unless it had to do with Rowena. He might even
be plotting a reckless visit to the girl. More trouble.
The kind he didn't need.

Yet they had found an unexpected ally in the countess, not to mention a steady source of food. Odd that
she insisted on a formal wedding, though he expected
they would be long gone before it could take place.
Still, he was glad to have her help in whatever form.
Perhaps with her assistance they could survive on the
moor until he completed his quest.

After their meal, the three of them plus Ting set
out for Lerwick, followed by their guard who trailed
them every step of the way. Despite this, Gemma felt
buoyed with hope by the countess's support. She
wanted to take it as a positive sign. Things might still
work out. Yet Drummond didn't have the satisfied
look of a man who had just dined well and anticipated
a bright future.

"We must be prepared for an attack. 'Twill come,"
he reminded her.

Her hopes plummeted, and she sighed, wishing he
hadn't ruined her optimism. "I will try, though I've
no skill in such things."

"I do. You may rely on me."

The warmth of his words encircled her, and she
reached for his arm, liking the way he crooked his

elbow to accommodate her hand. His left hand closed over hers in a possessive gesture, and desire swirled within her. He offered his protection so freely, yet he did not share what was in his heart and mind.

At least he wasn't William Fermour. She was relieved to have escaped marrying the earl's choice. Yet she couldn't live with a man of so taciturn a nature. Not forever. What to do?

The hard question gnawed at Gemma. She admired his warrior's body, his muscles honed by disciplined use. His strength, so basic and primitive, spoke of self-sufficiency. He needed no one, and she longed to be like him. To cast off her role as a woman, which society saw as weak.

Yet her predicament had naught to do with gender. The men under the earl's rule were as helpless as she. They needed an outsider's strength and cunning just now, and as she'd been blessed with a thunder god, she should be content.

He was an asset, not a husband. Keep the situation in perspective, her mind advised.

As they advanced down the Lerwick high street, doors closed, and she realized people had heard about them. The earl's reach was long and word traveled fast.

Drummond seemed immune to the disappointment. "Shall we find your friend?" he asked.

"Aye, Sibilla will help us identify all those with fourteen-year-old children."

Drummond again tucked her hand in the crook of his arm, his expression as calm as if they were out to enjoy a Sunday stroll, not on an important quest.

Gemma realized she had been holding her breath and forced herself to fill her lungs. They were in no immediate danger. She must not panic. Not yet.

But once they arrived at her friend's cottage, Sibilla seemed nervous as they talked. Why did her elderly friend fidget and stare at Drummond and Iain so? Why did her married daughter start when she entered the cot and saw them with her mother?

Gemma supposed the earl inspired fear in everyone. She could think of no other explanation. Taking the list Sibilla had prepared, Gemma selected the first family with a fourteen-year-old child and directed Drummond to the harbor area.

As Drummond walked ahead, Gemma took Iain's arm, then purposely slowed her pace so they fell behind. "What did Rowena say?" she asked him in low tones.

Iain's face bloomed into a delightful smile. "She loves me."

"How wonderful for you. What else?"

"She's going to slip out tonight to meet me."

Gemma didn't like the sound of the plan. Not now that they had a guard, but Iain clearly had his heart set on it. "I would like to see her as well," she said.

"You would? Why?" Disappointment tinged Iain's tone.

"I require news of various castle matters." Gemma did wish to communicate with the countess, but she was more concerned about the pair meeting unattended. She knew Iain well enough to realize he was set on seeing Rowena. Even if Gemma begged him not to go, even if forbidden by Drummond, Iain would find a way. From what Gemma had seen, babes could result from such trysts.

Iain studied her for a moment, as if searching for a reason to deny her request but failing to find one. "You're worse than Drummond," he grumbled at last.

"He would just forbid you to see her, not offer to go with you." Gemma fought to contain her smile. "And you would go even if he forbade it, wouldn't you?"

Iain nodded stubbornly.

Just as she had thought. "Now Iain," she soothed, "I must discuss my uncle and the countess with her. Truly."

Iain pulled a face. "It's supposed to be a lover's tryst," he complained. "If you're there, 'twill ruin the romance."

Gemma sighed heavily. Nothing in her life was romance. Sex, perhaps. But never romance. "My apologies, Iain, but duty prevails. I might as well play the romance ruiner for you, as well as for me."

He snorted. "Ye're having yer share romance, to judge from the other night."

"One night," she retorted, embarrassed to know he had listened, though he couldn't have avoided it.

"Two," Iain said.

"How do ye ken?" She was sure he couldn't be certain.

"I could smell it on the pair o' ye when ye came back to the cot." Iain smirked.

Gemma was beginning to understand why Drummond objected to Iain in love. "Whatever it is, 'tis not romance. I'm not the sort of woman men try to romance."

"He's romanced ye more than anyone else since I've kent him, and that's been years," Iain said with sincerity. "Drummond Storie's never romanced another woman afore ye."

This touched Gemma and she wanted to hear more, but Iain's use of a different surname for Drummond demanded immediate investigation. "Why do you call him Storie?" she asked. "His mother's name was Storie? And his father was a Graham?"

"His mother was Elizabeth Storie, but our father was from a branch of the Graham clan. His name was William Mosley. Will, for short."

"But then Drummond's name should be Mosley, not Graham," Gemma puzzled. "When his chief wed his mother to his father and made him legitimate, he should have taken his father's name. How did he come to bear the Graham name?"

"Didna he tell ye? If ye're wed to him, I think ye're entitled to the details."

As she shook her head in the negative, Iain frowned, as if disapproving of his brother's secrecy. "My apologies, but ye'll have to ask him, then. 'Tisna my tale to tell."

Vowing to ask Drummond at first opportunity, Gemma and her party approached Lerwick Harbor. The shops and quay teamed with men on shore leave from the Dutch and German fleets fishing for herring in the North Sea. They came every summer, and the town loved them. They boosted trade, bringing an influx of gold and silver coins from the Continent as the fishermen bought fresh meat and vegetables, the women's knit stockings, cheese from their goats, and any goods they thought might sell when they returned home. In the bustle of business and raucous men infesting the harbor area, Gemma was grateful to have two stalwart men escorting her.

The cot of Margret and William Everiegarth had a view of Bressay Sound, beyond which lay Bressay Island. The day being fair, Gemma bid Ting stay outside and they approached the door. "Hello, Margret," Gemma called. " 'Tis Gemma Sinclair come to visit with two friends."

"Gemma Sinclair, I havena seen ye for months," Margret's voice wafted from within the cot. A moment later she appeared at the door, her kertch askew on her gray-streaked hair, her apron crooked, a welcoming smile on her lips.

The smile disappeared as she caught sight of their party. Clapping both hands to her mouth, she shrieked and raced back into the cot.

"Great heavens, I'll see what's wrong. You wait

here," Gemma said to Iain and Drummond. She followed Margret into the cot, concerned for the woman. "Margret? Are you unwell?"

The woman dropped into one of two basket-backed chairs by the fire, moaning.

"What is it?" Gemma knelt and placed a hand on the woman's shoulder.

" 'Tis the father of my eldest child, that's what it is," Margret groaned.

Gemma wisely refrained from commenting. If the father of her eldest child was not William Everiegarth, she would pretend to forget the information immediately. Yet she could not believe that either Drummond or Iain had fathered a child on Margret Everiegarth, who was a good twenty years older than Drummond.

"You canna have met my companions," she said, trying to reassure her by being sensible. "Have you?"

"Aye." Margret paused. "Nay," she contradicted, moaning again. "I couldna ha' met them. They be too young."

"They are Iain Lang and Drummond Graham, visiting the islands from Lowland Scotland," Gemma explained. "They willna harm you."

Margret sat up and looked at her for the first time. "Lang?" she repeated, seeming mystified by the name. "Graham?"

Gemma didn't know what to make of the woman's puzzlement, so she merely nodded.

"Let me see 'em, then." Margret heaved to her feet, seeming to gather her courage.

Gemma rose and summoned Drummond and Iain to enter the tiny cot. Margret met them with wary eyes. After scrutinizing them in silence, an inspection that both endured with patient acceptance, she bid Drummond sit on one of the chairs by the fire.

"I pray you, wait outside," he said to Gemma and Iain as Margret took the chair next to him.

As Gemma left the dim cot, she glimpsed the two

putting their heads together, whispering. They seemed to know one another, or at least to know about each other. What did it mean?

She sat with Iain by the kale yard, trying to be patient. Had Drummond been here before and met the woman? But she had thought this his first visit to the islands. The question gnawed at her. Would Drummond explain this tangle to her? Or would he remain silent, his usual habit?

Drummond finally emerged an hour later. Margret did not show her face, not even to bid them good-bye, though she had been friends with Gemma for years.

"Is she the woman we seek?" Iain asked as his brother approached their seat.

"Aye, it seems she is *one* of two *women* we seek." Drummond sounded exasperated.

Iain cursed. "I feared this."

"As did I," Drummond muttered, tucking the knit stockings he had bought from Margret into his already bulging pack.

"Did you give her gold?" Iain asked, staring at the pouch strapped at Drummond's waist.

"I gave her silver in payment for her wool goods. Her husband will suspect nothing. I'll see that she has more in the future, but her husband provides well for them. She is one of the fortunate few."

Gemma looked from one to the other, baffled and not a little vexed by their mysterious exchange. "I thought you were looking for a woman to deliver a message. If this is the woman and you delivered the message, is your mission not done?"

"It is not done." Drummond drew out the words, tingeing them with resentment.

Disappointed and every bit as baffled as before, she persisted. "I know you have not been to the islands in the past, yet Margret seems to know you."

"I have never been to the Shetland Isles, nor have

I ever set eyes on Margret Everiegarth before this day," he agreed heavily.

"Then how is it she knows you both?" she appealed to Iain.

Iain did not answer. He looked with a frown to Drummond, who gazed off at the busy Lerwick Harbor, a mix of annoyance and consternation on his face.

"Isn't anyone going to explain this drama to me?" she demanded, frustrated by their silence.

Drummond refused to meet her gaze. "Soon," he muttered. "You'll know as soon as I can make sense o' it myself. Let us get on with the list." He glared at the earl's guard as they continued on to the next cot.

Concerned by this new event, Gemma perched on a three-legged stool in the cot of James and Maryara Gutteromson while Drummond coaxed information from Maryara. The three older children were away with their father, helping to rebuild a town dyke, as was the responsibility of all when required. Their absence offered a convenient solitude.

If Drummond had found the woman he sought, why was his work not done? What did this mean for their departure from the islands?

Vainly she tried not to cough as smoke rose from the fire and drifted toward the hole in the roof ridge. How could Maryara abide it? she wondered between discrete attempts to clear her throat. Why didn't she open the door to air the chamber—though she supposed the bairns would wander out if she did. Glad she had left Ting outside to browse in the yard, she eyed Iain, who sat across from her, wiping his tearing eyes.

Wondering how many women Drummond must now find, Gemma gazed at the smoke hole in the ceiling. She didn't like the look of it. Loose straw thatch bristled around the hole. A stray spark could easily ignite it. The network of straw simmons supporting the thatching sagged between the rafters as well. This roof needed repairs before it collapsed on their heads. Yet the family probably had too little money to pay their rent, else their laird would have done it by now.

The scent of goat and pig drifted from the adjoining byre that served animals, and Gemma tried not to be uncharitable in her thoughts. Thin, tired-eyed Maryara must be unable to keep up with the work. Her two youngest children, perhaps two and three years of age, crawled about on the clay floor in little more than tail clouts, despite the coolness of the day.

One of the children, a boy, toddled over to her and reached up with inquisitive hands. "What cold fingers you have, dear," she crooned, gathering him onto her lap. He smiled, touching Drummond's cloak wrapped around her shoulders. "Gracious, your toes are cold as well. Let me wrap them in my warm cloak." She glanced at Drummond as Maryara opened a wooden chest and produced her spinning. It wasn't the best they'd seen, but Drummond would buy it, and Gemma was glad.

What didn't make her glad was the tumult of feelings within her as he questioned Maryara. He was so patient, so concerned about how she had met her husband, her thoughts on love and loyalty and her past. Yet the intimate offerings only flowed one way. How Gemma wished to hear answers to the same questions from Drummond's lips.

Without his answers, she thought through what she did know. She knew that Drummond searched for a woman on behalf of his family. Someone in his family, a man, had told him he had visited the Shetland Islands and met a beauteous woman, most likely a romantic relation.

Did it not make sense that, being members of this man's family themselves, Drummond and Iain resembled this man? Margret Everiegarth had seemed to recognize them. It would explain her statement that she knew yet did not know them.

Then there was Drummond's father, the man he refused to discuss. Will Mosley had sired two children out of wedlock. He had refused to wed Drummond's mother until forced by his chief. Given such a past, he might have sired other children out of wedlock. Had Will come to the Shetland Islands years ago and sired a child on Margret Everiegarth?

Gemma pictured the woman's eldest son in her mind, the fourteen-year-old John Everiegarth. Though he had dark hair like Margret, Gemma thought he might resemble Drummond and Iain.

It meant that Drummond had come to the Shetland Islands to find the illegitimate child of his father. What a noble undertaking. Except that Margret had seemingly told him there was more than one child, and from his comment, Drummond intended to find this second half sibling.

It made sense, yet held dire implications for Gemma. Did it mean he hadn't come from the king? Had Drummond appeared by coincidence on the island when she most required aid?

Drummond Mosley. Drummond Graham. She had thought him her salvation, sent by the king. Who was he really? Chaffing under the weight of the mystery, she listened as Drummond spoke to Maryara, establishing that she was not one of the women involved with his errant father. How many more women must they interview to eliminate them as well? Every woman with a fourteen-year-old child on the islands?

A loud thunk on the roof startled Gemma from her thoughts. She looked up. Tongues of flame licked at the edge of the smoke hole.

"Fire!" she cried, staggering to her feet beneath the weight of the child.

# *Chapter 21*

"O utside, everyone," Gemma shouted, gathering up
the Gutteromson child and racing for the door.
Drummond reached it at the same time, but to her horror, it refused to budge. A shove from his massive shoulder should have popped it open, but it stood firm.

"A curse on ye, Patrick Stewart." Drummond
banged the door with his fist, then turned to study the
tiny chamber, his angry face a sight to behold.

Gemma bit back a cry as she realized the meaning
of his curse. The earl's guard had not just been assigned to watch them. He must have blocked them
inside, then set the fire.

Her anger matched Drummond's as she eyed the
growing blaze that ate up the dry straw around the
roof's smoke hole. Her gaze leaped to the sagging roof
she had noticed earlier. "Can we get out this way?"
she cried, gesturing.

"We'll have to. Iain, help me." Drummond pushed
past a stunned Maryara as the smoke thickened and
the bairns began to cough. Iain rushed to help him
swing the heavy wooden settle to a position beneath
the weakened roof. Drummond vaulted onto the seat
and tested the sagging thatching. Reaching up, he
punched through the straw thatching with a savage
smash of his fist.

Maryara shrieked, then subsided into coughing as

he whipped out his dirk and began to cut the network of supporting simmons. Within minutes, he had cleared a space through which a child might pass.

Gemma found a peat cutter and held it up. "Can you use this?"

He grunted assertion and set to work with the sharp blade of the special spade, enlarging the hole.

Maryara shrieked again. "The roof is fallin'," she cried. Flaming straw landed on her shoulders, setting the back of her cotton kirtle alight.

Iain and Gemma launched themselves at her simultaneously, hauling her away from the collapsing section of roof and beating out the flames with their hands. Gemma worked awkwardly, holding the frightened, clinging bairn in one arm as Maryara bent over to shield her other child in her arms. When the flames were out and they turned back, Drummond had disappeared.

"Bring the bairns," he ordered, his face appearing at the hole in the roof.

Gemma clambered onto the settle and lifted the boy as high as she could above her head, praying that Drummond could reach him. Without a squawk of protest, the child disappeared through the hole in Drummond's arms.

"The other bairn. Quickly." Drummond's order was terse.

Gemma held out her arms to Maryara, who passed her the whimpering younger child. Gemma's lungs burned from the smoke and she felt as though she were choking as she lifted the child up to Drummond. The heat in the cot was rising. Sweat dripped from her brow.

The second bairn vanished as quickly as the first. Then it was Gemma's turn. How would she reach the hole? It was well above her head.

"Give her a boost," Drummond shouted, gesturing to Iain.

As Iain grasped Gemma around the thighs and thrust her upward, more of the roof behind them collapsed in an avalanche of flaming straw. Propelled by terror, Gemma stretched for Drummond's hands.

His hands locked around her wrists, and she felt Iain let go as she rose in the air. Before she could get a handhold to help, her head cleared the hole in the roof. A gust of welcome fresh air hit her in the face as Drummond shifted his hold to her arms. He hauled her onto the roof on her belly.

"Easy now. Dinna kick. Ye'll knock down the rest of the roof," Drummond warned as she struggled for a foothold. He unceremoniously pulled her the rest of the way by the back of her skirts. "Slide to the ground while I get the others."

She barely managed to turn feet first before sliding down the bundled straw thatching. She hit the ground and collapsed to her knees, remaining there for several minutes, stunned. Then she rallied and staggered to her feet. Several townspeople had gathered in a semicircle before the flaming cot, staring at her. Two women held the bairns, and they all gazed in awe at Drummond as he pulled first Maryara, then Iain from the burning cot, then leaped to safety.

Drummond knelt by Gemma as the smoke took its toll and coughing racked her.

"Are ye hurt?" he asked, patting her on the back.

She shook her head miserably as she gazed with watering eyes at the cot.

The fire crackled with lusty pleasure as it devoured the straw. The bairns cried, frightened though unhurt by the tumult. The sea broke on the rocky shore nearby, as rough and angry as the feelings in Gemma's soul.

A heavy peat cart that didn't belong to the Gutteromsons blocked the door to the stone cot. The earl's guard was nowhere in sight, but not one of the townspeople had dared to push it away from the door and liberate them. The fire had been no accident.

They saw Maryara and the two bairns safely entrusted to a neighbor, then sought her husband and the other children. Gemma stood by, grateful for Drummond's caring, as he gave James Gutteromson a gold coin that would pay his rent many times over. She felt badly for the family, knowing their loss had been caused by her and Drummond's presence in their home, yet his generosity was unprecedented, as always.

Gemma was glad to return to their cot as the supper hour approached. She collapsed on her blanket, shaken and drained by their brush with near death. The earl had attacked her first with her own interest in Drummond, then with his guard at the castle last night, now with fire. Though her determination could match his in matters of will, she admitted she might prove no match for his extensive arsenal.

"Lie down," Drummond urged. "No ill will befall you as long as I'm here."

Gemma looked down at her shaking hands. "We were almost grilled alive."

"But we were not, and the earl will continue to be unsuccessful in his attempts to kill us. I promise."

She appreciated his reassurance, but his steadfast belief in his own infallibility did not stop her trembling. "We canna remain here. He might try the same thing with this thatched roof. We must move."

He rose and covered her with the other blanket, tucking it snugly around her. "Well and good to propose a move, but to where? At least here we canna be blocked inside, as we have no door."

She could not enjoy his humor, nor his calm acceptance of the attack. They must move, though their choices were limited. "There are other places," she murmured, clasping his arm to keep him near. He sat down beside her and rubbed her back as she clutched the blanket. "Sheltered bays. Deserted islands used only for grazing sheep. A sea cave that I know. We must move every night. . . ." She trailed off, too spent to go on.

"A good idea, but later." Drummond smoothed her blanket with a reassuring hand. "I want you to sleep awhile. I'm going to sit outside. When you wake, we'll see what the countess has sent us for supper."

"Please wait." She sat up again, urgency gripping her. "Is Margret's son—"

"My and Iain's half brother," he finished for her, seeming willing to explain at last. "Fifteen years ago, my father visited these islands and seduced a woman, producing a child. I came here to find the woman and help her if she and her child were without support. What I didn't know, what Margret told me, is that my father most likely seduced another woman and may have produced another child. As he left her, he said he'd found a bigger fish to catch before he departed. Since she heard he spent time hanging about Scalloway Castle, she suspects 'twas someone there."

His grim statement, the angry tightening of his jaw, did little to relieve her mind. "I canna think this woman would still be at the castle," she said.

"No' if she had an illegitimate child. She would have been cast out, so we cannot know where to find her. Damn my father." He cursed roundly. "He lived to seduce women and had dozens. At times, I suspect he had them without the seduction, getting them to a solitary place and taking advantage of them without their consent."

Dozens? Gemma shuddered, realizing the implications for his life, not just his mission in the islands. "Do you look like your father?"

"Very much in height, coloring, and features. Iain is like him in coloring and somewhat in features."

It explained Sibilla's and her daughter's uneasy reaction to Drummond and Iain, as well as Margret's shriek when they had first appeared. They had all met Will during his visit to the islands, Margret with disastrous results.

"So, Gemma Sinclair, you longed to understand me better. I hope you find your new knowledge interesting." He slipped from her grasp and strode through the door of the cot.

Gemma sank back on the blankets. She had suspected something unpleasant would explain why Drummond had said their search was not yet ended.

Each revelation showed her more of what had molded Drummond's character. Each disclosure was more unpleasant than the last. And he clearly did not expect what he revealed to appeal to her.

Single-minded in his intent to do something about the earl's latest murder attempt, Drummond saw Gemma settled in the cot. As soon as she drifted into slumber, he bid Iain guard over her and set off for Lerwick again.

The guard, forced to choose between remaining at the cot or following him, chose to follow.

Let him, Drummond thought. He welcomed the man's report to the earl. If his lordship truly believed him to be from King James, he would be terrified by what Drummond was going to do next. But Drummond had had enough of the nobleman's diabolical machinations.

At Lerwick Harbor, he scanned the ships at anchor and identified the one he sought. Satisfied that the captain of a certain German fishing ship was likely visiting the town, he went from one ale house to the next, seeking him.

"Drummond Graham! 'Tis good to see thee," the burly German captain greeted him. "Art thou here buying wool?"

Drummond gripped the calloused hand offered and

shook it with warmth. "Well met, Hans Kleman. I am indeed buying wool, and Shetland's is said to be the best. 'Twill sell for a fine price in Edinburgh, where we last met. And you? Catching many fish?"

"Oh, ya. Many herring. I know you rescue my countryman und his crew from der wrecked ship." Kleman signaled for another mug of ale and bid Drummond sit.

"People on this island talk too much," Drummond muttered, taking a place on the bench beside Kleman and accepting the ale brought by a lad.

"So 'tis true. You are the hero but take no reward." Kleman chuckled, seeming to enjoy the idea of a champion refusing his due. "What shall I do mit you? Force you to accept a favor, ya?"

"There is no need to force me. I need a favor, ya." Drummond grinned back, infected by the man's joviality. "Will you be stopping at Edinburgh on your return to Germany?"

"Oh, ya. Ve stop in Edinburgh first. Then home to Hamburg."

"Excellent. Here's what I need." Drummond told the German everything, ensuring as he did so that the earl's man heard nothing but saw his every move.

Gemma awoke later, feeling refreshed and ready to tackle the new challenge. Drummond's latest spectacular rescue had inspired her.

They had faced probable death, yet he had saved three adults, two children, plus himself with no more harm than Maryara's singed kirtle and a few scratches and blisters. Despite the appalling nature of the legacy left him by his father, he undertook to right the wrongs he saw. He stirred her imagination as no man had in her past.

But they must hurry to find this second woman. Time was running out.

The sun had sunk lower in the sky, indicating the

advent of evening though it would never set completely. The midnight rays bathed the land in a golden radiance that turned it into a magical fairy realm. Beyond the entrance to the cot she saw Drummond's broad, muscular back, solid and reassuring as he guarded her sleep. Despite her dilemma, she felt a stirring of appreciation for his faithful vigilance.

She rose and stood in the entry, tying her bodice laces where they fastened in front. Drummond sat on a stone, watching the earl's guard, who sat on his own rock farther down the hill, gazing malevolently back.

Gemma crossed to the broad, flat rock and sank down beside Drummond. For years, her life on Fair Isle had been beautiful, but for the last six, living in the grip of the tyrant on this island had changed her. Rather than wanting to hide from this difficulty, she felt driven to confront it. She could not change the legacy left to Drummond by his father, but she could help him set lives aright.

"I'm awake," she announced.

He nodded without taking his gaze from the guard. "I heard you moving about."

"Where is Iain?"

"He went to bathe in the sea. The eastern shore, not near Scalloway Castle or the earl," he added as she started to express concern.

Reassured, Gemma took his arm and rested her head against his shoulder. "We must interview more women on the morrow."

"You still wish to be involved in this"—he gestured in frustration—"this wild goose chase?"

Gemma nodded firmly. "The women of the islands are my friends. If another of them has been wronged, I wish to see her cared for. Now that I understand whom we seek and why, I can narrow the field further. We can limit our search to destitute women with fourteen-year-old children. Those who are secure can be left in peace." She paused, giving him a moment

to assimilate her decision. "I do need word of my
uncle, of course. For me, his safety comes first, and I
must depart the island with him at first opportunity,
but until then, I will assist as I can."

"Marione will bring word about your uncle when
she comes with the food basket."

"Tonight, we must find a way to lose our guard, then
move to another location to sleep," she continued.

"A sensible idea. Your sea cave?"

"The interior is dry, but getting there is not. I think
we had best choose something on the main island tonight. Time will be too short to go to the cave. We
should move to a different place each night."

They lapsed into silence, during which Gemma
chaffed. She ought to admire the way the low-riding
sun turned the grazing sheep on the hillside to gold,
but this evening, they failed to hold her attention.
Drummond had not thanked her for deciding to continue assisting him. She would not ask for thanks. He
was her only hope of saving her uncle. She would do
what she must.

"Are you not going to question me further about
my kin?" he finally said.

"I was going to wait for you to volunteer what
you wished."

"Alexander Graham is my kinsman and our chief."
He launched into a recitation in a tone of indifference.
"Just after my father died, I learned that he and his
cousin, Will Mosley, had been switched at birth. Since
Will was my father, I was really a Graham, not a Mos-
ley.'Tis why I bear the name."

Confused by this unusual confession, Gemma shook
her head to clear it. "Why in heaven would they be
switched?"

"Their mothers switched them," he continued, "my
grandam and great aunt, because a gypsy fortune teller
prophesied that my father would be unfit as leader of
the clan. He would have been, too. He was a reckless,

corrupt, depraved, self-serving . . ." He sputtered as
he trailed off, as if words were inadequate to describe
the despicable nature of his parent.

"You needn't tell me this if you dinna wish," she
protested, wondering what prompted this unusual confidence about his past. Perhaps their narrow brush
with death had loosened his tongue.

"Everyone agreed the chief should keep the name
and the place, despite the switch at his birth," he continued, relentless in conveying the details. "Now he's
wed to an Englishwoman, Lucina Cavandish. They
have two children and another on the way." He
glanced down at her briefly before returning his gaze
to the guard. "You'll be pleased to know that they
breed horses."

She released him and sat upright, excited by the
idea. "Do they breed ponies?"

"Nay. Lucina loves long-legged English steeds and
Barbs and Arabs from the East. There's profit in riding horses."

"I like any kind of horses, but ponies have their
special purposes. There could be profit in them, as
well."

"Given a chance, Lucina would probably adore ponies. She loves any kind of horseflesh."

Gemma tucked away the information for later consideration. "If your father and Alexander Graham
were switched at birth, is it not true your father should
have been chieftain?"

"Aye. Alex was actually the third son, so the fortune teller foretold more than my father's bad character when she advised that the two be switched. She
must have seen the death of Alex's two elder brothers
as well. I suspect she saw many things, of which this
was only part."

His forthright discussion of such sorrowful facts,
which he had clearly come to accept, saddened her. It
also worried her. He hinted at worse to come, and

what he had just confided was already odd and ugly as it was. "You say that your father should have been chieftain. Why did you let your cousin Alex keep the place instead of taking it yourself?"

Drummond sent her a swift, assessing glance. "Angling to be wed to the head of a clan?"

Gemma grinned. "I'm already wed to a hero. I don't need a chieftain."

He ignored her. "You're entitled to know everything about my odd family. We only learned of the switch after my father died during a treasonous attempt with the Earl of Bothwell to assassinate King James. My Great-Great-Aunt Isabel finally told the secret she'd kept for years, and Alex's old nurse verified its truth. Alex offered me the place, but the clan was used to him. I told him to keep it and the name Graham and I swore my oath of loyalty to him. His upbringing prepared him better than mine to lead."

Grieving for his undeserved fate, Gemma touched his hand.

He remained stoically unresponsive.

"What of your mother?" she asked, drawing back. If he resisted her touch but seemed inclined to talk, she would let him.

"As I said, my father, Will Mosley, seduced her, then refused to wed her. Clearly he was a fool, for that reason as well as others, for she was industrious, beautiful, and well worth marrying. My father was free to choose a bride, and the chieftain, Jock Graham, wouldna have objected to their making a match. But my father refused."

"She is happy now, is she not?" she probed.

"Aye. Since I was my father's eldest bastard, Alex arranged a marriage by proxy so she was legally wed. This happened just before he died. Now she lives at Castle Graham as part of the household. She used to be a weaver, but Aunt Isabel taught her to use the

family charmstone for healing, so she has a new purpose in life."

"Do you disapprove of her using this charmstone?"
Gemma asked cautiously. She had heard of such crys-
tals, said to have miraculous healing powers. They
were good magic, so she couldn't think why his mouth
tightened as he spoke.

"Why should you think that? The Dunlochy Charmstone has been in Isabel's family for years. My mother
does great good with it, especially since Isabel's health
is failing due to age."

Gemma smiled faintly. "I think it because your
mouth turned down as you told me. I'm guessing that
something about it troubles you. Does she heal the
people she sets out to help?"

"Generally, though she is judicious in what she
promises, as Isabel taught her. She doesn't give false
hope."

"She sounds wonderful. You must be very proud
of her and happy she's found her place among the
Grahams." Gemma couldn't resist another question.
"But I'm wondering, has she ever tried the charmstone on you?"

"Oh, aye. When I broke my arm a few years ago."
He touched his left wrist, suggesting that was the
place.

"I mean for your other ailment." When he gazed at
her quizzically, she gathered her courage. "You have a
bad case of melancholy, Drummond. Has she ever
tried curing it with the charmstone?"

A brittle silence ensued, and Gemma felt certain
she had gone too far.

Drummond shifted on the rock, turning slightly
away from her. "The charmstone canna help me with
that. You now know what I must accomplish here in
the islands," he gritted out, his gaze glued on the
guard. "Imagine that task compounded a hundredfold.

Imagine the area I must search for my father's offspring expanded to the length and breadth of Scotland. He even went to the Continent once or twice.
You dinna suppose he remained celibate while there,
do you?"

Her heart sank as she realized the enormity of his
task. "Do you mean you've found other half siblings
before John Everiegarth?"

He nodded. "My father didna just enjoy seducing
women. He enjoyed sowing his seed and reaping the
results. He owned every one of his illegitimate offspring if no one stopped him. He made us beholden
to him and required that we work for him in return
for sustenance. Iain's adopted father forbade such influence, but my half sister Elen was not so fortunate.
Nor were a half-dozen others I can name. In the years
since my father's death, I've found more than ten others I hadn't known existed."

And he would find many more in the coming years,
Gemma realized. If his father had indulged in carnal
relations both because he enjoyed seducing women
and because he wanted offspring, the number of children he had sired could be staggering. Little wonder
Drummond was melancholy.

"I see you are speechless with admiration for my
quest in life," he observed.

For once, she groped for words and found none.

"But now you understand why I have never taken
a wife. What woman would wish to follow me around
the countryside, sitting patiently whilst I woo other
women to confide in me."

"Is it so bad?" she ventured.

"Bad?" he scoffed. "I'm a wanderer, sworn to travel
the land for I know not how long. No woman is so
demented as to commit herself to that."

He was trying to warn her away, Gemma realized.
Unsure how she felt about it, she took a practical tack.

"Someone should have locked up your father and thrown away the key."

Drummond grimaced. "Alex did lock him up several times, but he always got out. He enlisted me and his other offspring to help him escape. I hated being part of it, but I did exactly as he commanded or suffered the consequences."

She could imagine what those consequences had been. As a vulnerable youth with a impoverished mother, he would have had few defenses against his father's demands. "Well, then, I guess we had best continue the search."

He eyed her in disbelief. "Ye *still* agree to assist me? After what I just told you?"

"The sooner we find the people you're looking for, the sooner my uncle and I can leave the island," she said simply.

He turned to look at the guard. His green eyes, usually brilliant with life and energy, seemed full of anger. "Aye, if we can stay alive that long."

# Chapter 22

Iain returned a short time later, proclaiming an excellent appetite. Drummond announced that he intended to snare a rabbit from a warren over the hill. They could roast it to augment their cold fare.

As he strode off, Gemma studied the earl's man with interest, noting his dilemma. First he started after Drummond, then retraced his footsteps to check on Gemma and Iain. Clearly he wondered what Gemma would be doing if he followed Drummond. He couldn't decide which of them to watch.

At last, he elected to follow Drummond and disappeared over the hill, leaving her unguarded. How interesting. She tucked the information away for future reference. It might serve useful later. It was certainly useful now.

"We should visit Rowena before our guard returns," Gemma said to Iain.

" 'Tis early. She willna be waitin' for me yet," he protested, his wet hair hanging in his eyes.

Gemma finger combed the unruly locks into some semblance of order. "If she's in love, she'll be watching for ye long before you're to appear." She finished arranging his hair and tapped him smartly on the shoulder. "We willna have a chance later. Let us go."

Iain agreed without enthusiasm, and Gemma was tempted to comment on the unlikely prospect of his having success with his romance. Her own romantic future seemed nonexistent after what she had learned from Drummond, but she elected to keep her mouth closed. It was no use belaboring the point. She would concentrate on showing Iain the subtle approach to the castle. He must not march down the track for all to see, as he had done the other day.

She instructed Ting to stay at the cot, then led Iain down the hill, away from the track. "We'll go the long way by the shore, out of sight of the castle, then follow the stone dyke that keeps the animals from the crops. 'Tis tall enough to hide our approach until we get quite close. From there—"

"We hide behind a friendly cow on the way to the dairy," Iain finished for her. "I know. I've done it before. I do wish it got dark here, though."

"It does," Gemma said. "In the winter it gets dark and stays that way for months."

"I meant now." Iain pulled a face at her. " 'Twould be easier in the dark."

Rowena apparently anticipated Iain, for she waited at the back door of the dairy. "The dairymaids are done wi' their work for the day," she said. "We have the dairy to ourselves."

Gemma eagerly began her questions. "How is your mother, Rowena?"

"Sore of heart."

That was understandable, given the earl's ugly deeds. "But her pains have no' begun yet, have they?" she pressed.

"Nay. But my father is like to give her pains. He's in a dither about the message yer husand has sent to King James."

Gemma stilled. "What message to King James?"

Rowena's eyebrows shot up. "Did he no' tell ye? Drummond went to the harbor at Lerwick today and was seen speakin' to a German ship's captain who is bound for Edinburgh. I heard my father an' mother arguing about it in her bedchamber. The king is at Edinburgh at this time o' year, is he no'?"

Gemma nodded, annoyed that Drummond hadn't told her. He had been busy while she slept, seeming to confirm that he came from the king after all. If it were true, one day the plight of the islanders might be eased. But now, the earl would be even more intent on devising an accident to end Drummond's life.

"My father doubled the guard on Gordie and Robert," Rowena continued, "an' he's startin' to attend more closely to Elizabeth and me as well. I had difficulty gettin' here. I'm supposed to be lying down wi' a sick headache. Och, I almost forgot. I took yer uncle extra dinner this noon for Master Brandie, the cook, and your uncle told me to tell Iain to tell you that he is well and very busy for many more days. I'm glad to tell ye direct."

Gemma breathed easier. "Praise heaven my uncle is well. And I'm very glad to know that the countess's worries have no' affected her health."

Rowena shook her head, her green eyes sad. "Her pains are no' come yet, but she keeps to her bed and speaks o' nothing but her plans for yer wedding to Drummond Graham." She darted a shy glance at Iain. "I should like to be yer bridesmaid, if I may."

"I should like to have you." Gemma was taken aback by Rowena's conviction that the wedding would really take place. "But I dinna think there will be a wedding anytime soon. Pray tell your mother to put it from her mind."

"Mother says there shall be, and Father's threats havena dissuaded her. She's set the date for the twenty-fifth of June and has demanded he pay for silk to make ye a special gown. She wishes to measure ye for it soon, an' she's orderin' all manner o' food for a great feast. Clothing for everyone else as well."

Gemma blinked, baffled by the countess's uncommon persistence on the subject, especially in the face

of the earl's opposition. It took a powerful force of
will to contradict him, and her ladyship had rarely
done it in the years Gemma had known her. Yet she
now seemed determined that this wedding take place,
which, unlike the handfast, would make Gemma's
union to Drummond irrevocable.

Gemma wasn't sure she wanted to be tied to him
forever. The man hoarded his thoughts like a miser.
At the rate they were going, she would spend a lifetime prying them out of him. He also traveled like a
gypsy most of the time. Could she live with that? She
didn't know. Could she live without him? She had
answers to none of these questions.

Flustered, she retired to the far side of the dairy
and sat among the crocks for butter, all other concerns
forgotten as the news fogged her mind. Did the countess really have the strength to make the wedding a
reality? If so, mayhap she should write a note and try
to dissuade her. Or speak to her personally.

Glancing at her love-struck young friends, she noted
how the pair held hands and gazed into each other's
eyes as Iain spoke with adamant fervor. He must be
proclaiming his love, and Rowena seemed to blossom
as she listened, her creamy skin glowing, reflecting her
happiness. With her red-gold hair, she looked like a
living flame in the gloom of the dairy. Iain's flame-
colored locks mingled with hers as he leaned forward
and brushed her lips in a chaste, reverent kiss. Rowena accepted his caress in silence, appearing awestruck.

As Gemma turned away to give them a modicum
of privacy, she reflected on how similar they were in
temperament. Rowena had always been sunny in nature and easy to know, just like Iain. But as they could
never wed, it seemed a disservice to encourage them.
As the eldest daughter of the earl, Rowena was des-
tined for a political alliance meant to cement relations
between the islands and the Highland chieftain's hold-

ings. Their hope for the future was as bleak as hers
with Drummond.

"Rowena, you will be missed if you stay any longer,
dear," she announced. "Pray give your mother my
love and tell her I hope to see her soon. My uncle as
well, if you see him."

Iain appeared crestfallen that their visit must be so
brief, but Rowena still glowed with the pleasure of his
presence. She pressed his hand before releasing him.
"Dinna fear. Our love will sustain us while we are
apart," she assured him. "We shall find a way to be
together. I ken it in my heart."

"We shall. I swear it." Inspired by her words, Iain
kissed her softly one last time. Then, with the same
agility Gemma had observed in Drummond, he peered
out of the dairy to locate the guard on the wall, waited
a moment, then slipped behind a big-horned cow.
With a handful of grass plucked from the yard, he
urged his chosen escort toward the dyke.

With a last farewell to Rowena, Gemma found her
own handful of grass for an escort cow and followed
Iain.

The guard sat on his rock, looking sulky as they
returned to the cot. Gemma avoided his glare as she
and Iain passed. Without a doubt, he was wondering
what trouble he had failed to prevent, but no one
would learn of Iain's tryst with Rowena. At least not
from her.

Ting trotted to greet Gemma as they drew closer to
the cot, neck arched, happy to see her. They exchanged hugs and nuzzles, but Gemma couldn't wait
to get to the cot. The mouth-watering aroma of
roasted meat drew her like a magnet, making her
empty stomach rumble in anticipation.

Inside, she and Iain found Drummond roasting a
rabbit he had spitted over the fire. Though the countess's basket had arrived, the prospect of the first hot

food in days appealed. Ignoring Drummond's disapproving expression, she pushed past him and began to unpack the basket.

"That rabbit smells wonderful. Is it almost ready to eat?" she asked.

"Where have you two been?" Drummond snapped. "Not strolling on the seashore, I presume."

"We did no harm, sir, so pray let it rest," Gemma said, setting out a trencher of bannocks and marmalade. "I'm so glad you're an excellent hunter."

His furrowed brow did not smooth. "You'll not evade the issue with pretty compliments. I thought we had an understanding. You were to tell me your plans before you did anything."

"Only if they were dangerous." Gemma resented his possessive attitude. "This was not."

"If you went anywhere near the castle, 'twas dangerous. Mayhap even if you did not."

"Ye'll no' blame Gemma," Iain cut in. "I went to see Rowena. She only came along."

"I guessed what you were up to, Iain," Drummond snapped. "I'll speak to you later. This is between Gemma and me. She's older and should know better."

"I'm trying to help," Iain said.

"You would be more help taking a walk to give us some privacy. Here, eat." Drummond cut a hefty haunch from the roast and thrust it at Iain. Succulent juices dripped from the meat as Iain eagerly accepted it and left the cot.

Alone at last, Gemma turned to Drummond. "I'm sorry you dinna like it," she said, "but I had to be there to oversee them. Iain would have found a way to go to Rowena, even if I had forbidden him."

His answering gaze was reproachful. "You should have told me about it, Gemma, so I could have handled it. I'm sorely disappointed in you."

It wasn't going to work. He would never understand her or agree with her reasoning as long as he believed he was in the right. "You'll be even more disappointed to know that the countess is ordering food for our wedding feast." She waited, wondering how he would respond to her diversion.

He turned back to the rabbit.

Gemma imagined he was analyzing the news as methodically as he turned the spit. He let nothing touch him personally, instead devoting everything to his quest.

"The earl willna allow a wedding ceremony," he said.

"I would agree that you are correct, but Rowena says the countess and the earl have argued about it and her ladyship has prevailed." She had managed to divert him, but she had also chosen this subject for a reason. "The countess is beginning plans for the ceremony and a great feast, including ordering cloth for wedding garments. We are instructed to prepare to be measured."

"Taking measurements doesna guarantee a ceremony." He poked the peat fire, rearranging the hot coals.

"No, but the earl is allowing the preparations to proceed," she pressed. "Either he's humoring her or he means to let the wedding take place. I suspect he wishes to tie us together to make us easier targets."

"He'll probably poison the bride ale. Get us both at once," Drummond muttered. "I say no wedding and there's an end to it. Besides, I'm all wrong for you, as you well know."

"Fine," she exploded, having gotten her answer and hating it. She jerked to her feet, upsetting the stool. "Make up my mind for me. Dinna ask me what I want."

He looked up from the rabbit, seeming surprised. "You want the wedding?"

"Nay," she shouted, stepping back, wanting to get

away from him. She wanted a wedding, but not like this. Not ever like this.

Her anger seemed to affect him at last. He unfolded his tall, sinewy frame and came to stand before her, hands on hips. "Then what are we arguing about if we're of like mind?" He appeared baffled.

"We're arguing because you insist on deciding for me," she bit out, clenching her fists until her nails bit into her palms. "I'm tired of tyrants. I've had all of them I can bear."

For an instant, she thought he would explode at being called a tyrant. Let him, she thought. She would welcome a shouting match.

Instead, with exaggerated formality, he offered her a small bow and backed away. "Pray forgive my presumption," he said with a hint of sarcasm. "Let us begin the discussion again. I think it a bad idea for us to go through with a wedding ceremony. What do you think, Gemma?"

"Thank you." She cleared her throat. "There will be no wedding. I do not wish to be wed to you," she declared with force. And why should she? If they married, he would stop at Castle Graham from time to time to see her, and she would have to sit there, bored to tears, doing nothing while he was gone. Oh, she might breed ponies. He had hinted at how Lucina kept a stud, but Gemma had already lived through one bad marriage. Enough was enough.

"And the next time you send a message to the king," she added, leaving the subject that mattered most for one more easily settled, "you could at least have the courtesy to mention it to me. Not let me learn it from someone else. Everyone on the island seems to know, save me."

"Ah, so that's what this is really about." He removed the spit from the fire and propped it against the stone wall of the cot. "Dinna feel badly. I doubt that everyone knows."

Must he take everything she said literally? Instead of dissipating, her frustration worsened, but she welcomed it. She needed to be angry with him. To stay angry. "You will be pleased to know your tactic worked," she flung at him. "The earl has doubled the guard on his sons."

"Ah." He pulled out his dirk and sliced meat onto a trencher from the countess's basket.

His bland response set her teeth on edge. "I want to rescue my uncle and depart, Drummond," she flared. "You may be able to hold everything inside, but I cannot. I'm going mad with uncertainty and fear. How many women do you have to find before we can go? Are you sure your father seduced only two? Mayhap it was ten. Or a hundred. Make it a thousand for good measure, and while we search for them, my uncle will be murdered, the earl will catch us, and we'll become his slaves or worse."

Drummond's expression changed abruptly, alarming her as he slammed his dirk to the ground. "I told you, I don't know how many women my blasted father seduced. Don't you think it troubles me, too?" He leaped to his feet. Gone was the rigid self-control, the calm mask of authority. "He's many years dead and I'm still cleaning up the chaos he spent a lifetime making. I may be the rest of *my* life at it, and I'm tired of it, do you hear?" he shouted, livid with emotion. "I'm weary to death of dealing with the results of his damned fornicating habits, lying to women, creating babes all over Christendom, using innocent children in his stinking plots. If someone hadna already killed him, I would have done it myself." He stood, chest heaving, fists clenched.

Gemma felt relieved by both their outbursts. She had suspected that strong emotions lurked behind Drummond's well-controlled exterior. He wouldn't be human if they did not, and she liked him best when he was human. " 'Tis my turn to apologize," she said softly. "I shouldna have said that about your father, but I'm glad you finally shared with me how you feel."

The anger seemed to drain out of him. "You are justified in being angry. So am I. I have no choice but to search for my half siblings, but you shouldn't have to suffer with me. My mission makes a shambles of what I wanted in life. You see what it does to those close to me."

Gemma's heart ached for him. Or was it aching from her own pain? "You need only tell me what you're thinking and feeling more often. As you did just now."

He shot her a skeptical glance. "You like it when I shout at you?"

"You weren't shouting at me. You were shouting at your father, as you wanted to when he was alive."

Drummond nodded slowly. "I wanted to, believe me, but he would have beaten me bloody for it. He did often enough for less." He returned to the rabbit, slicing off another leg with his dirk and thrusting it at her. "Here, eat while 'tis still hot."

As Gemma accepted the savory meat, their hands touched. He looked up, his gaze locking with hers. The desire in his charismatic green eyes struck her with the impact of a gale wind. Heat swirled within her, pooling deep in her belly and between her legs. She wanted to rush into his arms and urge him to put his hands . . .

With an effort, she took her portion and found her stool, then urged him to eat his share. But a moment later, as he left the cot to fetch them both water, she put aside her trencher. Closing her eyes, she pressed both hands to her temples and struggled with disappointment.

What use was it if Drummond shared his feelings with her? For a moment he had shown her the private man behind the mask. A man of passionate emotions and noble ideals who made her heart race. But it did not help in the overall scheme of things.

The cork for the earl's secret chamber would arrive soon, and her uncle's days would once more be numbered. Beyond that, she could see little, but given Drummond's mission in life and how it had shaped him, any future for them looked bleak.

# Chapter 23

Drummond scolded Iain soundly for trysting with Rowena, wondering as he did so why disagreements with Gemma couldn't be managed as easily. With his brother, he could explode, put his issues on the table, and Iain would apologize and promise to do better. Oh, he would sulk a little. Insist he'd had to do what he'd done. But they were friends again as soon as it was over.

With Gemma, it was infinitely more complicated. When he had demanded her obedience, something he wanted only so he could protect her, she had twisted the discussion in another direction entirely. She had goaded him until he'd lost his temper, a rarity for him. Only after he'd blurted out his innermost feelings had she returned to being the sweet, intriguing woman he so desired.

That was the trouble. The more he shared with her, the more she rewarded him. He wanted to continue, but what was the use if he had no future to offer her? It wasn't fair to either of them.

Despite the passion that sizzled between them, a wife needed more. He must leave her alone.

Hating the decision, yet trusting it was for the best, he prepared for the night. Mist had descended on the island, so thick it blotted out the sun. Visibility reduced to a few feet in all directions.

Appreciating the cover, he bid Iain and Gemma pretend to settle for sleep. After an hour, they slipped out the single window, away from the guard and up the track. Drummond wished them as far away from the guard as possible, but they were all too tired. They walked for a short time, then spread their blankets in the shelter of a stone outcropping.

On the morrow, they would return to the cot. The guard would never know they had been gone. Unless he tried to kill them while they slept.

"I'm glad I took Ting to the pony herd earlier." Gemma yawned and stretched, seeming not the least upset to be without a roof for the night.

"She's safest there for the night," Drummond agreed. "Are you comfortable?"

"I'm not *un*comfortable." Gemma reached out one hand to touch his cheek, rubbing the backs of her fingers against the growing length of his beard.

His body tightened in response. Her simple gesture misted his mind with desire until all other thoughts became as foggy as the terrain. He ached to bed her on the spot.

"Well, *I* am uncomfortable." Iain kicked and wiggled beneath his blanket. "There's something sticking me in the back."

"Probably a stone. Cast it away," Gemma advised with a chuckle. Settling on her side facing Drummond, she pillowed one hand beneath her cheek. "God'den, Iain. God'den, Drummond." With a contented sigh, she closed her eyes.

Drummond marveled at Gemma's composure. She really did love this island.

"I didna object to the cot, but I canna pretend a rock is a shelter," Iain groused, glaring at the outcropping. He groped for the objectionable stone and hurled it away. "I dinna think I'm going to sleep a wink."

Neither would he, Drummond thought. Not with Gemma so close.

They returned to the cot the next morning, bringing Ting from the herd. Drummond emerged, pretending he'd just arisen from a deep sleep. Their guard had drawn near their abode, presumably to keep the door within view. He lay curled on the ground, snoring blissfully.

Drummond cleared his throat and the man jerked awake. He scrambled to his feet and backed away, obviously mortified at being caught violating the requirements of duty. He would have been more mortified to know where they had been.

"Oliver Tulloch," Gemma said, leaning against Drummond, as if such intimacy were commonplace. "The garrison captain must have been desperate to send him. He's been punished so often for falling asleep on duty, we've all lost count."

The odor of smoke from her clothing, mingled with her heady woman's scent, wafted to his nostrils. Her shining silver hair lay on her shoulders against the blue bodice, softly disheveled, reminding him achingly of their lovemaking. Emotions seethed within him, all the more disturbing for being unfamiliar. An unaccustomed desire beset him—the wish to put down roots and make a home with this woman.

"Your clothes need washing," he said, quelling his rising wish to capture her in his arms. "You smell of yesterday's smoke."

"So do you. Are you offering to be washerwoman?" She gathered a handful of his shirtsleeve in one hand and tugged, her grin contagious.

How could she smile at a time like this? Yet he found himself smiling back. "Mayhap, if we had some soap."

What he really wanted was to remove her clothing,

under the pretext of washing if required, and enjoy her nakedness. He wanted to show his appreciation that she hadn't turned tail and run since learning of his dismal mission.

But they had no soap, and the guard and Iain were present. He forced himself to begin the morning's tasks instead. As he drew water for the pony to drink, then for Gemma and Iain and finally himself to wash, he banished all thoughts of Gemma from his mind. Their future was uncertain at best.

By the time Marione emerged from the fog, his appetite clamored full-fledged for attention. He quickly relieved her of the kishie full of food on her back.

Gemma ran to meet her. "God'den, Marione. How are folk at the castle this morn?"

"God'den." Marione shifted from one foot to another, as if nervous energy flowed through her veins. "They're nay good." She stopped long enough to embrace Gemma. "Nay good at all."

"Tell me everything, Marione," Gemma urged as she led the way into the cot.

Drummond followed with the kishie and placed it so Gemma could unpack the food.

"The earl found out Lady Rowena saw the young gentleman last night." Marione nodded toward Iain.

"Why would he think that?" Gemma asked before Iain could give himself away with a foolish avowal that he had seen her and intended to continue doing so.

"I dinna ken. Mayhap he slapped a confession out o' her. He can be fearsome." Marione grimaced. "She says she's no' hurt, but the earl's locked them all up."

"Locked up whom?" Gemma asked. "Do you mean Rowena?"

"I mean all the children. They're under lock and key in his chamber. Naught may come out. Naught may go in, save him and us maids to take them food and empty the chamber pots several times a day. Gor-

die has his two nurses, but 'tis all that are permitted
regularlike. Six people crammed in that chamber, and
the children not even allowed to see her ladyship,"
Marione concluded with a vigorous nod.

"Oh, dear. This is sad news." Gemma gripped a
loaf of bere bread to her middle, forgetting to placing
it on the stool.

Drummond gently relieved her of it and put it with
the rest of the food.

"And you say he doesna let them out at all?"
Gemma asked anxiously as she plunged her hand back
into the basket and brought out their usual pot of
herring. "But they need exercise and fresh air."

"He says they canna come out, not ever, until the
king's man is gone." Marione shot Drummond a
glance. "No' that I believe for a moment ye would
hurt a hair on the children's heads, sir," she said
politely.

Drummond *had* wanted the earl to be nervous. He
hadn't expected it to happen because of Iain and Rowena's tryst, though. It was also worrisome that his
lordship's concern had an adverse effect on the children. Cooped up in a chamber, they would inevitably
wear on one another's nerves and quarrel.

Gemma had evidently thought of this, for she
seemed anxious as they went about their day. True to
her promise, she narrowed the list of women he must
question, cutting the number in Lerwick by half. Still,
the list was long, and he tried to work with speed.
Now that they suspected the woman had once served
at Scalloway Castle, he was able to question each on
that score. Those who had no prior castle connections
could be eliminated. He went through eight interviews
before the time of the evening meal arrived.

None of the eight women had known his father,
although several had evidently seen him during his
visit to the islands. They reacted to his and Iain's ap-

pearance, although not as violently as Margret had. Drummond eliminated all eight as his father's conquests.

The mist still hung on the hillside by the time the sun had made its brief journey around the sky. Never setting. Ever shining. Its work never done.

Drummond was starting to feel as if he, like the sun, could never rest. After the long day, they still must find a place to sleep that night. He didn't trust the earl not to burn the thatched roof over their heads.

"We should change abodes again, madam," he said to Gemma as they finished their work at Lerwick for the day.

"I fear for the countess and the children," she answered. "May we return for the evening meal, then slip out of the cot again like last night?"

Drummond agreed, considering it the easiest way to evade their guard. The man had trailed them relentlessly the entire day.

Back at the cot, they found Marione and their food basket waiting for them. Unfortunately, the news she brought was bad. "The countess wished to see the children today, but his lordship forbade her. She were so upset, I feared for her."

"Oh dear." Gemma wrung her hands in distress. "Marione, I wish I could help."

But she could not, and as Marione departed, Drummond had to draw her aside and gently remind her of their priorities. She seemed resigned as they ate their meal, but also unusually quiet. At his suggestion, she once more took Ting to the pony herd. The three of them again pretended to settle for the night.

After an hour of feigning sleep, Drummond rose, roused Iain and Gemma, and they slipped out the window. Gemma led the way up the hillside. The mist had thickened, covering their escape.

"Where are we going this time?" Iain asked. "I didna sleep at all well last night. 'Twas chill, out in the wind."

"We'll go to a broch for the night," Gemma answered. "It has no roof, but the high walls will keep out the wind."

"It sounds like a type of bread," Iain complained. "Canna we go back to Scalloway Castle and rescue Rowena?"

"No' tonight, Iain." Drummond strove to remain the voice of reason in the midst of the increasing madness. He didn't relish sleeping in a place he couldn't see to examine for safety, but he would not say so as they had little choice.

"It's not a type of bread," Gemma explained. "It's an ancient fort built by people who lived here centuries ago."

She wouldn't be so cheerful, Drummond thought, after another night in the open with only a blanket. Though the weather was mild, if it rained, they would get wet.

But the misty weather did not turn to rain as they arrived at a loch. Clambering into a boat dragged up on the shore, Gemma motioned them in. Drummond took the oars, with Iain in the stern. They hit land after a brief journey, and Drummond saw little more than high stone walls as they anchored the boat on shore.

True to Gemma's promise, they were sheltered from the wind within the walls. Better still, grass and wild thyme wove a lush, fragrant carpet dotted with primroses and marsh marigolds.

The fairy queen of the isles spread her blanket amid the haze of pink and gold, stoking his desire as she removed her stiff bodice and lay down. She held out an arm, beckoning to him.

"Not tonight." He spread his own blanket, sat down, and rolled up in it.

"Are you sure?" She grinned mischievously.

"I'm sure I want to accept your generous offer, but 'tis best we get some sleep." He didn't mention that he would be unable to stop if they started. "Later, you'll see the wisdom of what I'm saying."

"You may be a hero, but you're not always right, Drummond Graham," she admonished, rolling up in her own blanket.

He sighed again. "Once we're away from these islands, everything will change, Gemma. You will find that life looks different."

"My life *will* change." The vastness of the impending alteration in her world seemed to strike her at last. She closed her eyes.

"That's right. You've never lived without the threat of the tyrant hanging over you. You canna understand," he said.

"That's not true." Her eyes popped open. "I grew up without tyranny. Fair Isle was a beautiful place, a land of birds on the wing and flowers in springtime and freedom. I was happy there with my family. I knit beautiful Fair Isle stockings in the patterns my mother had taught to my older cousins. I sold them to fishermen from Norway and Germany, who loved my work. I was glad to be alive."

Her words captured his imagination, and he saw her in his mind's eye, a wild bird herself, flying across the land on feathered wings. He ached to reach out for her. "Your life wouldna be like that, either, if you were tied to me," he said brusquely, determined not to give in. "Leave off, Gemma. I've had all I can tolerate for one day."

Not only had he had all he could tolerate for one day, but the night didn't hold much charm for him either. As she settled with a contented sigh, he grudgingly admitted that she seemed to be taking everything in stride, adjusting even better than he had to their odd and often uncomfortable days and nights.

Which made him wonder . . . Was it possible his wanderer's life might suit her?

But then he remembered being cold, wet, and tired.

How often he slept in the open and got soaked in rain or dusted with snow. How he had no home to call his own. No woman could be happy with a steady diet of such a life.

Despite his conviction, he longed to bed her again. His body never stopped its demands that he claim her. But it wasn't right. He didn't want to bind her to him any more than she was already.

In truth, he dared not bind her more closely. The more he had of her, the more he wanted her. It wasn't fair to her.

He shifted position on the hard bed he had made by choice and now must lie in. How he longed for Gemma's comforting hands on his body.

Instead, he had nothing to look forward to but the nightmare waiting for him just beyond the edge of sleep.

# Chapter 24

*H*e held the little brocade pouch in his shaking hand.
Even though it was invisible, the charmstone within
held him in its thrall. No matter that he had been sent
to master it. It would master him.

*Touch*, it dared him. *Touch.*

He wasn't supposed to look at it. He was supposed
to take it to his father. But he had to see. As he had
carried it through the darkness, it had seemed to call
him through the cloth.

Tempted beyond bearing, he tipped it from the pouch
into his palm.

Pain! Scorching fire!

It seared his flesh, and he jumped in agony, knocking
it to the floor. It rolled into the corner where it smoldered at him, an eerie, unwinking eye. Nausea set his
head spinning, and he feared he would be ill all over
his mother's scrubbed kitchen table.

*Thief*, the Dunlochy Charmstone accused. *You will
burn.*

He did burn. The odor of charred flesh seemed to
permeate the air. Clenching his teeth, he gripped the table
with his good hand, and wished he had never looked.

Gradually the room stopped spinning and he dared
to examine his hand. Not a mark on it.

Nothing.

Except the guilt still burned him, eating him alive . . .

Drummond jerked awake, sweat pouring off him. Sitting up, he wiped his brow and tried to still his pounding heart.

By St. Andrew, the dream again. He had thought it gone seven years ago when he'd seen the charmstone returned to Isabel Maxwell. What had begun for him as a boy had ended once he'd become a man. He had played his part in seeing the stone safely back to one who could use it for good.

Yet on this journey, the dream returned. It hung over him like a vulture, waiting to pick his mind down to bare bone. How he hated it. But it was back with a vengeance, and it was no use trying to escape.

"What is it, dear?" Gemma's soft voice, the unexpected endearment, startled him. Her hands slipped around his waist from behind, tender and comforting. She held him, and he felt her press her warm cheek against his back. "A nightmare?"

"Aye." He leaned back against her, hating his weakness, yet craving her touch.

" 'Tis all gone now. Put it from yer mind." He felt her rise to a kneeling position behind him. She placed a palm on each of his temples and massaged with gentle pressure, as if willing away the nightmare. So small and fragile, those hands, yet fraught with such power. At their last encounter, it had been sexual. Now it was soothing, chasing away his pain.

Beneath her touch, he gradually relaxed. Tension fled. "Lie down." With the softest of voices, she urged him beneath his blanket. "Sleep."

It had been so long since he had let anyone offer him solace. Fixing his gaze on Gemma, he burned the memory of her serene smile into his mind. Closing his eyes, he carried her tranquility with him as he drifted back to sleep.

Drummond awoke to find that the sun had burned off the fog. Gazing over at Gemma, he saw that fine

silver lines of dew outlined every stem and blossom
encircling his slumbering Fair Isle bride. He watched
her sleep, the fine fringe of her lashes brushing her
cheeks. Such peace she had given him in the night.
How he wished they could claim that serenity together
for all time.

But peace was not the order of the day for either
of them. Upon their return to the cot with Ting, the
guard sat glaring, clearly humiliated that they had
eluded him in the night. Good. He had not dared
report their absence to the earl for fear of punishment.
Food would not be forthcoming if those at the castle
thought them gone.

Food did come. Marione brought it, along with
news. The countess was anxious about the children,
who remained under lock and key. The earl was angry,
punishing people left and right. Gemma's uncle
worked in the far wing of the castle with none permitted near him. And there was naught they could do
about any of it.

Drummond persevered in his interviews, and they
passed an anxious day. Iain was grumpy, claiming he
had slept but little at the ancient ruin. Gemma was a
blessing, though, as her presence seemed to make the
work go faster. The women seemed more at ease. As
an experiment, he directed her to ask certain questions, and in her gentle way, she drew the women out.
They finished the list of women at Lerwick in record
time and moved north.

That night, they slept in the Cave of Bressay. They
left the main island in a small boat Gemma borrowed
from its noost, saying it belonged to a friend who
would not mind. As they entered the yawning hole
that gaped in the cliff wall, the vaulted cavern glittered
purple and green. The true color of the rock was un-
clear as reflections from the water shifted and
changed. As they rowed away from the sunlit outer

world, the cavern narrowed, then curved, plunging them into darkness. Gemma lit the lantern.

" 'Tis gloomy in here." Iain gulped, the sound echoing off the cavern walls and still water.

"Aye. So gloomy, no one will think we sleep here this night." Gemma sounded practical and not the least frightened.

"If you say so, but might we choose another place for tomorrow night?" Iain begged.

"If you like. But I'll sleep soundly knowing the earl canna guess where we lodge," she said.

"We're no' gang to sleep on the water, in the boat, are we?" Iain asked with a shudder.

"Nay, Iain. A nice sandy cove lies ahead, with a chink in the rock that lets in light. You can see by it that we're on dry land."

"Good," he muttered. "Because that's about all we'll have."

Drummond didn't mind the cave, but the long walks required to reach their sleeping place each night, the need to choose places where Ting could follow or to take her to the pony herd, then the return to the cot for food and news, drained their strength. It also left less time for his search, and Gemma's uncle must soon be rescued.

Despite the nightmare constraints under which they worked and lived each day, moments of bliss took Drummond by surprise. At the end of the fourth day, as they topped a Shetland hillside, he found a glorious view spread at their feet. Sapphire sky met azure water, and frothy waves crashed on a pristine white beach. Seabirds wheeled on high, their cries mingling with the roll of the surf.

Gemma stood gazing out to sea, her radiant smile illuminated by the sun, her long silver hair whipped by the breeze. Unable to resist, he encircled her shoul-

ders with one arm and pressed her to him. Her inquir-
ing gaze made him want to do more. But more was
not their destiny.

Seeming to sense this, she pointed at a sparkling
burn rimmed with gold flowers that laughed and chattered over rocks on its way to the sea. "Look, marsh
marigolds." She caught his hand and urged him to a
run down the hill. "Let us pick some to make a
crown."

A short time later, with a crown of gold perched on
her silver hair, Gemma raced Iain and Ting along a
sandy spit to their sleeping place for the night, another
cave along the western shore south of Scalloway. She
belonged to this land of azure sea and shining sands.
If only the earl were not driving her away.

As Drummond approached, she greeted him, laughing merrily at Ting's cavorting in the sand.

"Yer crown is crooked." He righted the wreath of
little flowers that had slipped down over her right eye.

"But my kingdom is intact." She caught his hand
and squeezed it. Then, with a meaningful smile she
moved away to light the lantern so they could venture
into the cave.

Was it her way of saying that she relished her last
days on the island? Or did she relish her time with
him, as he did with her? All the more bittersweet
because it must end?

"Ye're doing well," he told her as they ventured
into the cave, the lantern throwing arcs of light around
them. Iain had remained outside, watching a sea hawk
floating on high. Ting had found something green to
munch.

"At what?" She stopped and turned her head,
catching a slanting ray of the lantern so that her blue
eyes glittered like sapphires.

"At talking to the women. I thank you for your
help."

"I would rather be doing well in a different area."

Her voice was plaintive, and she fixed her gaze on the lantern.

"What area is that?"

She turned to look at him. *You,* her eyes said, though her lips remained still.

How he longed to agree. Once more the unfamiliar urge to put down roots assailed him.

He took the lantern and set it on a rock, then kissed her until they were both breathless with desire. He longed to make her promises of stability and caring, but it was futile. He must not promise the impossible. His legacy demanded that he wander the world.

Late the next day, as Drummond sat before the cot, hooves thunked on earth and an approaching vehicle creaked. A pony cart rattled up the track, driven by one of the Scalloway castle stablemen. The countess sat on the seat beside him, wrapped in a blue cloak. Marione's dark curls were visible just behind her.

"Your ladyship, you shouldna be out of bed." Gemma rushed down the track to meet them. "The cart's shaking is surely bad for you." She waved at the stableman, who reined the pony to a halt. Ting trotted up to greet the pony, and the two touched noses, clearly acquainted.

" 'Tis nay great thing," the countess insisted. But she was so rotund, she could scarce bend over to catch Gemma in a hug. She scowled at the earl's guard before turning to Drummond. "Introduce me to yer bridegroom, child," she ordered Gemma. "I've no' met him in the flesh."

"So you have not." Gemma seemed suddenly shy, a blush as subtle as the wild sea pink flooding her cheeks. "My lady, may I present Drummond Graham of Castle Graham."

As he bowed over the lady's hand, Drummond felt the countess assess him with brilliant green eyes. The lady's face looked strained, and her hands protected her huge, increasing belly. Her ankles, encased in knit stockings but visible above heelless slippers, appeared swollen as well.

"Do ye agree to wed wit' my companion, Gemma Sinclair?" she asked.

"If she wishes it," Drummond said, knowing that Gemma did not wish it. Nor should he wish it, for her sake.

"An' you'll remove her from the Shetland Isles?" the countess pressed.

"I've agreed to take her back to Scotland whether she weds with me or no'."

"She wants to wed wi' ye, do ye no', Gemma?" The countess adjusted her cloak.

Gemma's color heightened further. "I'm sure I do not know if—"

" 'Tis settled," the countess interrupted. She thrust out an imperious hand. "Help me down, Jakob."

The stableman jumped to his feet. "My lady, the earl said—"

"I'm taking a wee walk with Gemma and her bride-groom," she barked.

The dull, unhealthy-looking flush suffusing her face worried Drummond. "May I suggest that you remain where you are, my lady, in comfort, and our friend Jakob may take the wee walk in your stead," he intervened.

"Excellent idea," the countess praised, leaning back against the seat. Her color returned to normal. "I pray ye fetch me some cool water from the well, Jakob. I feel a thirst. Marione?"

"Here, my lady." Marione had been sitting in the bed of the cart, knitting.

"Gang wi' him," the countess ordered as the driver climbed from the seat and set out for the well. "Will ye help her down?" she asked Drummond.

Drummond lifted Marione to the ground, which seemed to fluster her. She scuttled away after Jakob.

As soon as the pair were out of earshot, the countess rallied. "Thank ye, Drummond Graham. Ye are the man they all say ye are, thinking of others' needs and comforts first."

"I try, my lady." He wondered what was coming next. Only something of monumental importance would have brought her all the way up the hill, in defiance of her husband's wishes.

"I require yer services, sir," she continued, pushing back a stray strand of hair whipped loose by the breeze.

"Any service I can render to Gemma's friend and protector, I offer with pleasure," he said.

The countess motioned him closer, but she did not speak softly once he was near. "Ye can help me kidnap my children from Scalloway Castle," she said in clear tones.

# Chapter 25

"Kidnap the children?" Gemma echoed the countess's words. "Has it become that bad?"

"Aye. His lordship is near intolerable." The countess's eyes misted. "The children canna be caged like animals. They need fresh air and sun, and he willna let them out, nor let me in to see them. He's like one demented. I ken 'tis a terrible thing I ask of ye, but I dinna ken where else to turn. I canna bear it anymore." She grasped Drummond's arm. "Ye will help me, Drummond Graham, will you no'?"

"I will do anything you deem necessary, your ladyship," he said with a dutiful nod.

"Thank ye." The countess released his arm with a sigh. "And Gemma, the children trust ye. They'll gang wi' ye when ye fetch them. Will ye lend me yer aid?"

Gemma's stomach clenched as she realized she must once more venture into the earl's lair, but for her friend, she would do it. "Aye, my lady. Anything ye ask."

"I perceive you have a plan, your ladyship. What is it?" Drummond cut in, seeming to sense Gemma's trepidation.

"His lordship sleeps in his tiring chamber, adjoining his great bedchamber where the children are," the countess explained. "Both chambers have doors opening into the corridor. I mun take the key from him, though he keeps it in the pouch at his waist even when he sleeps. I canna think how I will get it from him without waking him, but I mun try. I can contrive for him to drink a mild sleeping potion, but 'twill no' make him senseless. He might wake if he feels me at his pouch."

"I will remove the key from the pouch, your ladyship," Drummond said, "if you can ensure our safe entry into the castle. Then Gemma and I will help you move the children elsewhere."

His offer, the grim confidence with which he made it, chilled Gemma.

"I will guard the way to his chamber mysel'." The countess beamed at him with appreciation. "Och, an' we mun leave Robert behind. He'll wish to remain wi' his father, but we will liberate Rowena and the wee ones."

"Where do we take them?" Gemma asked. This question worried her the most.

"The Cheyne house on the voe has been empty for years," the countess said with surety. " 'Tis isolated and I crave a timber dwelling with a tight slate roof. 'Twill suit."

"What is a voe?" Drummond sounded as if he suspected it of being dangerous.

"The word is old Norse," Gemma explained. "It means inlet. 'Twill be a healthful place for her ladyship, away from the odor of the castle garderobes." *And from her power-obsessed husband,* she thought.

"Is the house hidden?" Drummond was clearly not yet satisfied. "Will the earl think to look for us there?"

"No' at first. The house is said to be cursed." The countess put forth the fact grimly. "None go near it, and none agree to reside there."

"You don't believe in this curse?" Drummond leaned forward, as if intrigued by her refusal to accept local beliefs.

"Gemma will tell you the story, but the curse was on the owner of the house, no' the house itsel'. I dinna believe it will harm me or mine, but his lordship's garrison believes it, being local men." The countess flicked a hand with disdain. "I've been in it, and it seemed a fine structure to me. Most o' old man Cheyne's fine furniture still sits there. I had Marione deliver some items for me no' long ago. Things I might need in case of an emergency, such as a comfortable feather bed." She winked at Drummond.

Drummond smiled back at her. "I see. But what if the earl does find you? He's bound to, given time."

"I'm certain he will, but I have some tricks up my sleeve. I havena lived wi' the man for nigh on thirty years for nothing." With a resolute tug, she straightened her lace-trimmed cuffs. "He willna move me back to thc castle. At least no' right away, and by the time he does, I hope ye will be prepared to depart. Ye mun leave this island, Drummond Graham, and take my Gemma wi' you."

"I shall, but I will not desert you in your time of need, my lady. Are you sure you would not like to leave the island as well?"

The countess folded her hands in her lap and contemplated them for a long moment. "I hate to think 'tis come to that, but mayhap it has." Her green eyes were moist. "I shall be more sure what to do once I am delivered o' this child." She held out her hand to him.

Drummond stepped forward and captured it in his own, bending to kiss it. "We'll see you safely through this, my lady. Do not fear. Bring as much food as Iain and I can carry, and we will liberate your children on the morrow."

The countess smiled her thanks, and Gemma saw her press gold coins into Drummond's hand. He tried to refuse them, but she would not hear of it. "For a cart to carry us to the house. Buy one outright, and a pony to pull it."

Gemma let her mistress arrange the time and place that they would all meet the next night, then saw her friend off to the castle with her tiny entourage. But as the cart creaked its way back down the track, she turned to Drummond with urgency. "Drummond, you and Iain will stay at the house with us, will you not?"

He shook his head as he pulled on his leather jerkin, preparing for their day of interviews. "Iain and I will stay outside the house, taking turns on watch."

She studied him, disliking the idea of relinquishing him, even if he was nearby. The possibility of the earl's men attacking him and Iain in the night was too frightening. Yet she supposed his plan was practical. They could more easily detect the approach of marauders if they were outside rather than in.

Always practical. Never feeling. Definitely never sentimental. The least he could have done was express regret. She had so relished sleeping at his side and had hoped he felt the same.

But if he did, he would subjugate the feeling. Emotions impeded duty, and duty came first. Although she admired his control, recognized it as essential in times of danger, it hurt to think he felt no regret.

"We will need to purchase a boat so we can leave the island," she said, following his example and staying with the practical. "Do ye have enough gold left, or should we ask the countess for more?"

He grunted noncommittally as he emptied the last two days of wool from his pack, loading it into a large cloth bag to keep it clean.

"We'll also need oil skins for keeping dry, jugs of fresh water, and things to eat that require no preparation." She ticked off the items on her fingers. "In case we're adrift for several days before we find land."

He did not respond at all this time, instead shoving

the wool into the bag with more force than necessary. When he had filled it, he stowed it in a corner of the cot. "I've arranged for a man to pick up this wool and put it on a ship to Edinburgh," he said. " 'Twill be delivered to the Graham clan's factor and sold. That's how I get my gold for these journeys."

Gemma frowned. "You're no' going to discuss your plans for escape with me, are you?" She tried to strip her voice of all emotion, but accusation wormed its way in anyway.

He came to stand before her, placing his hands on her shoulders. "Gemma, lass, the less ye ken, the better. If the earl manages to capture you, despite my efforts to prevent him, he could force you to tell him all."

Her heart sank. Though he was right, she hated having less than his full trust. It seemed symbolic of their entire relationship. He was wary and private at all times, building reasons like barriers to keep her out. Nor did she like parting with him. Living each day with him, waking to greet him each morn, had been a delight. Now that it must end, she realized she had not fully appreciated their time together. Nor had she appreciated all his skills, it seemed. "Drummond, why did you offer to take the key from the earl's pouch?"

He stepped back, his hands dropping away. "You once asked the trade for which I prepared," he said with icy irony.

"You did not answer at the time."

He picked up the empty pack and hoisted it onto his back. "So it seems I owe you an explanation. My father apprenticed me to the best cutpurse in the south of Scotland. By the time I was ten, I was a master at the trade, if you wish to call it one."

Gemma felt as if the breath had been knocked from her. "You were an innocent child," she gasped.

"A child, aye, but no' so innocent," he said. "My mother quarreled with my father over it, but if she didn't allow my 'education,' he punished her. Sometimes directly, sometimes through me. I knew she felt it was wrong. She explained to me in detail that I must do as my father directed but never use my skill for evil once his influence was out of our lives. But as a child, I couldn't imagine anything ever being different. So I used my skill as he bade me, and sometimes I used it for things I wanted as well. I was a child, with a child's faulty judgment."

Gemma imagined his mother's agony, praying for the day when the father of her child would leave them in peace. "Clearly you never put it to evil use since your father died." She was silent a moment. "But the nightmare plagues you?"

He met her gaze, his eyes hard as emeralds as he stood at the door of the cot. "I hate using my skill in this way, but for you and the countess, I'll venture whatever is required to achieve a just end."

As they found their sleeping place for that night, Gemma grieved for Drummond's past and the sacrifice he would make for the countess. His corrupt father had taught him a skill that had scarred him for life. For the sake of the countess and her children, he would call forth that skill once more.

"Are you not out of practice in your, um, skill?" she asked Drummond as they walked south from Scalloway. "I ask only out of concern for our success," she added.

His lips tightened. "Nimble hands are good for many things besides thieving. For instance, catching trout in a shallow stream without a hook and line. Weaving. Darning."

"You've done weaving and darning?"

"You sound as if they're not a man's tasks."

"Most men do not consider them so, but I would respect one who undertook them anyway."

"If I was interviewing a woman and saw she required assistance, I offered to help. Why not?" He shrugged expressively. " 'Tis all exercise for agile hands."

Her gaze slipped to his hands, and she wished she could invite him to exercise his agility on her, but no good could come of their intimacy. The sooner she believed it, the better.

"Where do we rest tonight?" Iain called from behind, where he walked with Ting, his concern obvious.

Gemma halted a moment to let him catch up. "An ancient, er, hut, dug into the earth and reinforced with timbers." She decided not to mention that it was a burial mound that had stood empty for centuries. Poor Iain was having enough trouble sleeping in their odd abodes.

"A hut, ye say?" Iain snorted. "First an ancient fort, then a cave. Next thing ye know we'll be sleeping in a burial crypt."

Gemma deemed it a good moment to hold her tongue.

The next night, Drummond left their cot openly, setting off up the track toward the moor. The guard followed him, assuming that Iain and Gemma would remain in the cot, asleep.

Drummond then eluded the guard and went to the castle by another route. In his absence, Gemma and Iain had retrieved the pony cart they had purchased. They met just out of sight of the castle, where Iain agreed to wait with the cart. Then Drummond and Gemma approached the earl's lair by the usual stealth and entered through the unfinished wing, away from the wall walk guards.

True to her word, her ladyship awaited them at the first stair. She was fully dressed, with several bundles of clothing for herself and the children assembled. Marione stood at her side.

Removing his boots, Drummond handed them to

Marione and mounted the stair in silent stockinged feet. Gemma removed her slippers and followed. In the corridor above, he advanced toward the earl's tiring chamber, the sixth door to the right, the countess had said.

Despite the cool night, sweat formed on his brow, and ugly thoughts in his mind. His mother's sorrow each time he had set out returned to him.

He didn't want this task. Not then. Not now. Thieves who were caught had their hands struck off, maiming them for life. He had practiced hard at his profession, determined to be good. He had never been caught. Not yet.

He froze as footsteps sounded on the stair above, coming down from the wall walk. Grabbing Gemma, he dragged her into what he thought was a guest chamber, praying it was empty. St. Andrew was with him. No one lay in the four-postered bed.

Ear pressed to the door, he listened. His heart beat louder than the footsteps. Had he missed the guard's retreat back up the stair?

"Is something wrong?" Gemma whispered, seeming to sense his disquiet.

What they were doing was wrong, but it was needed to set other wrongs aright.

"I know ye dinna want to do this," she continued.

An understatement.

"But the children are being abused. 'Tis for the best."

"Hush," he commanded. "I canna hear the guard return."

"If ye wish to change yer mind, we would understand," Gemma persisted.

Was she mad? They had come too far.

"What did yer father make ye steal that troubles you so?"

He snapped his gaze to her face. She was perceptive yet innocent. Despite her association with the earl, she was untutored in the ways of evil. He turned back to the door. "He made me steal the Dunlochy Charmstone," he hissed, his nerves at the breaking point. "He had no idea how to use it, but he wanted it, and I took it for him. Now will ye be silent so I can listen for the guard?"

In the stillness that followed, he wondered what she thought of him. He dared not look at her to find out. At last he heard the footsteps pass again. He waited a full minute, then eased the door open a crack. No one was in the corridor. Was the guard hiding, waiting for him to emerge?

He would have to take the risk. "Wait here. If someone comes, close the door and ye'll no' be seen. When I come out of the earl's tiring chamber, ye can join me."

He moved swiftly, giving her no chance to protest or ask more questions. His candle guttered as he crept into the earl's tiring chamber and placed it on the floor. His lordship lay on the narrow bed, his mouth open, wheezing with each breath.

The countess said he had drunk the potion she added to his wine. He might be roused but would not wake of his own accord. Not unless Drummond touched him wrong.

One hairy leg emerged from the linen sheet, as if his lordship had become overwarm in the cramped chamber, surrounded by his wardrobe. Brass pegs on the wall sported a colorful array of robes, short gowns, furred cloaks, and doublets. The odor of musk hair pomade wafted from an open armoire that bulged with more clothing. The rich goods of a rich man who was spiritually bereft. So bereft, he exploited people, then locked up his children, fearing revenge.

The door at the far end led to the bedchamber and the children, but it was locked with a bolt from the bedchamber side. The countess said she had tried, unsuccessfully, to enter that way.

Drummond moved with fluid slowness, testing each floorboard before transferring his weight. Nothing creaked. He credited the new wing and a new floor for that miracle. At the bedside, he crouched to study the earl and how the pouch lay.

His lordship had thrown back the coverlet and linen sheet from his upper body, again as if uncomfortable from the closeness of the tiny chamber. The belt holding the pouch ran around his middle, tanned leather against the white of his sleeping shirt, the pouch nestled to the right. Unfortunately, he lay on his right side, his left hand protecting the pouch. A difficult position.

With caution, Drummond slipped one hand into the space between the earl's left hand and his right arm. He eased the pouch's closing strap from its loop. Simple, that part. But opening the pouch flap would be harder. If pushed back fully, it would touch the earl's belly, and a touch might wake him. It was impossible to tell how much it would take, and Drummond had no wish to know.

He eased the flap back with his fingertips.

The earl snorted and shifted.

Drummond pulled back, watching the flickering eyelids, his heart in his throat.

*Be prepared to bolt,* his master had taught him. The old Scots cutpurse with a patch over a grisly, empty eye socket had rehearsed him for hours immeasurable. How to approach the unsuspecting prey in a crowd. The seemingly accidental jostle. The swift cut of the knife to lift purse or pouch. Concealing the booty was also important. And how to bolt. Drummond had learned that part especially well.

He stood rigid, his lungs holding air, aching to draw breath.

The earl settled, breathed again rhythmically.

Drummond slowly filled his lungs, then maneuvered forward. The earl had shifted position. He now rested flat on his back, the pouch more exposed. The flap had loosened, falling halfway open against his round belly. Could that glint be the key showing beneath the flap?

With one smooth movement, Drummond touched the glint of metal, closed two fingers on it, and drew the key from the pouch.

Relief bathed him in cool sweat, so unlike the earlier heat that had brought moisture but no relief. Grasping his candle, he pinched it out and glided from the chamber.

Outside the door, Gemma awaited him, her eyes anxious. She started forward as he held up the key. Grasping his hand, she pulled the key from it, but instead of turning to open the door, she carried his hand to her lips. She kissed it with fervor, then pressed it to her cheek, her eyes closed. She understood about the charmstone. She cared for who he was now, not what he'd been and done as a child.

Euphoria lifted him to the heights before he forced himself back to earth. She could not, must not, go beyond caring. He did not wish to hurt her any more than he already had.

In a dozen steps, they reached the door of the main bedchamber where the children slept. Gemma unlocked it with the key.

"I'll wake Rowena but no' Robert," she whispered. "He's like to alert his father."

"I'll send up Marione," Drummond mouthed to her, forming the words without a sound. He turned and glided along the corridor.

At the foot of the stair, the countess hung on Marione's arm, her expression strained in the gloom.

"All is well," he assured her. "Marione, pray help Gemma bring the girls and Gordie."

The countess nodded. "Robert will wish to stay with his father. If he wakes, tell him the girls and the baby mun be wi' me. He loves me enough to stay silent for that. Go, Marione."

As the girl hurried up the stair, Drummond pulled on his boots. A moment later, Rowena descended the stair, carrying Gordie wrapped in a blanket. Marione, behind her, carried a bundle of clothing and a birthing stool. Gemma brought up the rear with a groggy Elizabeth.

"Did Robert wake?" the countess asked. She eyed the birthing stool with distaste, and Marione quickly concealed it with the bundle.

"Robert slept like a stone, Mama," Rowena said.

"Where are we going?" Elizabeth reached for her mother, seeming anxious. "Why is Gemma here? Papa said she'd been bad."

"She's always been my good friend, lamb," the countess said, embracing her. "We're going to stay in the lovely Cheyne house, the one you admired, with the slate roof."

"Will Papa mind?"

"Bless you, lamb. He'll want what's best for me, and being together, you and me, is what I need most," she assured her daughter.

Elizabeth held out her arms to her mother. "Carry me, Mama."

"I canna carry you just now, lamb. Let Drummond Graham do so." Her ladyship backed away, holding her belly, and Gemma hurried to support her.

Drummond stepped forward, and Elizabeth consented to let him carry her.

"Let us hasten." The countess beckoned them forward.

Bearing the child, Drummond led them, prepared to show the countess and her children how to leave their own home by stealth.

# Chapter 26

The long journey in the night tired the countess. Gemma was glad to see her settled at the big timber house on the inlet north of Scalloway. True to her ladyship's assessment, the house seemed nothing out of the ordinary. The man who had lived in it was another story entirely.

Marione made up the bed in the great chamber with fresh linen, and her ladyship collapsed into it, blessing her foresight in sending the featherbed ahead.

Drummond and Iain went outside to scout for signs of human presence and game. Within a short time, Gemma and Marione had the rooms tidied and the food they had brought stored in the larder. Then they helped Rowena and Elizabeth arrange a sleeping chamber together, along with a place for young Gordie. Gemma and Marione occupied another bedchamber together, and the house was full.

Late that night, as Gemma sat with Rowena before a peat fire, she listened to the rain drumming on the stout slate roof overhead and was grateful that they were dry. On her lap, Gordie grabbed Ting's ear and tugged it, delighted to have the pony for a playmate again. Ever tolerant of his curious hands, Ting nuzzled the bairn's toes, making him gurgle with laughter.

Gemma thought with longing of Drummond. He

and Iain would be vigilant in watching the house, yet she worried. Were they damp and uncomfortable in the byre behind the house? Would the earl find them? Would he attack when they least expected it?

One anxious day passed, then another. They saw no sign of the earl or his men, or of anyone besides men on a fishing boat far offshore. Gemma set to work cooking, cleaning, and washing for the countess with Marione's help. She tried not to worry overmuch about her uncle, but she wondered if the cork had arrived and whether Simon Brandie was feeding him enough.

Rowena played with Gordie and Elizabeth, the three taking long walks on the sandy beach and in the meadow near the house. The countess sat in the sunshine and watched them, a smile on her lips as they romped and laughed among the wildflowers. Ting grazed nearby on sweet meadow clover, seeming to enjoy the countess's company. The family seemed to be rediscovering the joy that life with the earl had stifled.

Gemma worked to keep Rowena and Iain apart, yet it was difficult. Drummond kept his brother under strict control if he was present. He often sent him hunting for game or fishing for their supper. But if Drummond left for any reason, Iain found an excuse to seek out Rowena. More than once Gemma stumbled on them stealing a kiss. Though she felt the shrew, she delivered a blistering reprimand to them both each time, but it seemed to do no good.

That afternoon, Gemma stood in the kitchen, scrubbing the cooking pot after noon dinner. Suddenly, she heard the countess shriek. Fearing her mistress's labor had begun, Gemma raced outside. She found her friend shouting at Iain. Rowena stood nearby, sulking. "Iain, be off. You've distressed her ladyship,"

Gemma exploded, furious that he could be so thoughtless. "You should know better, especially at a time like this. Go guard the other side of the house."

"If the earl comes, 'twill be from this direction," Iain pointed out stubbornly.

"Then *we'll* see him and warn you. Don't you think we have eyes? Off with you at once, and no arguments." Her anger increased as the countess buried her face in her hands.

Iain left them, dragging his feet and casting longing glances over his shoulder at Rowena. Gemma thought it best to put Rowena out of harm's way. "My dear, may I ask you to fetch Gordie from his nap? I hear him crying in the bedchamber, and Marione is walking on the beach with Elizabeth."

With a sniff and a wounded expression, Rowena obeyed.

As she departed, the countess looked up, her expression tragic. "Gemma, I dinna like Iain's interest in my daughter. I dinna scorn him for his birth, but they're no' right for each other. You mun believe me."

"I believe you, my lady," Gemma said, meaning it. Each time she saw Rowena and Iain together, a vague uneasiness hovered at the back of her mind. Yet she could not define the reason for it.

After that, the countess watched her daughter like a hawk. She either kept her daughter with her or ensured that she was with Gemma or Marione. A new tension sprang up in the house that Gemma regretted, but she felt it couldn't be helped. The two were not right for each other.

One thing was right, however. The house, the fresh air at the voe, and the solitude suited them all. No signs of the curse feared by the locals plagued them.

"What is the story behind the house?" Drummond asked Gemma on the third day. He had decided he might safely go to Tingwall to continue his sibling search and purchase a few supplies.

Gemma sat making one list of women for him to interview, another list of women who would know others to interview. "When old man Cheyne wasn't so old, he took a young mistress, despite the fact that he had a wife and five children," she began. "The young woman died when she bore Cheyne's stillborn child. After she was buried, her mother marched out here to the house and cursed old Cheyne, saying that he and his would never again thrive. Just as she predicted, one by one, his children died of illness or accidents. His wife died last, and he was left alone in this house beside the sea. He kept to himself for many a year until he, too, died. No one dared to take up residence here or work the croft, so it has been fallow all these years."

"Do you believe the house is cursed?"

She thought a moment. "I did before I came, but having slept here for several nights, I must admit I dinna feel a thing. As the countess said, 'tis not the house that is cursed. 'Twas the man himself, but the folk in these parts believe 'tis both." She grinnèd ruefully. "Perhaps I'm insensitive, that I dinna feel anything."

"Insensitive? You?" Drummond's gaze moved slowly over her body, daring her to be insensitive to the thoughts clearly moving through his mind.

The tingling awareness of him began in her mind and spread to every part of her body. Dizzying, heart-stopping awareness. She wanted to shed her clothes and divest him of his. Here. Now. To touch hard muscle and harder arousal. To look into his passion-glazed eyes and urge him do what he willed. What they both willed. Anything to keep passion alive for as long as she dared.

But she was a coward, she supposed, for she did none of those things. Instead, she handed him the list and forced herself to bid him a cheerful good day. She wished him luck and sincerely hoped he would have it, but he found no trace of another woman who had been seduced by Will Mosley. Not that day or the next.

Late in the afternoon of their fourth day at the voe, the countess's labor pains began. Gemma started up from her knitting, displacing Ting's head from her lap. "Iain has taken Marione with him to fish for our supper," she said to the countess, remembering how Iain had grumbled and Rowena had pouted when she was not allowed to go with them. "I can walk to the nearest croft and ask someone to fetch the midwife from Lerwick. Surely she will come and not tell anyone where we are."

"Nay, 'tis only the beginning an' I want ye wi' me." The countess clutched the arms of her chair, her tense expression signifying a pain. "No need to disturb the folk at the next croft, especially since 'tis so far away. Nor Rowena and Elizabeth."

She gazed out the window at her daughters, who were picking wildflowers near the cliffside with Gordie. Then she leaned her head against the chair's cushioned back and closed her eyes, an expression of patient suffering on her face. "I've borne four live children and miscarried many others. I ken what to expect, as does Marione. The midwife has been instructing her. Why do ye think I brought her wi' me? Ye've seen many foals birthed. We can manage together, we three."

Gemma gripped her own chair arms, wondering if this was wise. If something went wrong and the countess or the child suffered, she would never forgive herself. Yet Marione had spent considerable time with the Scalloway midwife of late. As the countess would not hear of bringing another person to the house, she supposed they must take the risk.

Having exhausted her last argument, Gemma sat in silence for several minutes. Suddenly, the countess flinched. Grimacing, she heaved to her feet. "My water is breakin'." She staggered, and Gemma rushed to support her. "Ye canna bear my weight," her ladyship warned. "I'm too heavy. Let me sit again."

"We must get ye to yer bed," Gemma insisted. "Lean on me and we'll go up."

"I canna mount the stair." The countess pulled at her skirts, which were wet up the back.

"Ting will bear ye. Won't ye, Ting?" Gemma clucked to her pet, who came willingly.

"I'm too heavy for yer sweet pettie."

"She's very strong. She carried Rowena home that time she sprained her ankle on the shore."

"I'm many stone heavier than Rowena."

"But 'tis not as far as Ting took Rowena. I'm sure she can do it. Sit sideways. I'll stand on the other side so ye canna fall."

"Can she bear me up stairs?" the countess asked, still doubtful.

"Ye've seen her go up and down stairs every day, following me about the castle," Gemma assured her. "Let us try. If she seems unable, we will stop. Come stand here, Ting."

The pony obeyed, for she liked the countess, who often caressed and spoiled her by feeding her such favorites as fresh carrots, turnips, and beets. Between the two of them, Gemma and Ting brought the countess to her bedchamber. Gemma stripped away her mistress's wet skirts and settled her between the sheets in a clean night rail.

"Thank ye, Ting." She caressed the pony, who whickered plaintively, as if she understood. "And ye, Gemma. Ye're such a good lass. I'm glad ye've found yer Drummond Graham."

Gemma plumped a pillow and placed it at her back. " 'Tis nothing permanent. 'Tis merely to lend me assistance for a time, as I require. As we both require."

The countess regarded her intently as Gemma gathered up the soiled skirts and tied them in a sheet for later washing. "Nay," she said. "That first time I saw him with ye in the great hall, I knew otherwise. 'Tis why I insist on the wedding. I wish my man still looked at me that way."

Gemma stopped, her hands full of linen. "What way is that?"

"As if he could make love to ye for days on end and never get enough."

Gemma felt blood flame her cheeks. "We have a certain attraction, but that is all. I doubt 'twill last."

To her surprise, the countess scoffed. "Drummond Graham will be true to the woman he chooses. He's no' like my Patrick, overindulged by his father, given everything he desired. Patrick once cared for me, but he's been seduced by power and forgotten about love. Now he cares only for the children I bear him." Her face puckered as another pain assailed her, and she gripped her middle, moaning.

Gemma thrust away the laundry and hastened to her side. "Hold my hand. As tightly as ye like. 'Twill pass soon."

The pain subsided, and the countess collapsed on her pillows once more, releasing Gemma. "Each time I'm brought to bed, I pray 'twill be easier, but 'tis nay such thing." She closed her eyes and squirmed into a more comfortable position.

As Gemma stood up, the countess caught her hand. "I never told ye, but—" She stopped and breathed deeply, as if steadying herself against another pain. It did not come, so she continued. "When yer mother died, I had just miscarried a child and hadna had Robert yet. I raised ye for a year like my own before his lordship sent ye to yer kin." Her voice lowered to a whisper. "I loved ye, Gemma. I still do. As a bairn, ye had the sunniest o' smiles and the brightest disposition. I could hardly bear to give ye up, though ye were none o' my blood. But ye needed me, having lost yer mother, and I kent yer aunt couldna give ye the time I could."

Gemma's heart contracted as she finally understood the full extent of her ties to the countess. "Now I know why I feel ye're like a mother to me." She embraced her friend. "The day I saw ye six years ago, when the earl found me a husband on the main island, I felt a kinship to ye I couldna explain."

"It fulfills my dearest wish to have ye in my life again," the countess confessed, clasping Gemma's hands, a happy smile curving her lips. " 'Twas my idea to find ye a well-to-do husband, though I never meant his lordship to choose one so old."

"Never mind, 'tis over now." Gemma excused her friend. "I'm wondering if ye knew my mother."

"Nay, nay," the countess said hurriedly. "I didna ken her personal-like. She lived in Scalloway village and I heard o' her death. And now, because ye've become like a daughter to me, I wish to see ye wed wi' a good man, though I know I'm like a harpy, drivin' ye mad." She patted Gemma's back as they hugged.

"I thank you, my lady, but do not trouble yourself about it just now. You need not."

"I think about it all the time, my Gemma," the countess assured her. "I'll see ye happy if 'tis the last thing I do. Why does Drummond no' take ye and depart? Ye could write to me of yer wedding rather than wait here for me to give birth."

Feeling guilty to heap more worries on the countess, especially at this time, Gemma told her of her uncle's imminent death. Then, trusting it was for the best, she briefly explained Drummond's personal mission that kept him on the island.

The countess blanched and gasped, seeming unable to get her breath.

"My lady!" Gemma caught her hand, feeling for her pulse. "What is it? Tell me, please."

Instead of speaking, her friend closed her eyes and turned her face away, inhaling in ragged gulps. She labored for several minutes, shaken by spasms of trembling.

Filled with concern, Gemma spread a blanket over her mistress, fearing she was going into shock. She raced for a cup of cool water. "My lady, can you drink this?"

The countess seemed to struggle within herself for a moment. Then she forced in one long breath and expelled it slowly. She repeated the process until the shaking passed. " 'Tis my bloody husband." She ground her teeth, her voice low with desperation. She opened her mouth, as if to speak, then shut it and swallowed, as if swallowing the words she wished to say. "What he willna do to further his own ends. Let me be delivered o' this babe and I'll help ye free yer uncle, Gemma." She evaded Gemma's gaze and fidgeted with the sheet, seeming to sink into weary resignation. "As for the other, I will help ye there as well."

Gemma's heart leaped with hope for Drummond's sake. Yet as she watched over her friend, concerned for her labor, a nameless fear gnawed at her. Questions had plagued her since they had come to the house on the voe. Ugly, uncomfortable questions that she had a feeling were better left unanswered.

She, too, took a long, slow breath and struggled to keep her voice even and calm. "Drummond will not stop until he finds every woman who bore a child by his father. I fear his determination is destroying any chance for his happiness, but it cannot be helped. He feels he must right his father's wrongs."

Another labor pain attacked the countess at that moment, worse than the prior ones. She clutched the sheets and fought for breath.

"Hold my hand, my lady. I'm here for ye. I love ye." Gemma sat on the bed and transferred the countess's grip from the sheets to her. She captured her friend's attention and helped her focus. "The babe is all that's important now. Think only of him."

"He's comin'. I feel him." Three hours later, the countess gripped Gemma's hand like a vice as she pushed to deliver her child. It hurt so, Gemma thought she would scream. The labor had not been long, but the countess's pain had been extreme.

"Och, the head has crowned. Ye're doin' fine, m'lady," Marione crooned, feeling beneath the birthing stool on which the countess strained. "Another push an' he'll be here, I dinna doubt."

Gemma sent up a prayer of thanks that Marione had returned soon after the countess's labor began.

"I mun rest." Her friend sagged against Gemma as the urge to push waned. "I'm sore tired," she whispered. "I wish this laddie were here now."

"You're sure 'tis a lad?"

"Verra sure," the countess affirmed. "I've always been right about my bairns."

"I'm sure he'll be here in a thrice," Gemma encouraged. " 'Tis going so quickly. And think how wonderful 'twill be to hold him in your arms." She had seen enough foals born to know that this labor was progressing rapidly.

"Not quick enough to suit me." The countess tensed, her mouth set in a rigid line. "Here comes the next pain."

"Push, m'lady," Marione admonished. "Give it yer all."

"I gave it all the last time," the countess muttered, gripping Gemma's hand again in preparation. "But I'll try." With a grunt, she applied herself to her task, then suddenly cried out in triumph.

Marione leaned forward as the babe's head, then his shoulders, followed by the rest of his body dropped without warning into her hands. "A big, brawley boy." She chuckled as she moved the child to the toweling on her lap. "As brawley as the day, m'lady. He's big an' perfectly formed." She wiped away the blood and white curdlike substance spotting the tiny body as Gemma and the countess craned their necks to see.

A contented though exhausted smile spread over the countess's face. "My laddie is perfect."

"That he is," Marione agreed as she finished wiping down the child. "Ye should be proud, m'lady. Five brawley children, three of them boys." With expert fingers, she cleansed mucus from the child's ears, nose, and mouth with pads of soft cotton. Then she assessed the still-attached umbilical cord as it pulsed with life.

"Run and tell Rowena and Elizabeth," the countess instructed Gemma. "I want them to hear the good news at once."

As Gemma left the room to obey, she heard the infant begin to snuffle and breathe on his own.

Upon her return, she found that Marione had cut the umbilical cord and was delivering the afterbirth. At long last, the countess was settled in bed, the new babe in her arms.

"I'll fetch some strengthening broth for ye, m'lady. Then ye mun sleep." Marione gathered up the soiled linen. As the door closed behind her, the countess motioned for Gemma to approach the bed.

"Look, love, he's as healthy as an ox. I've decided to name him Malcolm." She glowed with pride as she partially unswaddled the babe to show Gemma his sturdy limbs.

"He's beautiful. He even has a fine head of hair." Gemma smoothed the dark fuzz covering the child's head.

The countess reswaddled the babe and urged him to her breast. She had refused the idea of a wet nurse, insisting that for once she wished to nurse her infant herself. A fortunate choice, as no wet nurse was available just now. "When the earl finds us," she said, "as he most like will, I intend to ask him—"

"Oh, no, my lady. You must not see or speak to him.

We will keep him away." Gemma didn't want to think of what the earl was likely to do to his disobedient wife.

The countess tsked. "I ken a thing or two about him that ye dinna. I can handle him. The worst he'll do is order me back to the castle and shout at me for a few days. He's never laid a hand on me since the day my father swore he would kill him in cold blood if he beat me. An' my father still lives. So"—she paused to draw a breath—"as I was about to say, when he finds me, you and the others will disappear and I will manage him. I will ask him to allow preparation for your wedding. 'Twill take place here."

Gemma knew her friend would be disappointed if she didn't marry Drummond, but she didn't wish to start an argument. She would not contradict this time.

"The preparations will allow us to gather provisions for your escape from the island, ye ken. I've no' forgotten your uncle. He will no' die."

Gemma fell to her knees by the bed, her heart overflowing with gratitude. "My lady, you are goodness itself."

"I'm a moral woman. I hate what my husband does."

"You ask for the wedding so we can use it as cover for the escape?"

"I have asked for the wedding because I saw your attraction to Drummond Graham. And his to you. The idea of escape came later. I hate to part wi' you, Gemma, but 'tis for the best."

"You could go to the king and ask for protection from the earl. For you and your children," she dared suggest.

For the first time, the countess nodded slowly. "If we can manage it, I would go. But to travel so far with so tiny a babe." She gazed down at Malcolm, who suckled at her breast. "I have time to decide. For now, tell me about your bridegroom." She motioned for Gemma to sit on the edge of the bed. "What do ye like about him most?"

Realizing she must humor her mistress, Gemma sat. "I suppose I like the way he sets people at ease and encourages them to confide in him. He draws them out so they forget their cares and become engrossed in telling the tale of their lives."

" 'Tis a rare gift, to listen well. I kent he would be right for ye from the day he arrived. What else?" She wore an intent look, as if she were asking for deeper reasons than curiosity.

Gemma ached inside. She didn't want to discuss the man who was perfection in many ways except in one of the most important, yet the countess insisted. Gemma shifted restlessly. "You heard the stories about him. He's a good man. Isn't that enough?"

"A good man whom ye love for many reasons," the countess insisted. "I want ye to understand them all, so say on."

Gemma flinched as the memory of Drummond's lovemaking rushed to mind. Blood flooded her cheeks. "Is that Gordie crying?" She started up, eager to escape. "He must be awake. I'll go to him."

The countess caught her sleeve. "Let Marione care for Gordie if he's awake. Think, Gemma. What stops ye from loving Drummond Graham?"

Gemma decided that saying it straight out was best. "He decides what's best for me and acts on it. Always. In everything. I resent it." She felt like a fool saying it. It sounded so trivial. Yet it was not trivial to be told what she did and did not wish in her life.

The countess patted her arm. "He's helped so many, he doesna trust people to care for their own needs. He thinks he mun do it for them."

Tears sprang to Gemma's eyes at the countess's sage insight. Unwilling to let her friend see them, she went to Gordie. As she gathered the warm, sniffling child into her arms, pain throbbed through her. She did not want to give up Drummond, but she did not see how she could compromise her ideals.

# Chapter 27

The brilliant sun of morning brought the earl to the voe, accompanied by three of his men. Gemma spotted him at a distance from the countess's chamber window.

"Marione, clean up this soiled linen," the countess ordered upon hearing of her husband's approach. She seized the reins of authority with unexpected vigor. "Gemma, I wish ye to take Malcolm and go at once. All of ye, leave the house and hide where they'll no' find ye. Dinna dare to return until ye see him ride away. Do you ken?"

"But, my lady, Malcolm will become hungry." Gemma disliked the idea of parting the newborn and his mother.

" 'Twill be only a few hours. Take the milk from that stray goat ye found. If Malcolm cries, dip a clean cloth in it and let him suck. Now do not delay."

Drummond shouted for her up the stair, and Gemma realized she had no choice but to obey. Taking the babe, she, Iain, Drummond, Ting, and Marione left by the back door and raced for the voe. They would hide among the rocks until the earl departed.

Gemma sent up a prayer as Drummond helped her down the winding cliff path to the sea. The countess was so sure she could handle the power-obsessed, punishing earl. For all of their sakes, Gemma hoped she was right.

Rowena stood at her mother's chamber window, watching her father approach the house. Mounted on his black stallion, he appeared hale and vibrant, a smile of ugly anticipation on his lips. Rowena trembled, remembering how he had seemed to enjoy slapping her. She would never return to the castle to be his victim once more. She would run away with Iain first.

"Elizabeth, child, hand me that bolster," her mother ordered, as calmly as if she prepared for an enjoyable evening of entertainment. Rowena watched in puzzlement as her mother stuffed the fluffy cushion under her night rail and settled it against her stomach. "Rowena, pray help me pull down my night rail, then cover me with the sheet and coverlet. That's right." She drew the covers up to her armpits. "I wish yer father to believe I'm in labor, ye ken. I want the three of ye to go into yer bedchamber and lock the door. Stay there unless I call ye."

Rowena nodded in mute astonishment, realizing that her mother meant to frighten her father. Like many men, he believed that males should never be present during the birthing process. Not only did such events belong exclusively to the domain of women, but a male presence could be bad luck and have a negative influence on the birth. That, combined with his discomfort about the cursed Cheyne house, would give her mother a distinct advantage.

Seeing the wisdom of her mother's plan, Rowena herded Elizabeth into the bedchamber and settled Gordie for his nap. But after she'd heard her father mount the stair and launch into a tirade, she opened the door. She had to listen. She must know what was said. Creeping across the passage, she stood at the open door, just out of sight.

"You stole the key from beneath my verra nose,"

her father raged. "From beneath my guards' noses. You had help, I'll wager. Ye couldna do it alone."

Rowena trembled. Her father frightened the living wits from her when he behaved like the devil incarnate.

"You think I'm so daftie, I canna manage on my own?" her mother stormed. "I did manage, Patrick, so ye'd best have a care." She issued this warning with seeming relish. "Gordie and the girls are well and shall remain well as long as they're wi' me. Now will ye leave me be?"

Peeking through the open door, Rowena saw her mother ensconced in the great four-postered bed, gripping her bolster-stuffed belly. Her father faced the bed, his back to Rowena, his rigid posture displaying his ire.

"I'll put guards all around the house," he vowed. "I'll see the bastard dead if he comes near my children again."

"No guards, at least no' so I can see them," her mother commanded. "They distress me, an' a woman in my condition shouldna be distressed. Why do ye think I came here in the first place?" She gripped the coverlet, her face turning ashen. "It's a lad, Patrick. Another heir to further secure the earldom. I've always been right about our babes, an' he's comin'. I can feel him." She moaned sharply.

Her father seemed to freeze in place. "Margaret, what are ye sayin'? Are ye—"

"I'm bringin' forth yer son as we speak," her mother hurled at him. "The pains started nigh on an hour ago. Ye come storming in here wi'out so much as a kind word. No consideration whatsoever." She released an agonized groan. "The pain grows worse," she cried. "The babe is nigh."

Her father stumbled backward, mumbling something that might have been an apology, though Rowena couldn't tell. As he turned away from the bed, she saw stark terror written on his face, as if the sight of his wife in labor frightened him to death.

The unexpected desire to giggle seized Rowena. She had never known her mother could playact. Nor had she known that childbirth frightened her father.

"I want Gemma. Will ye send me Gemma, Patrick?" Her mother moaned.

"Tell me where she is an' I will," he growled.

"What do ye mean, where she is?" Her mother reared up into a sitting position, looking alarmed. "I thought she was living in the cot on the moor. Ye have a guard on them. Are ye telling me she isna there? What of Drummond?" She yelped suddenly, as if the news had brought on new pain. Falling back on the pillows, she thrashed her head from side to side, her hands restless on the coverlet. "What have ye done wi' them? Oh, what have ye done?"

"I havena done anything with them." Her father fidgeted, clearly distressed. "They've all disappeared, including the damned pony."

"If I hear ye've hurt my Gemma . . ." her mother cried.

"She isna yer Gemma."

"She's like a daughter to me and well ye know it. She's more my Gemma out of love o' my heart than she is yers. If I hear ye've hurt a hair on her head, Patrick. If ye do, 'twill be on your immortal soul. Oh, God . . ." She shrieked and gripped her belly, her face twisted with pain.

Her father backed closer to the door. Rowena retreated into her bedchamber and pulled the door to all but a crack.

"I've no' hurt her." Her father sounded defensive. "I didna do a thing to her."

"But ye tried," her mother accused. "I heard what ye did. Ye tried to kill her. Shame on ye, Patrick Stewart. God will punish ye, an' me for being yer wife."

"I had to do something. I didna trust her," he snapped. "She tried to murder a man just days ago."

"She did nay such thing," her mother barked. "Ye think I'm a fool, Patrick Stewart, to believe yer twaddle. But I ken what yer doing, and I'll no' stand by and let ye blacken yer soul."

At her bold words, he roared with rage.

Rowena cringed, all desire to giggle gone. She knew all too well the deadly anger smoldering in his eyes, as he frequently turned it on her. Behind her, she sensed Elizabeth frozen with fear on the bed.

"Whatever ye think, ye're to keep yer moue shut about it or suffer the consequences," the earl shouted. "Do ye ken I could be ruined, my heirs murdered?"

"The king doesna want to murder yer heirs, Patrick," her mother retorted. "If he ever takes action against ye, he'll want *yer* hide, for flaunting his authority."

"Even if Gemma were wi' ye, 'twould not save my Gordie from that bastard madman, Graham," her father exploded, using her words as a torch to light his wrath.

"*Yer* Gordie," she shot back. "As if he werena mine as well. As if I would let anyone near him who would do him harm. I would give my life for my children, so ye can trust my judgment. But *yer* judgment is failin' ye, Patrick." She turned her face away from him. "Ye're no' the man I wed all those years ago."

"Nay? That lad was a soft-headed romantic who could achieve nothing." He snarled from across the chamber. "Ye love havin' a grand castle to live in as much as I. Ye love having servants an' fine gowns. Who gave ye all yer fine geegaws, eh?" He gestured at her lace-trimmed night rail.

Rowena imagined the tears that must be pooling in her mother's eyes.

"I loved ye as ye were, Patrick," she said. "Better than any o' those things."

"And ye dinna love me anymore? Is that what ye're trying to say, woman? I'm cut to the quick. See me bleed?"

He didn't care anymore. No feelings touched him. Only his lofty ambitions, his need to wield absolute power over his domain. He didn't love her or Elizabeth, nor even Robert and Gordie. They were important only for what they represented as part of his dynasty.

"If ye dinna care what I think or feel, at least respect my wish to be safely delivered o' this child. Here. In peace. Wi' Gemma." Her mother staunchly refused to concede the point.

Rowena didn't think she could be so brave in the face of her father's anger. Admiring her mother, she held her breath, awaiting his reply.

Her father cursed, but he sounded thoroughly cowed. "Who's going to birth this babe?" he demanded.

"Marione, ye great gawking idiot. If ye'd gang away, I could get on wi' it. Now get on wi' ye, an' dinna come back until the morrow."

He seemed to hesitate, and her mother screamed in sudden agony.

Her father bolted from the chamber, and Rowena barely had time to pull her door shut. As it closed, she glimpsed her father, his head drooping, signifying defeat.

"Ye can stay in the house," he called from the passage.

Rowena's hopes rose.

"I willna post guards within yer sight, but there will be guards," he added, "an' I want to see ye delivered of a bonnie man child on the morrow, and I want to see him healthy, or that Marione is a dead woman."

For a moment, she heard nothing. Rowena hung on to the door handle, praying. *Do not think to look for me. Or for Elizabeth or Gordie.*

He stomped down the stair. The front door slammed so hard, the entire house shuddered.

Tears of fear and anger spilled down Rowena's cheeks as she sank onto the bed beside Elizabeth. Her little sister regarded her with wide, frightened eyes. Rowena gathered her into a hug, knowing her sister did not understand all that had taken place. But she would be frightened just the same.

Their father had altered irrevocably over the years, becoming harsh and cruel. He treated her mother as if she were little more than a child-bearing vessel. He would wed Rowena to a barbarian if she didn't escape, and she would end just like her mother, tied to a monster. Though he seemed to love Elizabeth, who knew what decisions he would make about her future if she could bring him power or land that he desired?

" 'Tis all right," she reassured Elizabeth, who clung to her. "Mama has managed Papa. We'll stay here for a while and all will be well." But she wept for herself, and she wept for her mother. They had both lost any semblance of security or peace in their lives.

Drummond had found a concealed vantage point from which to watch the house during the earl's visit. After less than an hour, he saw the man emerge and ride away. As the countess did not accompany him, he assumed that all must be well. But guards had probably been set.

To be sure, he circled far and climbed the side of the hill looking down on the approach to the house. Sure enough, three men sat around a fire, roasting a duck. Creeping closer, using the many rock outcroppings for cover, Drummond watched.

"What the devil are we doin' here, eh?" one grumbled. His words drifted to Drummond on the sea breeze, despite the distance. "Guardin' a woman who's birthin' a babe. Seems a waste to me. She's as like to run away as I am to fly off this island."

"I dinna ken, but ye'll no' catch me near that house." The second one shuddered. "My grandda said a ghost walks its chambers and moans in the night."

" 'Tis no' a ghost," the third argued. "My grandam says strange accidents happen. Her ladyship is like to fall down the stair and break her neck. 'Twas what happened to Cheyne's wife. Snapped it clean in two."

"Well, I'll sit here, fine, but no' closer," the second repeated.

"Here is good enow," the first affirmed. He appeared to be their commander. "His lordship said to let no one pass. Nay trouble wi' that."

Drummond left them, melting away up the hill and over the crest. The guards, believing they guarded no more than a woman laboring to bring forth a child, would give him no trouble. He chuckled as he realized the men were afraid to be within sight of the house itself. He could come and go as he pleased.

"I bought us some time," the countess said with pride to Drummond as Gemma placed Malcolm in her arms. Recognizing his mother's scent at once, the babe wailed and butted at her breast.

"Dinna go. We mun talk, Graham." The countess bid Gemma raise the sheet so she could nurse the babe. Drummond politely moved to the window and turned his back to give her privacy.

"When will his lordship return?" he asked once he judged them settled.

"On the morrow. I think it safe for Gemma to be here, but no' the rest o' ye. No' even Marione. I will ask him to let the pair o' ye wed here at the house, then order all manner of odd provisions, including supplies ye'll need for yer escape. He'll think it the whim o' a nursing woman and grant them."

"Very canny, my lady," Drummond praised. " 'Twill fulfill most of our needs. I will walk to Lerwick on the morrow to see to the rest."

"In a few days, when we've amassed what we need, I will return to the castle and check on yer uncle, Gemma."

Drummond heard the strain in her voice. "Will you come with us when we depart, my lady? I would convey you to the king's court."

He heard her sigh from behind the linen screen. "I would like to go, but my babe is so small. I canna think he would survive such a journey."

# Chapter 28

Gemma spied the earl the next day, riding across the meadow toward the house. The countess accepted his approach with a calm that did her credit.

"Gemma, I pray ye, brush out my hair on my shoulders. His lordship likes it that way. Rowena, can ye find my best night rail? 'Tis in that bundle o' linens I brought. Marione, off wi' ye, lass. Tell Drummond and Iain ye're to hide for an hour or two. Elizabeth, my pettie, sit here on the bed so yer papa can see ye. Rowena, fetch Gordie an' let yer sister hold him. 'Twill sweeten yer father's temper to see them, but ye had best remain in yer chamber."

Rowena quit the chamber, seeming all too happy to avoid her father.

A short time later, festooned in white lace, holding little Malcolm, the countess pinched her cheeks, as if she wished to look her best for the meeting. "Gemma, ye may listen, but keep out o' sight unless his lordship asks for ye," she warned. "If he does, show yerself and agree to anything he says. Dinna fear, no matter what 'tis. Ye'll soon be beyond his reach." She sighed as she gazed at her infant son, who regarded her with serious, wide blue eyes. "Ye have yer father's eyes, laddie. I hope ye grow to be generous and loving, as he once was. A pity he changed."

Gemma agreed, though she found it difficult to be-

lieve that the earl had ever been generous and loving.
She entered the bedchamber with Rowena and waited
for the earl to arrive.

"Where's my new son?" the earl bellowed, racing
up the stair.

As he entered the countess's chamber, Gemma
slipped into the passage, taking a position where she
could see without being seen.

"A brawley laddie, as healthy as they come," his
lordship crowed in triumph, lifting the child in his
arms as expertly as if he were accustomed to handling
babes daily. "Ye've done me proud, Maggie. Now we
have three laddies to keep the Stewart line intact."
His face ruddy with delight, he displayed the babe to
Elizabeth. "Look, Elizabeth," he chortled. "Look at
yer new little brother."

"I like him, fine, but he canna kiss yer cheek like I
can." Elizabeth giggled, gazing coyly at her father.

The earl boomed with laughter and offered his
cheek to be kissed. "There's my Elizabeth. Ye ken
what's what." She pecked his cheek, and he dropped
a kiss on the top of her head and ruffled Gordie's hair
with his free hand.

The countess beamed at him from the confines of
her four-postered bed, as if she'd never been happier.
Gemma marveled at the contrast between her expression now and her prior grim determination. Rowena
had told her of her mother's skill yesterday with play-
acting, but seeing it still surprised Gemma.

The earl had altered as well. Seeing his new son
seemed to soften him, at least for the moment.

"If yer so pleased, Patrick, ye might give me a kiss."
The countess beckoned with a lace-clad arm, her smile
warm and welcoming.

He moved to her side, babe in his arms. Sitting on
the edge of the bed, he bussed her loudly on the cheek.

"And a boon?" She lowered her gaze demurely as
she stroked the velvet trim on his doublet.

"Aye, a boon," he agreed with enthusiasm, clearly satisfied with what she had done for him. "Whatever ye name. Ye've earned it."

Margaret patted his cheek. "That's my Patrick. Ever generous, ye've been to me. I want my brass bathtub. Right there." She pointed to the hearth. "So I can bathe afore the fire."

"Ye're coming back to Scalloway," he stated, his eyebrows drawing together in the beginning of a frown.

"Oh, aye," she agreed placidly. "In a few days, when I'm up an' about again. But afore then, I crave a bath." She patted his arm and pouted. "Please, Patrick. My tub?"

"Oh, verra well," he conceded. "I suppose ye crave yer favorite dinner, too."

The countess clapped her hands like an excited child. "Would ye send it to me? Fresh young leg o' lamb? An' some jugs of fresh springwater from the well by the castle. The water here doesna taste near so sweet."

"Come back to the castle an' I wouldna have to send to ye," he complained.

"A woman who has just given birth canna be up and about," she told him, tapping his cheek with a saucy smile. "A few days, lovie. Nay more."

"Oh, verra well. What else?"

"A berry tart," she said, a dreamy look in her eyes. "Will ye send me Simon Brandie, Patrick? To make a fresh tart, right here? I crave berry tart hot from the oven like I never craved it before."

He agreed grudgingly, and Gemma recognized that this was a ritual. She recalled something similar after Gordie's birth. Each time the countess brought forth a live, healthy child, the earl apparently expected to indulge her.

Silently, she blessed her ladyship's cannyness. She had deliberately made up a reason to summon Simon

Brandie, the cook. The man would bring news of her uncle.

"One more thing, lovie," the countess coaxed, kissing her finger and tapping her husband's nose with it. "Ye've already granted me this boon, in a sense, so 'twill no' be hard for ye."

"If I've already granted it, then 'twill be an easy pleasure to grant it again."

He grinned at her, and for a moment Gemma glimpsed the young man with whom her mistress had fallen in love. A generous, congenial, laughing boy who gave freely to those near him.

The countess caressed his cheek. "Thank ye, pettie. All I want is for Gemma to wed her laddie a wee bit sooner than we planned. This comin' Sunday morn would suit fine."

Only four days away. From her place in the outer chamber, Gemma held her breath, awaiting the earl's reply.

The earl seemed unsurprised by the request. Rising, he faced the door. "Get in here, Gemma Sinclair," he boomed. "I ken ye're eavesdroppin' in the passage. Her ladyship requires ye."

With a start, Gemma leaped into the chamber and skidded to a halt, impaled on his imposing stare.

"How did ye get the wench away from my guard on the moor? He never saw her depart, yet she disappeared. An' now she reappears here." He narrowed his eyes to suspicious slits as he stared at his wife.

The countess smiled up at him, all innocent guile. "I sent for her, naturally. We love each other, and she came at once, to help me wi' the babe. Did ye no', Gemma?"

Gemma nodded, remembering the countess's warning to agree with everything she said.

The earl swore, as if he sensed a lie but knew he couldn't force his wife to admit it. "Where the devil is Drummond Graham? Here as well?" He scanned the chamber, as if expecting Drummond to pop out of the woodwork.

The countess tilted her head with an air of uncertainty. "I think he's in Tingwall."

"He's been spotted in Tingwall," the earl agreed. "Does he agree to wed?"

"If ye'll let me send for him, we'll be sure, but the last he an' Gemma spoke, he was eager for it," the countess said with tranquil conviction. " 'Tis my dearest wish to see her happy. The ceremony should be in the parish church in Lerwick, with a modest feast after held"—she paused, as if thinking it through—"here. Why not? Since they are no' castle folk, 'tis more fitting, and the view is lovely. The guests will all be servants, so they can feast outside at trestle tables set on the grass, whilst we take a meal inside."

Neither of them considered the local superstition about the curse on the house, nor did they consult Gemma's wishes. She stood in silence, fuming. She had to remind herself that the countess acted a part and must be excused, but the earl did not. Such high-handedness came naturally to him.

"If ye can make Graham comply, I agree on one condition," the earl said to his wife's proposal. "They mun live at the castle and serve ye. Drummond can be yer bodyguard, Gemma, yer handmaiden. See that Drummond agrees. In writing."

He stared at Gemma, and she winced inwardly. If Drummond agreed to serve the countess, he essentially served the earl and could not continue to be the king's man. One could not serve two masters.

Cunning move. His scheme was more effective than killing them both, for that could bring down the king's wrath and suspicion. This would convince the king that all was well under the earl's rule. If Drummond wrote to the king that he wished to wed and live in the realm of the very man he'd been sent to investigate, it had to be so.

The earl tapped one toe, and Gemma realized he was waiting for her response. Her stomach jumped with nerves, but she steeled herself to reply. "I know Drummond will sign whatever paper you prepare on the day of the nuptials, my lord," she said. "May we proceed with preparations? We wish to be wed at once."

The earl's questioning gaze bored a hole into her soul. He sensed a lie behind her statement that Drummond would agree, but he could not know for certain. She straightened her back and willed him to believe her.

"Very well. Sunday, as ye say," he snapped, his patience worn thin. "In three days, I expect ye back at the castle, Margaret." Having delivered the order with the rapid fire of a pistol, he dropped the newborn infant into his wife's arms and strode from the chamber.

Gemma raced to the window. Below, she saw him mount Black Jupiter and race away, the wind whipping his hair.

She felt as if the devil had sealed her fate. He, the master liar, could tell she lied. Now she must take desperate measures. She and Drummond must assemble their resources, rescue her uncle, and depart the island before they were bound to the earl for all time.

Only four days remained before Gemma's wedding. Simon Brandie came to the house to make berry tart and brought news. The cork had arrived and her uncle was halfway through his work with it. Though the cook didn't know where or how it was being used, everyone knew Lawrence Bruce had sent for it and gloated over its arrival. Gemma's uncle would be killed as soon as his work was done.

A knot of tension ached at the base of Gemma's neck as she went about the preparations for her nuptials, pretending nothing was wrong. She didn't want to select food and drink for the feast after the ceremony, or choose the prayers and music for the church service. She wanted to assemble fresh water for their journey, in case they missed land and were adrift for a time. She wanted to procure the boat and begin to load it.

Instead, she must act like an eager bride. If she didn't do her part, the countess rose from her childbed to do things for her, wearing herself out. So Gemma threw her energy into organizing a wedding that would never take place.

Yet her heart was in her throat as she stood in a magnificent kirtle and bodice that had belonged to the countess. The seamstress fussed around her, checking the alterations of the blue silk that frothed with Flemish lace.

How she wished she truly had nothing on her mind save being united with Drummond. Instead, she must face the reality that they would never wed. She must worry whether they could successfully free her uncle and escape. She must guard against any hint of their plans becoming known.

"Ye mun take the gown wi' ye," the countess instructed after the seamstress had departed. She was out of bed today. It was sooner than Marione advised, but she said she felt fit. "Wear it at yer church wedding in Scotland."

*There will be no wedding,* Gemma thought, unwilling to say the words aloud. The preparations over which she labored were naught but a screen, meant to hide their true purpose. No matter what she wished, she could not change it.

"I ken what ye're thinkin'." The countess hugged her. "But dinna give up before all hope is gone. Experience changes people. Sometimes for the worse, but sometimes for the better. Keep yer faith.''

Gemma leaned against her friend, appreciating her strength.

"Has Drummond found a boat?" the countess continued.

"Nay, my lady. He's still searching for his sibling," Gemma admitted.

"Tell him to cease at once and obtain a boat for ye."

"I'm sure he'll find one." Gemma turned back to the looking glass that had been brought from the castle, pretending to admire the blue silk. "This is his last chance to find the woman. He feels he must spend every moment possible searching for her." Gemma had felt anxious about this very subject, but Drummond had refused to give up.

The countess raised a hand, signifying that she understood. "Tell him I know who the woman is. He need seek no more."

Gemma struggled for a moment, unable to take this in. A thousand questions clamored in her mind to be asked. "You know who she is? Are you certain? Is there a child? Are they in need?"

"She *was* seduced by William Mosley." The countess rearranged the lace trim on the skirt, then fell back to study the effect. "She is not in need. I've seen to that. There is a child, and I will arrange for Drummond to meet them both, mother and daughter, before he leaves the isle." She pursed her lips as she regarded Gemma. "Ye need something at the throat. I will give ye a pearl necklace. 'Twill be just the thing."

Gemma's eyes misted. "Thank you, my lady. Yer kindness overwhelms me." She hesitated.

The countess smiled. "But ye wish to know who this woman is and where she can be found."

"Drummond would be relieved to know where to find her," Gemma admitted.

The countess shook her head. "One thing at a time, lamb. Ye have preparations to make for a perilous journey. You need oil cloth to keep off rain, rope, food, blankets, containers for bailing. We mun devise reasons why we need these items for the wedding feast and have them brought here in the next days. And Drummond must procure a goodly sized boat. No' too large, but large enough to take ye to the mainland. Tell him I will see that he meets this woman. But for now, we have other work. Only three full days remain."

Gemma slipped away early that evening to the sea cave where Drummond and Iain were staying. Since the earl had found the countess, they no longer needed to guard the house. Instead, they amassed supplies for their escape. In the sheltered cove, hidden from prying eyes, Gemma settled on a sun-warmed rock, with Drummond on one opposite.

"I've found your other sibling," she said.

He leaned forward, his startling green eyes both eager and skeptical. "You managed that while confined to the house?"

"How I managed it is not important. The woman and her daughter are found."

"You're sure she's the one?"

"The countess assures me she is. She was mistress of the castle at the time of your father's visit. She would know if a woman in her household became with child."

"Do they require assistance?"

Apprehension grew in the pit of Gemma's stomach as he studied her. What if the countess was mistaken? "She says they are not in need of assistance, but you will meet them both."

"When?"

"In the next day or so. But just now, she wishes you to obtain the boat as quickly as may be."

"You say they need no assistance, but did the woman wed?"

"I dinna ken, Drummond." Now that she had shared the few facts she knew, they seemed pitifully meager to her as well. Yet she trusted the countess.

"I need to know if she's happy," he insisted. "I canna leave the island if I'm no' sure. I wish to speak to her myself."

Pain stabbed Gemma at this reminder of how he needed to control situations, unable to trust others to handle them. Yet he understood what mattered, putting the woman's happiness first. "The countess would not share more details."

"Are you certain she speaks the truth?" he demanded more harshly, becoming annoyed. "She's not just trying to take care of the problem so you can depart?"

Gemma's certainty wavered. Could this be the countess's tactic? Was she convinced they would never find the woman? Yet Gemma refused to believe this of her friend. "I do not think so. Please, Drummond," she pleaded, "will you just find us a boat?"

"I already have." His eyes flashed with irritation.

She felt immediately guilty. For doubting him. For nagging him. But she resented his not telling her sooner. "May I see it?"

As he stood slowly, the muscled movement of his calves and thighs beneath taut fabric transfixed her. She wanted to stare at him all day, because soon she might never seen him again.

He held out a hand. "Come, then."

She took it, let him pull her to her feet. But despite his strong grip, she felt alone, as if she were slipping from the rock in Scalloway bay into icy waters, buffeted by fierce storms.

He led her to where jagged rocks sprouted from the rocky shingle. A moderate-sized sixern sat concealed behind the barrier. "Iain and I hauled it up here to keep it from floating away. We'll have to turn it over if it rains." He hopped in, stepping over the thafts, chasing away a gull that perched on the bow. "It has a mast, a tiller, and six oars, though only four will be used. One each for me, you, Iain, and your uncle. Ting doesn't count since she cannot row."

"You mean to bring Ting?" Despite her resolution to stay at arm's length, appreciation drove her to him. She clambered over the side of the boat and flung her arms around his neck in an embrace that nearly unbalanced him. "Just when you've been so difficult, you surprise me with your generosity."

The expression on his face was unfathomable, but not his action. He bent to kiss her, demonstrating with lips and hands what his words did not. They said he wanted her, and Gemma wanted to abandon all scruples and revel in his touch. She wanted the wedding for which they prepared.

Yet what had seemed so simple when she had first given herself to him had become impossibly complicated. It would never work.

Still, she gripped his shoulders, kissing him back. She wished she could forget everything save the exhilaration found in his sleek, masculine grace.

But she had made her decision. She must say farewell to such things.

As he began to raise her skirts, a prelude to lovemaking, she broke from his embrace and moved away. "Where will you keep the boat?" she asked, stripping all emotion from her voice.

"Here." He indicated the cove. " 'Twill lessen the ease of pursuit if we keep it where no other boats are kept." He reached for her again.

She climbed out of the boat, nearly falling in her haste, engulfed by her sorrow. "I must return to the countess. She does not know I slipped out."

"Come back later."

"I'm needed."

In his eyes, she read agreement, and the foundation of her resistance weakened.

*Stand firm and apart,* she warned herself.

He did not try to touch her again. "Tell me when you have supplies assembled. Iain and I will fetch them and pack them in the boat." He stepped over the side onto the sand.

"I will. The countess is having me order the things we need for the journey, making up excuses why they are needed for the wedding, then having me hide them among the other goods gathered for the feast so they go unnoticed."

Pain lanced her as she spoke. When she left the island, she would leave behind not only the land of her birth, but the ties that bound her to Drummond.

Her marriage had been an idyllic adventure that couldn't last in the harsh light of reality.

# *Chapter 29*

D rummond felt uneasy about the many forces at work on the island.

The countess and her wedding plans.

The earl complying for his own reasons, scheming to catch them in his snare.

Lawrence Bruce driving Gemma's uncle at his work.

Iain and Rowena plotting to slip away so they could be alone together.

Gemma moving away from his touch.

The other problems he could deal with, but this last had cut him to the quick. He knew what it meant. Gemma agreed with his decision. He had convinced her that his manner of living was unsuitable for her.

He must help her find some solid farmer or tradesman instead. A man who would give her a home, love, stability, things a woman required.

Except he couldn't see Gemma with a tradesman or a farmer, a plodding fellow, uninspiring and drab. Perhaps an expert craftsman, skilled with his hands and coveted for his abilities. Could she be happy with that?

*He* couldn't. The idea of another man touching her filled him with outrage. He wanted her for himself.

Visions of Gemma formed in his mind's eye. Gemma walking among the wild ponies on a night of thunder magic. Gemma running races with Iain and

Ting on the sandy beach, her silver hair flying, her feet nimble. Gemma smiling up at him, laughter on her lips and in her eyes, a flower crown hanging over one eye.

That night on the moor, she had been his alabaster goddess of the island, magnificent in her nakedness. The midnight sun had illuminated each of her tender curves. Must he vow never to experience her quick-silver beauty again?

The closer they came to the day of the wedding, the more he was tempted by the thought of going through with the ceremony. If only he could forget his never-ending task.

But if he'd ever made a noble choice, now was the time to do so. With her sorrowful birth and her bad first marriage, Gemma needed stability and love. A husband at her side, steadfast in his devotion. He must help her find it, see her safely settled, and go his way.

How he wished he could be that husband. He wanted to hurl away his commitments and do as he damn well pleased, not be bound by his father's choices made years ago.

Yet even if he managed to provide the one thing Gemma needed, he had none of the other. He knew nothing of loving with an open heart. He must stay with choices suitable to his abilities. Control must rule.

He returned to the problems at hand, saddened but resolved. Lawrence Bruce had found the cork to line the secret chamber more quickly than expected. The man looked forward to completion of the chamber so he might destroy the master mason who had made it.

This bloodthirsty attitude raised Drummond's ire, and he anticipated thwarting it. With pleasure, he would turn evil aside and blow it away like dust on the wind.

In three more nights, he would spirit Andrew Crawford away from Scalloway Castle. He would hoist the sail on their tiny vessel, and he, Iain, Gemma, and

Crawford would sail away from the Shetland Isles, never to return.

But before he went, he would meet the woman his father had seduced, as well as a new half sibling. Wondering when the countess would arrange it, Drummond counted his remaining gold coins. Whether the woman had wed or no, he would help her. Then he could depart with a clear conscience. His work in the Shetland Islands would truly be done.

On the day before his wedding, Drummond went with Iain to the hill above Scalloway Castle to watch the countess return to her husband. Though the earl had agreed to let the wedding take place at the Cheyne house, he had insisted that his wife return to the castle beforehand.

The pony cart bearing her, Gordie, the new babe, Rowena, and Elizabeth drew up before the main gates at midday. The earl emerged in person to give his new son a triumphant welcome. Rowena avoided her father, using Gordie and Elizabeth like shields as they alighted from the cart.

Iain frowned. "She's sore distressed to return to the castle. I pray her father doesna slap her again."

"I pray so, too." Drummond wished he could remove both Rowena and the countess from the earl's control, but he didn't see how he could if the countess didn't agree.

"When are we to meet this woman our exalted father seduced?" Iain asked.

Drummond had been wondering the same thing. "The countess didna say. There's little time left."

"Is Gemma still at the house on the voe?"

"Aye, with Marione. The plan is for them to walk to Lerwick on the morrow for the ceremony, but by then . . ." Drummond did not speak aloud of their plans. It seemed bad luck to do so and he had sworn

Iain to silence. It would take so little to upset the delicate balance they had prepared.

"I'll wager ye canna wait to make her yers. I envy ye." Iain complied with one agreement while breaking another. Drummond had asked him not to speak of Gemma, but his brother refused to listen.

" 'Tis a heavy responsibility to wed," he muttered, deliberately missing Iain's point.

" 'Tis a joy to love a woman."

"Not if you fall in love with a different one every five minutes."

"That's unfair," Iain protested, recognizing the veiled criticism and looking aggrieved. "Celia's father felt she was too young for marriage. Sarah really was too young. I ken that now. Dorothea was pledged to another, though she didna love him. And Marta—"

"Marta *was* wed to another," Drummond finished for him. "You had no business falling in love with her."

"How was I to ken that when we met? Once I did, I set her free, and I was also free to seek love elsewhere," Iain explained matter-of-factly. "Ye condemn me, but you ken little of how to love. Only how to possess."

Drummond *did* want to possess Gemma. It seemed he'd wanted her from the moment they'd met. How it had happened so quickly, he didn't understand, but it didn't matter. It was over between them. Done. "Ye'll have to say good-bye to Rowena tonight," he warned Iain, trying to be gentle.

"I refuse to believe it."

Typical of Iain. To hope for something that was completely hopeless, going on faith alone. For the first time, Drummond sympathized with the pain Iain must have felt at losing the women he loved over and over, though he still couldn't understand his brother's willingness to repeat the experience.

At the same time, he remembered that he wasn't in the same danger as Iain, since he wasn't in love. Iain's daft preoccupation with the object of his affection couldn't begin to resemble how he felt about Gemma. Nor could Drummond consider harboring such feelings for more than one woman in a lifetime. It was too excruciating, this need to make her his.

Drummond heard nothing more about meeting the woman his father had seduced and his half sibling. The countess seemed to have forgotten. He hated to leave without fulfilling his reason for coming to the islands, yet he dared not delay. Andrew Crawford's life would be forfeit if he did.

In the middle of the night, their last night in the islands, Drummond woke Iain, as planned, and the two stowed their blankets in the sixern. They crossed the island and, evading the wall walk guards, entered the castle through the partially completed wing. Leaving Iain in the screens passage as lookout, Drummond went to the kitchens.

Embers glowed on the two hearths of the cavernous stone chamber as he entered in silence. From the pouch at his waist, he drew Gemma's key to the storage chamber where Andrew Crawford was locked. Inserting it into the lock, he twisted it.

The key turned noiselessly, showing that the lock was well oiled. He stepped inside and closed the door. As he lacked a candle or lantern, he saw nothing in the pitch-black chamber, yet he sensed something amiss. Despite his quiet entry, Andrew should be stirring. Instead, utter silence greeted him. He felt alone in the tiny room.

Minutes later, Drummond ascertained what he had suspected. A soft whisper, followed by a groping inspection, told him the chamber held naught save sacks of oats and bere. Andrew was not there.

Trepidation shot through Drummond as he spun on

his heel. Back in the great hall, he found Iain gone from his post. Damn the lad, he'd gone to find Rowena.

Knowing her chamber was near the countess's, Drummond raced up stairs two at a time. As he turned down the corridor, he bumped into Gemma, followed by Ting.

Gemma wore a traveling pack for their voyage and carried a lantern. Ting had a pack strapped to her back.

"Why are you here?" he demanded in a whisper. "You were to wait at the boat." Andrew Crawford's absence from his cell had disturbed him. This change in plans made things worse.

Grasping his arm, Gemma opened a door and pulled him into a lavishly furnished antechamber. "The countess told me that you would meet the woman and your sibling tonight." She closed the door. "I thought you might need support, so I am here."

Loyal, caring Gemma had come to support him. Though the timing was rotten, he needed to meet the woman and his sister. "Where is she, then? We have little time."

Instead of leading the way, Gemma pulled a letter from the purse at her waist and thrust it into his hand.

"This is not a good moment for reading letters." He thrust it back to her. "We must—"

"Pray look at it.'Tis from your father. Here is his signature." She unfolded the letter and pointed to the place.

Drummond stared in surprise at his father's familiar scrawl, illuminated by the lantern Gemma held. "Why do you have his letter?"

" 'Tis a love letter. He wrote it to—" She broke off, as if she dared not say the name aloud.

"He wrote it to me." The countess's voice sliced through the silence of the chamber with unexpected clarity. Drummond turned to find her in the entry to the adjoining bedchamber, a wax taper in one hand, the skirts of her blue night rail gathered in the other. She advanced toward them. "He called me his darling Maggie and gave me this ring." She dropped her skirts and held a dull gold circlet to the light.

Drummond froze as he recognized one of several dozen such inexpensive baubles his father had commissioned to convince the women he seduced that they would wed.

"I once had a bonnie love wi' my Patrick." Her eyes had a distant, nostalgic look in them. "But it didna last, so I found another. A passion as grand as a woman could wish.'Twas an illusion as well, but at least I had it for a time."

Rage caught Drummond unprepared as full understanding of the countess's meaning broke over his head like a storm. This was the woman he sought. This, the beauteous maid his father said he'd seduced during his visit to the isle. But she was no common wench working in a tavern or the wife of some poor crofter, as he'd expected. She was the wife of the highest lord of the land, and an honest, caring woman at that.

Disgust, pity, and regret coursed through him. How dare his father trick such a woman into believing he loved her? He wanted to retch as he remembered the tactics his father had exercised on inexperienced, innocent women to convince them they were the center of his world.

Wishing with all his heart that he could change the past, he lifted his gaze to meet hers. Given her husband's character, how had she even considered betraying him? How had she dared?

"Oh, aye, I dared." The countess spoke as if Drummond had voiced his concern aloud. "I dared, for when I was four-and-twenty an' past my first youth, my Patrick took a doxy. A beautiful young lass as fair as the morning sun, ye ken. Not that he'd never touched another woman since we'd wed, but this one he kept beneath my verra nose and got her with child. He didna care how he humiliated me. I was to bear it, to hold up my head before the household, the village, the entire island, and pretend I didna ken. So I had my own grand love some years later, and one o' the children he thinks is his is nay such thing."

She lifted her chin in defiance as Drummond stared. He had been so absorbed by the shock of imagining his evil father seducing the noble countess, he had forgotten the child of the union. "Do you mean to say—"

"That's just what I mean," she confirmed with a resigned nod.

By St. Andrew, which of the children was it? Drummond thought swiftly. The eldest, Robert, was the very image of the earl. He could not be the love child. Little Elizabeth was only five, and Gordie far too young. But what of . . .

Unbidden, the image of red-gold hair and piercing green eyes leaped to his mind's eye. Rowena. So like her mother. So unlike the earl.

With the image came another. Rowena with Iain, walking on the moor, their hands close but not quite touching. Both had slanting green eyes and fiery hair.

Drummond flinched as he admitted that Rowena, fourteen years of age, with her red hair and green eyes, was the resulting love child. He should have made the connection sooner, but he hadn't. The countess also had red hair and green eyes. He had assumed the daughter resembled her mother and had left it at that.

Rowena was the half sibling he sought.

He wanted to sink to his knees, to weep with anger and frustration. Of all the women he had met on the island, he had never suspected the countess would be the one he sought.

A second realization thundered hard on the heels

of the first. Iain believed himself in love with a girl who was his own half sister. It was a disaster. Drummond must get him off the island at once. But first, despite the pressure of time, he had a duty to perform. "My lady, I am deeply sorry my father wronged ye," he said. "I came here to find the woman and do what I could to make it up to her. I am at your disposal."

She inclined her head, again with such a forgiving air, it nearly broke his heart. She would have borne his father's betrayal with just such nobility. She was a gentlewoman through and through, refusing to acknowledge her pain. "There is naught that ye can do," she said. "And I have my sweet Rowena to cherish. Yer father gave me a great gift in that child."

Drummond knew his despicable father would have claimed parentage of the girl if he'd been able, forcing her and her mother to be beholden to him. At least the countess's high position had spared her that fate. "Again, my lady, I am at your disposal. How may I serve you?" he said.

"Ye canna serve me. Ye must depart," she said with her usual no-nonsense approach. "You have no time to lose."

"Ye are correct in that, but we have a bit of a problem," he admitted, knowing they must find Andrew Crawford before it was too late. Stepping to the door, he opened it to check the corridor. And found Iain.

"Are we ready?" Iain asked in an eager whisper, entering the chamber. "Rowena has decided she wishes to come with us. We can take her to the king in Edinburgh, aye? The king will intervene in her father's plans to wed her to that monster. With yer permission, of course, my lady." He bowed to the countess.

The countess moved toward them, her night rail rustling. "Laddie, I've wanted to tell ye. Ye canna love Rowena because she's yer half sister."

"Eh? Is this some sort of a jest?" Iain turned to

Drummond, shrugging as if mystified. "What does she mean by such a thing?"

"I'm sorry, Iain, but 'tis no jest." Drummond took Iain's arm, wishing he could spare him the pain to come. "Listen to the countess. She has just shared this secret with Gemma and me."

Iain looked at Drummond, then at the countess's determined expression. "No' a jest?" he faltered.

"I'm afraid not," Drummond said as gently as he could.

The blood drained from Iain's features, and he staggered backward. "Nay. I canna believe it. If we were siblings, I would have sensed it."

The countess set down her candle, took the lad's hand, and pressed it between her own. " 'Tis sorry I am, to be the one to tell ye. But 'twas I who had an affair wi' yer father all those years ago."

A cry issued from beyond the open door, and Rowena stumbled through the opening. She was fully dressed and cloaked for traveling and carried a bundle under one arm. "Mother, what are ye sayin'?" she wailed. "How could ye have kent Iain's father? 'Tis a lie." She clasped Iain's other hand and studied him with feverish eyes, as if hoping to disprove the idea.

The countess stared at her in confusion. Clearly she had not meant her confession to be overheard by her daughter. She released Iain and pressed her hand to her heart for a full minute. Then she seemed to gather her wits. "I fear 'tis true, child. Yer father was Will Mosley, the man who also sired our two guests."

"Nay." Rowena carried Iain's hand to her cheek as tears brimmed in her emerald green eyes. "How could this be?"

"What she's saying is that Iain and I came to these islands to find the illegitimate child of our father, Will Mosley," Drummond said. "Unfortunately, you are that child."

Iain faced Drummond, a desperate light in his eye.

"I want proof," he cried. "I willna believe it otherwise. I refuse."

For an agonizing moment, a thousand emotions bombarded Drummond. He did not wish to hurt Iain, yet he must not love his own sister. It was unthinkable. "We have as proof our father's letter to her ladyship, clearly written in his hand and signed by him. 'Tis dated fifteen eighty-four. Look for yourself."

As Iain examined the letter, Drummond forced his own anguish deep inside to deal with later. Nothing must stand in the way of their escape from the island. But to do that, he must overcome this difficulty and gain everyone's cooperation.

"Is this true?" Iain asked the countess, a last, desperate hope that she would deny it flickering in his eyes.

She hung her head in mute desolation. "Ye ken how he was, yer father. He could charm the sun out of the sky if he took a mind to it."

Iain clutched his stomach and moaned.

Drummond ached for him. Once more, their wicked father reached from beyond the grave to ruin his children's lives.

Rowena dropped Iain's hand and backed away, tears streaming down her face. Iain started toward her, then checked himself, looking confused. "Damn. I havena even the right to comfort her anymore." He staggered to a corner and sat down, looking bereft.

The countess embraced her daughter, her composure crumpling as well. " 'Tis sorry I am, child. I tried to stop ye from fallin' in love wi' him, but I was too late."

Rowena seemed to rally. "Mama, I want to go wi' them. If I am no' the daughter of an earl, I dinna have to wed the man that Father—that is, the Earl of Orkney—chose for me. I need endure his abuse no longer."

The countess turned to Drummond, nodding.

"There's somethin' ye can do for me, then, sir. Will ye take her wi' ye?"

"Of course, my lady. There is room in the boat for one more."

"But what will you tell the earl, my lady?" Gemma protested, speaking for the first time during the confrontation. She had stood in silence during the revelations, a dazed expression on her face. Now she recovered her animation. "He believes Rowena is his daughter and he has a legal right to claim her. In truth, he does have that right, as she was born during your marriage and acknowledged as his. Rowena is legally his daughter, despite her true parentage, but if he knows the truth, he might do something terrible." She gripped Ting's mane hard, betraying her fear.

"He willna want her once I tell him the truth," the countess said with conviction. "Rowena mun go and find a new life, free of all fetters. I had the affair with Will Mosley. I alone mun take the consequences."

A ring of steel outside the chamber interrupted. The countess faltered as everyone whirled to behold the earl, a towering figure of darkness, standing in the doorway with drawn sword.

Drummond whipped his own sword from its scabbard and stepped forward to meet him. Expecting Lawrence Bruce or members of the garrison to follow, he prepared to defend the women as best he could.

The Earl of Orkney strode into his wife's antechamber. Ting laid back her ears and started toward him, snorting angrily, but Gemma held her back.

"Stand aside, all o' ye," the earl thundered, facing the countess. "I have a right to deal with my wife's transgressions as I see fit. Ye ken the fate o' unfaithful wives, Margaret. Are ye prepared to take the responsibility ye claim to want?"

# Chapter 30

The Countess of Orkney swayed for a moment, staring at the figure bearing down on her. Then, as if gathering courage, she lifted her chin with regal pride and advanced to meet her husband.

"Ye ken the fate o' unfaithful husbands, Patrick. They have their wives' scorn, and ye should have had mine when ye took a mistress and flaunted her under my nose. But even though ye broke my heart, I couldna scorn ye. I never stopped lovin' ye. In a sense, I understood yer desire, for she was fair as the dawn, wi' her silver hair and graceful ways."

With a twisting in his gut, Drummond recognized the new truth the countess was about to reveal and moved closer to Gemma. How he wished to protect her. But he now knew that Gemma would never hide from the truth. He encircled her waist with one arm and prayed for strength. For both of them.

The level of energy radiating from the countess increased as she crossed the chamber to lift strands of Gemma's fair hair so that it shown in the lantern light. "Even though ye betrayed me with Janet Sinclair, Patrick, I couldna help but love the child of yer union. She was so fair, and she needed me, but ye wouldna let me have her love. Ye robbed me of her and everything else ye could, and I've had enough o' yer hunger for power. I care for ye, I mourn the loss o' what we had, but I willna tolerate yer evil ways more."

Gemma turned white as a sheet. Drummond felt her tremble. "He's my father?" she gasped, pointing at the earl with a shaking hand.

"Aye." Margaret sighed heavily. "Ye ken that yer mother died a few weeks after giving birth to ye, God rest her soul. As I told ye, I cared for ye mysel'. Raised ye 'til ye were a year old. 'Til *he* interfered." Resentment tinged her voice as she narrowed her eyes at her husband. "You sent her to her aunt and uncle on Fair Isle. I suppose 'twas where she belonged. She was nay kin o' mine, but I'd grown attached to her sunny smile and her affectionate ways. But even then ye couldna let her live in peace," she accused her husband. "Ye married her off to Alexander Thomasson, using her beauty as a bartering coin, the way ye use so many people. 'Tis why I want her to wed Drummond Graham, and so she shall. She deserves a brawley bridegroom, no' another ald man."

Drummond saw disappointment, despair, and betrayal in Gemma's eyes. Releasing Ting, she slipped from his supporting grasp and advanced on the earl. "I always wondered why you took such an interest in me. Why didn't you tell me you were my father?" Her voice quivered with suppressed fury. She brandished the lantern at him. "You, of all people, had the power to avoid condemnation if you acknowledged me. But you chose to use me for your own purposes, marrying me off to encourage one of your men without ever giving me your love or even your name. How could you?" Ignoring his sword, she gripped his arm and shook him, torment riddling her face. "I know you're capable of love. You love Elizabeth. You love your wife in your own twisted fashion. Why do you make yourself so hard of heart?"

The earl's mouth twisted with anger at her accusations. In a swift motion, he drew back his left hand and struck Gemma hard across the left cheek.

She reeled from the blow. Drummond leaped forward to disarm the earl, but a streak of white charged past him. Ting sank her teeth into the thigh of the man who had so often abused her and now attacked her mistress.

The earl shrieked. Chaos erupted in the chamber. Drummond lunged for the earl, knocking the sword from his hand. "Iain, assist me," he shouted as he tackled the man and bore him to the floor. Ting released her hold and backed away, ears pinned to her head, her tail switching furiously.

As Drummond grappled with the earl, Iain mastered his thrashing legs and sat on them. Rowena pounced on his right arm and pinned it to the floor. She had to use both hands and all her weight to master him. Drummond sat on his chest and confined his left arm.

"I always wondered why ye never strapped Elizabeth for misbehavin', as ye did me when I was younger," Rowena muttered to the man she had believed was her father. "Now I ken why. Ye never liked me."

"Now I ken *why* I never liked ye," he spat. "I couldna believe I sired ye, with all that brazen red hair and defiant will. And ye're *not* my get. Ye're a bastard brat."

"Yer father was James the Fifth's bastard brat. That makes ye a bastard brat as well, one generation removed." Rowena refused to crumble at the derogatory name he had called her, instead displaying the very defiance to which he objected.

"How dare you," he roared, surging against his assailants' grips. "I'm the grandson to a king. Yer father was an unprincipled whoreson who passed his base nature on to his bastards. Ye deserved the strappings I gave ye. Ye still do."

"Ye'll never touch me again." She shook with wrath. "I'm leaving the island with Iain. We canna wed, but I can care for him as a brother. But ye never understood caring. All ye wanted was to wed me to someone who would bring ye more power. Well, ye can wed Elizabeth to that Highland monster ye chose for me. Yer so fond o' her. See if you can find it in yer heart to wish such evil on yer pride and joy. I hope I never see ye again."

He snarled at her, and Drummond had heard enough. "Come, help me tie him to that chair."

With Gemma's and the countess's help, they dragged the earl, kicking and fighting, to the heavy chair. Gemma produced rope from her traveling pack, and they tied him to the high back, the massive arms, and the thick, turned legs. As they worked, Patrick Stewart called Drummond a dozen filthy names.

"Find something to gag him," Drummond told the countess. "He's making so much noise, he'll bring the garrison down on us."

Rowena cheerfully produced her handkerchief.

"Here's mine to tie it in place," Gemma volunteered.

Drummond applied the gag, muffling the earl's shouts. The countess took her place at his side, smoothing back his hair and patting his shoulder, seeming to enjoy his confinement.

Drummond offered her a slight bow. "Your ladyship, I invite you to accompany us."

"I accept. I'm taking the children and leaving ye, Patrick. All save Robert. He's too far corrupted by yer hunger for power to be my child anymore, but the rest o' us will seek asylum at the court o' King James. Queen Anne will no' turn me away. Farewell, lamb. An' dinna ye dare try to force me back to ye." She kissed his forehead as the earl reared back, straining against his bonds, shouting into his gag, his face mottled with fury.

"Go quickly, your ladyship, and collect the other children," Drummond directed. As she hurried away, he drew Gemma into the passage, out of the earl's hearing. "We must find your uncle," he said quietly, giving her no chance to interact further with the earl, whose betrayal would soon hit her hard. "He's not in the storage chamber, as you said."

Rowena tugged at his sleeve as she joined them. "I know where he is," she whispered. "I saw Lawrence Bruce take him to the new wing earlier. He was surely up to no good."

Gemma grimaced. "You dinna suppose he locked him in the secret chamber?" she said.

"He probably did," Iain commented from behind, seeming morose but ready to execute their escape plan. " 'Twould be like him, to condemn the maker o' the chamber to death in his own work. Wi' all that cork lining, no one would hear him shout for help." He paused as Drummond shot him an accusing stare.

"How did *you* learn of it?" Drummond demanded. " 'Twas a close secret."

"From Rowena, who guessed it from talking to Gemma's uncle and watching him work in the new wing when no one was looking." Iain sighed. "I know I canna keep a secret, Drummond, but this one doesna matter anymore, does it? For certes, I've had my share o' surprises tonight." He exchanged regretful glances with Rowena. "I still canna believe you're my sister, but I suppose 'tis why we were drawn to each other from the start. But no' in the usual way. I was so awed, I hesitated to kiss ye."

"Ye were awed by me?" Rowena looked pleased. "In what way?"

"Ye're so learned," Iain said. "Ye read Latin and Greek. 'Tis too much for a lass."

"Ye dinna think a lass should read?" Rowena asked in surprise.

"As my wife, ye wouldna have need o' such things," Iain replied matter-of-factly.

Rowena gaped. "I wouldna have wanted to give up my learning just because we wed." She planted both hands on her hips. "Iain Lang, are ye prejudiced against intelligent women?"

"Nay," Iain retorted. "I just like a woman I can talk to as an equal. Ye're more than my equal, always quotin' great books by men I never heard o'. I'm a carpenter and a fightin' man."

"Well, I'm glad I found out before we made the mistake o' being wed," Rowena said in a heat. "I thought ye liked the things I told ye from books. Ye led me on, Iain Lang. 'Tis—"

"Enough," Drummond scolded, exasperated by their squabbling in the face of terrible danger. "We must free Gemma's uncle and leave the island at once."

Gemma was already moving down the passage toward the new wing. Drummond shepherded Rowena and Iain before him. They might still encounter the earl's minions. They were far from being free yet.

Passages remained empty as they traversed the castle in stealthy silence. It was as if the earl had ordered his men to stay in their beds on pain of death. Perhaps he had, Drummond speculated. His lordship had seemed to know they would come to the castle that night. He could have planned to murder them and wanted no witnesses to his crime.

In the new bedchamber, Gemma set to work, pushing and prodding the carved ornaments adorning the wood-paneled wall. Nothing happened. No panel slid back to reveal the secret chamber within.

They could not even be sure her uncle was confined there. Lawrence Bruce might have brought him here to complete some aspect of the work, then killed him and buried his body outside. He didn't mention this possibility to Gemma. He didn't like to think they might miss their opportunity to escape.

"Why does it not open?" Gemma cried, voicing his frustration as she banged the wall with her fist. "He said these two ornaments operated the mechanism, save they do not."

"Why don't we chop down the wall?" Iain suggested. "I could find an ax."

" 'Tis solid hickory, Iain," Rowena said with a disdainful sniff. " 'Tis so thick, 'twould take hours to chop, and 'twould make a great deal o' noise. Then there's a stone wall behind it, an' ye canna chop that."

Iain made a face at her. "Why are ye so practical at a time like this?" he complained. "Canna ye see that Gemma is distraught?"

"I'm just explaining why yer idea is bad," Rowena argued. "A thousand pardons if ye canna take the truth."

Annoyed to the limit of his endurance by their squabbling, Drummond ordered them to be silent. Gemma leaned her forehead head against the wall, sobbing. Ting hung her head in sympathy. "Oh, Uncle, I wish ye could hear me," she wept.

They dared not linger in the castle much longer. He must do something or they would miss their chance to escape. Grabbing a chair, heedless of the damage it would cause, Drummond crashed it against the wood-paneled wall.

A moment passed, then a dull thud answered from the other side. Gemma straightened and regarded the wall with hope. "Uncle," she cried. "Are you there? Tell me the sequence." She pounded the wall where Drummond had hit it, wincing at the pain to her fist.

A responding thud sounded. Andrew Crawford was probably pounding the wall with all his strength, Drummond thought, to make any noise at all. The layers of cork, stone, and wood would be so thick.

Gemma followed the directing thuds to a new ornament next to the original two. "Ah, the left and right
ones move together, as he told me, but another is
involved. I need a third hand." With both hands occupied on the two ornaments, she jerked her head
toward a third. "Someone push that flower to the
left."

Drummond pushed the ornament as directed. Nothing happened.

"Try to the right. There!" she cried in triumph as
a panel slid noiselessly back.

Andrew Crawford poked his head through the
opening. "Thank God ye're here. I thought I was
done for."

Gemma fell on him, weeping with relief. "Come
out." She helped him squeeze through the narrow
opening, then stood on tiptoe to deluge him with
kisses. "You're my true father, Uncle. You always
have been, though I just learned that the earl sired
me."

Crawford staggered to a chair and sank into it. He
was breathing hard, the sweat trickling down his face.

Gemma caught up a cushion and fanned him with
it. "Here ye're near suffocated in that closed chamber
and I'm fussing about nonsense. Ye need air, Uncle."
She fanned harder.

He breathed deeply for a few minutes, then seemed
to revive. Catching the cushion, he tossed it aside and
tugged her onto his lap as if she were a mere bairn.
" 'Tis no' nonsense, Gemma, if ye've learned yer true
parentage." He pinched her cheek affectionately.
"How did ye find out?"

She linked both arms around his neck and kissed
him on the forehead. "Her ladyship told me. In front
of his lordship. I was so angry, I shook him. And Ting
bit him." She reached out to pat the pony, who was
ever near. "Good girl."

"Great heavens, and Ting lived to tell the tale?" Crawford cast his gaze toward the door, as if expecting the furious earl to burst in any second.

"He's tied to a chair just now, with a gag in his mouth." Gemma described the earl's captivity with obvious relish. "He can stay there forever, for all I care. Ye're my real father, as I said. I love ye." She kissed his cheek.

"And I've always loved ye like a daughter, child." Crawford returned the caress. "I didna want to keep the truth from ye, but he insisted. 'Twas his loss. He'll never understand what he missed."

"Did you always ken he was my father?" Gemma asked. "From the time I was born?"

"Aye," he acknowledged. "From the start. He's a wicked, wicked man, hurtin' his wife, then hurtin' ye by holding back the truth. I only did as he said because I kent that yer auntie and I loved ye more than he ever could." Crawford glanced up at Drummond. "But what shall I do now? The man means for me to die."

"We are prepared to depart the island at once," Drummond hurried to assure him. "Ye must accompany us, sir. Once beyond the earl's reach, we can discuss yer wishes. Ye may not find it safe to return to Fair Isle. Does your family need ye?"

"My children are all grown and wed," Crawford said. "My wife, God bless her, is in the hands of her Maker. I accept yer offer to leave the island."

"Fine. Rowena, Gemma, help the countess with the children. We must away." Drummond had had enough drama. The earl would be found or would break free of his bonds soon. He wanted them away from the castle without delay.

Their journey north to the boat took place without mishap. Drummond didn't trust their ease of escape. They had made such a noise and taken so much time at the castle. Yet no guards had descended on them, even during their fight with the earl. His lordship must have another plan to stop them if his murder attempt failed—something they would not expect.

But he must not waste time trying to guess the man's intentions. He would face the trouble when and if it arrived. For now, he must concentrate on the task at hand, which was difficult enough. Marione had joined their party. The countess assured him that the earl would abuse the girl if she were left behind. How would he manage eight people, two infants, and a pony in an open boat?

Insanity, but it must be done.

# *Chapter 31*

Gemma helped lead their party to the cove, feeling exultant yet fearful. Everyone save the countess and Marione, who carried Malcolm and Gordie, pitched in to pull the concealed sixern toward the water. Ladened with the supplies Gemma had accumulated, the boat cut a deep track through the sand and into the shallows.

The waves rolled and swelled, and their boat tossed, as if sensing trouble ahead. The ever-present wind keened in fitful gusts. Dark clouds had gathered to block the midnight sun.

"Is the water too rough?" Gemma asked her uncle as he returned to shore from launching the boat.

He shook his head, worry drawing his eyebrows together into a frown. "I would like it smoother, but we can still row, and the wind will speed us on our way."

Full of trepidation, she watched Drummond carry the countess to the boat as it rolled on the waves. Her uncle followed with Malcolm as Drummond returned. He drew Gemma aside.

She leaned against his chest, needing a moment of respite in his sheltering arms. Her mind whirled. She had received answers to the questions plaguing her. As she'd feared, none were good. Iain and Rowena were brother and sister. No wonder the countess had been against their love from the start.

Fortunately, instead of turning it into a tragedy, the pair had responded with the amazing resilience of youth. They now squabbled like siblings over every whipstitch. Still . . .

Her world spun, unsteady on its axis, and she clung to Drummond. The countess's revelation about her parentage had shocked her most of all.

"I canna believe he refused to admit he was my father," she whispered against Drummond's leather jerkin. "Once I was part of his household, I saw him daily, yet he never said a word. I was nothing to him but chattel."

"Many nobles think of women that way. Dinna let it pain ye." Drummond's arms tightened around her, and she was grateful for his wish to relieve her pain. "Your uncle is your true father," he said. "Blood means nothing to the earl."

"It should mean something." Gemma held back the tears, hardening her heart against the man who had hurt her and others so often over the years.

"Some people think their blood kin exist for their own personal benefit."

She knew he was thinking of his father.

He smoothed back errant tendrils of hair from her forehead, tilting up her chin. "Gemma, I have something important to say to you."

She gathered a deep breath and held it, sensing a momentous confession was imminent.

"If anything happens to me on this journey," he said heavily, as if he believed it would, "I want ye to ken that a German ship awaits us just west of the Island of West Burra. The captain, Hans Kleman, is my friend. Get to him and he will convey you all to safety."

She expelled the breath, her mind in a muddle. This

wasn't what she'd expected, yet it was wondrous news. But at the same time . . . "Kleman is the German captain everyone says you spoke to at Lerwick Harbor?"

He nodded in agreement, his eyes watchful.

"You didna send a message to the king?"

"Hans has been fishing offshore. He hasn't gone anywhere near the king. At least no' yet, but he'll sail us to Edinburgh."

"You arena from the king?"

"I've never been from the king," he said with a trace of impatience. "I've only met him a few times. He knows who I am but only because my cousin insisted on explaining how his and my father had been switched. Other than that, he doesna ken me from a stump in the woods."

"Why do you confide this in me now?"

"Because I felt I should not be the only one to know our destination."

"You didna have to tell me about the king."

"Nay, but I felt I owed it to you, in case something happened. I wanted to tell you sooner, but I was concerned that if the earl captured you, he would force it out of you. Then nothing would have stood between you and death. There is still that danger, but I suspect if we dinna elude him tonight, nothing will save us." He paused, looking upset. "Damn it, why are you crying? I know I canna make you happy, but I dinna purposely try to cause you pain."

Gemma's confusion cleared as she realized what he was trying to tell her. She caught his hands and kissed them, laughing through her tears. This private, solitary man never shared his thoughts or plans with others by choice. Now, for the first time, he chose to share them with her. "I'm no' crying," she insisted.

"I think I can tell if you're crying or not." He drew her back into his arms and kissed her wet cheeks. "I dinna want to make ye cry. I never wanted that."

"I canna help it." She captured his face between her hands and gazed at him a long moment, then kissed him hard on the mouth. "I'm crying because—"

He groaned, a guttural agony wrenched from deep within him. "Whatever you're about to say, stop. I have nothing to offer you. Do you understand? Nothing that you value."

She had no time to argue with him. "I'm crying because I'm so relieved that ye arranged for the ship," she lied. "Ye must tell everyone." She kissed him a last time, then took his arm. "Come. Do it now."

"Everyone?" he asked with obvious reluctance.

"Everyone. 'Twill ease their fear. They believe we must row all the way to the mainland in this modest boat. We were willing to take the risk, but think how they will be heartened to know a full-size sailing vessel awaits with cabins to shelter them."

A jubilant mood swept their party at Drummond's announcement. Everyone worked with greater speed, but the darkening sky worried him. The midnight sun, ordinarily so brilliant, had disappeared behind a massive black thunderhead, leaving them in true night. As he carried Marione, then Gemma to the boat, he studied the choppy waves and hoped they would not be stirred higher.

As if he divined Drummond's concern, Iain stopped quarreling with Rowena long enough to carry her to her place. Andrew carried Elizabeth to the boat, then returned to place Gordie in Rowena's lap. Rowena sat next to her mother and Malcolm. Gemma took the tiller seat behind them.

Then Drummond and Iain lifted Ting over the side. The pony had never been in a boat. She rolled her eyes and trembled with fear but did not resist. She obeyed Gemma's soothing command to lie down between the thafts at the countess's feet.

Satisfied that the women and children were in place,

Drummond had Iain and Andrew help him drag the boat through the shallows until it stopped scraping the sandy bottom and floated free.

Drummond climbed in last. He and Iain placed the pegs of their oars in the rooths.

"I can row," Rowena offered. "I ken how."

"Later, if required," Drummond said. "Just now, we must get underway."

As they left the shore and Andrew hoisted the sail on its mast, the blood ran icy in Drummond's veins. Another sixern, twice the size of theirs, appeared to the north. It headed straight for them. The earl's plan became plain.

He would see them all drowned.

The perfect murder. Clean and impossible to trace.

"Adjust the sail to catch the wind," Drummond shouted to Andrew. "Row, anyone who can."

Rowena urged Elizabeth to the thaft between her and her mother, placed Gordie in her lap, and grabbed an oar. Despite his need to manage the sail, Andrew pulled out his oar as well, as did Marione who sat on the other side of the mast, sharing the thaft with him.

Gemma gripped the tiller and prayed, but the larger sixern gained on them. Waves slapped against their bow and spray showered them as they plowed through the water, making good speed.

Behind them, Lawrence Bruce gained on them, grinning with diabolical pleasure. In one hand, he held a pistol, in the other, a long pole with a great grappling hook on the end.

"My lady, do ye ken the use o' the tiller?" she asked the countess, panic turning her voice shrill. "Can ye change places with me so I can row?"

"I'll have to." Crouching low, the countess shifted to Gemma's seat. Gemma helped her steady Malcolm in the crook of her right arm, then took her own place behind her uncle and on the same thaft as Rowena.

The countess gripped the tiller with her left hand, a fierce expression on her face.

"They're gaining. Row, Gemma." Rowena pulled at her oar, her eyes lit with terror. "I willna go back. I'd rather jump into the sea."

Gemma jammed her oar into its rooth and plied it with all her might, for she knew Rowena could not swim. The addition of her power to Rowena's shot their craft ahead.

"I'll no' return either," Andrew grunted, putting his back into his oar. "I'll take my chances with the deep."

Though her uncle could swim, Gemma rowed with all her strength, hounded by a fear and fury she hadn't known she possessed. The freezing water would make swimming difficult, especially at this distance from the shore. The women in skirts would have no chance at all, nor would the infants unless the earl had ordered Bruce to save his sons.

The pitiful effort of all six rowers and a small sail did nothing to aid their escape. The larger boat gained on them.

Bruce handed his grappling hook to one of his men and leveled his pistol at them. "Give it up," he shouted. His voice swept to them on the growing wind like a malevolent howl.

"Get down," Gemma shouted. She pulled Rowena to the bottom of the boat with her. The babes cried, sensing their terror. The countess bent double behind the high stern, protecting Malcolm yet still clinging to the tiller. Marione crouched with Elizabeth and Gordie on the bottom of the boat. Gemma quaked, knowing this left Drummond as Bruce's easiest target.

Her uncle suddenly shot to his feet, waving his arms. The boat tilted to a dangerous angle.

The pistol exploded.

Gemma's world narrowed on her uncle as blood

spurted. He collapsed in a heap on the bottom of the boat.

"Nay" she wailed, climbing over the thaft, her heart in her throat. Where was he hit? Desperate, she turned him to find an ugly, oozing wound in his forearm. She yanked a strip of ruffle from her smock, mopping the blood, trying to see the wound's severity.

"Row. Dinna trouble wi' me." Her uncle clenched his teeth to bite back the pain. " 'Tis no' that bad."

" 'Tis bad enough." Relieved to know the shot wasn't fatal, Gemma knotted the ruffle around his upper arm and pulled it tight to stop the bleeding "I love ye, Uncle. Hold fast." She clambered back into her seat and grabbed her loose oar.

"Row," Drummond bellowed as Bruce leveled his second pistol at them.

"Underwater reefs ahead," Rowena cried.

Gemma's breath caught and a chill raced down her spine as she saw the dark, underwater mass rushing toward them.

"We'll pass over them. Guide us straight on, my lady," Drummond shouted. "Our hull is not as deep as theirs."

With five rowing and the countess steadying the tiller, they careened for the reef.

Bruce steadied his aim and the second pistol exploded.

Drummond lunged sideways against Iain, barely avoiding the shot.

Bruce fumbled to reload his pistols as his six rowers pulled on their-oars. The gap between the sixerns narrowed.

They hit the reef first. The jolt reverberated through Gemma, and a horrible crunch rose above the wind as wood scraped on rock.

"Row, but no' too deep," Drummond ordered, plying his oar.

Gemma dipped her oar, once with caution, then more deeply.

"All together," Drummond directed.

They pulled together. Their sixern ground on the reef for a terrifying moment, then shot forward, free.

Wood scraped on rock behind them as they cleared the barrier. Bruce's sixern hit the reef and hung there to the hair-raising crunch of splintering wood. His men pushed in vain with their oars to free their hull. The waves worked against them, driving their deep bow against the sharp reef.

Bruce bellowed with rage, unleashing both his pistols.

Their discharges boomed, stopping Gemma's heart, but the metal shots fell on open water. Lawrence Bruce could no longer do them harm.

Gemma concentrated on rowing, driven by her anger. No wonder men battled like the Furies in war. Something dark and dangerous had seemed to shoot through her blood, blinding her to all but survival. She realized she would have done anything during their encounter to save those she loved from Lawrence Bruce.

"Everyone, keep rowing," Drummond ordered. "We need to get these infants into shelter from the damp night." He turned the sail to catch the wind. As Bruce's craft shrank in the distance, he fixed his gaze on the horizon. His jaw set, his body moving rhythmically, he plowed his oar through the choppy waves.

Marione paused to comfort a snuffling, frightened Gordie and Elizabeth, hugging both children to reassure them, then resumed work with her oar. With the wind in their sail, the sixern moved with speed.

Naught but the sound of wind and waves ruled the cloud-darkened night as Gemma rowed in time with the others. They all glanced over their shoulders often, their gazes fixed on the silhouette of the Island of

West Burra. As they rounded the north end of the island, Gemma sighted a ship ahead. She wanted to faint with sudden exhaustion and relief.

She felt like a sleepwalker as they bobbed beside the German ship. Sailors scrambled to help them on board, their guttural German a welcome confusion.

The countess elected to be lifted to the deck, her infant son in her arms, in a thick fishing net hoisted on a crane. Gemma looped two slings of heavy canvas under Ting's belly, reassured her, then saw her lifted as well, eyes rolling with fear.

Her uncle sat up and insisted on helping the sailors arrange the fishing net to lift him to the ship. Relieved to see him up and moving, Gemma followed, climbing a rope ladder after Iain.

It was hard going up the steep side of the ship to a dizzying height. She collapsed on the deck, hugging her knees with one arm, holding on to Ting with the other, dazed and spent.

All was not well in her world, but one thing was certain.

They were saved.

# Chapter 32

Drummond thrust his way through the milling sailors, searching for Gemma. His first priority had been to assess Andrew Crawford's wound and see that the metal shot had passed in, then out of his arm, leaving a clean wound. Then he saw him safely into the hands of the ship's physician. Next, he had checked on the countess and her children and found that Captain Kleman was installing them in his own cabin. He had seen Gemma and Marione arrive safely on board the ship.

But now he must find Gemma. To hold her in his arms. To tell her . . .

To tell her what? He couldn't tell her anything. Except that he was glad that she was free of tyranny at last.

She sat on the deck near the crane, holding on to Ting, her forehead pressed against her knees. He pulled her into his embrace, urging her arms around his neck.

Ting butted against him, as if needing reassurance, too, and he looped one arm around the pony in a brief embrace before he turned to concentrate on Gemma.

Her lips tasted of salt. Whether from tears or the sea spray that had battered them during their frightening escape, he couldn't tell, but she had been crying. He kissed her over and over, willing her to feel the same fury he felt at having to give her up. He kissed her until she was gasping, her exhaustion turning to passion.

"Thank you," she whispered as he pressed her to his heart, kissing her hair. "For giving me my liberty. 'Tis the greatest gift anyone has ever given me."

What could he say?

"Speak to me." Gemma pulled back to see his face, cupping his cheek.

"I'm trying. Give me a chance, will you?" he groaned, finding her lips again, drinking in her sweetness as if dying, unwilling to let her slip away.

She sighed deeply at his ardor and refastened her hands around his neck. "I canna read your thoughts, Drummond. I am a stupid mortal and require you to communicate with words."

"What do you want me to say? I love you, Gemma, but it canna be. I'll see you have a tocher so you find someone more suitable. For now, I'll settle you with Lucina at Castle Graham."

The admission cost him. He writhed at having to confess his failure. Yet he could not provide this tender, valiant woman with all she deserved.

How he wanted to offer himself anyway. What little he had would always belong to her.

She seemed to struggle, her face reflecting a mixture of pleasure mingled with sadness at his admission. Her faint smile suggested she'd known of his love long before he'd realized it himself, yet she did not profess her love in return. "Why would Lucina want me at Castle Graham?" she asked quietly.

"She will. I guarantee it." He was relieved that she broached such a tepid subject, instead of pressing him into further declarations he could not honor. "With your knowledge of horses, the question will be whether she'll agree to let you out of her sight once you've met. She'll insist you live at Castle Graham and have your own breeding stock. I'll even find you some ponies like Ting to breed."

But he would be gone, and he knew she didn't want to stay there without him. Yet what choice did they have?

"Are you sure I wouldna be a nuisance in the household?" she asked.

He drew a deep breath, praying that he could influence her decision. " 'Tis a very large household, well able to accommodate another person. I'm positive that they would consider you a welcome asset. Lucina, Alex, and my mother will all love you. Trust me on that, if nothing else."

"Very well," she said. "I agree to accompany you to Castle Graham."

Relief flowed through Drummond. The place where his heart lay in his chest, cold and heavy, warmed the tiniest bit. He could give her a home, if not his heart.

The voyage to Edinburgh was uneventful, the weather fine. The countess and her children enjoyed the view from the spacious stern cabin. Gemma slept with Marione in the first mate's cabin. Drummond, Iain, her uncle, and Ting slept between decks with the captain and first mate.

The next morning, Gemma helped the ship's physician clean her uncle's wound.

"You see"—the stocky German pointed to the raw red flesh in the middle of the hole piercing her uncle's arm—" 'Tis beginning to knit in de center, as it should."

Relieved, Gemma urged her uncle to eat the fresh food Captain Kleman had stocked for them, including delicacies for the countess and her children. He even had carrots and hay for Ting.

They arrived at the bustling port of Edinburgh on the morning of their second day at sea. As they disembarked and Drummond conveyed them to his cousin's town house in the city, Gemma realized her favorite blue kirtle was torn, dirty, and out of style. She stared from the coach window at row after row of brick or stone houses, awed and not a little intimidated.

"A grand, impressive sight, eh?" Drummond remarked as they rode. "But no' to your taste, I'll wager. You miss your island. I regret taking you away from it. I've always thought of you as the queen of the isles."

She turned her gaze from the busy city streets to study him in surprise. "There will always be a special place in my heart for my home island, but that doesna mean I canna fall in love with a new land. We passed many beautiful places on our way here. I know I could come to love Scotland as well. The sandy beaches looked so pristine, the woods so cool and green. I believe I dislike cities, 'tis all."

He appeared relieved. "Then you'll love the countryside around Castle Graham. I know some beautiful wild areas I'll show you. Green meadows full of sheep and wildflowers. Ice-cold, sparkling burns pouring down steep mountainsides. Solway Firth streaked with color at sunset."

"Such a poet you've become." She smiled her praise. "I believe I am already in love with them, just as I loved my home of Fair Isle."

*But not as in love with them as I am with you,* she added to herself.

The countess settled her children at the Graham town house, then wrote to Queen Anne at court. A cordial reply came back, inviting her to attend upon Their Majesties. A full day was spent procuring suitably elegant garments for the countess, Rowena, and Elizabeth.

Then off to court went the Countess of Orkney and her four children, with Marione in attendance. She returned with an invitation to move to the queen's lodgings at Edinburgh Castle. Anne Stewart was appalled by the treatment her kinswoman by marriage had suffered at the hands of her husband. She granted the countess asylum at once with King James's approval.

The countess, as it turned out, had raided her husband's counting house before she departed. With the earl's funds, she ordered tailors to the house the next day to outfit herself and Rowena further for court life. She insisted on ordering several garments for Gemma.

"Ye risked yer life, helping me escape," she said over Gemma's protests. "Ye keep refusing all repayment. A few new kirtles and bodices are the least I can do."

Gemma's uncle, with his skill as a stone mason and his wound healing nicely, found work at once. "Gemma, my heart, I've changed my name so the earl willna find me. An' I've found work, buildin' a great house for a wealthy gentleman."

"Ye'll make it a splendid one, I know, Uncle." She kissed him, happy for his good fortune.

"An' in another week or so, when my arm is healed," he continued, "Captain Kleman has agreed to sail me to Fair Isle. I'll bring yer Cousin Ester back wi' me, as well as all yer other cousins and their families, afore the earl thinks to punish them for my escape."

Gemma wept for joy to know that her family would be nearby. "I'll help you get them settled," she promised, "when they arrive."

Later that day, in the countess's tiring chamber, her ladyship insisted that Gemma try on her serviceable new garments.

"When is the wedding, Gemma?" she asked as she stepped back to admire the simple, but well-tailored, blue kirtle and bodice.

"There canna be a wedding." Gemma sighed, hoping her friend would not press her further.

"Och, men are thickheaded at times, but yer Drummond has a good heart. Has he no' admitted he loves ye?"

Memories of his declaration nearly overwhelmed Gemma as she nodded.

"Ye mun help him see what is best for ye," the countess advised. "Ye told me once he is so accustomed to making decisions for others, he forgets they might be capable o' making their own."

"Hello, may I come in?" her uncle called, interrupting their tête-à-tête.

"Enter," the countess bid him. "I was just saying to Gemma that some people dinna ken that others wish to make up their own minds about their lives."

Her uncle nodded in agreement. "Aye, she's right. Drummond will just have to come to see."

Suddenly, Gemma realized they were both right. She knew what she must do.

Having chosen her path, Gemma rode to Castle Graham in the company of Drummond and Iain. Her greatest fear was for Ting. She worried that her pet could not keep up with their long-legged mounts.

To her gratification, her stalwart companion proved their equal. Apparently her life on the rugged island and her time with the wild herd had toughened her. She raced at their side, taking joy in their wild gallops. She tossed her head with glee, and Gemma knew they both reveled in their freedom. Oppression was gone forever.

Drummond had sent word ahead to Castle Graham of their pending arrival, and Lucina and Alex welcomed Gemma with kind cordiality. Lucina greeted her with a special enthusiasm, urging Gemma to the stables with her after she'd only been there an hour. She seemed thrilled to meet another female who shared her love of horses. They spent long hours in the stables during Gemma's first se'nnight at Castle

Graham, talking horses, caring for ill and injured horses, riding horses.

During that se'nnight, Gemma also learned that Drummond would soon depart once more on his journey.

Where was he going? she'd asked him.

To Argyll, he'd replied. His father had spent some time there ten years ago.

Iain had elected to remain at home this time. He'd had such a shock over his relationship with Rowena, he did not wish to depart just yet.

Drummond frowned but said nothing, instead spending more and more time alone, gathering supplies for his travels.

Gemma laid her plans.

Gemma was in the stable the morning of her tenth day at Castle Graham. She heard a step behind her and looked up to find Drummond standing in the doorway, the sun at his back, making a halo around his fiery hair. "Gemma?" he called. "I've come to say good-bye."

She came out and pirouetted. "Do you like my new gown?" she asked with a coaxing smile.

"Rather simple, but serviceable, I suppose. Plain blue?"

"Very serviceable. This light wool is comfortable on cool summer nights and cozy as the winds of autumn begin to blow. Do you like my boots?" She pulled up her skirts to reveal stout leather boots with tough leather soles.

"No' for dancing, I take it." He smiled with indulgence.

She detected the sorrow in his eyes. "Nay, they're boots for walking," she advised him gently. "I've broken them in during the last se'nnight. I can walk all day in them, but they also have good heels that will stay in the stirrup during riding."

"Ah." He appeared puzzled, as if he didn't understand why she was showing him these things.

She laughed and swirled her cloak around her
shoulders. "I also have a warm cloak with a deep hood
for keeping off the rain. 'Tis of good wool and should
hold up well as autumn comes on."

"Very nice. That shade of loden green suits you."

She suppressed laughter. "Ting has something new,
too. Would you like to see?"

Deeper puzzlement etched a frown on his face. She
wanted to laugh for joy. "Come here, Ting." The
pony's hooves tapped on the wood floor of the stable
as she stepped smartly out of the stall. She wore a
harness to which two new packs were strapped, one
on each side. "In here, I have changes of clothing,
water, food, a few personal items such as a comb, a
small looking glass, and linen toweling." Gemma patted the packs, then Ting, with pride.

Drummond grew grave. "Gemma, why are you
showing me these things?"

She moved to his side, took his hand, and smiled
up at him. "Because I'm going with you to Argyll.
And on your next journey after that, and on the one
after that. The castle is fine, but you know I've never
loved castles. I feel cramped and long to be in the
fresh air. If your purpose in life is to wander, my
purpose is to wander with you."

The bemused expression on his face lifted. Joy took
its place.

"Can you truly mean this?"

"I love you, Drummond Graham. My heart belongs
with you. I long to wander the world with you, wher-
ever your quest takes you."

He clasped her to him so hard, he crushed the
breath from her. She didn't care. She flung her arms
around him and clung to him as she'd never clung
before.

"God, I love you, Gemma Sinclair." He paused, as

if anxious about something. "But what about all these people who need you? Your uncle. The countess and her children. You willna be in one place long enough to take care of anyone."

She laughed. "We've helped them find ways to take care of themselves. Now all I need do is take care of myself. And you."

"Most women want a church wedding with all their family present. A fine dress. A great feast after. What of those things?"

"I am not most women. I am *your* woman, and this is what I want. I want a clergyman to marry us legally in the eyes of the church. I will wear the beautiful dress that the countess had made for my wedding. Beyond that, I crave nothing except the open sky and your hand in mine and Ting at our sides."

He gathered her into his arms. "And you would be truly happy with so little?"

" 'Tis not so little. Your love is so much to me, I've never been happier than I am right now, loving you," she answered simply.

Taking her hand, he led her, both of them laughing, into the sun.

# *Epilogue*

Gemma drifted into consciousness slowly, aware of Drummond's warm length pressed against her beneath the coverlet. As she stirred, he lifted her hair and kissed her neck.

The wavy pane of glass in the window admitted a slanting ray of early morning sun, illuminating their bedchamber at the tiny Argyll inn. Plain whitewashed walls. A simple washstand. One chair. And a wide bed with a thick feather mattress.

"You didna have the dream, did you?" she asked.

"I've never had it since that night I told you about the Dunlochy Charmstone and you didna care," he assured her. "I believe you can stop asking every morn."

"Very well. I shall stop. But only if you will kiss me everywhere, Drummond. Will you? Now?" she murmured, loving the drowsy pleasure of lying at his side.

He chuckled. "The question is not will I kiss ye. The question is, could you stop me if ye wanted to." He kissed the back of her neck again.

"Here, Drummond. Will you kiss me here." Gemma pointed to her throat.

Drummond kissed.

"And what of here? Could you bear to miss here?" She raised the covers and pointed.

Drummond kissed yet again, becoming more enthusiastic.

She sighed with pleasure. "And what of here, Drummond? Ye wouldna wish to overlook this spot."

"Nay, never." Passion flared in Drummond's eyes. He bent his head and kissed her, a long, languorous caress with hands and lips.

She stretched, luxuriating in his touch. "My breasts feel odd this morn."

"Odd? How so?"

She shrugged. "I dinna ken. As if they were ripe berries, longing to be plucked."

"They are that." He attacked, growling with mock hunger.

She laughed and they tussled until at last Gemma sat up.

"Ugh." She gripped the edge of the bed.

"What's wrong?" He moved at once to her side.

"I feel odd. Dizzy."

"Nauseous?"

"Aye, I suppose. I felt it yesterday morn, but by the time I'd broken my fast, 'twas gone."

"What of your courses?" He tucked long strands of hair behind her ear and kissed her cheek, then her mouth.

"What of them?"

"I've never noticed ye to have one." He pulled aside the robe she wore and nuzzled her breasts.

She flapped a hand languidly. "All the excitement. And the shock. I've been through enough to frighten the courses out of any woman."

"Gemma, my dear, you havena stopped having courses from shock. You're carrying my child." He turned her to face him. "I've suspected it for a while."

She stared at him, feeling truly shocked now. "No. I cannot be with child. I'm barren."

"You are clearly *not* barren. I never quite believed it."

A wild joy seized her. It was a miracle. A gift from above. "With child? Me?" She touched her belly with awe.

"You, Gemma Sinclair. With my child. Our child." He chuckled, then sobered. "We must return to Castle Graham at once."

"Why? I've always heard that mild riding and walking is good for a woman who is expecting. We're in no hurry. Why should we go?"

"They're no' good for a woman in her ninth month."

"I'm no' in my ninth month. I may be stupid, but I should hope not so stupid to be that far along and not guess."

"You're no' stupid." He kissed her nose, her ears, her hair. "Never stupid. But you will be in your ninth month eventually."

"Eventually, but we have time. We can do what we came to do in Argyll, then return to the castle in time for me to bear the child. When he's a few months old, we can set off again."

Drummond put down his foot. "I willna hear of it. Not until he's a year old, perhaps more. Iain can go in my stead. 'Tis his turn."

She stared at him again. Not since the night Drummond Graham had appeared in her life, a thunder god bringing her aid, not since she had learned the Earl of Orkney was her father, had she had so many surprises. *But you're a wanderer,* she wanted to say. *You swore it on your life.*

He rolled his eyes. "Dinna look at me that way. I think I'm entitled to stay home with my wife while she bears a child and the child grows up."

"Home? You have a home?"

He grinned a bit sheepishly. "If you're willing to share space with close to a hundred people and can tolerate a stuffy castle, I consider Castle Graham my home."

"I suppose I'm used to stuffy castles," she teased, lowering her eyes demurely. "But are you sure you trust Iain with the task? He doesna seem inclined to go on any quests just now."

"If not, I have plenty of other half siblings who can take a turn in cleaning up our father's sordid affairs. Elen and my other half sibling, David, for instance. They've expressed an interest. Let them go."

"They're not as good at questioning women as you are," she tested him.

He slammed his hand on the bed. "Damn it, they can learn, just as I had to. If I want to stay at Castle Graham with you and our child, I will."

"You will? With our son and me?"

"A son?" he marveled. "Am I going to have a son?" He kissed her. "Gemma, I refuse to leave your side for a minute. Can you be sure 'tis a son?"

"I cannot be as sure as the countess was when she told her husband."

They both laughed, remembering how the countess had tricked her husband into thinking she was in labor.

Gemma sobered first. "I dinna really know if 'tis a boy. I'm still getting used to the idea that I'm not barren, but I would like a son who looks just like you."

"A bonnie laddie, to carry on the Graham name. But I would love a daughter just as well, Gemma. One who looks like you."

Gemma nodded, smiling so wide, she felt positively beatific. Ting, hearing they were awake, came over to nuzzle her bare toes. "She wants to go out."

"Fine. I'll open the door. The folk downstairs will see that she goes out."

He let the pony out the door, then closed it and tumbled Gemma back beneath the warm covers. "I want to make love to my bride from Fair Isle."

"And give us both thunder?" Gemma asked, reaching for him.

"And give us both thunder magic of the best kind," he agreed.

# Author's Historic Note

Patrick Stewart, Earl of Orkney and Laird of the Shetland Islands, was a real historic figure who inherited the earldom from his father, Earl Robert, an illegitimate son of King James V. The history books verify that, like his father before him, Patrick Stewart abused the islanders. He found excuses to confiscate their land, executed them for supposed crimes, falsified weights and measure in the marketplace to increase taxes collected for his own coffers, and forced the local people to work as free laborers building his great castle at Scalloway. As several historians remarked, the islanders remember the Earl Patrick with the same sentiment that many people reserve for Hitler.

Lawrence Bruce was the half brother of Earl Robert, sired by the same mother but by different fathers. Historians verify that Bruce, accused of murder in the Highlands, fled to the Shetland Islands where one of the earls, either his nephew Patrick or his half brother Robert, gave him asylum. There, he established his personal base of power, even going so far as to build his own castle at Muness on the Shetland Island of Unst. In reality, Bruce and the earl were opponents vying for power on the islands, both struggling to amass more land and the homage of more servants and tenants than the other.

Andrew Crawford is another real historic personage, a stone mason whom Patrick Stewart had build his great castle at Scalloway. Within the castle, the earl ordered Crawford to build a secret chamber. In real life, the earl murdered Crawford after he finished the secret chamber, but since all things are possible in fiction and since this is a romance, I arranged for Crawford to be spirited away in secret by his loving niece, Gemma, and her beloved, Drummond Graham.

Although the history books I consulted waxed eloquent on the subject of Patrick Stewart, in only one out of over a dozen reference books did I find mention of his wife. At that point, I e-mailed the Shetland Islands. In these days of the Internet, what a marvelous resource it is. I was thrilled to discover the Shetland Times Bookshop, located at www.shetland-times.co.uk. From them, I bought several photographic books depicting the beauty of the Shetland Islands, which were shipped to me by air and quickly received. I also struck up a discussion with the delightful bookshop manager, Edna Burke, who is a native Shetlander and traces her ancestry back to the time of Earl Patrick. For details about the history of the earl, she referred me to a book called *Black Patie: The Life and Times of Patrick Stewart, Earl of Orkney, Lord of Shetland*, by Peter D. Anderson, published by John Donald Publishers, Ltd, Edinburgh, 1992. Although this book is out of print, I obtained a copy via interlibrary loan and soon learned that Earl Patrick married a widow, Margaret Livingston, daughter of Alexander, sixth Lord Livingston, and together, they had one child, Elizabeth. For the purposes of my story, I decided to do some creative work with Margaret and Patrick, blessing them with five children, although in reality they had only Elizabeth. Robert, the earl's only son, was actually the illegitimate son of an Orkney woman named Marjorie Sinclair. With her, the earl also had two more children, presumably both girls. This is how I selected Gemma's name, making her a

Sinclair, although of course in my story Gemma and Robert are half siblings rather than siblings. I also advanced Black Patie's age a bit to make him a more formidable villain. In 1599, the real Patrick Stewart would have been approximately 34, as his birth is said to have fallen somewhere between the summers of 1565 and 1566.

I presented the rest of the earl's history as accurately as possible, even to the occasional use of the storeroom off the kitchens as a prison. Although Earl Patrick was a friend to King James VI during his younger years and in favor while serving at court, the power he gained in the Orkney and Shetland Islands apparently did corrupt him, for he was called to Edinburgh in 1609, probably more to account for hints of treason rather than his unkindness to the Orkney and Shetland people. He was finally tried by the council, and in 1615, executed for "tirranie and opressioun" and for suspected treason. This happened one month after his son Robert was put to death for starting a rebellion against the king's men in Orkney. In keeping with my stories that present history with a woman's touch, I like to think that a woman like my Gemma Sinclair was, at least in part, responsible for bringing the earl to justice.

The Shetland Islands are, of course, the original home of the Shetland pony, and herds of the delightful animals roved the meadows and moors for many centuries. I named Gemma's pony, Ting, after the town of Tingwall, as well as after the Lawtings, which were the legal councils that governed the islands, though they were dominated by the earl's creatures during his rule.

Early in its history, the Orkney and Shetland Islands belonged to Norway and Denmark. Hence, the many customs, traditions, and place and people's names are from the old Norse. But in 1468, Christian I, who had betrothed his daughter Margaret to James III of Scotland, pledged the islands to pay part of her dowry. In 1472, they were annexed by Scotland. Before that event, the Shetland Islands were virtually self-ruled since they were so far from the capital of Norway. Little wonder the islanders resented the rule of the Scots earls.

The story about the Cheyne house being cursed was drawn from Shetland folklore. It seems that once a place was cursed, no one would go near it. The story I read was from James R. Nicolson's *Shetland Folklore*, published by Robert Hale, Ltd., though the croft in question was not named as belonging to a particular family. I chose the name Cheyne at random, with all apologies to any Cheynes still living in Shetland.

If you enjoyed this story, I hope you'll let me know via e-mail at jlynnford@aol.com. You can also write to me at Janet Lynnford, PO Box 21904, Columbus, Ohio 43221, but I'm able to answer e-mail faster. And do look for my next book from Onyx, when I return with the story of Angelica, the second youngest of the Cavandish siblings.

# Glossary of Scottish Words

**bere**          barley

**brawley**       handsome or attractive

**broch**         an ancient fort from prehistoric times, found on many northern islands

**byre**          a cow barn, or, in a small cot, the chamber for all the animals

**cot**           short for cottage and what the Shetlanders called their homes

**cottar**        a person who lives in a cot

**croft**         a small land holding run by a family

**crofter**       a person who possesses a small land holding

**cuddie**        a basket

**dyke**          stone walls built to keep sheep and cattle out of crop areas

**kale yard**     a fenced or stone-ringed oval for growing kale

**kishie**        a large basket made to wear on the back, usually for carrying peat

**noost**         a place to store boats, a mooring

**rauckle**       headstrong

**rooth**         the part of the gunwale with a clamp of hard wood or iron where the oar works

**sixern**        the six-oared boats of Norway, the

|            | Shetland Isles, and the other northern countries |
|------------|--------------------------------------------------|
| **simmons** | ropes of twisted straw used to support and tie down a thatched roof |
| **thaft**   | the bench or seat in a fishing boat where the fisherman/rowers sit |

Turn the page for a sneak preview

at

# Janet Lynnford's

next Scottish romance

# Spellbound Summer

Coming from Onyx Books

August 2002

*Argyll, Scotland, 1600*

Geddes MacCallum, fifth Laird of MacCallum, wagered that a battle could have raged around the Englishwoman and she would pay it no heed. She stood knee deep in the rushing water of the burn, looking happier than any woman had a right to, given what she was doing.

Her spade flashed in the sun as she wedged it into the gray muck of the bank, levered a chunk loose, and dumped it into a waiting bucket. With her apt expression and her dirty clothing, she reminded him of a child making mud cakes.

She was no child though. The womanly curves beneath the drape of her clothing made that plain. She had tucked up her practical brown kirtle skirt to reveal slim, enticingly bare legs. Though the fabric of her simple bodice was brown linen, its excellent cut emphasized her small waist and graceful movements as she bent and straightened, harvesting muck from the bank.

Geddes frowned as she paused to push back an errant lock of shining brown hair. Her gesture streaked her creamy cheek with mud, though she didn't seem to notice. Nor did she seem to realize that she was in danger. The burn ran between his land and that of

Angus Kilmartin, Master of Fincharn. Everyone in the area knew that only five months past, he had vanquished the Kilmartin in a deadly battle over the right to Castle Duntrune, but the Englighwoman was not from this area. She could not know that his four men, stationed along the burn, watched for marauding Kilmartins, anticipating their attack. Or if someone had told her, she didn't care.

She was more interested in digging clay.

It was a dangerous attitude for a young gentlewoman, traveling with naught but a young male escort and an old man to protect her. Dangerous, but intriguing, to find such daring in a female.

He moved closer, intent on seeing more of her.

As he approached within hailing distance, Geddes stared at her hair, the rich, dark color of cinnamon, bundled in a careless knot at the nape of her slender neck. It sagged as if it were about to tumble down, yet its dishevelment did not lessen the provocative quality that held his interest.

Her manner fascinated him most of all. With singleminded concentration, she riveted her gaze on the bank, as if her entire future lay before her.

Geddes stepped forward, thinking it high time she attended to the ruling chieftain.

"Greetings," she called, shifting her gaze to him and waving in a salute. "You must be the other local laird." She smiled, and a sparkle danced in her eyes.

Despite the mud streaks on her cheeks, that smile nearly bowled him backward as she offered him friendly apreciation. The charming dimple that appeared in her rosy cheek accentuated the good-natured humor in her face.

Geddes didn't know what to make of her. Women didn't look at him with impersonal friendliness and appreciation. Nor did they refer to him as "the other local laird." Women behaved in a seductive or obsequious manner, depending on what they hoped to gain from him. He was known, after all, as the Rakehell of MacCallum.

He glanced at his men to see if they'd noticed. The four members of his garrison studied the meadow opposite and the wood behind him, as they should. But he didn't doubt they were listening to his exchange with the Englishwoman. By nightfall, every word he and the maid uttered would spread around Duntrune.

Geddes watched her as she fished for her spade in the burn and retrieved it, futher wetting her skirts in the process. Seeming untroubled by her dripping garments, she hoisted a load of gray sludge aloft and waved it at him. "Look! I told you I would find the clay, and I did. Isn't it wonderful?"

Strictly speaking, she had not told him. She had told his tacksman, Dougal Dunardry, who had questioned both her and her young Scots escort last night, then told them to clear off. But here she was still. The hump of blanket reclining under yon tree was, he judged, her young escort, Iain Lang. Not much protection just now, though by all accounts they'd been here all night. His wish to sleep might be understood.

As they had not obeyed Dunardry, he had decided that someone with more authority must send them on their way. He would do it now, whilst the young man slept on. "This was my grandsire's favorite place to fish. I dinna appreciate your digging it up without my leave, Mistress Cavandish." He adopted a curt manner that most people found intimidating.

She dropped the gray chunk into her bucket, propped the spade against the bank, and shaded her eyes against the sun with one slim hand. "My apologies, but the Kilmartin laird said in his letter that this land was his. He gave me permission to dig, so I did."

His impatience dissolved, replaced by incredulity. "You exchanged letters with him?" The villain had written to her and said she might dig, so she had come? How naive could she be? Worse yet, how naive were the pair who served as her protectors?

"That side belongs to Angus Kilmartin. This side is mine. If you take clay from here," he stabbed one finger at the bank where she dug, "you must have my permission first."

She turned her attention to where he pointed. "I do apologize for trespassing. I learned of the change in landowners yesterday, but truly, I thought it did not matter who owned it since neither of you is interested in the clay. If you would but look at it, you would understand why 'tis critical that someone put it to use. Look how lovely it is." A dreamy expression transformed her features from attractive to beautiful. With her gaze locked on her heart's desire, she beckoned him with the spade.

Geddes had never had a reason to look at raw clay at all, let alone notice the match to this particualr specimen. But her obvious fascination intrigued him. Against his better judgment, he moved closer to study what appeared to him to be little more than mud.

"It took us half the night to uncover it"—she caressed the pale gray muck with gentle fingertips, ignoring the fact that it was laced with tree roots and stones—"because we took care not to erode the bank into the stream. We wouldn't want to dirty folks' water down the way." She shot him a glance, as if to see whether he appreciated her conccrn for the land.

He did, though he would rather she not dig at all.

"Have you ever seen the like?" She took a chunk of the clay in both hands, wet it with water from the burn, and began to roll it between her palms. Despite the mud beneath her short, pearly nails, Geddes realized she had the hands of an artist. They were lithe and clever, clearly accustomed to molding natural materials to her will.

He had always appreciated artistic skill, whether in

males or females. Just because he lacked such skill himself didn't mean he couldn't enjoy it in others. Her clever hands were the perfect complement to the idealism shining in her eyes.

A pang of regret twisted through him as he remembered how he, too, had once been similarly idealistic, hoping to achieve the impossible, ardent in his efforts to convince his father to believe in his dreams. How painful when his tower of hope had come crashing down. If only hers did not have to do the same. . . .